Fortunate Abandonments

I am grateful for these people. I do not take for granted their support, and for always being there for me.

I'm especially thankful to have an extraordinary husband, Harry. He has, and does challenge me always to make me be more fearless in my writing. He has given me a beautiful life and always has my back.

I am grateful to my lovely, kind niece, Becky Higgenbotham for all she takes care of in my day to day life. My life would not be the same without her.

My sister, Colleen, for all those play school days growing up in the schoolhouse she set up in our cow shed on our farm. She was a strict English teacher - "It's not ain't, it's isn't," rang out.

Danielle McKlveen, a special thanks for her efficiency in all I ask of her. Her many, many retypes of my late night edits. When I call, she finds it and takes care of the problem. I could not write if she were not in my corner.

For the open intelligence of Bob Babcock and his lovely wife, Jan, and the artistry of Mark and the grace of this family at Deeds Publishing for my book. They are not only professional, but funny and kind. My deep, heartfelt thanks. I am indebted.

The wonderful artwork of Teo Aladashvile. She awes me with each stroke of her brush.

Jerry Brown Schwartz

Fortunate Abandonments

JERRY BROWN SCHWARTZ

DEEDS PUBLISHING | ATLANTA

Copyright © 2023 — Jerry Brown Schwartz

ALL RIGHTS RESERVED — No part of this book may be reproduced in any form or by any electronic or mechanical means, including information storage and retrieval systems, without permission in writing from the authors, except by a reviewer who may quote brief passages in a review.

Published by Deeds Publishing in Athens, GA
www.deedspublishing.com

Printed in The United States of America

Cover design and text layout by Mark Babcock

Artwork by Teo Aladashvili

This is a work of fiction. Names, characters, businesses, places, events, locales, and incidents are either the products of the author's imagination or used in a fictitious manner. Any resemblance to actual persons, living or dead, or actual events is purely coincidental.

ISBN 978-1-950794-99-7

Books are available in quantity for promotional or premium use. For information, email info@deedspublishing.com.

First Edition, 2023

10 9 8 7 6 5 4 3 2 1

AUTHOR'S NOTE

Character Driven Realistic Literary Fiction

My Grandmother Monterey, her two sisters, Great Aunt Dessie and Great Aunt Azzie were separated as children. Few facts are known about their lives. The real facts were buried with them.

One can only imagine the heartache they experienced at being separated. Never knowing if they would ever see one another again.

Eventually they did reunite, in their mid-twenties. After they reunited, nothing could separate them except death. Their younger brother played a large part in the family bond.

I wanted to give them a life, even if it is created from my imagination. Each one was an interesting character, and a loving part of my life. I want the reader to take each one's journey of their difficult social lives and the human conditions that controlled their lives, and how their abandonments all take a fortunate turn. This is a journey with the Darnells through four generations.

Jerry Brown Schwartz

Contents

VOLUME I: The Darnell Children: 1

    Chapter 1: A Fortunate Abandonment   3
    Chapter 2: A Moral Man   14
    Chapter 3: Star Attraction   25
    Chapter 4: A Broken Soul   37
    Chapter 5: Moving Forward   43
    Chapter 6: Cal   60
    Chapter 7: Goodbye to Circus Friends   73

VOLUME II: Building Lives & A Town   77

    Chapter 8: Heading Toward A Home Without Wheels   78
    Chapter 9: Busy Days   94
    Chapter 10: Sparsity   112
    Chapter 11: A Good Doc Comes to Darnell Dr. Francis Charing   137
    Chapter 12: Mickey's Spirit Lives On   156
    Chapter 13: The Circus Statue: a Town Celebrates   159
    Chapter 14: Gray Clouds Over: Protected Earth   166
    Chapter 15: Big Sister: Monterey   178
    Chapter 16: Folly   195
    Chapter 17: Garrison Anne Polly, The Woman With All First Names   202
    Chapter 18: Growing   218
    Chapter 19: Lee's Mornings   233
    Chapter 20: Walks with Doc   238
    Chapter 21: Gap Captures Hearts   242
    Chapter 22: Today Just Feels Different   245
    Chapter 23: Sparsity's Walk   259
    Chapter 24: Gap and Starling   261

Chapter 25: A Forever Goodbye	284
Chapter 26: Monty Arrives: at Grand Central	304
Chapter 27: Monty and Jazzy	315

VOLUME III: Plaid Patience   *323*

Chapter 28: Grand Central Welcomes: Plaid Patience	324
Chapter 29: Monty's Letter Sent: to Papa and Gap	334
Chapter 30: The Right Foster Home	344
Chapter 31: Plaid and Hanna	358
Chapter 32: Monty Lets Go	364
Chapter 33: Notice of Plaid Patience	371
Chapter 34: Plaid Goes Home to Georgia	377
Chapter 35: New Sounds	396
Chapter 36: Plaid Vignettes	419
Chapter 37: Plaid Talks Foster Homes	460
Chapter 38: A Better Man	479
Chapter 39: Goat Kidding	501
Chapter 40: Tess Tells Girlean	504
Chapter 41: Spring Comes to Tess	514
Chapter 42: Protected Earth Lives On	518

FORTUNATE ABANDONMENTS

List of Characters

Mr. Darnell: Husband of Tansy and father to Tansy's four children
Tansy: Mother of Monterey, Dessie, Azzie and Little D
Monterey: The oldest child of Mr. Darnell and Tansy
Dessie: Middle child of Mr. Darnell and Tansy
Azzie: Third child of Mr. Darnell and Tansy
Little D: Youngest child of Mr. Darnell and Tansy, later to grow up and be called Papa Lee
Mr. Ward: The circus owner, builds the town of Darnell and buys 1,000 acres in Georgia
Birchard: Little People, perform for circus
Mickey: wife of Birchard
Szabo: Strong man in Mr. Ward's circus
Protected Earth: The 1,000 acres, is named Protected Earth by the new owner, Mr. Ward
Cal: Owner of Cal's Hub in Darnell and love of Mr. Ward
Liza: Cal's daughter
Silas: Real Estate Lawyer in Darnell
Dilsey Somerset: A southerner who is short time friend and lover of Cal and father of Liza
Sam: Longtime citizen, friend, and an occasional lover of Cal
Runaway: In charge of the horses and stables on Protected Earth
Emilio: Worked on Protected Earth
Maude: mule
Chase and Talker (dogs): Bluetick hounds of Mr. Wards
Sparsity: An albino girl, taken in by Mr. Ward, becomes a special person to Mr. Ward and family

Granny Dahlia: Raised Sparsity, Granny dies, Sparsity heads out on her own at twelve

Doc Charing: English Dr. answers Ad and becomes the loved and much needed only physician in Darnell

Leeward: Son of Birchard and Mickey, grows up to become the caretaker of all protected earth.

Folly: Son of Birchard and Mickey. A little person

Leeward: Husband of Tess

Tess: Mother of Girlean, wife of Leeward, lover of Ajay

Ajay: Mixed race, father of Girlean

Garrison Anne Polly: Lover of Papa Lee, Mother of Gap

Gap: Papa Lee and Garrison's daughter, mother of Monty and lover of Starling.

Starling: Handsome Gemologist. Loner, and father of Monty of Gap's lover at seventeen

Papa Lee or Papa: Was Little D, but as an adult was called Papa Lee

Monty: Daughter of Gap and Starling. Granddaughter of Papa Lees and Mother of Plaid Patience.

Seamus: Worked on Protected Earth

Plaid Patience (or Plaid): Child of Monty, grandchild of Gap and Papa Lee

Jazzy: Friend, Protector, and lover to Monty in New York

June Light (or June): Social worker in New York, and friend to Plaid Patience

Hanna: Bag lady in central park

Mr. And Mrs. Millhouse: Plaid Patience's foster parents in NY

Girlean (or Girl): Mixed race child of Tess's and Ajay's

Monterey, Dessie, and Azzie

"Then we sat on the edge of the earth, with our feet dangling over the side, and marveled that we had found each other."

— *Erik Dillard*

For my Grandmother Monterey, Great Aunt Dessie, Great Aunt Azzie, the joy of hearing your voices and laughter, as you three drank muscadine wine and played cards on the back porch.

VOLUME I
The Darnell Children

CHAPTER I

A Fortunate Abandonment

Under normal order of events, the circus would be a happy, joyful, and laughing place for children, but this day was overshadowed by a hateful deed. A father abandoned two of his children at the circus grounds. The father yearned to be of the carriage trade. He was an over-wearied, wretched man. His showy horse-drawn carriage came to a slushy, abrupt stop in the soupy, early, wet morning. Once handsome, his skin, teeth, and soul now yellowed by cheap whiskey, smokes, all-night gambling, and by indifference and resentment to work and his four children, Mr. Darnell, now a widower, was left with four children. He set his goal to rid himself of that responsibility.

The carriage door opened and a red-haired girl of twelve jumped out, landing smack in the middle of a mud puddle. Not jolted, she quickly turned back to the carriage door, reached in, and lifted her six-year-old brother out. The air was wet and bitter cold. She shivered, then ignored her discomfort and pulled the boy in tight to her body and sheltered him.

The driver's mordant words followed the two children, "You two, be off with ya! Out of my life, a condemned life I've lived." His whiskeyed voice held no concern except for himself. The horses bolted as he hit their backside with his cruel whip, their breath blasts of white mist remained in the frigid air. The carriage splashed muddy water onto the children which only added to their misery. The two children stood shivering and clung to each other. One may ask, why were they not more distraught at being thrown out like garbage by their father? They whispered to each other, "It's for the best not to ever see him again — no matter what the future holds."

Their father, Mr. Darnell, had married the outstanding, beautiful, socially positioned Tansy DeLamore. He had enticed her with his dashing good looks and a fabricated story of temporary estrangement from his well-placed family. The adamant objections of her skeptical parents enhanced his appeal. To Tansy, ultimately, forbidden desire led to their elopement. His calculated hope was that the marriage would not only elevate his social status but would also allow him to share in her family's wealth. This was not to be. The DeLamore family was resolute in their daughter's unfortunate choice of a husband. Their well-educated, cultured daughter was excessively naïve. Still, she deserved an honorable husband.

For years, they had carefully cultivated a select field of desirable suitors for an advantageous match. However, with Tansy's elopement with the penniless swindler Darnell, their plans for their only child's future were shattered. The DeLamore's talked into each night, blaming themselves. Where did we go wrong? But no answers were reached to ease their pain.

The DeLamore's heartache created such a stony hardness in them that Tansy was disinherited and cast out of her family. The situation caused her great unhappiness. Any desires she had or expectations of her family's acceptance of her husband were lost. The fears of her parents proved true. Not wanting her parents to know what an awful husband Darnell was, Tansy tried to change him and prove them wrong. Over the next few years, she did receive pleasure from her children and with each birth, Tansy gave thanks. They provided her with reason to greet her days. Mr. Darnell, frustrated by the failure of his scheme, became increasingly surly and abusive to his wife and children. Tansy's health of body and mind started to degenerate.

Her ruinous marriage continued to spiral her downward. She now lived each day for her brilliant, beautiful children. All the hours she spent on training and educating her girls would pay off. As the family grew more impoverished, her three girls—Monterey, Dessie, and Azzie—had to help support the family. The three went into the streets performing. Tansy had taught the musically inclined Dessie to play her cherished violin. Azzie, the youngest, did acrobatics of great skill and loved the applause she received.

Monterey, the eldest, sang with the voice of an angel. At first, she and Dessie performed together but quickly learned they could bring more home if they split up and worked in different areas. It took courage, but their need was great. They soon learned to face their fears for the good of the family. The girls brought home coins for the family coffers. No matter how hard the girls worked, they were still children and could not take in enough money to support the family.

A bit of luck came their way when their home was to be foreclosed on. A close friend of Tansy's parents, who happened to own the bank, let the Darnell family continue to live there. Tansy was grateful and suspected her Mama and Daddy, who still refused to meet their grandchildren or accept their daughter's marriage, were secretly making the mortgage payments. She accepted the generosity and asked no questions.

Mr. Darnell, on rare occasions, did bring in a few dollars from his writing. People that read his published works gave him decent reviews, but his lifestyle would wash out his talents.

He did manage to keep up his one pride, the fancy carriage and horses Tansy's parents had gifted her with as a wedding present. He saw that the horses were well-fed and groomed and the carriage shined. More care was given to the carriage than the wife and children.

From an early age, the fearless, athletic Azzie helped to feed and exercise the carriage horses. She would feel the powerful animal move beneath her and imagine that she was running away. The other children were afraid of the horses but Azzie loved the feeling of escape as she indulged in her secret thoughts of cantering into a new life.

Through the years, Darnell's desperation to constantly elevate himself and his failure to achieve this increased his resentment even stronger toward his wife and children. When Tansy became pregnant with her fourth child from a night of wifely duty, Mr. Darnell was outraged. He foisted even more anger upon his entire family. The physical and verbal abuse grew as his frustration increased.

Tansy was bedridden through most of her last pregnancy, but times were so grueling, she was forced to bundle her children up as best as she could and go out into the winter weather to call upon her parents. Tansy's father said, "Tansy! Our dear Tansy, is there any way that we can persuade you to come home? That no-account Darnell has never and will never provide for his family."

Tansy looked around at the home she grew up in with caring and fun parents. How could that love have turned to so much disdain for her? Their disappointment hit them all in the deepest part of a person.

Her mother stood sobbing in the background. She said softly, "Come children, have some hot milk and a meal." The three girls followed her into the kitchen, all the while looking back toward the parlor to check on their mother. Tansy reassured her daughters with a weak smile.

Tansy continued her conversation with her father. "Father, I am in no condition to engage in a quarrel. Will you provide?" Tansy felt her baby kick strong as her belly pushed against her worn, long, black, wool cape. Her concerns were for her children. Hard times had absorbed most of the family's wealth. Mr. and Mrs. DeLamore both agreed to finance food, coal, and clothes for the children each month. However, Father gave his solemn word on financial assistance. He would not create any circumstance for Darnell to receive DeLamore money to support his ungoverned ways.

Tansy and the children walked home with their hunger satisfied. For the first time, Tansy talked to the girls of her parents' sorrow and why she was cast out of her family. The girls, feeling their mother's pain, said, "Mother, please don't worry. You don't have to explain. It hurts you so badly." They all joined hands and were thankful for any relief that their grandparents gave.

Tansy went into childbirth a weak, dispirited woman. She died giving birth to a son. She left a loving note for her parents and had a separate, personal goodbye talk with her children. Monterey delivered the note to the DeLamore's. Mr. DeLamore handed the note to his wife and said, "We lost our Tansy when she married that horrid man. We were deprived of knowing our grandchildren, but we will do what we can. Our resources have become bare." Their father was rarely around and didn't even show up for Tansy's services.

The girls continued living with an embittered father and a newborn to care for. Monterey, being the oldest, took over management of the home and secretly hid away a few dollars they still earned in the streets and the pittance that the DeLamore's sent.

The girls felt great sorrow for the loss of their beloved mother but felt at last she was peaceful. Never again would she have to live in fear. They didn't understand how their sweet mother could have loved their father, but she had been connected to him in a peculiar way. The girls often talked among themselves of their mother, how she loved them and devoted time to make sure they were educated. Tansy had left a strong influence on her children. Each child grew to have strongly marked qualities. The girls dedicated themselves to see that the baby boy, Little Darnell received the same early education their mother had given them.

Time passed rapidly. All staples stopped coming from the grandparents. Monterey sent Azzie to check for the problem. Azzie arrived at the DeLamore house to find that it had been boarded up. A neighbor informed her that the DeLamore's were consumptive. They died within a few days of each other. No, they did not know where they had been buried and the bank had taken ownership of the property. Azzie returned with the sad news.

The sisters felt robbed of never being given a chance to know their grandparents. Monterey spoke, "I know they would have been proud of us."

Monterey, once more, did what was necessary to care for and protect her sisters and Little Darnell. The next six years for the Darnell children focused on scrounging up food. Monterey saw to their education. They stayed out of their father's way. There were no more even remotely good family times with their father. How he obtained his money for drinking and an outside life, they didn't know. The children had not been taught any kind of religion, so faith didn't play a part in their survival. The four would huddle together, dreading the sound of the horse and carriage being put away for the night. Often in his drunken grimness, he would use his belt on the girls.

They protected their younger brother. On one occasion, when Little D wandered into the room when their father's violently destructive behavior exploded on the girls, he turned toward the small boy. The three girls overtook him and took the strap away. Monty didn't yell. She said in a definite voice, "Father, if you ever so much as harm a hair on Little D's head, you will regret it. The harm that will happen to you is beyond imagination. Azzie, you and Dessie put Little D back to bed." Mr. Darnell finally passed out, muttering in slurred unintelligible rage.

The girls often played out ways as to how they could punish their father for this past cruel treatment to their mother and now them. The best times were when he lost consciousness. Evil thoughts entered the girls' heads. "How would life be if he disappeared?" "Why couldn't he have died instead of Mother and our grandparents?"

No one had the answer.

The children managed to survive. One thing the father did provide was his love of books in all areas that a person needed for a good education. Monterey took advantage of this and pushed her siblings to read, read, and read more.

A change took place when Mr. Darnell started courting a well-to-do widow. The widow enjoyed the company of his often-extravagant display of manners and dress, but she refused to take on the responsibility of four children. Darnell soothed the widow's doubts by a fictionalized story that his dead wife's sister desired to raise his beloved children. The rich widow believed the yarn and set about making wedding plans. Their father then set out to rid himself of his children. With no concern for their happiness or welfare, he came up with a solution for each one.

First was Monterey, the oldest. Mr. Darnell answered an ad from an aging man named Mr. Andrews who advertised for a wife, mostly to care for his children. His devoted wife, he wrote, passed away and he needed a smart, attractive wife. He would provide a safe home and generous pay to her parents or guardian. Mr. Andrews paid several visits to their home. One day after a visit, Mr. Darnell said to Monterey, "Mr. Andrews needs a young woman to care for him and his household. He has looked you over and wants you for his wife. He sees you are stern-faced and much too tall for a girl but, all in all, he thinks you are a fine, strong-looking, young girl. Forget your foolish dreams of becoming a teacher."

At this point, he took her book from the table and threw it into the fireplace. Monterey looked in horror as the fire tore through her favorite book and turned it to ash. She thought, 'Just as my future looks.' Mr. Darnell then unbuckled his belt and pulled it into his hand. Monterey knew the pain of the belt. She still had the strength to defy him. The thought of leaving her siblings tore at her heart. She pleaded, "But Father, I am still a child. I know nothing of being a wife. I won't leave with Mr. Andrews! I won't! I am going to be a teacher. I am needed here." Monterey stood paralyzed at the thought of being a wife to any man. She thought of the promise she made to her mother on Tansy's death bed. "Mother," she had vowed, "I will give my all to educate my sisters and Little D." Monterey remembered how Tansy had held her newborn for a few minutes before letting go of life.

Mr. Darnell's face became distorted, his yellow teeth throwing spit, his red hair and red-veined face coming closer to Monterey. The old stench of stale, cheap whiskey filled her nose and the room. He turned from her to bolt the door. She continued her screaming and pleading. The other children, hearing their beloved sister's terror, beat on the door. When he didn't open, Dessie ran to the barn to retrieve an axe. Azzie and Little Darnell continued to plead for their father to open the door.

Dessie returned shortly. As the children moved away from the door, she assaulted the door with all her might. The axe finally broke through. The door opened. Little Darnell ran to Monterey; he clung to her legs, feeling the wetness of blood on his small hands, begging his sister not to leave. The pain of the children's suffering at the thought of being parted was unbearable for each sibling.

Then there was a silence as Monterey gathered her siblings around her. With extreme courage, she spoke to the crazed man, "Father, you may bend our bodies, but never, never will you destroy our souls or separate us in spirit! And someday, you'll get what you have coming. When that happens, Father, you will remember me."

Her father tore Little Darnell from her, knowing the young boy was the girl's frailty. As he left the room, he said, "Monterey, I expect you to be ready within the hour. Mr. Andrews will arrive for you." Feeling she had no place to turn for help, Monterey consoled her sisters, "Please know I feel this is for the best that I follow Father's order. I fear for each of us. Never forget our beautiful mother and her teachings. I will hold each of you dear in my heart and thoughts always. We will reunite one day. Know that when I say my prayers, my words will be for each of you, every day of my life."

Mr. Darnell returned to the parlor with Monterey's bag. She could endure no more. The carriage driver handed an envelope to Mr. Darnell. Just like that, Monterey was gone. The solution to rid himself of Dessie came as he rode back from visiting the widow. He passed a band of gypsies camped alongside the river. The gypsies were in the business of bartering and Mr. Darnell needed two new horses for his carriage. He had an exotic-looking, talented daughter, a gifted violin player. Though most of Tansy's fine things had been sold, she had managed to keep her violin for Dessie. Tansy gave her music lessons and she practiced when her father wasn't around, but he'd discovered her talent. She would be a jewel for the gypsies. An opportunity presented itself.

Dessie went willingly after a tearful goodbye to Azzie and Little Darnell. Riding to the camp, Dessie thought, nothing can be as horrible as living with my father and I may get a chance to run away and find Monterey. And so, it was. Dessie stood on the riverbank while Mr. Darnell negotiated her fate. His high voice trickled down as he argued over the terms. The gypsies sealed their deal and her father hitched up his new horses. Dessie stared at the man that was her father. The sorrow and pain she felt was for her sisters and brother. If her father never took another breath, she thought, there would not be one tear shed for his soul. Her father rode away without even looking back. Walking into the camp, she heard laughter and happy fiddling. The joy in the camp drew her in like a magnet. Just like that, Dessie was gone.

The other two children who remained would be his biggest problem, Darnell thought as he rode away from the gypsy camp. On his way home, he noticed a bright colorful sign nailed to the side of a barn. It read, "MR. WARD'S SENSATIONAL EXTRAVAGANZA OF

CIRCUS PERFORMERS." He stopped the carriage. Holding his head, he cried out, "What kind of man am I to give my children away?" His remorse was short-lived. He thought of his rich widow, waiting for him to come to her unencumbered with children. "A selfish man I am but I deserve a richer life! This might be my last chance!" He tapped the horses with his whip and headed home.

Darnell didn't need further information. Focused on his goal, he reasoned, "The circus is a perfect place." Night was approaching. He figured early morning would be the precise time—before the circus awoke.

Azzie held Little D protectively as she watched her father's carriage retreat into the morning fog. Only twelve years old, the overdeveloped, red-haired Azzie posed a striking figure. She thought, we are free, all of us are free from evil, never to feel the sting and pain of his belt or see his ugly face. For the first time since her mother's death, even in her present position, she felt a smile on her face. The circus felt like a way of hope for her and Little D. A fence surrounded the area.

In the foggy morning, Azzie could not see whether there was a gate to enter the area. She bent down to Little D. "I am going to lift you up over the fence. Keep your hands on the fence. Can't lose you, Little D." Over he went and then she climbed the fence. Smells of sawdust and animals filled the damp air, along with different sounds of animals drifting through the morning mist. She liked it. Walking closer in, Little D held on tightly to her.

She could barely make out the circus sign that was fairly visible in the fog. With a cheerful voice, she said to Little Darnell, "Look, Little D! We are at the circus!"

The boy answered with cold trembling lips, "Azzie, I like the circus. But I will miss our big sisters. Will we ever see them again? Can we find them? They would like the circus."

Azzie felt pain for her much-loved little brother. Anger smoldered in her heart. She thought if she had that axe, she would chop their father up and feed him to the big circus cats. But she smiled and thought, they would probably spit his wretched body out. The taste would be so awful. She spoke to reassure Little D, "Hush, Little D. We will be okay. Monty and Dessie love us and would never have left on their own. They will be happier, as we will be. One day, we will see them again, I promise. I'll protect you." She took his hand and walked toward the entrance to the big tent.

Little D tugged at her hand and said, "Can we see the lions? And Azzie, I will never give up until I find our sisters."

"Sure, Little D. Now come along." And just like that, the two belonged to the circus.

CHAPTER 2

A Moral Man

Mr. Ward's circus brought entertainment into the big cities and small towns. Being a moral man, he felt an indebtedness to the folks in each town where his circus performed. He hired locals for odd jobs. When the circus started arriving, some reached their destination by horse-drawn brightly painted caravans and some by train. Tents had been set up, sheds and fences had to be built to secure the complete area. Horses required stalls and an exercise area was established for the animals.

Wonderful, colorful wagons that housed the performers were secured. Temporary jobs gave the citizens badly needed earnings. People would travel long distances to see the circus and sometimes to work there.

Extensive advertisements in the form of exciting posters were displayed on anything available, barns, trains, trees, and on the front of businesses. The posters showed big cats, beautiful women flying through the air in sparkly, scanty outfits, and bare back riders on Arabian horses performing death defying feats. The circus brought entrancement, allurement, and play in towns.

Opening day of the circus, there was a lavish parade down main street that lured young and old, beginning with clowns' antics, followed by waving, costumed performers, some riding an elephant or horses, and wagons bearing cages of exotic animals. The parade ended with the iconic wheeled calliope playing the siren song to come to the circus.

Mr. Ward was held in reverence by his performers. He paid well and provided good food and housing. Also, he praised and respected each performer for their talent and dedication to him in the success of the company. Some of the performers traveled with their families. Others only saw their family twice a year. Mr. Ward understood their sacrifice.

The two abandoned Darnell children approached the large tent. Azzie said, "Hush, Little D. It looks like a child with a lantern is coming toward us. Let's be very still." Little D stopped his chatter and pulled in close to his sister.

The swinging lantern steadily approached, the fog giving the light an eerie glow. A deep voice rang out, "Hey, you two, stop. What are you doing here this time of the morning?" Azzie then saw that the lantern was in the hands of a little person. The voice bellied the man's size.

He softened when he saw children before him. "Don't be afraid. I am Birchard. I work for the circus. You both look cold and I bet hungry. How about some warm milk and bread?" Birchard did not start asking the children questions. His kind heart was more concerned about their welfare — their history would come out later.

Little D spoke before his sister. "Yes, Mr. Birchard, we are hungry. Our father left us." Birchard found it odd that the children didn't appear to be more upset. Why wouldn't they be, if they had just been abandoned by their father? He stepped closer to the children.

Birchard said, "Come along. This wet morning is chilling my bones. Also, how long have you children been out in the cold?" Not waiting for the children to answer, Birchard continued, "I will take you to Mickey, my wife. She will see that you are both fed and changed into some warm, dry clothes."

Azzie thanked Birchard. The children gladly followed him back to his tent, where Mickey, Birchard's warm hearted wife welcomed them. The couple's wagon felt cozy and warm, with a big pot belly stove right in the middle.

Azzie looked around; the furnishings were of miniature size.

Mickey spoke, "My, my. Birchard, dear, who are these children?"

Azzie liked Mickey's voice. A gentle voice, she thought, and besides, she was pretty with dark hair like Dessie's.

Birchard replied, "They will have to tell us who they are. All I know is that they say their father left them at our circus grounds."

At five-feet-two, Azzie towered over Mickey's three-foot frame. Mickey reached for the children's hands. "There's plenty of time to tell us your story. Let's get you out of those wet clothes and into a warm bath to warm your bones. What are your names?"

Azzie replied, "Mrs. Mickey, I am Azzie. I am twelve. Little D is seven. There are four Darnell children. Father got rid of us all." She started to cry, then composed herself.

Birchard moved chairs in close to the stove while Mickey got some warm blankets. She let Azzie change behind a drawn curtain. Little D did not want to let his sister out of his sight. The miniature couple sensed the young boy's fear. They spoke with Azzie as she changed out of her wet clothes to reassure the boy. He needed to hear that his sister was okay and that she wasn't going to leave him.

After the children were fed, she kept them wrapped in warm blankets, washed their clothes and dried them by the stove. Birchard spoke, "Mickey, darling, I must inform Mr. Ward about the children."

Azzie in a now constant chatter with Mickey, stopped and directed her words to Birchard and asked, "Who is Mr. Ward?"

"Mr. Ward is the circuses kind-hearted owner."

Suddenly anxious, Azzie asked, Mr. Birchard, "Mr. Ward won't send us away or try to contact our father, will he? Little D and I wish to never see our cruel father ever, ever, ever, ever again."

Birchard didn't know how Mr. Ward would react to the news, so he didn't answer Azzie, but said quietly to Mickey, "I'm leaving for a short time, Mickey." He kissed his wife and left.

As he walked to Mr. Ward's tent, Birchard thought of how Mr. Ward had treated him like a son and had given him both the opportunity and responsibility to earn the respect of other performers. He spoke out to no one and said, "He never let my size deter him. I have tried to live up to each task. When Mickey and I have a child one day, the child will be named after Mr. Ward."

Birchard moved quickly, anxious to deliver the news of the children. Birchard thought of the dastardly man who put two beautiful children out into the cold, to possibly freeze to death. Whatever brought that father to do such a deed? Birchard brought his thoughts back and pulled the small bell outside Mr. Ward's tent. Mr. Ward's strong, direct voice gave a quick response. "Yes, Birchard, come in."

The two together were a site of interest. Birchard stood at just over three feet, while Mr. Ward was over six feet tall. No two greater, trusted friends ever existed. Birchard was Mr. Ward's contact with the other circus performers in the outside world.

Mr. Ward's reclusiveness was not class distinction. None of his actions was anything but kind. As the ring master, he showed the behavior of a great stage star when he walked into the center circus ring. Birchard never tired of hearing and watching Mr. Ward start his introduction in his black top hat, soft red Italian wool tailed coat, and knee-high black boots shined to perfection by Birchard himself.

The reverberating sound of his voice was carried throughout the large tent.

"Ladies and gentlemen, welcome to Ward's greatest show of circus performers." He would then go into describing each act, leaving the crowd in anticipation of each act to follow. His own history was a deep secret, which he never chose to make known. An avid reader, he traveled with a well-stocked library. He was versed in a wide range of subjects from agriculture, animal husbandry, and politics. He did not believe in organized religion but knew the Bible thoroughly and read it often. When Birchard passed his tent, Birchard often observed Mr. Ward on his knees in prayer. Mr. Ward's shadow loomed large over him.

Mr. Ward, a cup of tea in hand, greeted Birchard.

"Come, come, Birchard. Sit." He pulled a special chair and a step stool over for Birchard. Mr. Ward then poured another cup of tea that he passed to Birchard with a jar of honey. "What brings you out so early on this wet freezing morning? My friend, you are always a welcome sight for good company, under any kind of weather."

"Thank you, sir." Birchard took a few sips of the hot tea. "Feels good. Two children were left at our grounds. They are with Mickey. Said their father left them. It's an odd thing they expressed no desire to return to him. The young girl is a beauty. The boy is a bit frail looking, but both are spirited." Birchard knew that he sounded nervous. He was. He didn't know how Mr. Ward would respond to him taking in the children and not wishing to report them to Wayward Children Authorities.

"Birchard, my friend, you do bring interesting news to the start of our day. Are they okay?"

"I believe they are enjoying a rest by the stove at present."

"Birchard, any ideas as to what we will do with a small boy and a beautiful young girl?" Mr. Ward considered their dilemma as he proceeded to get dressed.

Birchard assisted him in setting up his shaving table. Birchard moved in quick, short steps, as was a little person's way.

"Sir," Birchard said, "That will be a decision only you can make. Once you meet them, I don't believe that you will choose to send the children back to whatever life they came from."

Birchard was pacing the room, watching Mr. Ward's every move.

"Birchard, you believe we should provide them with a home? After the children have rested, bring them to me. I would like to discuss how they ended up here. It is unfathomable that a person could abandon their children. Let's do this before the performance tonight. Better still, bring them to the breakfast room. I will meet them, and we can introduce the children to all performer families. Because by taking in two new persons will most likely affect each one, so I feel it's only right to take all responses."

Birchard never desired to bring unpleasant tidings to Mr. Ward. Today was not the time to inform him that Mickey was with child. Birchard knew the importance of his and Mickey's act to the circus, so he made the decision to wait for at least a few more weeks. He knew Mr. Ward would be happy for them, but also knowing how it would affect his circus.

"Yes, Mickey will see that the children are cared for and ready to meet you. Mr. Ward, most of the tickets are sold. We will certainly have a full audience tonight. S.R.O. Mickey and I will perform our new act. It is perfect." Birchard placed his hands on the chair and lifted himself down in a swinging motion.

"Your new act is frightful for me to watch. I need you to set my mind at ease," declared Mr. Ward.

Mr. Ward rose from his chair, the lantern in the tent cast his 6 foot 4 shadows across the tent, putting Birchard virtually in the dark.

Birchard stepped aside into the light and said, "Never would I put my Mickey at risk."

Birchard wanted to perform the new high-wire act without a safety net. He felt sure of their act, but Mr. Ward cared more for his friend's safety than for the extra excitement created by not having a net.

Mr. Ward leaned down to shake Birchard's forceful hand. "Thank you, Birchard, for your trustworthiness. I rest easier knowing that you and Mickey are close by."

Birchard excused himself and headed to check on Mickey and the children. Walking along, he no longer needed a lantern. Daylight was showing itself. He glanced down the formed alley created by the wall of caravans. People had started to mill about. He never got tired of the circus saying its good morning, the different languages, strong coffee smells, animals yawning, and music coming from the bands. It was the sound of life.

Birchard rarely let his mind rest. His thoughts ran to Mr. Ward who lately seemed to carry around a serious forlornness evident since their recent talk. He knew Mr. Ward's pioneer heart longed for land to build a farm and a town. He revealed his dreams one night after they had overindulged in some local white lightning.

"Birchard, I am ready for a bucolic piece of land that is waiting for me to use its resources to help build a town. I'm ready to wake up in familiar landscapes. I pray you and Mickey will consider sharing the dream with me. I believe it's getting close to the perfect time."

Recalling that specific conversation, Birchard lifted the door flap on his tent and smiled at the happy sounds of children's voices coming from inside. Soon he would hear his own child's laughter. His thoughts soared at the thought, of his child running to greet him as he walked through the door.

Mickey was reading to the children, and fine looking they were. The girl spoke, "Mr. Birchard! My brother and I thank you and Mickey for your kindness. Mickey gave us permission to address her by her first name. Please we beg you, don't send us to an orphanage. Mickey has informed us that it's Mr. Ward's decision. May we talk with Mr. Ward?"

Azzie stopped talking, walked over and took her brother's hand, and came back to Birchard. "Forgive my rudeness, but we must see Mr. Ward. I know after he hears our story, he will not send us away. We don't seek charity. We will work hard. I'm an excellent horse rider and quick learner. My little brother is very smart, he already knows his numbers and he rarely cries or complains. Our father does not want us. He is a very cold person." She then turned back to Mickey and said, "Mrs. Mickey, please tell Mr. Birchard what my body looks like." Birchard didn't have a chance to get a word out.

Mickey reached out and took the girl's hand. She said, "Dear Birchard, this girl has been beaten often. She has fresh wounds and old scars. You must do what is necessary. Mr. Ward will listen to you. We cannot under any circumstance return them to a tormented life. This is one time we must insist."

Birchard could never refuse a request from his wife. He adored her and placed great value on her opinions and wishes.

Birchard spoke, "Mickey, Mr. Ward requested that we bring them to the dining tent. We will have breakfast with the other performers, and then Mr. Ward will meet Azzie and Little D. Now, I must take my morning walk and check on feeding the horses and the new baby elephant, our food supply, and all my many tasks. I will meet up with you and the children in the dining tent." Birchard reached and got a writing tablet and pen and adjusted his hat. He left for his grounds check.

'Mr. Ward is the wisest and kindest person I've ever known. At first, he will answer no. But then he will say, convince me. No doubt, he will make the right decision,' Birchard thought as he completed his morning check of the circus. His rounds included checks for big cats, performers welfare, costumes, and the general wellbeing of each person and animal. It was a huge job. But Birchard was up to it.

The children caused a stir among the performers when they entered the morning breakfast tent. Mickey was holding Little D's hand. Azzie's fiery red hair haloed her captivating face. Porcelain skin dotted with freckles showcased eyes that showed no fear. Her battered existence probably contributed to her fractious forward character, and her straight, defiant posture.

The performers were in pockets of chatter when Mr. Ward entered the dining tent. It was not typical for him to join them for breakfast. He sometimes ate with the performers in the dining tent at night after the last show. Mr. Ward used the time to give them praise for their performances and his thanks for their collaboration in making Ward's circus successful.

Mr. Ward walked among the tables, giving good mornings. He then went over to Mickey and the two children. Mickey introduced the children, who each stood and extended a hand. The two children kept standing until Mr. Ward said, "Please sit." He quickly directed a question to Azzie, "Why did your father abandon such handsome, bright looking, and mannered children as you both appear? Is he mad?"

Azzie's face became animated with anger. She said, "Yes, and Mr. Ward, our mother died giving birth to my brother. After she died, my two older sisters took care of us and schooled us. Our mother had been a lady of society. Father was bitter that our mother's family disinherited her for marrying a no-account like him. He was just after her money and her status. He thought money would make him into a gentleman of high standing. He also blamed us children and took his bitterness out on us. We ate and had clothes because my middle sister Dessie played her fiddle at private parties and street corners. My oldest sister Monterey sang on the street corners, and I did acrobatics in the park. Monterey begged local merchants and town officials for help. Father then sold Monterey into a loveless marriage. Our sister

Dessie was bartered to gypsies for two horses. Little D and I were left at your circus fence. And that's that, here we are."

Mickey handed the fiery girl a glass of water as she put her hand on the girl's arm, Mickey asked her, "Azzie, do you wish to rest? This must be painful."

"Oh, no! Mrs. Mickey please, if you and Mr. Ward don't let us stay, that would be painful. We can't go back to our cruel father. You have seen my body, please! Please, Mr. Ward, keep us!" Azzie fell down on her knees. The tent of performers were in total silence. Not a fork was lifted as the girl pleaded.

Mickey gently touched the girl's head and said, "Azzie, come, dear."

The young boy was crying. He crawled under the table and came out on the side next to Mr. Ward. His voice was trembling, but he managed to explain himself well. "We are strong and used to hard work. My sister can ride a horse like no one else. You have horses, don't you, Mr. Ward? And I can shine shoes like a mirror. You have shoes, don't you, Mr. Ward?

Azzie spoke up. "It's okay, Little D. We're staying, right, Mr. Ward? You wouldn't send us back to such an awful life, would you?"

Mr. Ward thought as he watched the children beg for a home, how their faces showed such lined concern. He knew the feeling of nausea that lives in your stomach. It never leaves, it lurks within your soul. Even through one may go on to have monetary security. Mr. Ward was still holding his dream, of an everlasting home place. He also knew the pain of being abandoned.

Mr. Ward made his decision, but let the children have their say. He stood then turned around, eyebrows raised, and slowly swept the performers and their families with his gaze, noting their silent pleas.

Momentarily, Mr. Ward locked eyes with Birchard, gave a barely predictable nod. "No, Azzie," Mr. Ward put his arm around the girl. He then reached and picked up Little D, setting him on his broad shoulders. With the ring master's voice, he said, "Let's all welcome

Little D and Azzie to our circus family." The children started intermingling with their new circus families and ate a most welcome, hearty breakfast.

The tent erupted in cheers. The performers, now giving applause, instead of receiving it, were a euphoric sight and sound.

Azzie stared at Mickey with huge eyes, unable to take it in. "We can stay?"

Mickey threw her arms around Azzie and rocked her, crying and laughing at once. "Yes, Azzie, you are staying."

Mr. Ward set Little D on the ground beside his sister. He called Birchard and Mickey to his side for a few private words. Children from the circus families crowded in, shouting their names, laughing, and dancing around in a happy bedlam. Mr. Ward, shaken and emotional, left the tent.

CHAPTER 3

Star Attraction

The appealing children were accepted into the circus with joy and interest. The gossip line on the circus grounds was active with questions: Who are the children? Will they become performers? Why were they abandoned? Will Mr. Ward adopt them?

The children possess huge, questioning minds and follow behind the many performers, wanting to know everything about them and the circus. They were the star attractions.

Azzie loved horses and, being an acrobat and a great rider, became spellbound by the bareback act. She would arise early to watch the bareback rider practice. Azzie asked questions and observed each and every movement of the performer. She eventually convinced the horseback professional to let her try a few acrobatic maneuvers on the horse. Azzie was a natural—fearless with natural rhythmic movements. She seemed to defy gravity. Azzie developed a special bond with a white Arabian horse named Princess. At each practice session, she would sail onto Princess's back. With Azzie's strong, muscular control and her beauty, she stood out.

Birchard knew Azzie had been hanging out at the bareback riders' practice sessions. He was completely struck with wonder when he walked into the main tent, catching her performing the bareback rider's complete act on Princess.

The regular performer, afraid that she would be in trouble for putting the 12-year-old in danger told Birchard, "I am with child and will be leaving the circus. Soon Azzie will be more than ready to take over my act. Yes! She is young but is a star performer."

Birchard could not disagree. In fact, Azzie was better than her teacher.

Birchard informed Mr. Ward about the bareback rider's condition and then told him about Azzie. "She is talented. I observed her. She has the act down and has added more daring moves. Would you like to view her practice tomorrow morning?" Birchard eagerly waited for Mr. Ward's reply. So did Azzie, as she waited outside Mr. Ward's tent for Birchard's word from Mr. Ward.

Mr. Ward was somewhat doubtful about putting the young girl into such a precarious act. He was aware of the attention the girl would attract. He was a showman and understood the need of an act to replace the one leaving. Mickey had made Azzie a sequined red outfit, almost the color of her hair. Birchard assured Mr. Ward once more that Azzie was ready. Birchard and Mickey had agreed that Azzie could live with them but did not have enough room for both children. So, Mr. Ward had Birchard build a bed in his tent for Little D. Mickey continued to assist in little D's care. Mr. Ward's voice was softer and filled with concern whenever he spoke about the two children.

Mr. Ward wasn't sure Azzie was ready at such a young age to take the responsibility of becoming a star attraction. "My wish is that we wait until we open in the next town. She can continue to train and take over the care of grooming not only Princess, but she can also help with the other show horses. If she handles these responsibilities, we will start advertising our new star. "Birchard, inform Mickey to arrange photos for Azzie's poster so they will be ready when we open." Birchard hurried out to inform Azzie of the news.

Birchard and Mickey kept Mr. Ward informed with all the concerns of the children. A tutor was brought in to aid with the children's studies. The boy was now eight and absorbed education with ferocity, but he was still having nightmares about being separated from his other two sisters.

Mr. Ward assured him, "Someday, Little D, we will find your sisters. I promise. I understand in the back of your heart there will live an unquenchable longing for your sisters until it's satisfied."

Often in the middle of the night, tired from long practice sessions and taking care of cleaning stalls, then putting down fresh sawdust and hay, Azzie was still tormented by nightmares of her father returning. Birchard and Mickey would often get up and console her. "You are safe, dear Azzie. He will never hurt you again. Mr. Ward would not allow him to see you or Little D," said Mickey.

On especially lovely nights, Azzie liked to walk the surface grounds when the stars were clear in the heavens. She would quietly leave Birchard's, take a walk, then enter Mr. Ward's tent, just to be near her treasured brother. Often times, she fell asleep on the floor beside Little D's bed.

Sometimes, Little D would wake up, feeling the presence of his sister. Reaching out, he would touch her hair and whisper, so as not to wake Mr. Ward. He would hand one of his blankets to her. She would take his hand and massage around each fingernail, as their mother did when she and her sisters were young and had nightmares. It always made them sleepy, and then she would tell a story to her children.

Little D said, "Sis, tell me a story about Monterey."

Azzie began, "Monterey had a long day, cooking and cleaning a very large house. Her husband, who she still calls "Mr. Andrews", because he was not her husband by choice, is expecting guests for the weekend holiday. She made your favorite, Little D, an exceptional egg white icing a mile high and golden brown from the oven for the banana pudding. It shines and entices all who enter the dining room with its inviting aroma placed on a walnut sideboard. Along with the banana pudding is a snowy coconut cake with candy cherries. As she places the last cherry on top, shaped as a heart she says, "These are for Little D—his favorite!"

Little D chimed in, "Was banana pudding your favorite?"

"Yes, but it was a rarity because we could not get bananas. Once in a blue moon, father did bring a stock of bananas home. Funny. Then sis wiped her hands on her rose embroidered apron, leaving cherry stains. Then she reaches for a pretty amber-colored decanter of brandy, gently takes a glass and pours it full. The glass is placed on her bedside table. She has her bath, brushes her long, dark, shiny hair and ties it back with a red ribbon. A box of blue stationary, a feathered pen, and paper are on her desk. She turns her brandy glass up and relaxes into the moment, then starts to write:

My dear ones, Dessie, Azzie, and Little D,

On this star bright evening, I close my eyes and use my precious gift of imagination to check that you are all safe, no matter where you rest your dear heads. My heart is full of love, reaching out, sending hugs and kisses. My dear sister Dessie, I know you are playing mama's violin and writing beautiful music. My darling little sis Azzie, do you have your lovely red hair in braids?

I know that you are performing somewhere. And my heart, my little Darnell, I am sure you have grown taller than those sunflowers that grew beside the fence in our backyard. As you put your heads down for a nightly prayer, know we will be together one day. Remember to smile when you think of me, your loving, devoted sister. Mr. Anderson is a good man and kind. He signed me up for a teacher's correspondence course and eventually, I can acquire my degree. His children are well-mannered and smart.

All my love,
Monterey.

Little D held back his sniffles. Azzie continued, "Monterey finishes her brandy, seals the letter, and secures it in her stationary box. She wipes away some tears, touches her heart, and places the letter box in her bedside drawer."

"Oh, Azzie! That sounded so good! I could see sis Monterey. Now I will tell you what sis Dessie is doing. She has her long, dark hair in braids with colorful beads of purple, red, and yellow braided in. When she plays the fiddle, her braids swing, and the beads hit together. Her fiddle is under her chin. She is standing under a million stars. She looks up and says, 'My beloved brother and sisters, this song sends my love through small breezes and a soft rain fall to shower over you all.' A campfire burns by her gypsy family's wagon."

"Captivating, Little D. You tell a first-rate story."

"Sis Azzie, can we visit them each night with a story?"

"We will try, Little D. Now, go back to sleep. I will stay with you until you do." She moved closer and hugged him. "I love you. Now, close your eyes. We must not wake Mr. Ward, that would be rude of us." She held his hand until he was asleep, then she left.

Mr. Ward was not asleep. He enjoyed the love expressed between the children. They brought a new spirit and inspiration into his life. He often wondered whether he had a sister or brother somewhere in the

States and often longed to reach out and have a loving hand enclose his.

Each performer in the circus felt pride that they were involved in some small way in the children's adjustment and how well both fit into circus life. Mr. Ward continually checked with the progress of the children's education. He relied on Birchard and Mickey to know the inner lives of the performers, like if anything was needed due to health problems, personal relationships, or loneliness for their families. They were loyal and kept him up to date on all matters. Birchard and Mickey were the headliners of the circus. The high wire act was the most popular act in the show. Mr. Ward often told them how indispensable they were to him. He would say this to Birchard when Birchard got distraught over the guidance of Azzie and Little D. Birchard worried that they should have more young friends, time for sports, and many other things that involved just being kids.

"Birchard, you worry too much. Remember, our circus has survived tremendous ups and downs. We kept on performing, did we not? Surely, we can adjust to raising these two children."

We cannot hold onto time, and it passes quickly. Mickey had lost her baby. After her recuperation, she was back to performing. The pain on her face was obvious. They wanted children before Mickey got any older. She gave more love and care to Little D and Azzie. Mr. Ward did not put Azzie in the first circus lineup. But because she was a beauty and extremely talented, after only a few weeks, Azzie became the most popular act in the circus.

Mr. Ward would often stand by and watch the young girl as she would take risk after risk. Her kinetic energy showed in acrobatics performed on the back of the horse, her head only inches from the ground as the horse galloped around and around the center ring. Mickey made Azzie dazzling, eye-catching costumes. Azzie shone bright as she pushed harder her death-defying feats, leaving the crowds gasping for their breaths.

Mr. Ward worried that Azzie was taking too much on. He asked Mickey to make sure that the girl was attending her tutorial. He did not want the young girl spending any time with certain older male performers.

Mickey and Birchard tried to keep a close watch on the headstrong girl. Azzie now had become the main attraction. She was billed as "The Amazing Blaze". Circus posters lined buildings, trees, boxcars, and barns with her likeness.

It was not publicized that The Amazing Blaze was only fourteen-years old. The private teachers that taught the children math, English, history, and social manners praised them to Mr. Ward as to how exceptional they were—a source of delight. He made sure that the children received an honorable education, as he also provided for all the children of the performers. The children's IQs were high, and their futures could be good and strong.

There was a promise, especially of Little D, to become a person of sterling character. The young boy's desire to learn was vast. Azzie showed little desire to advance her education. Her emotional shell was hardened. Mr. Ward, Mickey, Birchard, and the other caring persons in the circus had not been able to breach it. The only person who softened her perfect face by his presence was Little D.

Little D was proficient in memory. He would particularize on each remembrance about his family. Mr. Ward would ask much about Azzie. He wanted to support her and give her safe harbor for her injured soul. Little D would say, "She looks like our father and has his fiery temper. She would challenge him, knowing a beating would surely follow. My sisters suffered so, but Azzie never cried, no matter how much father beat her. Will she be happy one day? Will she, Mr. Ward?"

"We will provide her with all she needs to have a happy life. You worry too much, Little D. Go find Birchard for me."

He watched the young boy walk away, carrying such a heavy emotional load. Mr. Ward understood Azzie's pain and why she had turned to men for some inner peace. The attention seemed to dull her pain, if only for a short while. Mr. Ward assigned some of Birchard and Mickey's duties to others so they would spend some more time with the troubled girl. Azzie's emotional state was starting to worry Mr. Ward. Being his star performer, Mr. Ward didn't want to lose her. Azzie was physically developing into womanhood at a startling rate. Mickey was making more sophisticated costumes and discarding the old ones. Azzie now stood at about five-foot-nine. She had just turned fourteen.

Azzie was protected with loving diligence by Birchard and Mickey. Her little brother and her fans adored her. Regrettable, the spotlight on the young girl created a problem for the circus and for Azzie herself.

As a star attraction for the circus, Azzie loved the attention. One handsome trapeze artist sought to share her spotlight. To Azzie's delight, he focused his attentions on her. Birchard had spoken to him on several occasions about staying away from the young, emotionally unstable star. Undeterred, the ambitious young man used Azzie's susceptibility and inexperience to gain domination over her. He was a back stairs seducer, knowing that after each of her performances, Azzie would wind down by spending time at the horse stables.

He waited for her. When she appeared, he would begin his sweet talk, enticing her with promises. He would rub the horses down, moving closer to her by inches so that she wouldn't put up defenses. Taking a bottle from his pocket, he would drink, and then offer it to her. "Come on, have some play. The hooch will numb your inner troubles." He pushed the bottle to her, his touch grazing her arm and lingering there.

The thought of inner peace was a huge enticement. She relinquished herself to him. Hooch, as the moonshiners called their White Lightening that the local stills made, was in plentiful supply, no matter where the circus traveled. The moonshiners congregated outside the tents of performers, plying their liquor trade.

Mr. Ward had started court proceedings to become the boy and girl's official, lawful guardian. The children went to court to testify against their father's habitual abuses. All went well for Little D. He took Mr. Ward's name, Lee, but he wanted to keep their Darnell name because that's who he was in good times or bad. Azzie chose to be on her own. She preferred her independence.

On occasion, Lee could be found sobbing, in deep pain. His friends in the circus listened to his sorrow. He would cry, covering his face with his hands. Rocking his torso back and forth, he cried, "I miss my sisters, Monterey and Dessie. We should be together. On my life, I vow to find them and bring them home." His pain was a child's pain of separation from his loved ones, but his determination was that of a mature adult. His circus friends didn't doubt him. He was a convincing and captivating child. Invariably, someone would hoist him upon their shoulders, trying to help ease the pain and make him smile. They knew Mr. Ward was doing everything possible to locate the Darnell sisters.

Days moved into weeks, weeks into months, into years. The everyday procedures continued — installing tents in a new town, caring for animals, constructing the animals' housing, feeding performers, washing the many clothes, purchasing food and safely storing it all, cooks preparing hundreds of meals each week. When the circus ended in each town, it was all taken down and packed up to head for the next destination.

The years were starting to spin by like a toy top. The performers of the circus received pleasures in travel. They got to relax and mingle with their friends and families. Lee Darnell, as Little D was called now, loved traveling time.

Mr. Ward would let Lee ride on top of the wagons. Sunrise, sunset, days and nights all gave amusement to his senses. Lee would arise early on a soft, dewy morning, crawl up onto the top of the house wagon, feel the air with his fingers and face, smell the aromas coming off the earth, and let his eyes take in the beauty as the wagon moved along to its next journey's end.

At night, he would count the stars. His wish was always the same. He would say, "Star bright, star light, I wish my wish may come true tonight. All my sisters will unite and make my family ever so right."

The wish and goodnight prayer never changed over the years. The gentleness of mornings or the evenings, the comforting sounds of the horses' hooves, and the voices of the performers that drifted through the night quieted his fears, Lee would fall asleep under a canopy of stars as the colorful caravan rolled along.

The years moved at a remarkable speed. Lee Darnell continued to excel in his schooling and was maturing into a well-rounded, young gentlemen. He was becoming adept in languages, picking them up from the culture of diverse performers—Russian, Spanish, Hungarian, and Italian.

The arrival of the circus into the next destination was known several days ahead. Mr. Ward had a special advertising crew who saw that most people even in the most remote areas knew that the circus was coming. Each night of their engagement, Mr. Ward's circus had standing room only.

Each person in the circus usually performed more than one duty. For example, the bareback riders, which now included their star, Azzie, groomed their horses and helped with keeping the tent stables scrupulously clean. The tent opened at both sides so the animals could receive fresh air. Stables were cleaned and fresh straw was laid. Each act of work was performed without any grumbles. All felt part of the roaming community.

Lee Darnell was grateful to Mr. Ward. His desire to live up to the highest standard and make Mr. Ward proud to call him his son made him give all of himself and more. As Lee grew, he was given more answerability and he lived up to each task. He would help Birchard keep the profit and loss books and payrolls. Lee also helped with odd jobs in every aspect of the circus. He vowed in his prayers to never let Mr. Ward down.

One of Lee's favorite times was when the circus closed for the night or early on a Sunday. He would finish his duties and then start a walk down the alley formed by the stables and the house wagons lined up along the land picked for the circus. Each wagon had steps leading up to it and a tiny veranda that folded off the side. Along the pathway, a liveliness of circus families came out. The animals had been cleaned and fed, performers costumes washed and hung up to dry to be pressed the next day, all acts performing apparatuses were secured, and then their personal lives began.

Most Sundays were set aside for the performers to spend on rest, family, or however they chose to take advantage of the day. It also gave the cooks a day of relaxation. Aromas of combined food cooking from different countries representing the performers soon filled the air. Lee would often have dinner with a family, making sure that someone notified Mr. Ward of his whereabouts. The big cat tamer, the strong man, and the family of clowns' makeup came off. The laughter of different, wonderful languages drifted into his ears.

Lee visited with as many as possible. His greeting would begin, "Wonderful! Wonderful performance! Your act gets better each time." Since he spoke some words from each performer's country, he would speak to them in their native language. They welcomed him into their families.

Often, Lee just knew that his heart would burst from the love he received and saw in his circus family as he shared their lives. The unverified rumor, or rumors in the circus, journeyed swiftly. "Is Mr. Ward growing weary and longing to fulfill his lifelong dream of finding a piece of land? Only then can he build a working farm of vegetables, wheat, and corn to make meal grits, raise chickens for eggs, breed horses, and have goats for his own line of cheeses and butters. Do you believe the rumor, Lee?" The performers would ask, figuring if anyone knew, it would be Little D and it would be useless to inquire with closed-mouth Birchard.

Lee, with a very protective voice of Mr. Ward, would answer, "I am sure that Mr. Ward will let each of us know if he ever sells the circus. His love of the circus and concern for his family of performers kept him from putting the circus up for sale even a few years back." Only Birchard knew for sure Mr. Ward's plans.

CHAPTER 4

A Broken Soul

B irchard informed Mr. Ward that he felt Azzie was pushing her whirlwind performances to the edge. He was afraid for her, and the impact upon Little D, if a tragic accident should happen.

Mr. Ward took Birchard's advice. Mr. Ward sat alone in the center ring tent, thinking that the years of traveling, the excitement of the people, and his family of performers had helped to heal his incomplete heart. He woke up each day with the excitement of the constant enthusiasm of his circus, the family of performers, and watching Lee grow into a good man. That's what brought him to the tent today. He was to watch Azzie's new, daring act that Birchard was so worried about.

Azzie walked in with a prance, and as did Princess. Knowing her worth, she held her head high. Azzie jumped from a brightly painted yellow box, with purple stars painted on it, onto Princess' back, feet landing firm. She acknowledged Mr. Ward with a wave and then proceeded with her act. Her body moved around the horse's underbelly, as princess trotted around the tent, then she picked up a purple ribbon from the sawdust floor of the tent with her teeth, continued around the horse, and returned to a sitting position.

She then stood proudly, arms stretched high, she waved the ribbon in the air, then tied it around her neck into a bow. Princess continued to race around the center ring. Chills went up Mr. Ward's back. Azzie continued her act in surging fluidity. She eased Princess to a stop, then hopped off and gave the white horse a kiss on the nose. A worker took the horse away, and Azzie walked out of the tent.

Birchard was standing outside the tent when Mr. Ward came out. "Mr. Ward, it seems that Azzie cares little for her life. Her loose behavior after show hours is also troubling. Mickey always waits up for her to return home. I feel that this extra stress is affecting Mickey's health, as well as my own. Mickey needs to get enough rest. The loss of our baby and worries about Azzie are beginning to tell. We have grown very fond of this girl, but I can't have Mickey at risk."

Birchard's face showed grave concern as he paced back and forth. His little frame now drooped; Mr. Ward noticed. Mr. Ward put his hand on his loyal friend's shoulder and said, "Very distressing. Birchard, I would appreciate any suggestions that you and Mickey have to offer. We must help her. I will talk with Azzie and tell her of my concerns. She has certainly breathed new life into the bareback riding act, but we can't have her running amuck. Neither Mickey nor you are expendable."

Birchard's usual strong, handsome face wasn't smiling. The sides of his mouth were down. His large cheek dimples that were visible most of the times, imprints of a formerly steadfast smile, had disappeared.

"I don't know. I just don't know. We love her as we would our own blood. I will bring her to your tent. If we can't control her, without the extreme stress it is having on Mickey, maybe give her a small wagon of her own, near another family." said Birchard.

"Thank you, as always, Birchard. I'll be in my tent. Don't worry. We'll work this out."

Birchard walked away, head down, headed toward the stables. There he found Azzie putting new sawdust down for Princess. When Azzie saw Birchard, she stopped and said, "No sermons, Birchard. My head aches."

"I'm sure it does. You haven't listened to me or Mickey. I know you are smart, and we understand about your anger. But the chance for you and your brother to look forward to a good life are real, don't I say! Do not put this opportunity in peril. I feel that you are being misguided."

"And who would be misguiding me, Birchard?" When she showed such snarky behaviors, it was as if a different person showed itself. "You just don't like him. I do what I want with my life. Don't tell me how young I am." All the while, she kept grooming her horse.

"Well, Mr. Ward wants to see you now. I did inform him of what I feel is self-destructive behavior. He's seen it himself. Do you really wish to die, Azzie? How will you explain things to your brother? Think over your risk! Mr. Ward wants to see you right now." Birchard walked away shaking his head.

Azzie started out toward Mr. Ward's tent with a swagger. The closer she came, though, her stomach tied itself in knots. She said to no one, "I know I act crazy. Mr. Ward is disappointed in me. God, if you do exist and are around, help me get rid of this anger and pain in my gut." She stopped outside Mr. Ward's tent, bent over and clutched her stomach. Then, she steeled herself and stood straight. Now fifteen, her height was approaching six feet.

She rang the bell at the entrance to Mr. Ward's tent. Lee was out of the tent, most likely somewhere in the walkway chatting with the performers. The circus closed its show on Sundays. Mr. Ward desired for his performers to have leisurely time with friends and family.

Azzie waited at the entrance to the tent. Mr. Ward came and held the flap open for her to enter. His size did not take away from the wise, kind man that shined from within.

"Hi, Mr. Ward," Azzie cheerfully greeted him. "I saw you watching my act today. I could almost look straight into your face. If I get any taller, Princess is going to be too short for me to do my act."

"Come in, dear. I suppose you know why I wish to talk with you. I have made some tea. Please sit. I did observe your act. Yes! You are an amazing performer; you and Princess perform as one."

Mr. Ward poured the tea and sat. Before he could ask any questions, Azzie began. "Mr. Ward, as everyone knows, I would give my life to protect my brother. What a relief in my heart, knowing that Lee will always have a safe home with you. The performers say he is becoming a replication of you. He wants to know and learn everything." She stood up and started pacing. "But Lee does have a sense of humor and loves to laugh. He puts smiles on faces with his gift of storytelling."

Azzie stopped and said, "I am sorry, Mr. Ward, if that statement was out of line. But I haven't seen you laugh often, forgive me."

Mr. Ward smiled. Azzie amused him. "Can't say I disagree. I don't smile often enough. Please sit. I am very concerned, along with Birchard, Mickey, and many more who have grown to love and respect you for how hard you work, now and during your apprenticeship. As a bareback rider, you have astonished us all. You've become our star. The circus needs you. We all wish to help you. What can we do? You are so young to be keeping company with men that will take advantage of your youth."

Azzie started to cry from deep within. Her body shook. Even though she looked like a woman, the child in her often came out. Especially when reprimanded by an adult. Mr. Ward was a good father figure. She felt shame at his displeasure with her. He did not try to console her. He felt ill at ease with the situation.

Mr. Ward sat back and waited. She finally spoke. "May I wash my face?" He pointed toward the bath area that was behind a heavy green velvet curtain.

While Azzie was behind the curtain, Mr. Ward weighed out possible solutions. He deduced that he must try to help Azzie. He had never felt comfortable giving solace to others, particularly women. Maybe we can find a good doctor who can help her. The demons that inhabit her teenage soul torment her. And maybe I've contributed to her pain. She carries a great load with the responsibilities placed upon her. Maybe her star status is too much for her to bear. It had been three years since that fateful day that she and Lee were left at his door.

Mr. Ward had grown to love Lee and Azzie. Lee was like his own son.

Mr. Ward was heavy with thought when Azzie came back. She looked composed, standing tall and once more unyielding. Mr. Ward said, "Please sit. I have a few things to say." She sat, her stiff composure gone once more. A child sat before him.

Mr. Ward pulled his chair in front of her and lightly touched her hand. He said, "Dear child, you have been given a great talent. You give joy to so many people. They travel great distances from small farms and larger cities just to see you."

He continued, "Azzie, I am not a saintly man, and know little about the human heart. But I do know something about carrying childhood pain throughout one's life. I believe that the fact a person has been created means our fate is written somewhere. You and Lee were brought to my circus by fate. Where you came from doesn't matter. Those scars are there. But you can heal and overcome. You have a home with my circus and with me."

Azzie stood and said, "Thank you for your love. May I give you a hug?" Mr. Ward put his arms out and encircled her. She simply said,

"I am sorry if I've hurt anyone. I don't deserve the loving care Mickey and Birchard have shown me day and night. I understand I am young, and I have problems. Would you consider giving me a small wagon of my own. Maybe next to the strong man, he can keep an eye on me." She pulled away and walked out. Not waiting for an answer from Mr. Ward.

Mr. Ward walked straight over to Birchard and Mickey's tent. He conferred with them about meeting with Azzie. He told them that he was very troubled by the doomed feeling that he was left with. He had hoped to reach her and to assure her of the love that so many had for her. As a businessman, his troubled thoughts about his star created a whole new level of the dilemma that was Azzie.

He did instruct Birchard to set up her own wagon, make it quite a pretty, colorful one. After all, she is a Star.

CHAPTER 5

Moving Forward

Lee and Azzie liked to climb high into the frame of the high-top tent, where a special spot awaited. This was a close, shared time for the brother and sister. Here they looked down, like birds high in a tree, undetected by the rest of the world. The nervous joy of being hidden so far above everything and the inner gladness of being together added to the excitement. They watched the excellence of Birchard and Mickey practice their dare devilry high wire act.

Mickey was back to her vibrant self, smiling gloriously while standing on Birchard's shoulders as they performed on a tight rope without a balancing rod. The certainty of Birchard's pirouettes and his high-wire bicycle ride with Mickey drew awed sighs from even seasoned circus workers. Perfection. This was a dangerous practice, but it was also what made them so exciting to their audience.

Azzie said to her brother in their high perch, "We are blessed to have Mickey and Birchard's love. Yet, I continue to worry them."

"Yes, Sis! Why do you?" Lee said with hurt. Azzie went back to watching and ignored Lee's question. He continued, "I better climb down. I don't want to be late again for my chores and lessons. My teacher will be looking for me."

"You go, Lee. Don't look down. I want to see Szabo the strong man lift the big cat over his head, now that the cat tamer has included Szabo in his act. Now that I have my own wagon, and Szabo has agreed to be responsible for me, things will be better. Birchard or Mickey will not have to worry. She turned back, facing the center ring just as the cat tamer was setting up his cage run to let the lions into the center ring cage. Lee was still on his climb down. Azzie touched her heart and blew love toward her brother. She watched as his bare feet touched the sawdust floor, then off he ran.

Lee remembered that he still had to help at the stables. New straw was needed, and clean sawdust had to be hauled from the large pile at the end of the rented fenced-in circus property. As Lee ran by the ticket taker's booth, he paused and hollered out, "How are sales? Are we sold out for tonight's performance?

The gentleman answered, "Yes, Lee. Standing room only. That empty Big Top will fill with the clapping hands of five thousand folks, and a large part of that audience comes to see your sister's act. She will receive the oohs and aahs for her breathtaking rides on those galloping horses. Her circus family feels that girl risks her life." Lee shifted his weight from one foot to the other. He was restless for the ticket taker to finish talking.

"Gotta run. Chores and my teacher waits," Lee called with a wave. He took off running.

Today, Lee was overly excited. Mr. Ward had informed him and Azzie that a traveler had brought information about a gypsy caravan that had set up camp by the river. A family of fiddlers and actors had appeared just outside of town. Lee could think of nothing else. He couldn't keep his mind on his studies.

He passed Szabo, the Siberian strongman. Szabo was headed toward the center ring to rehearse with the cat tamer and the big cats. Szabo said, "Hey Lee, slow down. Come and talk a minute with your old pal." Lee detoured to speak to his friend.

"Sorry, Strongman. I should have said, 'Hello! Hello! Hello!'"

Szabo took hold of Lee's clothes and picked him up. Lee was dangling in the air. The strongman said, "Now, tell your friend. Why all the excitement?" He set Lee back down to earth and crossed his tree-trunk arms.

Lee laughed, gave the big man a quick hug and said, "Szabo, it really may happen. Gypsies are camped by the river. It could be that my sister Dessie is with them. If not, then maybe they've seen her at another camp."

Szabo answered in his odd little voice for a giant of a man. "I will be seated beside you during the carriage ride. Mr. Ward has informed me that we will take one of the horses and a few more bartering items. Mr. Ward would barter the whole circus, if he knew it would return your sister."

"Thanks, Szabo. See you in the morning!" Lee ran on, thinking how glad he was that Szabo would be with them. And he didn't mention a word of Azzie saying she now has her own wagon. And Szabo has taken on the duty of looking after her. Was this too much to ask of him? I guess not. Thought Lee, Szabos spirit is large.

The carriage was at Mr. Ward's tent at daybreak. Everyone had their nicest clothes on. Azzie was in a long grey wool skirt and jacket of soft beige. No matter his attire, Szabo's clothes were always straining at the seams. Each of his huge biceps was the size of Azzie's waist. His size was as large as his heart. He securely tied the lead rope on a lively sorrel to the back of their carriage.

Mr. Ward was dressed in grey pinstripes and a fine felt hat. Lee felt uncomfortable in his new suit and bow tie. But he smiled happily and said, "No finer looking family will ever greet Dessie. She'll be proud of her new family that has come to claim her. Bow tie it is. Then later, back to barefoot and overalls."

All gave a laugh at Lee's jokes. He chattered non-stop. "Will Dessie leave with us? She will be happy to see us, won't she, Mr. Ward? Do you think she knows what a star Azzie has become? Maybe she's seen the posters."

Mr. Ward tried to calm Lee by talking about the passing landscape.

But Lee always brought the subject back to Dessie. Azzie sat silent. She often withdrew into dark moods. She was excited about thinking she may see her dear sister, but also brooding that Mr. Ward apparently had not talked with Szabo about her now living next to his wagon. Her wagon had arrived and was painted blue, the trim in an orange and yellow. She loved it. The carriage rolled along. The soft sound of the horses' hooves on the road was soothing.

The closer they came to the camp; they could hear music and smelled the campfire as the cooking odors and the music traveled down the river. Approaching the camp, Lee's heart was pounding in his chest. He felt small but much protected in the company of Mr. Ward and Szabo.

Two men stopped the carriage as it neared the gypsy camp. Szabo, looming large in the driver's seat brought the horses to a gentle stop. "Did you come to barter goods, or to hire entertainment, gentlemen?" The colorfully dressed man in red and purple kept one hand in his vest as he asked them questions.

Mr. Ward asked, "May I step down from the carriage?" Mr. Ward presented an imposing figure. One of the men walked forward and shook hands with Mr. Ward. Mr. Ward explained who he was and why they had entered the gypsy camp.

"We are trying to locate my adopted children's sister." The other man had joined them and asked, "Why do you believe she would be here?"

"The girls' father had bartered a business agreement with a family of Gypsies when the girl was fifteen. I have desperately tried to contact anyone who could help to reunite the four children. Two are with me. But Dessie, as she was called, was a beautiful, dark-haired girl with a very robust personality. She has a rare gift with the fiddle."

"You are welcome to our camp to meet our families. We do not have a young girl that fills your description. Still, it's possible that someone in our group may have seen the girl in another Camp."

All were quickly out of the carriage. They proceeded to follow the congeniable man into the camp.

Azzie was as if frozen; no emotions showed. Lee was flickering with hope. Even if Mr. Ward was assured the men were truthful, Lee could no longer remain quiet. In a pleasing tone, he spoke. "Please, sir. I gave my promise to my sister that I would not stop looking for her. May we talk to the other families? Maybe someone has heard about her. We miss and want to see her. If Dessie doesn't want to come, we'll be sad, but we'll understand."

The man answered, "Young man, you are free to walk around our camp and freely ask about your sister. Regardless of any gossip you may have heard, our families will not hold any person against their will."

Lee looked toward Mr. Ward for his consent. "It's fine, Lee. Take Azzie with you."

In the meantime, Mr. Ward instructed Szabo to get the extra horse that they had brought. "We leave the horse as a gift for your hospitality, and in the hope that you will spread the word about Dessie. You may send word through the circus. Someone will know how to get the news to me."

Mr. Ward shook the man's hand. Azzie and Lee were given hugs by the man's family. They hadn't seen Dessie, but they said, "We will get word to you. You have our promise."

A disheartened four walked back to their carriage. The strongman gave encouragement. "Our circus family is strong. Each performer has spread the word about Monterey and Dessie. It will happen, kids." The giant man tapped the horses gently with the reins, and they were off.

On the ride back, Lee was dejected. Azzie was silent. She had only spoken a few words the entire trip. Mr. Ward spoke. "Lee, Azzie, I would like to hear some remembered things about Dessie. I believe some talk would make us all feel better."

Azzie said. "Let Lee start. I have a different thought about the situation after our visit today."

Lee spoke. "Dessie would play jubilant pieces on her fiddle that she composed. Sometimes when playing wildly, her long, dark hair became entangled in the fiddle strings, and a string would pop. We all laughed together. Her large, dark eyes danced with her music. She loved bright colors—purples, orange, and green flowing skirts. I hope that she is dressed in bright, beautiful colors every day."

Azzie spoke. "When we worked the streets for money, Dessie liked playing her violin for the people who gathered. When father bartered her away, he said, 'Strange, she didn't seem to mind.' I believe Dessie may be happy living with the gypsies. She had a deep mystery about her and wanted to travel. Dessie would often sit at a window and look out with a yearning. I believe she had been in that camp -- I'm absolutely certain of it. I felt her presence so strong today." Azzie's gaze was direct as she turned to Mr. Ward. "I really felt it."

Lee was looking distressed as he listened to Azzie's comments. But he said, "I never thought she might be okay with the gypsies, but why not? I am happy and would not want to leave Mr. Ward."

"Lee, let's be glad for Dessie. I believe she carried a gypsy soul. And may not wish to leave. We know in the deepest places of our hearts; she will always hold us close."

Mr. Ward commented, "Let's hope both your sisters are living a gratified life. I believe they still want to make contact with you both. We will continue our search."

Szabo, who had slowed the carriage down while the serious conversation was going on, tapped the horses into a trot. The rest of the ride home was silent of talk.

Upon their return, as the carriage approached, their circus family had gathered, each one showed an impatience to hear good news. But the look on Mr. Ward's and Lee's face told the story: No Dessie.

That night Lee crawled into the security of his bed and pulled the covers over his head. His heart-felt mushy. Every night he said prayers, giving blessings to all his circus family and Mr. Ward. He heard Mr. Ward moving about the tent. The temporary wood floor that was built to erect the tent on moved as the large man walked about the room. Lee thought the motion was soothing as he felt his bed move ever so gently as the floor went up and down. He fell asleep.

Mr. Ward continued to restore his confidence. He was determined; he would find Dessie and Monterey.

The bell outside Mr. Ward's tent rang early. It was an earnest clanging. "Much too aggressive for Birchard or Mickey," Mr. Ward thought as he slipped on his robe.

It was Birchard. "Come in, Birchard. Never have you rang my bell with such vigor."

"Sorry. Serious news," Birchard said.

"Come and sit, Birchard. I'll make some tea with a little morning brandy. I could use it also. My night was restless." Birchard turned the lamp up, then lit a lantern, giving the room more light.

Mr. Ward served the tea on a silver tray. He pulled a chair in close to Birchard, set the tray on a green velvet tufted footstool, then brandied and honeyed the tea. Both gulped a large swig.

"Feels good and soothing," said Birchard. He sat his cup down, and then he broke down. His voice trembling.

Birchard said, "Azzie has left. She ran off with that dandy of a trapeze flyer. My Mickey is distraught, thinking if she could have given more time with Azzie, this may not have happened. I had advised that trapeze flyer on several occasions to keep his distance from Azzie. But Azzie is her own person, hard-headed as they come. Being a full moon, I thought that may be why the big cats were making such an uproar.

But when I got up to check, I found notes at our door. The lanterns were left lit at the horses' stable. Two of the larger horses are missing. She didn't take Princess." She wrote in our note, 'Please tell Mr. Ward, all in me says thanks for taking me in, and giving me a chance to become a star. I hope I came through. Forgive me, but the voices in my head are telling me to move on. To quiet them and my pain, I feel I must go. May my months' salary pay for the two horses—Azzie.'

Birchard put his face in his hands to cover his tears. Then he composed himself, reached into his checkered vest, and brought out two envelopes. He handed both to Mr. Ward, then glanced toward Lee's bed. Lee set up and spoke.

"Hi, Birchard. You are visiting early. I had a bad dream that one of the big cats escaped. Azzie was crying that she was afraid for me."

Birchard quickly rose, walked over, and sat on Lee's bed.

Mr. Ward, rubbing his head, said, "Lee, we have distressing news. Azzie has left. Birchard believes the disappointment of not finding Dessie sent her over the edge. I am sure she will explain in her letter she left for you. Would you like me to read it, or do you prefer to be in private?" Mr. Ward put his hand on the boy's shoulder and one on Birchard's.

"Mr. Ward, I would like you, Birchard, and Mickey to be here when I read Azzie's goodbye letter. I know she loves me and would never intend to hurt me. Her heart for so long has been broken. I forgive her even before I read the letter." Lee got out of bed. Mr. Ward, then Birchard, bent forward and rocked him in a huge hug. Lee was now twelve years old.

The tent bell rang softly. Birchard said, "That will be Mickey."

Mr. Ward let Mickey in. "Hello, Mr. Ward. I am here to see Lee. How is he?" Mickey's voice was soft and soothing.

Lee listened as Birchard talked to him. Lee leaned down to let Mickey give him a hug. At twelve, Lee was tall and sure to be over six feet within a few years. Birchard and Mickey excused themselves. They would return later, when he was ready to read his sister's letter.

Mr. Ward heated some milk and cocoa. They both had a cup of steaming hot chocolate, and then Lee went back to bed. Pulling the covers over his head. Mr. Ward said to him, "Rest easy. I will be right here at my desk."

The lantern cast shadows throughout the tent as Mr. Ward pulled the curtain around his desk and took out his journal. He opened his letterbox and placed Azzie's unread letter inside.

He wrote: *Sell this circus! My star performer is gone, leaving Lee in a terrible state of another heartache. Birchard and Mickey are ready to raise a family. Yes! I will contact that Frenchman who is interested and is willing to purchase at my asking price. Tomorrow, I will take the carriage and check out that land our circus caravan passed. The land contained mixed forests, a river and rolling overgrown pasture lands that can be cleared. I will meet with my performers and inform them of my intentions. I enjoy seeing the words on paper, that I am making sure plans. Each performer will receive a nice share of the sale for all their years of loyalty.*

The very tall, regal man closed his eyes to indulge himself in a rare imagining.

He saw stretched out farmland with beauty and resources, boasting virgin forests, glowing spring-fed creeks, hidden valleys, a productive river that flowed lively, capable of supplying all the crops with water, a small swimming hole, take his shoes off, feeling free to stop and take a bath in the pond. Then wrap in a blanket and have a few whiskeys—fall asleep and wake up with a splendorous view of trees that could be milled for homes, wagons, heat for homes, and on and on.

Mr. Ward opened his eyes and felt good about his decision to sell. A glance where Lee slept made him think about his own abandonment. He felt surprise at the anguish that was still with him and could make his heartbeat race. He had been left aboard a ship in a trunk when he was three years old. He could still feel the soft red velvet that the trunk was lined with, where he had to put his face next to the air holes to breathe. Only parts of the people who walked by were visible — a hand, the eyes of a child, pieces of clothing. Never will he understand why he didn't cry out or make any kind of noise. Maybe as a captured animal feels, when being transported to the unknown but with no control over where they will be released.

The last memory that he had before waking up in the trunk was hearing lots of voices and people crying. Then, a sudden quiet. The room was completely dark. Someone walked into his room. The figure said nothing. Then, it was gone. Scared, he got out of bed, dragging a small quilt. The house was large and cavernous. Two small lights flickered ahead. He walked and crawled until he reached the end of a long hallway.

He climbed up onto the bier. Startled, he found his mother sleeping. She didn't awaken when he looked into the casket. He slid down, then crawled under the coffin. He curled up in the quilt and fell asleep. He felt safe being close to his mother. When mother wakes up, I'll be right here, he remembered thinking. Instead he woke up in a red velvet lined wooden trunk. On a ship halfway around the world. Who was his father, what kind of person would put a child into a trunk on board a ship headed out to sea.

Someday I will reveal my life to Lee, he thought. Mr. Ward brought his contemplation to the joy of tomorrow when he could check out the thousand acres for sale along the river. How could I be bitter about my childhood? Look where it has brought me, he mused. This sale is going to happen. He continued to write.

I know this land even before I set foot on it. I have gone over and over it, closed my eyes and lived it. My friends Birchard and Mickey and Lee will accompany me. The pain Lee is feeling for Azzie may abate for a short while on our journey. My hope is the excitement of our new life may help calm any worries.

The circus was scheduled to remain only two more days, then on to

Atlanta. Tickets for all seating were sold out, standing room only. Mr. Ward was concerned after losing his star bareback rider. They barely had enough posters to announce their engagement, as most of the posters had featured Azzie in some way. New posters were ordered.

Birchard assured Mr. Ward that each act would add new features to fill in the gap, and that he would be pleased. The five thousand that packed the audience each night would not feel let down. Each act was polished and ready.

By the end of the day, Mr. Ward was confident that all was well, in spite of Azzie's defection. A thousand times throughout the day, he's heard their credo, "The show must go on!" Azzie had been well aware of the importance of her contribution to the circus. How could she have left them all without notice, without their star attraction? She let them down after being welcomed into their lives, their livelihood, and their hearts. Yet, Mr. Ward knew that the circus as a living entity would survive without Azzie, or indeed without him. He was content. And in his heart, he realized how very sick Azzie was mentally. So, he could not be mad.

Morning came, Mr. Ward greeted the new day with enthusiasm. He said to Lee, "Get dressed, Lee Darnell. We are going to purchase some land!"

One only had to speak, and Lee was wide awake, an attribute which Mr. Ward liked a lot. Lee bounded out of bed and dressed quickly, questioning Mr. Ward the whole time.

"Are we quitting the circus and going to look for Azzie?"

Mr. Ward responded. "Lee, I am selling the circus, buying some land to live out our lives on. I will hire people to look for Azzie. Even if we find her, she may wish not to return."

"Will Mickey and Birchard be moving with us? And Szabo—what about Szabo?"

"Yes, Mickey and Birchard want to start a family, and they both feel that their high wire act is too great a risk for a pregnancy. They are looking forward to raising children in a home without wheels. But Szabo — no, son. He loves the circus and the performers have been his only family for many years. He feels a strong sense of duty to the performers and the success of the circus."

The bell rang outside Ward's tent's entrance. Mr. Ward spoke through the tent wall. "Be right there, Birchard." Lee's heart lifted for a moment, he thought Birchard was going to tell them his sister Azzie had returned.

Mr. Ward decided he would not ask Lee if he had read Azzie's letter. He knew that Lee, at his young age, should not be pressured. Daylight had just broken through. It looked to be a splendid day in spite of the sadness that overshadowed the circus. Azzie would no longer be a part of them in the physical but would forever remain in their hearts.

Mickey had packed a lunch. Blankets were neatly folded on the seats to give relief from the early morning dampness. The four friends were off. The sound of the horse's hooves left the graveled area and headed for the countryside. Mr. Ward sat with Birchard. Lee was happy to be in Mickey's attentive care. She was full of fun and interesting stories, and plus, she was a good listener. Mickey made him feel important.

Lee moved his face from side to side for the feel of the dewy breeze. He sniffed the smell of the dirt road and the surrounding countryside, not forgetting in his heart the loss of his last sister and the disappointment of the gypsy caravan claiming to know nothing about his sister Dessie. Mickey kept her hand on his arm.

Birchard gave the horses a gentle tap as they passed a poster on a barn advertising 'The Blaze Bareback Rider'. When Lee saw it, he asked, "Mr. Ward, should we stop and remove it?"

Mr. Ward answered, "No, Son. It's all right. The advertising team will be along to remove it when the circus closes. And often the farmers want the posters to remain."

In spite of their disappointment and shock over Azzie, they enjoyed the wonderful countryside. At noon, they stopped to eat lunch beside the river. Mr. Ward and Lee saw to watering the horses.

Within minutes, Mickey and Birchard had set up a refined, celebratory picnic, including a folding table with folding wooden chairs, a delightful linen tablecloth and wine. This was Lee's first taste of wine. Mickey teased, "Only a taste, young man," and produced a jar of lemonade for him. Mr. Ward told them about his dreams for their new home. All were jubilant. They devoured their picnic feast in high spirits. And Mickey announced she was once more pregnant.

Mickey sang out, "Birchard and I are ready to plant our feet into a permanent piece of dirt. We've always wanted to settle down and raise lots of children."

Mickey, Birchard, and Lee danced in a circle to express their joy. "A real home, a real home," they sang over and over, then fell back and lay laughing on the grass. Mr. Ward stood by with a smile, enjoying their antics. They packed up the table and chairs and continued down the red dirt road.

They arrived at what seemed to be a settlement, consisting of a small train station and a store that included a post office, feedstore, a restaurant of sorts, and general store. A few nondescript buildings fleshed out what apparently served as the center of the settlement. The horses approached the town at a slow walk. A charming rock bridge badly in need of repair crossed over a rolling creek. All in all, the place looked unfinished but welcoming.

Mr. Ward said, "Stop, Birchard. I want to feel the spirit of this place." Birchard reined in. It was a bright a day as God could make it. The carriage was silent. The leather creaked as the horses shifted and snorted. No one in the carriage moved or spoke for a few minutes.

Lee was the first to break the silence. "I like it here. They have a train station. Not many buildings, but Mr. Ward, you can build buildings." Lee looked at Mr. Ward.

Mr. Ward nodded to Lee in response. "Okay, Birchard, continue to that building with the sign on the porch." It was a plain board building. Cal's Hub, Post Office, Home Cooked Eats, General Store, Feed, and Saddlery. Several horses were already tied to the rail in front of Cal's Hub. An impressive carved statue of a life size pinto stood in front of the Hub. Birchard tied the horses and carriage to the shady side of the hitching rail.

Lee hopped down. "I will water the horses and rub them down."

Mr. Ward stepped down, and then helped the other's down from the carriage. A pleasing to the eye, silver-haired woman dressed in overalls appeared and walked down the steps to Mr. Ward. It was unusual to see a woman in pants, At the neck of her white shirt was a striking blue and white cameo brooch. Her hair was in one long braid to the side. She had a lined tan face that showed hard work. Her brilliant sky-blue eyes looked straight at him. She was tall, good posture, and extremely attractive, thought Mr. Ward.

"I am Cal." She spoke directly to Mr. Ward with no embellishments to her greeting.

"Good morning, Cal. I am Lee Ward." Mr. Ward extended his hand to Cal, then turned to Birchard and Micky and introduced them. "That's my son Lee, taking care of the horses." Each one smiled at Cal. Mr. Ward realized that Cal's welcoming hand was still in his. Her hand was strong and calloused, speaking volumes about hard work. Suddenly self-conscious, Mr. Ward released her hand. Her warmth stayed in his hand.

Cal was direct. "Are you folks from the circus a few miles over? Sure, don't look like you're from around here. Enough prying. Come on in. I'll get some food started for you all."

Birchard, Mickey, and Lee had grins on their faces. They had never seen Mr. Ward enamored with a woman. This was certainly an unusual, interesting lady. Mr. Ward did not meet their eyes. They all climbed the steps to the porch.

Mr. Ward said, "We did have a breakfast picnic by the river, but that seems hours ago. Something sure smells good." He pulled the squeaky screen door open and stepped aside. Cal entered first, followed by Birchard, Mickey, and finally Mr. Ward. The atmosphere in the Hub was warm and lively, but intensely curious as the people inside turned to look at the strangers in their midst.

Cal pointed to an empty table. She said, "I'll be quick. Want to wash up? Over there." She pointed to the other end of the room, close to the American flag that hung over the Post Office. "Don't mind the folks. We are always overly curious about strangers." Cal made a motion with her hand to the folks in the pub. Suddenly, everyone resumed whatever they had been doing. Cal rattled off the day's menu. They ordered. Cal went into the kitchen. Soon, she returned with their steaming plates. "If you want anything else, just holler."

Lee Ward was not a man who lingered when plans called for a decision to be made. His inner thoughts were fast and furious. His spirit of excitement made him feel totally alive. He liked all that he had seen, especially the attractive lady who owned the pub. Well, he thought, what a surprise for my well laid plans. The four ate their food, with comments and questions going back and forth about the land, people, work, the train station, the presence of a school, doctor, vet, and so on and on.

Cal now busy with her customers, let her eyes return often to the bearded, dark-haired, tall handsome, well-dressed man. He caught her eye, and she approached their table.

Mr. Ward stood up and spoke. "The food was divine, and we thank you for a very warm welcome. Cal, is there an attorney in this town, or someone who handles land sales?"

"You will find out, Lee Ward, most of our citizens wear several hats." Cal gave a holler to a man now repairing the screen door. "Silas, Mr. Ward he needs you to close a land deal."

"Are you looking at the thousand acres that runs along the river?"

Silas asked through the screen door from where he knelt on the other side, pliers in hand.

"That's it, Silas," Mr. Ward said. He would have preferred to broach the matter in a private conversation. Once more, the pub was frozen with heightened interest. Mr. Ward filed this information in his thoughts. This was indeed a small town, with all the trimmings. Cal again made her hand signal for everyone to butt out. They did. However, Lee noticed that though everyone resumed eating, they ate silently. We're sure enough fodder for their conversation, he thought, and redirected his attention.

Silas collected his tools into his battered toolbox and walked next door to another unpainted building. Mr. Ward settled their bill.

Cal followed the four out onto the porch. She placed her hand on Mr. Ward's arm. "If you would like to see the land, I could have someone ride out with you."

"No thanks, Cal. My heart tells me that this land and I belong together. I know this land. My imagination has taken me to every part of it. I don't think there will be many surprises."

Silas was back. He sat on the steps, spread out his papers, then briefly reviewed the land and the asking price. Mr. Ward was a master negotiator. Studying the map of the property, he asked well thought out questions, then countered with an offer. Silas was out of his league. Luckily for him, Mr. Ward was fair-minded as well as being a highly experienced businessman.

"Where is the pen and ink? Let's seal this deal." Thus, sitting on the wooden steps of the Hub, Mr. Ward, circus owner and a man of vision, became the owner of a thousand acres in the most picturesque land in Georgia. Birchard, Mickey, and Lee were spellbound at the swiftness of all that was happening.

Birchard finally spoke. "Mr. Ward, looks like some mean-looking clouds rolling in on us." The clouds had blown in while they were inside the Hub.

Cal offered her new friends her cabin. "You all are welcome to my cabin for a few days. I will sleep on the porch, which I often do anyway. My little girl Liza prefers it too. Please feel free to accept."

Mr. Ward expressed his thanks. "No thanks, Cal. We still have a few more days to run a circus. Lots of people depend on us. I will return after all is settled there. My understanding from Silas is that there's a habitable cabin on the land by the river. That will be fine for lodging for now, but could you arrange for someone to check the cabin for supplies? Then supply it. Maybe a builder can add more sleeping bunks if needed." He felt at home with Cal, as if they had known each other for a long time. He knew she could handle anything, and I hope a circus man.

"Lee Ward," Cal said in a voice of familiarity, "I can get all the local workers, fine tradesmen. They need work. I am damn capable of taking care of clearing the land for a main house. I know the land. Perfect spot on it for a real house. You game?" Cal had walked close into Mr. Ward. He had let his eye wander to a small girl playing on the porch with two dogs. "My daughter Liza," Cal said.

Mr. Ward put out his hand to the tanned, slim, straightforward, and rather sexy looking woman. He replied, "Cal, I believe I just met a new friend. You have my trust." Mr. Ward went to his carriage and retrieved a leather pouch and handed it to Cal. "This should take care of wages for the workers, supplies, and any other needs. We will see you very soon."

Cal reached down and gave Birchard, Mickey, and Lee a strong hug. She touched Mr. Ward on the arm. It was a strong arm; the muscle was ridged. She thought I want it around me, holding me. His hand was on her shoulder, he removed it then turned to Lee and said, "Take the reins." Everyone waved goodbye to the onlookers who had by now gathered on the porch. A few of them waved back; the rest just stood and looked on, stunned.

Lee lifted his arm and waved, "See ya soon."

CHAPTER 6

Cal

Cal was someone you wanted on your side. She fiercely protected all that she loved, her child, town, private life, all animals, and June bugs. This was a sore spot with Cal. Kids had a habit of attaching a string to the leg of the shiny green beetle. Then holler with glee when it would open its wings and fly around and around. She would walk up to a group of hollering children, take hold of the string, and untie the June bug and say to the kids, "Now! That's it, don't let me catch you all throttling any more June bugs. Their purpose on this earth is not to entertain bored children."

Her welcoming log cabin was nestled behind the pub. Red shutters outlined the windows and red plaid curtains peeked through. The door was never locked. However, the shotgun over the rock mantle was loaded. "My prayer is I never have to use that thing, but if I do...."

With her newly screened porch, she was proud to own the only screened porch in the community that the pest mosquitoes were kept out. It often served as her bedroom on balmy nights. The highly lacquered red iron bed was readied with line dried and ironed linen sheets on a feather mattress. She also gave it up to down and out souls. Could be an overnight drunk husband locked out by a fed-up wife. A troubled teenager, wanting to runaway but not that far. Mostly anyone needing to ponder a heavy trouble. All was okay unless Cal felt the person was harboring a downright meanness.

Her actions were to provide a safe haven, until they gained strength to get back to a kicking life.

No citizen of the town went against Cal. They may have disapproved and whispered behind her back, but that's as far as their courage took them. There was especially one porch guest that caused quite a stir in town. His name was Dilsey Somerset.

When Dilsey exited the train in Divine, he wasn't thinking about it being the south. And how he would be received. His Cherokee roots were on his mind and all his research had brought him to this area, along the river. He felt he owed it to his mother. A stranger was always checked out by the locals when exiting the train. Dilsey was no exception. Sam, a longtime citizen of the area, was picking up supplies at the station when the train rolled in. "May I direct you somewhere, Sir—I am Sam." Dilsey stuck out his hand in friendliness.

Dilsey removed his stylish wool grey hat, and said, "Yes, I am possibly looking for some work, as I explore my family roots."

"What kind of work," Sam asked, not giving any attention to 'my family roots' information the handsome interesting looking man had just spit out.

"I can do stonework, iron work, if you have a blacksmith in town that I could work with. I can create gates and fences that will beautify this village and will stand forever."

"Yes, we have a blacksmith, and I am sure he would welcome help. I don't know how much he could pay you."

"I am set up okay financially. My father passed away and saw that I was taken care of. I will gladly invest in the blacksmith's business if needed."

Sam said, "In the meantime, let me introduce you to Cal at the Hub. Get you a meal, and Cal can figure out what's good for your situation."

"Any luggage," Sam asked.

"Just my canvas bag and banjo."

Sam looked at the Indian looking man and felt a little reluctant to introduce him to Cal. But, that's not my call. That's Cal. No one decides for her.

Dilsey was certainly outstanding with golden skin and standing tall, walking with the stride of a warrior. His Indian roots shined through. Even though he was dressed in stylish clothes and spoke with what Sam reckoned was an English accent.

Dilsey Somerset was not typical. His father was a mapmaker from England. His mother a Cherokee. The father had traveled the southern states. During his travels he fell for a lovely Cherokee woman name Ayita. They were married by a proselytizer, who was traveling throughout the south. Sadly, "Principal People" as the Cherokee referred to themselves, had been moved to Oklahoma but, "Ayita" meaning "first to dance" and her mother and father had taken up residence in a small community outpost.

Ayita became pregnant shortly after her marriage to Mr. Somerset. The marriage was short lived, because Ayita died giving birth to their son. Saddened of heart and missing his homeland, Mr. Somerset's intention was to take the baby boy and move back to England. He felt the English would be more open in accepting the boy, and not treating him like a half breed.

Dilsey was educated and was well informed on his bloodlines. But he wished to know more about his mother. He had talked with his father that someday he wished to return south and follow up on his mother's history. After his father died, he sold the business, took a few belongings and his beloved banjo, and headed south. He ended up in the small settlement and living on Cal's porch. The citizens accepted him and his expertise in different trades.

One would say Cal was the pulse of the settlement. Cal's porch was to become Dilsey's home for two years. Under Cal's protection he was accepted. Word got around about his woodworking and iron working skills, keeping up with the demands for kitchen tables, rockers, gates, private cemeteries, enclosures, front porches, etc. Since Cal had a newly screened porch, she had ordered the screening from up North. The screened windows and porch was a much sought after luxury of which few people enjoyed. The screens almost became a full-time job for Dilsey. The citizens saved their pennies for this luxury.

Dilsey built extraordinary children's rocking horses, painted with brightest colors like Indian ponies. The children loved them.

In fact, a craved life-size statue of a pinto pony graced the hitching post at Cal's Hub. It was quite the talk of the citizens. Dilsey's artistic designs were showing up throughout the town and countryside, including the front door security iron gate for the bank. Dilsey could take care of just about any artsy task. Some folks whispered that Cal was one of those tasks. Several months after Dilsey moved away, Cal gave birth to a beautiful baby girl. The whispers certainly increased. They may have disapproved of her behavior; but kept their whispers low.

Once a few church going ladies decided to call on Cal after her beautiful baby girl was born. They had marched toward Cal, with self-righteous looks on their faces. But inside was just a burning curiosity if Cal had bedded Dilsey Somerset and now paraded his beautiful baby girl before the whole town. Cal didn't give a damn what they thought. The growls of the church ladies walking into the Hub, their noses turned up, their starched under-skirts giving a little swishing sound, but their courage took a rapid turn to meekness as Cal approached them.

One whispered, "We will make sure we place Cal's name in the prayer tray at church." In unison, they all replied, "Yes" and they gave a tight smile and asked Cal how she was doing. Cal didn't answer their questions but said, "Doing honey baked pork chops with English peas and chunky tomato sauce. Banana pudding. Sweet tea. Anything else, ladies?" One lady spoke, "No, thank you. Lunch sounds lovely."

Sam, who was seated close-by, gave a huge grin as he observed Cal poring a shot of white lightening in each church lady's sweet tea."

"Well, maybe we will have another sweet tea."

Cal poured their glasses up to the rim and was holding back a laugh.

When Dilsey Somerset left, he had left a journal of his life with Cal. "Someday, Cal when you feel it's the right time, read it. Just maybe someone will come along and will write my story. I held nothing back. I may never reach my family roots, but it's my dream. They may one day know who I am from these extensive notes. All my efforts in finding any of my Cherokee family have died."

Cal's thoughts went back to the last night she spent with Dilsey. Cal had stacked more logs on the fire, enjoying the crackle of logs. She had poured two large whiskeys, then said, "Dilsey Somerset, you are one of the finest, smartest, and shall I use the term sexiest men I have ever met. I will treasure my time spent with you and honor your notes and keep them safe. Life for sure can take strange turns. You are always welcome here, and that includes your family. We know the history of the Cherokee people and their removal from their land. I believe most of the citizens of this town feel the same way. You have earned their respect."

He knew Cal was good at her word. The two friends had sat up all night—talking, drinking, and singing. While Cal played her guitar, Dilsey Somerset made his banjo sing. The two made satisfying music together. But it was that time that comes in most relationships when one knows it's time to move on.

Cal fell asleep and when she awoke, Dilsey Somerset had left. There was no mention of her being pregnant. If Dilsey even suspected, he kept silent.

Cal walked out onto the front porch, engulfed the morning air, then set about placing the notebook in a safe place. First, she wrapped a lace cloth around it, stored it in a wooden box, then pried a board behind a cabinet loose and secured the box. Nailing the board back, she felt Dilsey Somerset's large spirit. "Yes! I will hold our last evening dear in my memories," she spoke to the morning.

Cal talked to herself about the searching man that had walked away. "My hope is one of your family will show up one day seeking information about you. If not, I will make sure before I die, my child knows her father. Safe travel, dear one. Your child will have a great life. No one will harm this child. Morally, you may consider my decision wrong, but I will live with it. I feel your load is heavy enough. Safe travels, Dilsey Somerset." She hammered the last nail, rubbed her hand across it and placed a kiss on the selected hiding place. Cal's sleep porch held many juicy stories which most likely would be buried with her.

Cal was proud of her accomplishments. She had built her cabin and the activity of the town took place at the Hub, Cal's place. She was proud of her coconut cake and loved to watch the faces of people as they took a first bite. Proud that she could figure out what was happening faster than most folks and have the problem solved while others were still pondering or scratching their heads.

Cal felt that God had chosen to bless her with this child. She would often say not that she went to church on Sunday's to worship, but to try to learn why did He choose me? Well, only He knows that. People would continue to gasp and gossip as to who Liza's father was. Cal gave up no information of a personal nature. Liza was her daughter, period. If a person treaded too close to her personal life, she would tighten her face and a small twitch would start in her left eye. Quickly, the person recognized the signs that they had chatted unwisely. They would say something to try to divert the situation at hand. "The weather sure is a-changing," then go on their way with no information, but at least unscathed.

Liza stood out: auburn curls surrounded her head, a prominent dimple in her chin, not as deep as her fathers, and golden skin.

Cal whistled as she worked. She finished putting the last dish away and secured the post office. Liza was asleep in her basket, Cal's two loyal dogs watching over her. Cal rarely let her child out of her eyesight. Underneath, she knew there were folks who disapproved of her maverick way of life, certainly not acceptable behavior for a woman. Cal picked Liza's basket up and walked out, followed closely by the dogs. She let the screen door close on its own.

The path home was short, but it was a pleasurable walk and always caused Cal to whistle her favorite tune, "Lil Liza Jane." Fireflies danced about. She smiled, reached out, and cupped a firefly in her hand and placed it on Liza's whisper-soft head full of shiny curls. "Here, Lady Bug," she told the sleeping child. The cooling night air caressed Cal's skin and the runoff brook from the river sang its sweet music. Cal stopped to watch a shooting star and resumed whistling her song as her thoughts now turned away from the past, and to the handsome Mr. Ward and his return.

Talking to the night, "Wonder if Mr. Ward had a wife. He said he was a circus owner with sold-out audiences. Now why do I care about that? Now he is the owner of 1,000 acres in Georgia along the river." And she knew, soon to be her lover. His fine-looking son possessed beautiful manners and correct words flowed easily from him. She didn't really see much likeness to his daddy, though. Well, maybe some of Mr. Ward's gestures. Yes, I noticed the handsome circus man's every move. The way he used his hands drawing most every word he spoke.

Mr. Ward buying the land was the most excitement that's been around here in years. Well, Dilsey had caused quite a stir and now with Liza being there and very much looking like her Indian heritage, they would always have a reminder of Cal's affair with the talented, handsome Dilsey.

Cal wondered if Ward was the kind of man that just showed up and knocked on the door at 3:00 in the morning; blazed up the fireplace, poured some shots of good white lightening, cooked some eggs, and said, "I had to see you now. Yes, unplanned sex—don't care for any part of convenient sex." Cal's door wasn't open to just anyone, she desired full listening from her lover, and it had to be her choice. But with Mr. Ward, she was sure it was an equal attraction. She asked herself, "Why do I feel so sure this man may well be my last lover? Love at first sight. Okay."

Cal entered her cabin. She never was tired of the feeling 'all's well' that comes from walking into the familiar.

Her dogs pushed in beside her. Two golden cats were curled up on the extended fireplace. The two rose and greeted her and Liza. A few live coals still glowed in the fireplace from the night before. Moving about in the darkness, doing things from habit, her head was full of thoughts of one particular man. She threw a few logs on the fire. It was quickly a blaze. After putting Liza to bed, she kissed her soft curls and said, "You are so dearly loved, my Liza Jane." The animals were fed and given some rubs. "Keep my Liza Jane safe." They understood and curled up close to the sleeping child.

Cal poured a fat whiskey, took a long, slow, warming gulp, turned down the lamps, picked up her worn guitar and strummed into the night with Mr. Ward on her mind.

Cal woke up at five, still in her chair. She checked on Liza, then walked out onto the small screen porch. The air felt chilly but good. She took in the dampness of the early morning. Only nature's sound played such perfect harmony to the ears. After a restless night, naughty thoughts of this new man kept filling her head. A mystery, that man, but what a formidable fantasy.

Moving about her cabin, the fireplace was still putting off nice, warm heat. She glanced at herself in a full-length mirror and dropped her robe. Not too bad... Not that anyone has seen me naked since Dilsey left town. But come to think of it, there was good old sweet obliging Sam last month.

She banked the fireplace, replaced the protective screen, and raised the window halfway for the cats. Cal pulled on a black turtleneck sweater and overalls with a small show of femininity—a pin. One of her dead mother's treasured cameos.

Cal ran her fingers over her mother's broach and thought how proud she was to be her parents' daughter, handsome C.C. and pretty Dot, was what most folks called them.

Cal was born a change of life baby. Her mother was reaching 50 and her father was much older than her mother.

She thought back of the secretive lives they'd lived. This came about because of their values. They felt different about social issues than their neighbors. But that's a part of my life I don't care to explore.

Yes! Daddy and Mama, I miss you both dearly. I only wish my Liza could have known you. She felt morning came much too early after a restless night.

With her thoughts running wild, she reached for a jacket on the way out.

The morning fog made little swirls around her as she walked to the Hub. Liza was fast asleep, wrapped on Cal's back like a papoose. She thought of her little Liza feeling warm against her back. Her child was the sweetest, never cranky, amused herself with play, now growing into the questioning stage.

Walking towards the Hub, the sounds of the frogs called out for lovers. "I understand your feelings." The herb gardens aroma filled her head as she hummed along. Her wide smile showed strong white teeth, lips free of lipstick.

A lantern hung from each corner of Sam's wagon. The lantern swayed from a breeze that came out of nowhere. A little chill went down Sam's back, but he shook it off. Sam sat on his newly padded bench. He seldom went out of his way for himself. The bones were getting tired and Cal pushed him to make himself more comfortable.

"Go get that seat fixed. A nice guy like you, Sam, should not be in pain. Give that old skinny butt some comfort." He stretched his long, gangly legs out and gave a big grin to the comfort he felt. He was thinking about all the noise happening in town, about the new landowner. A Mr. Ward had purchased a thousand acres that blended into the riverbank for miles, a place God had made perfect. Sam had to admit, that piece of land had been waiting for some time for the right person.

Sam talked to his horse, "I remember when I hunted there with my daddy, often he would skin a rabbit right beside the river, cut a roasting stick, and say, "Pick up some dry wood, Sam, for a fire. My boy and me are going to have some good eating."

"Yeah! Miss my Pa but since Pa died, I can't seem to go out and shoot a rabbit anymore. I even have to hire a man to kill the chickens. Oh well, go and soften my heart with age. Can't say that I like it much that Cal lights up when talking about that Mr. Ward."

Sam looked forward to his early morning rides to deliver goods to Cal. Sam's horse pulled his ears back. "Yes, boy, I can get long-winded, but thanks for listening."

The fog was thinning somewhat. He had seen a light come on in Cal's cabin, then it had moved to the side porch.

Sam's vision was limited as his horse and wagon rolled slowly through the morning fog. The horse halted as the hoof's touched down on the graveled lot in front of Cal's Hub.

Sam had been supplying Cal's Hub and general store for years with fresh vegetables in season, a constant supply of chickens dressed for the frying pan, eggs, and milk.

He admitted since his beloved wife had gone to Heaven, he and Cal had sex in the Hub, enough times for him to be encouraged it could lead to something more. Cal could be hurtfully honest. She would say, "Sam, a woman has needs; maybe more than a man." She was unusual. Well, according to society's standards. But all who knew Cal understood she didn't give one flip what anyone else's standards were. He took out his pint jar for coffee mixed with whiskey. Sure, keeps my bones warm. He tossed some down, thinking, what would my Lily say about me sitting here, throwing down white lightning so early in the morning and lusting after Cal?

His arousal was strong for the severely independent, sexy Cal. In all the 28 years he had been married, his life had been routine. As an adult, he didn't take the time to look at this exciting land he lived on. He labored hard most every day to see his family was taken care of. One light in his life was now Cal. Her attitude itself was a turn on. She desires satisfaction and Sam was more than willing to take on the job. He longed for it to be permanent. After making love, she would get up and walk away, sometimes saying, "Thanks, Sam. That was good. You are an upright, fine man. Your Lily was blessed to have had as fine a man as you." Then she would pour a cup of coffee and go about her business. She stirred up feelings and thoughts he never felt before. He wanted her to never leave his side. Sam felt Liza needed a daddy. He cared less about any gossip. If Liza was Dilsey Somerset's child, Dilsey was a fine, honest man who just happened to be part Cherokee Indian. But Cal said, "No! Sam, I do appreciate your kindness to take care of us but I ain't a saint. My, my! Why would you want to wake up with me? I am not that pleasant in the morning, or night for that matter."

"Who needs pleasant? I had pleasant for 28 years," Sam had replied. Cal smiled, thinking about Sam's response.

The birds were out early. Their morning song sounded good for her mood. A familiar, kind voice said, "Been waiting for you, Cal."

"Hi, Sam. Been, here long?"

"It was nice. I took a snooze and dreamed of you. You okay?"

"You know me, Sam. Always okay. Are you in for some coffee, whiskey, and coconut orange lime four-layer cake?"

"Sounds like the perfect combination except for one thing."

"Oh, Sam. Don't you go getting romantic on me."

Sam gave a small laugh, then said, "Shall I unload the supplies?"

"Oh, let those supplies wait. Come in. I got the feeling you could use some good talk."

"Yep! You are a clever and pretty one, Cal." Sam felt himself blush red with such a forward remark. Cal secured Liza into a playpen. The dogs moved in to watch over her every move.

They had coffee, whisky, and cake but Cal pulled back today on the intimacy. "Sam, you have been a loyal, dear friend and I don't mean to hurt you, but my free love side has been cut off. I am deeply in love. Yes! It's quick but I am so sure this is it. There will not be anyone else for me."

Sam pulled back and with a downcast face, he said, "I will always be here for you and Liza."

Cal had taken on the obligation of getting the old cabin ready on Mr. Ward's newly purchased land and also to clean land for Mr. Ward's new home. She asked Sam for his help in hiring workers.

Sam's reply was, "No problem, Cal. People need the work and wages. I'll get right on it."

Sam, like all the folks in town, just went about and got the job done, once informed. Not even taking in their own feelings, even if they didn't approve of the work at hand. Someone needed them to do a job.

Cal found herself continually making a visual search toward the crossover bridge, the entrance into town, for Mr. Ward's wagon. She felt Mr. Ward would be enlivened about the process that was about to be completed in his absence. Even though the town had always sustained itself quite well, the main work in town was farming vegetables for markets, both close and distant. There were small cattle ranchers close by, but now there were new promises in the air.

Mr. Ward was lured not only by his dreams but by virgin timber, the river, and the abundance of opportunity Georgia land provided. He appeared willing to bring this town along with his dreams. He needed little encouragement to be interested in nature. The citizens would be informed about Mr. Ward's feelings on his relationship with the land. We will work to educate our schools and meetings to hear the citizens out and their dreams for their town. And also, to protect the environment.

He wished to live a coexistence with the wilderness. His ethics would be applied in the building, planning, and farming. He would see no exploitation of his land and its resources. No clear cutting of the forest and return something, not just take. The people were hunters, but only for what they used.

A letter arrived from Mr. Ward. Before reading, Cal lovingly looked at his handwriting. She traced the beautiful penmanship. Capital letters swirled and curled to form a wonderful message. The letter contained a long list of future projects for the town. A P.S. at the bottom of the page read, "It's going to be grand to see you. You have inhabited my thoughts every day." Also, some more dollars to begin projects were included. He mentioned that he had noticed areas along the creek and river where huge piles of rock sat waiting. "Cal, try to start a competition with the town's children to bring these rocks to town. We are going to have our town boast a stone sidewalk." At first, the citizens thought it was a joke. But it evolved, not as an object of amusement, but as an outright competition. Everyone chipped in their labors… rock piles, picks, rakes, shovels, buckets of sand. The old red clay and board path in town was taking on a new face. Cal got Sam's help in keeping tabs for their pay. As the sidewalk materialized, the town's excitement grew.

Their goal was to complete the stone walkway and have it welcome Mr. Ward upon his return. The citizens wanted the charming town to grow. As Cal read off Mr. Ward's list of future goals, they got a glimpse in their minds. "Our fine new stone sidewalk will carry citizens and visitors by shops where ladies and gentlemen will be able to find most anything they need without stepping off Main Street. Using our citizens' variety of skills and talent, we will flourish. A new schoolhouse, library, and a brand spanking new railway station will be built. All this will spring up from the soil the town now rests on!" All seemed eager for the return of their exciting new citizen. Well, maybe all but Sam.

CHAPTER 7

Goodbye to Circus Friends

Lee awoke in the middle of the night and noticed that Mr. Ward's lamp was still bright. Still heavy-eyed from sleep, he rubbed his eyes, sat up on the side of his bed, and called down to Mr. Ward, "Father, are you alright?" The heavy, green velvet curtains were drawn around his desk. He pulled one side back to answer Lee. "Yes, son. Just going over as to what I will tell each one tomorrow morning. Get some rest. Enjoyable dreams."

Mr. Ward reopened his mind into a mélange of different thoughts, going back to all the years his circus had been his home and family. He realized he had vicariously lived by the way of watching his performers fall in love, get married, have children, lose loved ones, cried, and laughed. Often Mr. Ward would walk among the wagon rows in the evening where the families would be cooking meals, socializing, playing music, and dancing. His lone, stately figure would tip his top hat as he passed by them, then he would move on to check on the many animals. He would stop at each stall or cage. He shared his love of all animals often with Lee.

Often, if anyone had been close by as he took his lone walk, they would have heard this wise man asking each animal in a compassionate tone, "Are you okay?" He said to Lee often, "The animals deserve the same devotion and loyalty as we do."

He thought of all the walks he had taken; no invitations came forth to join the performers. As much as he had their respect, held in the highest regard, a line was still drawn between boss and employee.

He continued to go over each person and what he would say to them. He has asked Birchard to have all the performers meet in the large tent early in the morning to share breakfast.

Ward realized it was breaking morning and he had been up all night. He shaved, got dressed, woke Lee, and stepped outside his tent.

He walked toward the lunch tent with a heavy heart. He met up with Birchard and after "Good Morning" was exchanged. Mr. Ward spoke, "I want to walk among my family of performers, look into their eyes, and shake each hand, then place an envelope with a share of the money received from the sale of my circus. Each performer deserves recognition for the tremendous job they do and have done through the years. I hope by my daily actions I have shown all the respect each one deserves, and I will repeat this to each performer, as well as the cook and food staff and the roust-abouts. All have made this circus the best in the world, and I thank them beyond words."

Birchard said, "Mr. Ward, your circus family will be happy for us. You have always done right by them."

Mr. Ward and Birchard stood in the center ring tent. Szabo entered, wearing an extremely oversized polka dot bowtie — a borrow from the clowns.

Mr. Ward laughed and Szabo said, "I've gotten dressed special for this sad and happy goodbye." He gave Mr. Ward a giant hug and held him. Tears fell hard from Szabo's six-foot-eight frame and dropped onto the sand floor, leaving their mark like huge raindrops falling from the sky. Szabo did not continue with the talk. He released Mr. Ward and left the tent.

The family of performers were entering the tent with downcast faces. After all had gathered, there were soft whispers, then silence. In his great orator voice, Mr. Ward started calling each one to him. When all the thanks were finished, he went into detail about his reason for selling. Each person was given their share of the sale. "To each of you I say, when I found my land, I stood and looked out over the expansive fields that lay flat for miles. On one side, great oaks; and along a ridge, green pine trees silhouetted themselves against the sky. When I walked in close to the river, I drew in a deep breath and took in earth, water, and forest's perfume. My life dream materialized. I must move forward to live it." As he continued to talk, soft sobbing was heard throughout the tent.

His voice and expressions showed he desired them to understand and share his dream. He continued, "I want to live my life out, building a town, and watching my son. Lee, grow into a man. We will build a teaching school where young people can learn a trade. A place so inviting, they will want to raise their families there, and conversation is abundant among neighbors and friends, along with kindness. Above all, kindness."

Mr. Ward turned his gaze toward Lee; also, Szabo had returned. Lee was holding Szabo's huge hand and using the tail of Szabo's shirt to wipe away tears. Mr. Ward continued, "We will miss each one. All are welcome to visit or live at our new home."

Mr. Ward turned and walked out of the tent, back to his quarters for private thoughts. He could hear Birchard talking, saying his and Mickey's goodbyes. Birchard introduced the new owner. The next few days were busy with preparation for their journey. Cal had sent word; the cabin was shined and supplied. All eagerly awaited their return.

VOLUME II
Building Lives & A Town

CHAPTER 8

Heading Toward A Home Without Wheels

Mr. Ward continued with non-stop talk for the future. The last letter from Cal read that when she "checked on the property, the men had sectioned off the fields, clearing them for cultivation and that men and women workers are eager to work. The people are still building their own lives. Southern people are strong and within a few years have made great progress in our small settlement. The excitement of our citizens has added a great enthusiasm for you to build their town. Your land is being cleared with tools, plows, and mules. A lifesaver for the people of the area, neighbor helping neighbor.

"The land is rich and the people are eager. I have made it clear that you welcome all that wish to work and be a part of the town and America. We understand it is backbreaking work, trees are cut, stumps hard fought with mules and ropes. The people have been through this before with their own land. Some areas are heavily wooded, with a buildup of fallen trees over the years. They will be cut along with root balls and burned, stones picked up and stacked to be used in your home or for dividing the fields. It is an exciting time to know that all comes from the land.

"I am and the citizens are waiting for your return with anticipation and hope. Your reassurance all workers will be paid top dollar and that you are thankful for each person means a lot to everyone."

Mr. Ward's excitement was not to be shut down, Lee had never heard his father so talkative and cover so many subjects. Mr. Ward continued, "Cal is tremendous. I never dreamed that, along with my land and town, I would also meet what I now believe to be the perfect woman for me. She understands that I have had to use subterfuge with some Northern states and foreign countries to stock my land. As you know, Lee, that goes against my beliefs. Some still seem reluctant to do business with the Southern states."

Lee was wise beyond his years and understood the complications of life more than ordinary, thoughtful adults. So even if he was a child, Mr. Ward included him in most of his dealings.

"Father, you have done and do what is needed for you to accomplish your dream. Now we are almost here," said Lee. He looked at his father with great pride.

"Even after the years have gone by, a lot of the Northern states do not wish to help the South in their rebuilding. But the willful Southern pride goes a long way. Their manpower was greatly reduced but, fortunate for the South, they did have many sympathetic people, all were not for slavery, but more for individual rights and some great women to carry on."

The ride to their new home seemed to move quickly. It was a special time for Lee and Mr. Ward, a closeness of respect and love that they were able to share. Mr. Ward pointed out to Lee as their carriage moved along, "It's important to be aware of the moment we are living in, look at all you are passing through at this moment. Yes! We're heading toward an exciting time. But we never ever forget the moments we are living in."

"Yes, father. I am with you, and I have seen every bird we have passed." Lee continued, "So what if the citizens are a super suspicious lot. I have a feeling Miss Cal will see that you don't encounter any unpleasantness. Yes, I am sure. Would I be too forward, Father, if I asked did you detect more than I just met you for the first-time politeness from Miss Cal towards you?"

Lee enjoyed Mr. Ward's laughter, which seemed to occur often since their first trip to make the deal for his new land. He didn't answer Lee's questions.

Mr. Ward brought the carriage to a stop. Birchard and Mickey pulled up close behind. Birchard spoke, "Looks like a pleasing spot for some lunch." All agreed.

Lee wiped the horses down, let them drink from a small stream nearby, hooked the horses on lead ropes to graze, while the four had food and talked of their new life. Mr. Ward, always quite formal in his everyday actions, unfolded a table and four chairs. Mickey shook out a white linen tablecloth, a box of China, and the food was enjoyed under a puffy white partially blue sky and perfect place settings.

"Lee, we may encounter possibly some self-appointed judges in our new small town."

"I understand, Father. I am sure we do carry an air of mystery, being circus folks and you being a Yankee, and our dear friends Birchard and Mickey. We are not a typical family."

Lee paused and looked at his father; did he sense a little worry on Mr. Ward's face?

Lee looked at his father and said, "But Father, when the people get to know us, they will see all of your intentions are only for the good of the town and its people."

Lee thought, I know one pretty lady who will be saying, "So glad you have returned safely," as she puts her hand on father's arm. Lee smiled inside, just thinking about his father being in love.

Lee tried not to let his mind revisit Azzie's leaving, but it did. His thoughts were of, "I should have looked after her. I should have spent more time with her," and on and on. But, deep inside, he knew there wasn't a thing that would have changed her leaving.

Mr. Ward picked up on Lee's thoughts. He said, "Lee, we can't change the past. When we recall pain, we experience it all over again. Life moves on, and us with it. I read a line somewhere that read, 'One doesn't wait for fairness, you just keep going.'"

"Yes, Father. I do understand. It's okay and I am all right."

The carriages and wagon rounded the curve, dogwoods were in full bloom. A perfect day, the air smelled of an early spring. Wood stoves puffed smoke out of chimneys.

A town welcomed four newcomers who wore smiles of anticipation. Mr. Ward's eyes searched out one special woman.

Birchard called out, as his carriage pulled up beside Mr. Ward, "I believe I see Cal on the Hub's porch, looking our way."

The truth be known, Cal had not missed a day watching for these carriages to round the bend. They had arrived. Cal's heart beat against her shirt. She wasn't a kissy feely kind of person, and neither was Mr. Ward, but when their eyes met, the story was told.

Lee could not contain himself, he hopped off the carriage, ran to Cal, and gave her a huge hug. Cal asked if they were hungry and everyone said no. They were too excited to see the land.

Cal put her hand on Mr. Ward's arm and said, "Give me a few minutes and I'll get Sam to watch Liza and the Hub. Then I will ride out with you to make sure the cabin supplies are all in place. I'm sure all is fine, but I'll enjoy seeing your first reaction to your new land. The mules and that fancy horse arrived last week. The barn is incomplete, but it gives the animals shelter. That's some beauty of a horse. He should sire many a colt. Not sure he likes the country life; the men say he is somewhat belligerent."

"Cal, we will partake of some sweet tea before departing and it's our honor to have you join us." All sat with Cal and enjoyed tea.

Cal asked Sam to watch Liza and the Hub. He obliged with sad eyes. They headed toward a new life, with Cal alongside.

The ride to the new land gave Cal time to talk with Ward and give him some information about their small settlement.

She said, "Our small settlement has been in waiting for a deliverer." Mr. Ward explained his circus had traveled through this area of Georgia before. He had been impressed with the land and the friendliness of its people. "I kept the land of Georgia on my mind."

Ward reached out and touched Cal's hand—It was never just a touch. She never wanted him to remove it. He said, "Cal tell me how you ended up here, in this part of Georgia and who gave you the wonderful name of Cal, that suits you so well."

She moved in closer to Ward. His hand still holding hers.

He saw Cal's eyes were misty, very unusual.

She started to talk, "Ward I am proud of where I came from. My Mama and Daddy were extraordinary. Born and raised in Savannah. But upon hearing in the 1820's gold was found in Georgia, they decided to look for a better life. They were lucky and discovered a small productive mine that gave them enough dollars to build a small house and a way station. The way station attracted people, they could get a meal, even stable their mules and wagons—and any repairs to their wagons—or new shoes for the mules.

Roads had become quite good because of the post roads. Mail was delivered by stagecoach to my parent's waystation. Then picked up by settlers in the area.

Ward was listening and said, "Were the people charged for these services. Sounds like your parents were progressive people. And independent thinkers."

"When I was born my Daddy, really was hoping for a boy to work alongside of him. But he got me. Mother named me Calean. Mama died when I was seven. Daddy heartbroken put his energy into building a small settlement. I worked right alongside my Daddy. Daddy changed my name to Cal, because he said I was tough and a fighter, "No girlies name for my daughter."

"Daddy died when I was sixteen. I was strong both mentally and physically and took charge. And I am still here. Mama and Daddy are buried on the small bill behind the hub.

Cal said, "Now when will I hear your story," as she put both arms around Ward.

"Yes! I often said to myself… I have found my future home. I will be back to lay claim to some river land." He reached out and touched Cal's hand.

"I had big dreams of having a town that gave citizens an even chance. No matter a person's color of skin, or shape of eyes, tall or short. I will rejoice to create the opportunity for them to have a good life." The idealistic Mr. Ward carried with him the wisdom and financial power to back his plans for a settlement to become a thriving town.

"Cal, I give my pledge to the land and its people. I shall put my personal monies into building a new rail station and rail links to bring goods and send goods out. We will have to have patience while waiting, but we will succeed."

Cal felt with all her being this would come to pass. "Ward, the first night spent on your new land will be an evening of low-key celebration. I feel I have done more than just ready the cabin. Hope you will be impressed."

When they entered the road to the land, Mickey said, "I have never seen any land so beautiful."

Cal watched for everyone's reaction. The day could not have been more perfect—clear blue sky, spring bursting forth, workers clearing stumps, fire burning dead wood, all to make space for homes, pastures, and more.

Cal spoke, "Mr. Ward, I do hope I haven't overstepped my bounds by building an extra room onto the cabin. I have factored in your privacy but also Birchard and Mickey's. I thought, why not just go ahead!"

Mr. Ward took Cal's arm and walked her away from the others. Yes, he was being bold. He felt time was not on his side. Why? He didn't know, but he wanted Cal to know his emotions. He said, "Cal, this was unforeseen. You are magnificent, not just in your abilities to take care of each thing. Well! I am just going to say it, you are the woman I have been waiting for and I believe you have strong feelings for me. I just need a yes or no."

Cal liked the way Ward focused on whomever he was talking to. At this moment, it was her. "Yes," she said. "I will see you tomorrow night for dinner in my cabin. I need to be in my own surroundings. This is different. Are you fine with that?"

"Yes, I will be there."

"My door will be open. Now, we need to go to work. I will introduce you to the men and women who will be helping you build your land. Then, I will head back to town. This is your time together. I will be here tomorrow with food and other supplies."

Mr. Ward didn't question her and rarely did anyone else. All that new Cal knew she had people's welfare in mind. She said her goodbyes and rode away. Ward watched her. How different Cal was than any woman he had ever met. Not only her mode of dress in buckskin trousers, which only played up her body even more. Yes! I can look at this woman forever. She disappeared around the curve.

As Cal road back toward the Hub, her thoughts were on Mr. Ward and the coming days.

Birchard picked out a place for the wagon and said, "Mickey, this is where our home will be."

Mickey wept on her husband's shoulder. He placed his hands on her stomach and their love and commitment shined.

As Lee looked out toward the green landscape, he said, "Oh, Father! How can there ever be a more impressive sight?"

Ward smiled and said, "There will be, son. This land will be protected and made even more beautiful. There is much land to be cleared for the animals, fences, barns, and our home, wells to be dug, trees, gardens, and a mountain of other things."

"Father," Lee asked, "can we walk some of our land tomorrow?" Tears filled his eyes as he was overcome with emotion. Lee now stood almost as tall as Mr. Ward.

"Yes, son," answered Mr. Ward, "Protected Earth is what our land will be called. We will not only protect the land, but we'll also put forth our best effort to protect every living thing in it."

Birchard walked over and joined the conversation. He said, "This will be a large task in the following years, but I believe we have the will and strength to make this happen."

Cal had sent a supper for the new citizens. After enjoying a fine Southern meal of fried chicken, mashed turnips, and potatoes sweetened with fresh butter, coleslaw, and of course, crusty buttermilk biscuits, they enjoyed a piece of Cal's lemon pie, with its mile-high merengue browned to perfection.

Mickey spoke, "Cal seems to think of everything." She wanted to see if Mr. Ward commented, but he said nothing. Mr. Ward looked around his land and dabbed his mouth with a linen napkin.

Birchard spoke, "Mickey is quite tired. We are going to wash up and retire under this beautiful sky."

Mr. Ward reminded Birchard an extra room was built onto the small cabin.

Birchard replied, "Thanks. Tonight, we will make ourselves comfortable right here." The little couple hugged and smiled.

Lee offered to put all leftovers away and wash the dishes.

Mr. Ward said good night and walked toward the cabin.

Birchard and Mickey fell asleep under a giant oak. Birchard, being mindful of Mickey's condition, awoke before daybreak. The night had been cool. He covered his beloved wife with another quilt and adjusted another pillow behind her back.

He refreshed the fire, which still glowed with hot coals. From long habit, he put water on Mr. Ward's shaving table that Lee had set up.

Mickey sounded restless. Birchard roused her from her dreams and settled her in the back of the wagon to get a few more hours of rest.

Water was heated for the rigged-up shower with a curtain to pull around for privacy. Another shaving table was set up for the rest of the men to shave—that is, those who choose to shave. Most of the workers now camped out in tents sported beards of all shapes and sizes.

Cal had a restless night and spent most of it pacing the floor of her screened in porch with a jar of moonshine close by. She had sent word to the wood craftsmen to please deliver Mr. Ward's dinner table. She so wanted it to arrive today. Cal had commissioned a large table to be built by one of the area's finest wood craftsman. It was her gift for Mr. Ward. Then thinking, on second thought, if it will fit in a small cabin. If not, she will have the workers build a cover.

Once more drawing on good old Sam's friendship, she left him in charge of the Hub. Cal had scooted home and changed into a high collar blouse and a new pair of buckskin trousers. She considered her reflection in the mirror for a moment, then unbraided her hair and brushed it slowly. Her hair hung in long, soft waves. But then she gathered it loosely into a high bun in the fashion of the day, adding her grandmother's dangling earrings that matched her broach.

Liza's curls, as well as the curls on her two favorite dolls, now sported ribbons. When they looked into the mirror, Cal remarked to Liza, "Just look at us! My, my!"

Liza giggled.

They stopped by the Hub to load up. Sam raised an eyebrow at

Cal's feminine appearance. Well, he thought, Cal looks beautiful, but this shows a different side to the woman I thought I knew.

The sumptuous food was carefully packed into the back of Cal's wagon. The carpenter's wagon pulled up to the Hub with the table covered in blankets and tied down in the back. Together, the wagons carefully arrived at Wards place. After a hearty breakfast, Mr. Ward, Lee, Birchard, and Mickey noticed dust clouds rising above the bend. Presently, a caravan consisting of several wagons appeared. Out front was Cal, bringing not only her friendship, but also supplies that had been ordered for Mr. Ward. Neighbors had packed their wagons, and then had come to lend a hand.

The men set about shaking hands with Mr. Ward and Birchard. They tipped their hats in respect to Mickey and started to unload the supplies.

Mr. Ward's eyes, amid this activity, was centered on Cal. He thought, she is one of a kind.

Mr. Ward said, "Cal, I like the style. You carry it all beautifully."

Cal did not acknowledge his comment, but her insides told a different story. This is what love is, her desire to be next to this man was almost uncontainable.

Cal unloaded a cage that carried a rooster. The attached note read, "Your wake-up alarm. His name is Upstart and he brought along six hens to get started with."

Mr. Ward had been expecting Cal to bring food, but not a table, more work hens, and two blue tick pups, which were now pulling on his pant legs. He was to find that Cal was an open-handed gift giver. One may as well enjoy her magnanimous nature because you could neither change nor out gift her.

Lee picked up the pups. "What shall we name them, Father?"

"Nothing comes to mind, but it will soon, I am sure. Let's wait," said Mr. Ward.

Mickey walked up and said to Mr. Ward, "Yes, I do believe you have met your match and we are all happy with your choice." Lee, Birchard, and Mickey had a wide smile of joy on their faces, they were happy for the boss.

Before nightfall, the men had the rock foundation for the main house completed. Water barrels were filled, stacks of stove wood had been sawed, split, and cut, then piled under a new shed, safe from wet weather. Also, a temporary place was built for Upstart the rooster and his hens. Lee didn't feel it was safe to release them to run free. The pups were brought into the cabin. Fulfilled dreams, love, and gratitude filled the air on the land, it was a glorious time to be alive.

After a long, hard day of physical work, some of the men left, others stayed in tents set up on the property. Mr. Ward informed them they were to be paid at the close of each day. Birchard and Lee handled the wagons. He thanked each one.

The blue tick pups followed Lee's every step.

Birchard and Mickey felt strongly that Mr. Ward would not be spending the night on his land. He asked Lee to saddle his horse. No one asked where he was headed. They knew.

The moon rose high over the horizon and the lovely evening was coming to a close. Cal had been working alongside the men, she stopped when they did.

"I better go," Cal said reluctantly. "If I don't leave now, I'll have to pull over and sleep in the wagon."

As Cal climbed up into the wagon, Mr. Ward courteously put his hands around her waist to help her up. Settling in the wagon seat, she looked down at him, giving him a smile.

He said softly, "Hike up the fire and pour us a drink. I will be along shortly."

Gathering the reigns and giving a light slap to her horses, she called, "Night, all," as the horses pulled out. Mr. Ward did not take his eyes off her until her wagon cleared the curve.

Mr. Ward, Lee, Birchard, and Mickey sat a while in companionable silence. Lee broke the silence and said, "It sure feels good to be home."

Mr. Ward said, "I will wash up and head for town. Thanks to each of you for all the hard work."

"Goodnight, Father," Lee said and headed for the cabin. "Your horse stands waiting." The blue ticks at his heels, Lee caught Upstart who had already escaped from his temporary home. He once more secured the area for the hens and rooster.

Mr. Ward smiled. Knowing Lee's love for animals, he said, "I'm sure they will be fine now."

Birchard and Mickey stood together outside, whispering love and longing to each other.

Mickey's pregnancy was showing after only a few months, Birchard was worried. He saw to it that she was not overtaxed and got plenty of rest. Mickey laughed, "Surely, Birchard, you haven't forgotten how I defied death on the high wire?"

"Yes, I know, but Mr. Ward has inquired about a doctor. There is a midwife in the area, but neither of us feels completely comfortable with just her. You have lost one baby. He said he is sending for a doctor before you were ready for labor. He is also inquiring far and wide for a permanent town doctor."

They made love under the stars and spoke of their new home and child to be. Birchard nuzzled the side of her neck. "You are my soul, Mickey. I can't lose you."

Mickey put her hand on his heart. "You never will." He lay there for a while and listened to Mickey's breathing. Mickey had wanted children for so long. Birchard only wanted her. But if children would make her happy, then so be it.

When there was a mere hint of morning's brightening from the deep darkness of the night, Mickey opened her eyes. "Hi," she said, her voice still full of sleep.

"Good morning. Did you sleep well? How is your back?" Birchard couldn't help himself from being overly concerned about his adored wife.

"I'm good, help me, will you? I don't know if I could do it on my own."

"Oh, so you do need me, after all," he teased, helping her to her feet. And so, their day began with this sweet, flirty manner that came so easily to them.

On the way to the cabin, Mickey said, "I've never seen Mr. Ward so taken with a woman before. I wonder if he knows how smitten he is."

Birchard responded with a gentle laugh. "Yeah, I spotted that too. Do you think she feels the same?"

"Yes," said Mickey. "Cal is not difficult to read; she speaks out as she sees it. I don't think Cal has any games going on. That way, they are a good match. We have seen so many women make themselves available to Mr. Ward. But he has never showed an interest in anyone. With Cal, he is different. We love Mr. Ward and I like Cal and I believe we will be great friends."

Mickey kept her hands on her stomach, as if always protecting the baby.

In the past, feminine attention was important in Ward's life, but at last, this woman, he said, is his one love; he knew with all his being. From the first time he met Cal, he talked about every detail of her face, figure, and manner. Her tan, muscular body, her lovely face lined by sun and maybe some hard drinking, her long, graceful hands that move as if dancing. All these things excited him, and he locked them in his memory.

Ward's ride into Cal's had been spent in heavy thoughts. Never thought I would marry, but now I can't see myself away from Cal. He immediately felt at home as he rode into the barn at her charming cabin. He put his saddle away, rubbed his horse down, and released the horse into the corral. He didn't see Cal. The door to her cabin was open so he walked in. Cal was standing by the open fireplace, a glass in each hand. She handed Ward a drink and started talking nonstop. He looked at her, just enjoying the aura around this woman, that set every inch of his body on fire.

He finished the drink, set down the glass, and said, "Okay, okay." He laughed. He shut her up by covering her mouth with his own.

Cal continued, "But I'm not done yet. I like a purpose to get out of bed every morning. For me, first is my child. My whole self says, Lee Ward, I never want you out of my life. Then there's work, good whiskey, having folks look at you with respect, decent food, my old guitar, my dogs and cats lolling about, a warm, open fire, smelling nature and trees, and yes, a clean man and pristine sheets on my bed and dried in the sunshine. A little sin thrown in… and Lee Ward, that's you. Also, a long exhausting ride on my horse, then brushing him down."

Mr. Ward stared at the ceiling and considered her point of view. Cal had made a pallet in front of the fire. As they lay, absorbed in their love, she broke the spell and grabbed her pillow and belted him with it. Laughing, he grabbed the pillow. They grappled with the pillow, rolling back and forth. The dogs growled. Cal shooed them outside, then threw herself on Ward with a purpose. A wrestling match ensued in earnest.

Mr. Ward found that he had all he could handle. Cal fought dirty. The playful struggle eventually evolved into something wild, erotic, powerful, exhilarating, and infinitely more agreeable.

Later, both exhausted, Cal said, "Ward, I don't know where your character came from, but I know I love it. Your most trivial movements, talks, and happenings, I record in my memory. Lee Ward, you have not asked about the father of my child." Her voice dropped to a whisper, "Have you wondered?"

"Of course, one can easily see Liza is part American Indian. But that's your business. You will tell me when the time's right. She is a beautiful child, and she is yours." He cupped her face with his hands and pulled her close. "I would be proud to accept the responsibility for

Liza's future. I certainly have the highest regard for her mother. Here and now, you have my word that I will see to it that Liza is taken care of. Her future and yours are secure. I understand this is our first night, but my head is clear, and I know what I want, and you are right there at the top."

Cal looked deep into his eyes. "Thank you, Ward. I am happy and feel my life is full, I don't need anything. But that is quite a commitment." She put her head on his shoulder and sighed. What he had just given her was huge. "Let's sleep on the porch bed. It's a star-studded night and I want to wake up and share the morning with you. And all my mornings. This is forever, a thorough, companionable relationship."

They moved to the porch. After they talked quietly for a while, they made love again. This time, it was soft, slow, sweet, and unbearably tender. Afterward, they'd laid there without speaking. Each silent with private thoughts.

It had been a day of hard work, new friendships, and a night of passion, they fell asleep in each other's arms.

The smell of coffee greeted him beside the bed. "Mr. Ward, I need to talk," said Cal. "For now, I feel our relationship is going to be together, yet separate. Because at this moment, the thought of not seeing you does not feel too good. I wasn't prepared for this kind of love, not sure if I believed it existed. But here it is."

"Cal, at least for now, my son needs some time to adjust. You were in my thoughts, no matter time or place. I know there will not be another for me. Now, give me a cup of that great smelling coffee?"

After getting dressed, they sat for a few minutes and finished their coffee. He walked arm in arm with Cal to the barn. They shared a long, hard, coffee flavored kiss. Further words were not necessary. No definite dates were set between them. Anytime was just fine.

Mr. Ward saddled his horse, mounted up, and rode away. His thoughts were, I am already missing Cal. Cal had left Liza with a neighbor only for the night. Ward felt no guilt for staying away from

Lee and the land his first night. He knew in his heart Cal was in for the rest of his life. And Birchard was always there to look after Mr. Ward's son, home, and business interests. In return, Mr. Ward repaid Birchard's loyalty very well, indeed. Besides his generous pay, Birchard always knew that anything that he needed, he had only to speak the word. But mostly all was provided without asking. Ward was a man in tune to his surroundings and the people in it.

Mr. Ward rode back at a full gallop. All kinds of thoughts were jumping back and forth. When he rode up, he saw Birchard working on the holding areas for the horses.

"Good morning," said Birchard, with a grin. "It certainly has the promise of a beautiful day."

"Yes, my friend."

"I'll wipe your horse down. He looks like he had a good ride." Birchard stood on his box and proceeded to groom the horse.

"Thanks. Looks like the workers are coming around the bend. Early risers like us." Mr. Ward walked into the cabin. Lee and Mickey were having breakfast.

Mickey asked, "Shall I set breakfast for you?"

Mr. Ward replied, "Yes, thanks. Hi, son. Another hard day is ahead, and I am sure there will be plenty more."

"Yes, Father," said Lee, "and I am looking forward to each one."

CHAPTER 9

Busy Days

Living on Protected Earth, the people were surrounded by staggering possibilities. One had only to look around and beyond.

A large variety of fruit trees were installed and planted with enough room that a horse and buggy could ride among them. Reason was a special time when all came into bloom. The fruit trees presented a harvest that needed workers. An enchanted place to just sit under a tree have lunch, or a Sunday setting for a family brunch. The workers, along with Mr. Ward's family, were given free range to enjoy.

Workers came from various backgrounds and lives. They were given a choice, to live in one of the cabins that now dotted the landscape. One-room cabins with a sleeping loft, fireplace, a pumping well for water, wood stoves for cooking and heating. Each cabin was well-equipped for living or a one-night stay. If a man had a family, Ward would accommodate and build an extra bedroom for growing children.

Some workers arrived by horseback or mule and wagon. Also, word had spread to neighboring towns that had men that needed work. And all were welcome. With a large supply of workers, Mr. Ward was able to complete the much-needed sawmill and school. He was seeking teachers that could teach skills that the children of Darnell could build on, to become doctors, lawyers, or entrepreneurs. Also, he knew many of them would become farmers, craftsmen, apprentices for young masons, furniture makers, painters, and builders.

He wanted the young people in town to think twice before moving to larger cities. Most could earn a good living for themselves right here in Darnell. Settling down in their hometown made sense. In meeting with the newly hired teachers and the parents in regard to the curriculum, they carefully selected the curriculum that best suited the further development of the town and the students. He stressed the importance of science. He believed that if a person understands the land, weather, and how connected all of them are, they will love it more.

Most of the people of Darnell appreciated and benefited from Mr. Ward's contributions to the town. However, some of the old timers resented all the changes that were made by someone who had arrived so recently. Even the town was now named after Ward's son. Occasionally this would surface in the editorial page of the small local newspaper. And each eagerly waited for Wednesdays and Fridays for their paper to be delivered. Not that it always arrived on that date, but now with the newest up-to-date printing press, the small paper had expanded. Ward wanted all citizens to receive their paper. When the farmers came into the rail station for supplies, they could pick up a paper. This was looked forward to, but it got there.

Mr. Ward was not disturbed by the editorials; he understood. He would seek out the author to discuss their opposing viewpoint. He felt that every effort must be made to show wisdom and respect for all the town's diverse opinions. Mr. Ward knew that the best course for the town's growth was cooperation for his project.

Some in the town said that Mr. Ward's sentimentality was his weakness, but no one could say with credibility that he didn't have the highest regard for each individual. The citizens felt they had some place to voice their complaints. The paper also had a reporter that gathered news for this small paper. She had posted a news box at the railway station and Cal's Hub. The citizens were asked to drop off any news they wished printed. The owner of the newspaper was Jacob Blackwell. He insisted when he hired the inexperienced Lannie that she must only submit things that could be verified for the paper.

Birchard was a huge part of everyday life, on the land and in town. Throughout Birchard's life, because of his small size, he had to go beyond what most men met up with. This was no problem; however, he would say as he tapped himself on the temple with his finger, "I am wiser, smarter, more secure in my knowledge, and all around a better man for the bias and adversities I have confronted."

It was a truth; Birchard knew his business. His answers came quickly and correctly when someone presented a problem that needed to be worked out. And he never backed away from a situation that needed to be taken care of.

Birchard came from a childhood of poverty and extreme suffering in his home country. He and Mickey grew up together and fell in love as teens. Not seeing much of an opportunity in the small, poor village where the two lived, they practiced their circus act. They sought out an uncle who had been a tightrope daredevil.

Birchard told the uncle, "We wish to marry and get out of this poverty. We love watching your act and ask you to teach us." And so, he did. The couple practiced long and hard hours and became outstanding. The uncle, seeing an ad in the local paper that auditions were being given by an American for Ward's circus, encouraged them to audition. Mickey had been taught by her skilled seamstress mother and made their outfits from some warm purple velvet curtains. They were a sight to behold.

Most of their small village went to the audition to cheer them on. The owner of the circus was Mr. Ward, the young and handsome American. He had been awed by the diminutive couple and they were hired on the spot. He brought them back to the United States. Never for one moment did he regret his decision. Mr. Ward came to depend on Birchard, not only as a top performer, but also as a friend, and later, a business partner. And now they were here, living on this piece of unbelievable land, to live out their lives.

Today Birchard as he had inspected the supplies and organized the daily workforce, considered the frantically running about chickens. Birchard called Lee to his side, "Lee, scatter chicken feed as a trail into the newly finished hen house. The nesting bins are ready for the laying of eggs. The hens will soon settle in. The hens are finding out of the way places to nest and have babies." Birchard told Lee with a smile, "We'll have fresh eggs from our chickens. I will feel such joy collecting each one instead of searching."

Lee agreed, then remarked, "Luckily, the pups Cal gave father are not interested in chickens or eggs. What do you suppose those pups are looking for in the woods? They spend hours in there."

Birchard chuckled. "Can't say, my boy. Maybe we have stirred spirits up by moving onto their land." Lee looked toward the edge of the forest and a shiver went down his back. He often felt he saw shadows move behind the trees. A light, warm breeze moved across the field of pines.

Birchard instructed Lee, "Mr. Ward says the men are also to be paid for the use of their mules, wagons, tools, and plows."

"I am excited about taking on more duties," said Lee.

Birchard felt Lee was now capable and physically strong enough to work as hard as the men. Lee proved himself more and more each day. On occasion he was still a child and his wanderlust would overtake him. He would become mesmerized by observing a bluebird and its habitat or watching a new species of a dragonfly beauty. "Come, Birchard! You must see it."

Birchard observed for a minute as the dragonfly dive-bombed, flew upside down, holding its just caught prey as Lee quickly drew the dragonfly in his notebook.

Birchard smiled to himself and thought, after all, a boy still needs to indulge in his youth on occasion. "Dig in on as many different chores as possible, Lee. We have so many artisans working here. We need to take full advantage of the opportunity to learn, learn, learn!"

"Yes, sir," replied Lee.

The morning activities were well underway. After breakfast, Mr. Ward and Birchard lingered at the dining table to review the progress on the land. Mr. Ward called out to Lee to join them.

Mr. Ward commented, "As I rode by the men this morning that had gathered, having morning coffee, I felt warm inside as I observed them talking and warming their hands by the fire pit. I like the Southern way of a morning talk before work starts. It sets up a comradeship between the persons that do the labor. A respect for the other man that one depends on, while both are straining, sweating, and toiling to exhaustion. I am honored to be part of these men and women. Sometimes, not a word was said for hours until the pieces of work were completed."

Mr. Ward continued onto another subject, "I had arranged the purchase of goats, cattle, mules, and the latest farm equipment before we left the circus. All have now arrived. The barns that house animals and the cheese-making building are completed. And all the animals are settled in. The fields are ready for grazing and others for planting."

Birchard agreed, but all the while kept rubbing his knee, as if in severe pain.

Mr. Ward added, "Birchard, my friend, let's hire more workers if needed. I want you to pull back from all the hard physical work. That swelling of your joints can't be good. Besides, Mickey needs you much more. I'd rather you oversee things now."

It was hard to believe what had been accomplished. Birchard said, "Cal said there is an Indian settlement about 30 miles from here. They need work something fierce. Cal's friend Sam calls on them regularly with supplies. He could inform them that we have work and housing available for men and their families. The cabins are ready for those who desire to stay on. I am told the reservations that have been set up are a disgrace."

Mr. Ward said, "Sounds like a fine idea. We will handle any problems. Do let the Indians know that they will be paid the same wages as the rest of the workers. And they have my backing, I will deal with and see that all accept them."

Lee, who sat quietly while Birchard and Mr. Ward discussed business, spoke up. "Father, may I show the Indians all the artifacts we have uncovered?"

"Yes, Lee," Mr. Ward enthusiastically responded. "Of course." He was ashamed that he was a part of a race that helped destroy the Indians way of life. "Maybe we can give a small part back."

Each time an area proved to be where Indians had lived, it was marked off and all were forbidden to plant, cut, or clear it. This occurred often by the river, where Indians would set up their camps. Most tribes had long departed from the land. Their spirits loomed large.

Birchard agreed with Mr. Ward's thinking and made note to move forward on more hiring.

Mr. Ward continued, "Mickey is now resting in her own home. My heart gladdens to see the two of you living well. She is deserving of the best, Birchard."

Mr. Ward spoke with pride as he watched the happiness on Birchard's face. "The rest of our furniture will be completed soon. He is a marvel, that carpenter."

The few remaining pieces of Birchard and Mickey's furniture would be built and scaled to their size. Every aspect of their home would be appropriate for their needs. Mr. Ward had Birchard and Mickey approve all the final plans for each piece as well as every aspect of their house.

Dinners were mostly, Mr. Ward, Lee, Birchard, and Mickey. Mr. Ward said, "This is our piece of Protected Earth. I know my life will be lived out here."

He looked into the faces of the three people who he held dear to his heart and saw they felt the same.

The coming of Mr. Ward to the small town had given hope, jobs, and inspiration to the citizens to utilize their varied skills.

The citizens now proudly walked on stone in the sidewalks throughout the town. Mr. Ward felt pleased that he had been right about the townspeople and their spirit.

Under Birchard's capable hands, he had quickly completed his main farmhouse.

Many immigrants, some with reluctance, that had fought in the war for the South and the North had stayed and settled in the area. The warmer weather was appealing and the resilience of the people. Many were fine artisans that had been seeking a better life in America. Mr. Ward harnessed their expertise, gave a decent wage, and opportunities to build a decent life to raise their families.

At first, the Southerners were suspicious and arguable towards the use of Indians, Yankees, and immigrants. However, under Mr. Ward's leadership, they soon accepted that all men held the same goals as them. They wanted a better life for their families. Mr. Ward did not place any judgements. His compassion and kindness for each one persuaded them over to the common goal to continue to build a town where citizens can live in harmony. Each could worship as he or she chose.

That's not to say he wouldn't encounter a mean, odious person on occasion, but they were becoming rare, and the men were in unison to get rid of this kind of person. "Our town does not want troublemakers' protests and ideas. That's how we will grow." Mr. Ward said.

Time was moving at a fast pace. Oftentimes, Mr. Ward would see Lee working alongside one of the men and not recognize him; he had become so tall and muscular. Mr. Ward had put men in charge of the new rail station. At the town meeting, with Birchard and Lee at his side, he told all the assembled townspeople, "I pledge to put my personal monies into building a new rail station and connector railways to link our town for controlled progress. Riverboats are back in full force. The farmer can bring in his produce, along with the cattle ranchers. At our next town meeting, all of our citizens — that includes anyone that has called this area their home — are welcome. Also, the Indians that are still left in the area, and all we now call friends and neighbors." When he had finished talking, there was a quietness in the new schoolhouse.

Lee continued to pray that his sisters were all alive and that he would one day be reunited with them. Mr. Ward had careful concern for any of his new ventures competing with his neighbors. Planning heavily on the almost newly completed rail line, he sought out markets beyond the scope of the locals to sell produce and goods. He believed that every man should earn a profit for his labors, be it a farmer, builder, retailer, cattleman, or banker. If a neighbor could not secure a loan on their own, Mr. Ward would co-sign, securing their loan. This was common practice for him.

Once, he made a small loan to a neighbor who was struggling to earn a living with his cornfields. The man and his wife took the money and made a moonshiner's still. They were soon open for business. They repaid Mr. Ward every penny, plus, they established a bartering system. All the locals who had business, personal or public, came to know Mr. Ward as being above board in his ethics.

The farm showed Mr. Ward's unrestrained vision for abundance.

He was a passionate man, with the taste for the flamboyant and colorful that showed up in all of his choices. Pin oaks were soon to be planted on each side of the mile-long drive, starting at the entrance and continuing into the farm, functioning as a welcoming guide.

In the main house, the specialty woodwork on the doors and large archway windows were of the finest quality. Pink marble was brought from the surrounding areas for the floor in Mr. Ward's study and studio. He had secretly longed for the day when he once more could pick up a chisel or paintbrush.

In his younger years, even though he was raised in the circus life, he had envisioned that he would be a famous artist or sculpturer. When his house was completed, he then had ordered several large blocks of marble. His chisels were laid out, ready to begin the first tap.

The soaring, 20-foot-high room had an immense stone fireplace, sun-drenched windows, and double doors of old wood shipped from Italy, opening into a courtyard paved with stone. The view took in the river, edged by the forest—all a gift to himself and Lee's future children.

Mr. Ward asked Cal to marry him, but she said no. He knew she was committed to him, but she liked her way of life. Mr. Ward presented no inclination of slowing down. "Our town has a great future," he said. "My son Lee will carry out my dreams and yours."

The much-awaited wood-carved green and gold sign "Darnell" would be placed on the handsome new railway station. Underneath Darnell read "A Town and its Citizens in Harmony."

But there were some disagreements with the soil on Protected Earth. From the first turn of the plow, it was evident that the dirt had been robbed of its nutrients. The previous owners had planted cotton there every year for decades. The man who owned it had never set foot on the land.

Mr. Ward stood on the furrowed rows and took a handful of the earth. He felt its texture and held it to his nose, inhaling deeply. A frown creased his brow.

"Come here, Lee." Lee stepped over to where his father stood. "This soil is exhausted." Lee bent down and took a handful of soil. He inhaled a faint aroma of freshly turned dirt. Shocked, he looked up at his father. "What's wrong with it? It doesn't smell like much of anything."

Mr. Ward scattered the dirt back onto the ground and declared, "We will work hard to restore the land to its sweetest. It will provide us and our customers with the nourishment essential for all of our lives."

Yes, the plows would turn up rocky areas. Those stones were considered an asset, to be used somewhere in an arch stone bridge, a stacked wall to separate field crops, or for the many wells that supplied water for personal use and for the animals and crops.

The one crop that was not to be planted was cotton. Mr. Ward wanted no part of the cotton industry.

All sweated from hard work. Their sweat dropped to the earth, enriching it with their toil, along with the glorious rain showers. The extraordinary mules plowed and pulled, their bent heads trudging through wind, extreme heat, and cold.

Birchard ordered blankets to warm and shield their backs after a hard day for the mules. Mr. Ward gave orders to wash the mules, rub their overworked joints with liniment, see that mules were rotated, and given some off days to spend in free-range pastures. Birchard saw that this was done. There were many busy days ahead for everyone.

The town was being built for present and future generations. The architecture was fashioned by what Mr. Ward had seen and admired in Europe. A place to load and unload livestock and produce was carefully designed for markets in Atlanta and beyond.

The new log cabin library was Mr. Ward's shining pride. A local artist made hand-lettered library cards for all of Darnell's citizens. The personalized cards were considered to be badges of honor to possess. In the back of the library was a room which offered accommodations to any person, be it neighbor or stranger, who had fallen on hard times. The room held a fireplace, bed, and food supplies. The only payment requested was that the person using the room would give back to the community in some way, such as raking leaves or helping paint or maintain the town's buildings. Many a guest had quickly taken advantage of the room in the back of the cabin.

The library was well stocked, from ancient and American history to Shakespeare, along with any new, emerging writers. Mr. Ward continually ordered new books for the library and donated from his own collection. He saw to it that Lee was also committed to keeping the library up to par.

The front porch on the cabin held as many rocking chairs as it could handle. It subsequently became a gathering place for people to gather and chat and to play checkers or chess.

The town flourished. Shops seemed to spring up from the soil. Eventually, the ladies and gents of Darnell could find most anything they needed without stepping off their charming stone sidewalk, which many of them helped to build.

Its people treasured and protected their town. The same level of care as one would give to a sick friend or a person wronged was given. The townspeople took their role of "citizen" seriously and the town continued to grow from their hard work, good judgement, and respect. Dogwood trees lined the streets, as did stone sidewalks and the railroad station in which they took great pride. All had been a shared commitment.

Mr. Ward, knowing that Lee would someday take his place in Darnell, was passing on to Lee his love for books and his values of honesty and of sharing one's knowledge and resources. These talks between father and son took place regularly. "Lee, my son, we must live out our beliefs. I believe that most folks, when given the opportunity coupled with a little effort, well—they can have a successful, joyful life. The right books can educate people and show them a good productive way."

Lee listened carefully. He honored the knowledge of his father. Mr. Ward's words would shape Lee's own thoughts, habits, and decisions throughout his life. This Lee knew, and it suited him just fine. He patterned himself after the father who lived out his high standards and operated from the foundation of love.

The memory of his birth father dimmed; it was a thought that the father of his biology, the hateful, self-serving, lesser man, had never existed. Lee was proud to call himself the son of the greatest man that he had ever known, Mr. Ward.

Life on Protected Earth was a busy life, for each of its inhabitants. This included all living things.

There were extremes, as in any life, or land. Rain could pour for a day, leaving the soil a mess, rotting vegetables, animals caught in quick sands along the river, difficult births. During all the building, Lee often asked to excuse himself from his studies. "Father, Birchard could use my assistance."

Birchard sat nearby, grinning. "Well, Mr. Ward, we can use every person who is able, even bird watchers."

Mr. Ward spoke, "We are installing the peach and apple orchards and the other specialty trees, like plum and mulberry will be added. Of course, at Lee's request, we will also plant a variety of berries."

Lee enthusiastically agreed. "Yes! Enough, father, so the birds can have their fill and some leftover for cobblers!" Lee cherished birds. He often forgot his chores because he got lost in watching a finch build a nest. He was an excellent artist, particularly good with minute details.

His notebooks of late were becoming extensive. He wished to preserve all the fragments of his days and observations with accuracy.

Birchard on occasion would find Lee's work tools sitting idle because he had become entranced with another viewing. It could be a robin teaching her babies to fly, or activities around a cluster of red buds or wild plum trees blooming in the springtime.

Birchard could shout, "Lee, up and about. I want to see a shovel, plow, or hammer in your hand. What is that pen and paper building for us?"

"Facts and memories, Birchard, which I will read, show, and tell stories about to your children and mine someday. By the way, when is Mickey due to have the baby?"

Birchard reached for Lee's hand helping him up. "Come, my friend. We may see a new baby any day."

The friends laughed because Birchard new Lee would drive himself beyond quitting time.

At days end, some of the men washed off in the pond. But Birchard made sure that the water was drawn from the wells and that the outside holding tank was full for the next day. Plus, families that lived on the land waved good day and went home.

Time seemed to move at a very fast pace. The main farmhouse was finally completed and shined with pride. Birchard and Mickey's newly built home was full of great joy and worry. They hoped that the birth of their child would be soon. Both were bursting with joy. Birchard felt evermore reassured, now that a town doctor was to be a permanent fixture in Darnell. He was well-advised of the situation of the town. The workers who felt too tired to travel back and forth each day slept over.

Cal and Mr. Ward were now a couple. Love and desire showed when in the presence of each other. Cal's daughter, Liza, adored Mr. Ward. She asked her mother, "Why can't we live with Mr. Ward?"

Cal answered carefully. "Because this is our home, Liza. I built it with my hands. I will never leave it permanently. It has nothing to do with our love for Mr. W. He is in our hearts all the time. You will understand as you grow older."

Birchard had finished clearing a piece of land along the pine tree ridge. There was no view of the river, but the sounds of the river sang beautiful in the distance. This was to be a special meeting place for lovers, or solitude if needed. Ward tried his best to think and believe in anything possible to make life good, healthy, and interesting for his family, loved ones, and all the citizens of Darnell.

It was a common sight to see families, people seated on the front porches, discussing their day—and sharing experiences with loved ones. Lee, his father, and Birchard was no exception.

Every thought he had about Cal, and in detail her conversations with him, he shared with Birchard.

He thought, "Would Cal be displeased with him sharing their intimate talk with someone else?" He would tell her he wanted no dishonesty between them. Total trust. He believed he could have this type of relationship with her.

One evening after a few brandies of front porch talks, Mr. Ward loosened up, "Lee, my son, you can always come to me with any of life's questions. But one area I'm not an expert on… that's women. Meeting Cal has changed all my rules. One can never prepare for love. It hit my heart and suddenly my entire life was different."

He also talked of his new land, but most of his conversation was about Cal. He had never confided any of his intimate life with anyone. Now here he was repeating over. "Without a doubt, from the first time Cal came into my view, every detail of her face, figure, and manner was locked into my memory. Her tan, muscular body, her lovely face lined by sun and hard drinking, her long graceful hands that moved as if dancing, all these things excited me. Most of all, besides her effortless beauty, was her fierce independence and her ethic for hard work. She matched me drink for drink." Cal's friendship would prove to be a good thing, along with her intelligence and quick wit.

Mr. Ward continued to talk—Birchard was a good listener. And besides, it did his heart good to know Mr. Ward was in love. Mr. Ward hadn't used the word love, but Birchard recognized it. As far back as he could remember, he had been in love with Mickey. He could talk about her for hours. Yes, his friend, and now partner, was lost in love. Birchard got up and poured two more brandies.

Now that a few years had passed and Lee was in his teens, he was allowed to sit with his father and Birchard and share in brandy when these front porch talks occurred. Special times to be pulled up in Lee's memory years down the road.

They often shared talks of old circus friends. Ever looming in the background was if the detective hired to find Lee's sisters had come up with any new information.

Darnell still could not mention his three sisters without his emotions running over. Tears ran down his face when he waited for an answer from his father. Mr. Ward said, "Lee, I am certain whatever their manner of being, they're still standing tall — and proud. And thinking of their siblings."

Before Lee started for bed he said, "Father Ward, the time since Azzie left us has sped by. I still awake in the night sometimes and think I hear her walking lightly across the floor. I used to love when there was a full moon. She would lift the tent door, her silver sequined costume catching the moon's light. She glittered like a star that had dropped from the sky. I would sit up in bed. Her rich voice spoke words of how much she loved me, 'I love you with baskets full of hearts'. She even had Birchard carve some small wooden hearts and filled a basket full of them."

"I understand!" Mr. Ward said. "I know you will always keep those hearts." Mr. Ward smiled; Lee's serious thoughts had sobered him up.

"Your sister protected you with a fierceness of big cats. Your welfare came first. She would shout orders to the older performers, 'Where's little Darnell? Find him now! Make sure he's safe.' Your sister was much loved and respected by all the performers. She earned her star position. Her acrobatic performance on the horses was frightening to watch. She refused to use a security rope. I am sure that your other two sisters had the same spirit. They will not give up either on finding you."

Mr. Ward saw the disheartened look in Lee's face. Mr. Ward asked, "Lee were there any happy, fun times with your sisters growing up?"

Lee then related some good times he remembered. "Yes! Oh yes, when my father was away. My big sister Monterey schooled me and my two sisters. When lessons were completed and it was a nice day, we would go out into our small backyard, remove our shoes, and walk in the little spring that ran through the yard."

"Each time our father left the house, my sisters dreamed a little laughter project. Big sis would holler loud as she could, calling for each of us—sending our name throughout the unhappy house. We went down the line, taking turns shouting out anything that was on our minds and hearts, good and bad, sweeping through the house, up and down stairs, sliding down the stair rail—laughing and protesting until we emptied our voices."

Mr. Ward was loving the delightful stories, "Tell me more, Lee, my heart gladdens that you and your siblings had some joy."

"If father passed out from a drinking binge, and a moonlit night appeared, my sisters and I would walk about like trying to avoid a trail of broken glass. We silently entered the backyard where leftover residue from mother's garden still existed, a large scarred old tree survived in one corner. We sat under it and my sisters described little stories of the garden. If early spring, we were lucky to see a bulb that burst forth. This stolen time was a magical time, and for a short time we were transported into a life of happiness…Father, before we say goodnight. May we talk about how you came to own a circus."

"Come, son, beside me." Mr. Ward pulled a stool in close. Lee's ears perked, excited to hear his very private father was going to reveal some of his past.

"After I was left aboard a large passage and cargo ship, my abandonment also became my good fortune. A generous man named Sir Henry Daglish was en route to Europe, taking his circus on tour. Sir Daglish had desperately desired children. He saw my situation as a blessing. He took me in, his servants took care of me. As I started to grow, his wife wanted no part of a child, much less a waif."

Lee said to his father, noticing Mr. Ward's face showed some sadness, "Father, I love that you are sharing part of your life with me, but it if upsets you, all is okay without me knowing."

"I feel good," said Mr. Ward and he continued. "Fortunately for me, but not for Lady Daglish, she contacted food poisoning and died. Since Sir Henry liked having me around, he didn't economize on my education. Tutelage was provided on board ship for the children of his circus performers. An excellent education was provided. Sir Henry's butler instructed me on being a gentleman. Learning came easily for me. Over the years I knew most every aspect of the administrative and the day-to-day dealings with the circus. It was a divine place for a boy, adventure at every turn. Animals from all over the world were aboard, performers from different countries, how could I ever be saddened of this privilege of being abandoned at such a place. Sir Daglish was high-standing, had a strong education, and was cognizant in so many subjects and trades. Who in life is so fortunate?"

"Sir Henry Daglish loved people, animals, excitement, and good food. He had especially taken a liking to Southern food, which Lady Daglish detested. He was a gentle-face man of never-ending kindness. But he made the mistake of taking in a malicious partner. The man was jealous of all of Sir Henry's life. The sweet Sir Henry came to the edge of his gentleman ways in his dealings with the likes of the partner. He bought the man out and was going to ban him from the ship when the ship reached port. But, with great dolorous, I tell you, Sir Henry was murdered by this devil."

Mr. Ward dropped his head down to his lap, his cry was of great sorrow. Lee had never seen his father shed tears. Mr. Ward's mourning was long overdue. He felt safe in expressing this side of himself to Lee, his son.

"Father, let's rest, it's late. We can resume our talk another day. I thank you for this talk. My heart always needs to hear about your life. At whatever time."

Mr. Ward said, "Lee, stay seated. I still have a few extremely important things to discuss. The new detective I hired is a good man and won't give up the search; if anything happens to me, you must promise you won't give up finding your sisters. All I own will be yours and my wish is that you will be able to help your sisters if they need or want anything."

Lee was touched deeply by Mr. Ward's commitment to bring his family back to him. With emotion in his voice, he gave his promise that he would never forego the quest. "I have learned so much about life, and as a child I did understand how strong and brave my sisters were. They stood up against such great odds." The two now sat with no talk. Lee rose and kissed his father goodnight.

Birchard being the overseer of Protected Earth, kept a busy schedule. Lee was at a special place in life with his life being influenced by special people. He knew all the people around him were helping while he worked to organize a life for himself. Then it was up to him to take it all some place.

And all of Lee's learning was now going to be given a new added twist, a new arrival was coming to Protected Earth.

CHAPTER 10

Sparsity

Birchard could see the ever busy, diligent Runaway through the stable windows, where steams of light were shining through. The warm rays of sunshine went into each stall. The horses were able to enjoy the warmth, positioning their bodies back and forth to find just the right spot. The barn had been built with great care, the stables were built suitable for the individual horses or mules. There was plenty of room for them to lie down and readily rise and turn around in comfort.

Charts were hung on each stable, where Runaway recorded the diet, composition, and quantities of their food. He also had notes from his monitoring for injuries and illnesses. The yard and back had plenty enough room for the horses and mules to run and play and a nice shelter for them to get out of the weather. Mr. Ward had seen that the animals were living in a perfect and healthy environment, just as all his past circus animals were taken care of from ear to tail, head to hoof grooming. Runaway's concerns were the same as Mr. Ward's. The health and mood of the horses and mules must be kept in a relaxing, hygienic, and stimulating environment; this was to ensure that the animals would be ensured an enjoyable and active lifestyle and remain free from disease. All who lived on Protected Earth knew the rules. Each time someone started for a ride, pads and blankets must be checked for cleanliness, no wrinkles where the saddle sits. Check the horse's hooves, quick check for objects that could get lodged into the bottom of the hooves, this was strictly adhered to.

Birchard opened the ease-of-use stable doors. Mr. Ward had seen most all buildings, doors, and windows were built so that Birchard would not be inconvenienced through his routine checks and everyday life. But all was to have good eye appeal.

Birchard walked in, "Good morning, Runaway, sorry to interrupt your chores but I need the wagon to pick up supplies at the train station. Maude will need another mule today."

Maude's ears perked up at hearing Birchard say her name.

"I will put Easygoing with her; he can tolerate her sometimes mean disposition. You seem in a hurry today, Mr. Birchard. If you like, I am almost finished in the stables. I can go into Darnell for you."

"No, I will be fine. I appreciate you sending your daughter over to assist in Mickey's care. I enjoy the ride into Darnell. Never do I tire of the landscape, and it gives me time to let my mind roam. It's a relaxing trip."

Runaway once more checked the mules all over before they left the stables. He felt Birchard had stress from the worry over his wife, Mickey. He stood and watched the barn doors as Birchard's wagon pulled out and headed toward town. Birchard had Runaway's respect and he marveled at the little man, who was really a giant of a human being.

Runaway had been with the family of Protected Earth from the beginning of building the land. A smart, handsome Seminole, Runaway showed his love of the land and all its inhabitants.

Birchard also welcomed Chase and Talker on his rides into town. The two were as much a part of Protected Earth as anyone. This morning he didn't see them close by. They knew every inch of the land and spent countless hours exploring in side-by-side walks and rides with Lee, Mr. Ward, and Birchard. The Blueticks were a joy to watch and spend time with. They were muscular and speedy, their heads were carried well up, their coats a little coarse but glossy. Chase, the male, weighed close to 80 pounds. Talker, the female, was considerably smaller, around 50 pounds. They possessed wonderful paws, larger than most breeds of dogs.

Cal had gifted the two Gascon blues, as puppies, to Mr. Ward, much larger than standard Blueticks. Loyal, loving, but their noses often led them on long adventures into the forest.

Lee would say, "They sniff out old, unhappy spirits and start to howl to let someone know about their find."

Today, Birchard had left the property without the Blueticks, but before he reached the end of the drive, Chase and Talker came running full speed and bounded into the back of the wagon, startling Birchard, but only for a moment. The two looked at Birchard as if to ask, "Why did you leave without us?"

He continued to remind the two that they were not to chase every small animal that crossed the road or came into view.

Birchard was hoping Mickey's special baby clothing had arrived, along with a special rocker he was having made for his adored wife. Any day, Mickey was to give birth. She had been ordered to bedrest. After going through another miscarriage, this was her last chance to have children. And soon, a much-welcomed new Doctor will arrive to care for her. The whole team had accomplished unbelievable tasks, making the land a feast for the eyes. Helping nature along, Mr. Ward often said.

Birchard met up with the town's midwife on her way to check on Mickey. He stopped his wagon to say hi and bring her up to date on Mickey's state of mind.

"On my way to check on Mickey. Who is with her?"

"Runaway's daughter. She felt fine this morning."

"Mr. Birchard, still, she is not to be left alone. Her health is in serious condition, as you well know."

The midwife saw great worry in Birchard's face.

"As you know, the doctor from Atlanta did not give us great news. He reported Mickey will be fighting for her life. Birchard, hurry back to your wife. She needs you by her side."

Maude was getting restless to move on and now contending with another mule by her side. Birchard talked to Maude, "Now Maude, enjoy the help you have today, we have a large load of supplies to pick up. Only thinking of you." Maude's ears went back, still not happy with the situation. Birchard smiled at the sassy mule. Birchard thanked the midwife for giving her time to care for Mickey. "I understand and I will return shortly."

Birchard reached town and pulled into the rail station. His supplies were organized by the new stationmen Mr. Ward had hired to load and unload the citizens' supplies as needed. He seemed to think of everything to improve their lives. Leaving the wagon at the station, he walked toward Cal's Hub. Chase and Talker were already on the Hub porch, eating a meal Cal had set up for them.

Cal, looking happy and tan, greeted Birchard with a hug. "Glad to see you, my friend. How's Mickey? I thought I would go see her and spend the night. Will do her good to have some company. Take my guitar, sing and play some uplifting stuff. What do you think, Birchard? Good idea?"

"She would welcome you with open arms. Thanks, Cal. I will let her know you will be coming. Could you pack me up a few pieces of that coconut cake? I have lunch with me."

"Sure, why don't you take a seat. I will bring you a special drink to relieve those nerves and I will send a cake along with you for all. Be right back. Take care, my friend. Don't worry, our new Doc will be here soon to take care of our precious Mickey."

Birchard could hardly think of anything else but the safety of Mickey. The Hub was busy and bursting with talk and good food. He sat finishing his drink. Cal's drink gave him a good little buzz. Chase and Talker had relaxed on the porch at his feet. Talker seemed to dream a lot, raising her head up sharply with ears back, lolling around, then right back to sleep.

The man from the rail station came looking for Birchard to let him know all was loaded onto the wagon. Cal handed him a box with a coconut cake, the post, a hug goodbye. Birchard walked to the rail station. Birchard had no awareness of someone hijacking a ride in his wagon.

While the wagon was being filled, a girl watched from a hiding place. She had seen Birchard pull up, intrigued, having never seen a little person. She watched how nice and kind he was to the men at the station. Giving them money even before they started to work.

"Yes! That's the wagon I will hide in," she said to no one. The men finished packing everything into the wagon and pulled it along with the two mules to a shady spot.

Sparsity checked out the area when clear. She hid amongst some boxes in the back of Birchard's wagon. She was feeling dizzy with not much air and it had been a while without food. The twins had packed some food for her before putting her onto the boxcar. But she had eaten it all rather fast.

When Birchard was about two miles out of town, a female voice came from the back of the wagon.

"Hello."

Birchard almost jumped out of the wagon. Birchard stopped, thinking it was maybe one of the spirits the dogs had chased out of the forest.

He gave a sharp "hello," without looking back to where the voice came from.

"Hello! Who are you? Where did you come from? Are you a spirit?" Birchard thought for a moment, his heart racing, having never experienced a spirit. Maybe a spirit does talk.

"No! I am a girl. I don't think spirits talk, but never heard them talk. I got off the train, crawled into your wagon, and hid. Oak and Pine, Granny Dalia's twins that helped raise me, gave me instruction to make sure I only attached myself to a nice, kind, working person. I watched how you treated the men who loaded your wagon. Besides, you were much smaller than me, I have never seen a little man before. Mostly just saw Oak and Pine, Dandelion, Tulip and Larkspur. The hunting dogs, as they were called, and of course Granny Dalia, and the many goats that gave us great milk, the candles, lotions, and soap made from their milk.

"May I stand and climb over to sit with you?" she asked.

"One moment. Let me calm the mules down. Maude doesn't take to strangers. Whoa! Whoa! Maude!"

He pulled the wagon to the side of the road. The girl answered rather assuredly, Birchard thought, for being in her awkward position. She climbed over the supplies and sat beside Birchard.

"Hi, I'm Sparsity. Just Sparsity. No last name."

"I am Birchard. You, Sparsity, take off that ugly-looking hat. You are upsetting my mules. Let me take a look at you."

"I was hiding behind some stacked boxes and looking around for a kind face."

"You sure are a skinny little thing, not sure what I should do with you."

"Where do you live, Mr. Birchard? Can I work for you? I'm really strong, can milk goats, make cheese, know lots about herbs for healing all kinds of ills, love all animals, bugs, trees, and dahlias."

"We will see what Mr. Ward, my boss, says. Can't really see how I can just leave you here, a young girl with no place to go. Now I can't promise that you can stay." Birchard felt sad inside looking at Sparsity, his memory ran back to Azzie and Lee. Thinking the girl must be hungry and Cal did give him some coconut cake, and he had water.

"You want some food, only have cake and water."

"Starved, and a little belly sick from eating that raw corn on the cob from the train car."

"Open that seat up and take out that cake." He handed Sparsity his pocket bone-handle knife.

As hungry as the girl must have been, she didn't gobble the cake down, her manners were nice.

Birchard thought, where did this odd-looking girl come from, white cotton candy looking hair that hung down to her waist in ringlets, off color eyes, almost looked pink, skin so white, as if it was never touched by the sun. You could see her veins running through her body.

"Mr. Birchard, would you please ask Mr. Ward about a job for me?"

Birchard felt Maude pulling her head up, wanting to move on.

"Okay, Maude, giddy up. Let's see about getting Sparsity a home. Start talking, Sparsity, and tell me all about your life up to this very point."

"Mr. Birchard, some folks are afraid of me, never having seen someone with white cotton hair, white skin, and my eyes an odd color. A man that was walking by our little shack, he asked for some water from that well. He kept staring at me. 'Why are you staring at me like that?'

I answered, 'Like what, Mister? I want to see you and listen to you when you talk. We rarely get a visitor. Granny was sleeping. I offered him some water, I wanted him to sit and talk but he declined and moved on very fast."

Birchard thought, it's true the girl's eyes dart toward one's every move, like an animal protecting itself. Birchard tapped his head with his fingers and asked, "Curious how come you speak so well, growing up with no school."

"Oh! I had school, Mr. Birchard. Granny was smart. She didn't come from a low country, her family put her out because she got pregnant and wasn't married. She was alone, walked the rails, hung out with hobos and ended up in the shack by the railroad tracks. She picked cotton with the blacks and made a little money to feed herself and her twin boys that were due. The kindhearted blacks helped her deliver her twins and set her up in the shack by the rails. They dug up bushes in the forest and planted them to hide the shack from any public annoyance. Her mind had become muddled after all of the years of neglect, but she taught the boys how to read and write and kindness toward nature and all creatures.

"She would say, 'Don't let anyone or anything let you become mean.' She never talked about her previous life. It was, I believe, painful. We read from the newspapers that the twins brought home and the cabin walls were lined with newspapers. In turn, the twins taught me. I am not sorry about being adondoned. Granny, the twins, and those precious black and tan hounds that kept me warm on that cold night when someone had left me on granny's porch. Granny's wisdom ran deep, she just knew stuff beyond ordinary people."

Birchard's thoughts were running as to how Mr. Ward was going to react. He felt sure Mr. Ward would not turn the girl away. Maybe he would check out her story and find her two uncles. "You sure can talk a good story."

Sparsity broke into his talk, "I hope I haven't been bad with manners; I do thank you kindly." The girl kept up her nonstop chatter. Sparsity talked with her hands, expressing every word. Her fingers were long and slender, the skin was thin and almost chalk white.

Birchard thought back to the village he grew up in and remembered how an albino boy took cruel taunts, often physical from people. Birchard, a little person, overcame this kind of treatment by performing on his unicycle, walking tight ropes from one roof to another, often he put his life at risk. His family were all little people, so his heart went out to this different-looking girl. She didn't speak like a backwoods person, her English was good, her voice was nice and soothing, not a child's voice. But can she chatter, with hardly enough room between words for her to breathe.

This enchanting girl was an innocent lost. She continued with sentences that seemed far beyond what he could see before him. Memorized words, Birchard thought.

"Who gave you that name, Sparsity, and what does it mean?"

"I'm not sure, Mr. Birchard. I never asked. Oakey, Piney, and Granny Dalia said I had strap marks all over my little baby body when they found me on their porch. The dog started a ruckus at daybreak because I started to cry. I crawled out from their protected circle. I rarely cry. Well, one time when Granny Dalia got real upset with me, I hit a brown thrasher with a sling shot and killed it. The bird was a mama with babies. Granny said all birds should be given great respect. She was especially fond of brown thrashers. She made me take care of the babies until they could fly. I was pretty sad to see them fly away, but it was my responsibility for my bad deeds. Granny Dalia and her twin boys were sure good to me. They gave me goat's milk with the bottle that baby goats often used when their mothers didn't have enough milk. Maybe that's why I'm so white and really different looking."

The girl kept up her chatter. Birchard was curious. He let her talk and she seemed eager to tell her life so far.

"You sure can talk girl—and speak real nice." Birchard could not help but smile at the girl.

"I am real clean—cleanliness is very important so one doesn't get sick or smell."

Sparsity eyed a mason jar of water in the basket and said, "Mr. Birchard, may I just have a little of this water to wash my nasty hands? That boxcar was dirty. Also, is this your drinking cup?"

"It sure is but you can use it." Mr. Birchard slowed Maude down.

"Sparsity, if you would like, I can stop beside the creek. There's a bar of soap under the seat with a towel. You can wash up at the creek."

"Oh, my! Thank you, Mr. Birchard! That would be so good."

Birchard stopped at a pull off that had a well-marked path to the creek. Sparsity quickly jumped out, ran down the path as if it was familiar to her. She bathed all exposed skin, soaped up her long, white hair and stood up with a yell. Shaking her head like an animal to rid of extra water, she proceeded to wash the towel, wrung it out, then ran back to the wagon.

"Mr. Birchard, thank you so very much. And thank you, Maude," as she gave Maude a kiss on her head, "for your patience. If Mr. Birchard lets me stay, I will give you a lovely herb wash and massage."

Birchard let her get settled, gave Maude the go-ahead, and headed toward Protected Earth with a surprise for all. Birchard said, "Take that folded quilt out and rest, then we can continue with talk."

She closed her eyes for a short time, but soon started once more with her nonstop talk. "I started to call granny 'Yes Granny' from the time I could talk. It's obvious—I answered yes to all the things granny said. 'Granny Yes' sent the twins on trips to barter with herbs and what else I'm not sure. The two of us stayed at the cabin. Granny put up lots of berries, sour crab apples, wild plums, and some stuff we picked from the field. I helped but then I would go into the woods to hunt rabbits. But I could never kill anything. 'Granny Yes' would say, 'My, my, child where do you get these funny ideas? People have got to live. You can't exist on the little plants and a biscuit.' But I did—and here I am. No, Birchard! I could never kill an animal. Maybe I could harm a real mean human?"

At this, Birchard felt a little uneasy with the strange-talking, different-looking girl. She continued, "The twins would show up with bags of stuff, even some books for me. 'Sparsity, someday you will leave this place - you will need to know more than just reading and writing. You will have to know people and their ways.' They were always looking out for me. One day, they came home with a big feed sack of Dalia bulbs—granny laughed and cried. I never thought those ugly bulbs would make such beautiful flowers. All colors, reds, yellows, pink, purple, most every color. When the Dalia's bloomed, granny set out jars and cans full of them in every corner of the old cabin—even our outhouse. What a sight, Mr. Birchard. Maybe we can plant some Dahlias at your house. Then I started calling Granny, Granny Dalia because she loved the flowers so much. She liked the name better, and said she felt pretty herself, being called after the beautiful Dahlias."

Birchard sensed even though this young girl was now without a home, she wasn't seeking anyone's approval. She was Sparsity and that's it.

"Granny wanted to make our old shack pretty. So, the twins made some whitewash from the lye and water.

"Only white?" I pleaded. "Can't we make a color?"

Granny told me, "Run to the field and pick some of those purple berries, the ones we dyed that muslin cloth with, for your bed."

"I was so excited, sure enough, we washed that old shack in the prettiest purple color. The sun and rain did fade it a bit."

"Sounds like your granny was very special."

"When Granny Dalia passed on, the boys who were not really boys, but grown men, but Granny looked upon her boys, and mostly that's how she talked to them. I loved them lots. Both taught me so many things and looked after me. Anyway, they buried Granny right smack in the middle of her pretty, variously colored dahlia bed. It's a pretty spot. She will like it, loving those dahlias the way she treasured each bulb."

Sparsity stopped, took a worn little hankie from her pocket, wiped her odd colored eyes, tears slowly rolling down her white cheeks. "Sorry, Mr. Birchard, would you like me to shut up?" She didn't wait for Birchard's answer, she rolled off once more. "Oh my, my. Yes, Mr. Birchard, I know the twins must be about the two saddest people in the world with Granny dead and me gone. It must be like I died also." Sparsity tried to stifle back her tears.

"I am sorry, Birchard. I promised Granny I would not cry. She would say, 'Now what good do those tears do, child? Just makes hurt worse.' Do you think so, Birchard?"

"I'm not sure, depends on what we cry about."

"She ruled the twins. But she loved them. Granny knew lots of stuff. She spoke real nice, taught me all about nouns and verbs. I'm a willing student and wish to know how everything works and what is its reason for being here on our beautiful earth. Even though Granny stressed that I should know all things on earth are connected and humans are connected just as much." Sparsity's voice was becoming slow, her head bobbing once more.

Birchard said, "Sparsity."

"Yes, Mr. Birchard."

"You can rest. It's okay. I will wake you before we reach Protected Earth."

Once more, Sparsity climbed back into the wagon bed. "Thank you, please wake me. I want to see everything before we get to the house."

Sparsity curled up on the quilt and fell asleep. Birchard gave a small laugh, listening to such a loud snore coming from the child. "Let's get home, Maude, with our surprise." Birchard knew Maude only responded to verbal requests. She did not like her reins to be pulled.

Sparsity was dreaming of her granny, talking to Granny at her burial site in the dahlia bed. Sparsity's heart was beating so hard, she felt it might pop right out of her chest. She asked, "Why? Why do the twins want me to go away? Granny, I am so sad that you passed on. I am on my knees. You were so good to me, treated me as you did your own blood. But Granny, I know every inch of these woods, fields, streams, pathways, fishing ponds, or crawfish, every healing herb that grows on the hillside. The twins say I am becoming a woman and they can't take care of me. Now that you're gone, they say it's dangerous for me to stay alone when they go away. The hounds and I went for a last walk. We covered every known piece of dirt. It's all painted in my memory. I spent some precious moments in the woods. I promised the twins I will go, come summer." Sparsity awoke from her dream and said, "Here I am, Birchard. No one wants me."

Birchard was now mesmerized by the white, cotton, ringlet haired girl with eyes so blue you would swear they were created with a piece of sky. "That's a powerful story you tell, Miss Sparsity."

"Yes! I know, Mr. Birchard. You should have seen Granny's dahlias. Colors that feasted your eyes and colors that lifted your heart, lilac, pink, near magenta, white, purple, red, and my favorite, a huge yellow the size of a dinner plate. Do you think if I get to stay at Protected Earth that we could plant some of those big, dinner plate, yellow dahlias? Dalia's they were all named pretty names; Glory, Fascination, Audacity, Magic Moment, and Purple Joy."

Sparsity didn't wait for Birchard to answer her question; she continued.

"The boys and I would sit and watch Granny as she took care of her dahlias, watered, and cut bouquets. Then we got to place them throughout the shack. The place by the creek, where we carried our water from, Granny had us place a large bouquet on a flat rock. All the dahlias were dazzling, belonging beside a castle. But our purple washed clap board shack was happy. Granny would say, 'We may live in a shack, but I bet the Queen of England doesn't have flowers as pretty as we do.'"

Sparsity once more fell asleep, which gave Birchard some thinking time.

As the wagon rolled along, Birchard pushed any thoughts from his mind as to how Mr. Ward would receive the new surprise. But things seemed to happen in a right way. As least, it had for him.

Maude was a formidable mule and had a mind of her own. More than once, Maude displayed her temper. She would take off in a wild gallop and at different times, the supplies would go flying. After a time, Birchard secured his supplies extremely well.

Maude's slight edge today made Birchard smile. Easy Going was quite different from Maude. He just did his job and tolerated Maude's temperament; even an occasional nip from Maude wasn't enough to stray Easy Going from his course. Birchard stopped slowly as to not awake the sleeping girl. He got out of the wagon, gave Maude some loving hugs and a few pieces of apple. He laid his head against Maude's warm body, closed his eyes, and let his thoughts drift back to when he found (Little D) Lee and his sister, Azzie. Surely, Mr. Ward will take this special girl as he did them. It will be hard to say no to Sparsity.

Maude was now at ease. Birchard climbed back onto the wagon. He sat for a minute and looked at the sleeping, snoring Sparsity.

The mules picked up their pace, knowing the wagon was getting close to the drive to Protected Earth. Sparsity awoke and said nothing for a few minutes. She ran her fingers over the flowers on the quilt, then neatly folded the quilt and placed in on the seat.

"Mr. Birchard, thank you for your kindness. I can't believe I was lucky enough to hide in your wagon. When the twins told me they were putting me on the train, I was afraid of what I might face outside. Who will understand me? I am so different. Granny says no one looks like me." The twins bowed their heads and were silent. The sweet hound dogs were howling as we walked toward the train that always came to a crawl along the sharp curve of our cabin. It was easy to hop on. So here I am, Mr. Birchard, happier than anything I could have dreamed." Sparsity threw her long legs over the seat to sit next to Birchard as they pulled into the road to Protected Earth.

"You will make it, Sparsity, and be an added plus to anyone's life. The right person—you will just know."

Sparsity opened the small, tattered bag she was carrying and took out another small flowered meal sack. She pulled out a very artfully made necklace and a leather cord with different shaped sky blue turquoise stones on it.

"Here, Mr. Birchard, this is for you. My many thanks you didn't throw me off your wagon. You will see I am meant to be here."

She had the necklace around Birchard's neck before he knew it.

"Sparsity, I must say you are gifted with words; they come off your tongue easy and pretty. Thanks for the necklace — I will treasure it."

Birchard was now completely enthralled by this spirited child. She sent his mind back to two enchanting children he found early one morning, abandoned at Mr. Ward's circus.

"Mr. Birchard, when Granny died, right there in her herb garden, there was a peace on her face. She was doing what she loved. The boys were lost when their mother died. They looked to Granny to give them direction each day." Sparsity continued her chatter nonstop. "Maybe you won't believe me but I knew you would be waiting for me. Uncle Oak and Uncle Pine said, 'Now Sparsity, don't look so down faced. Someone will be at the first rail station. When that train stops, you get off, move like a fox, see all around you like a grasshopper, and make no noise like a butterfly. The right person will be there.' And there was your wagon, with the nice, pretty quilt with wildflowers on it, folded on the seat. For a moment, I focused on the quilt's beauty, but quickly curled up between the feed sacks. Oh! I forgot I did give your mule a kiss on the nose, can't resist any of God's creatures."

"Stop!" said Birchard. "All those pretty words are not going to win me if you don't tell me the truth."

"It's all true. No reason for me to lie. You won't regret letting me come along. I am here to live forever."

"Let's say you are. Who's Uncle Oak and Uncle Pine? Who names a person after a tree, anyway?"

"What's wrong with being named after a majestic, beautiful tree?" Sparsity waited for Birchard's answer. "Where did you come from, Mr. Birchard? And why are you so little for a man?"

"I am a little person, born a little person, and will die a little person."

"I like you. What are the mules' names? I love animals. I read that a woman gives her heart to a human man. I'm going to give my heart to all animals. I know lots of stuff. I never hit anyone, but I did hit a mean bobcat that tried to get my pet chicken. I feel so safe and proud I chose you, Mr. Birchard. Maybe you won't give me away."

Her thoughts ran back to the only folks she had known, Granny, Oak, and Pine. They worked hard to do little things for her so one day she could live with regular folks.

"Sparsity, can you cook?"

"Yes, squirrels, rabbits, and quail. But Mr. Birchard, I can't skin them. I feel so sorry, they are dead, no longer can they run, jump, or have babies. You won't make me skin anything, will you?"

"No, I understand. I can't either."

"Mr. Birchard, I don't take up much room, I can sleep behind a stove on a quilt. Pine told me I had what folks call quick wit. The walls of the shack were covered in newspapers, from strange places. After I learned to read, I'd read every word on that wall. Time tells who a person is. One book the brothers stole for me was about flower gardens in England. I can work in the garden. I am really strong. The twins are good, you won't report them to anyone. I sure miss the flowers and the dogs. They dressed me like a boy so no one would hurt me. Why would someone want to hurt me, Mr. Birchard?" Not waiting for Birchard to answer, Sparsity said, "I'm not a moocher, I will work hard for my keep."

Birchard had not spoken in a while. The girl kept on chattering away—back and forth she went on.

The wagon reached the second gate to Protected Earth. Maude stopped at the gates but before Birchard could even get out to open the gates, Sparsity had jumped out of the wagon and had opened the gates. She gave Maude a hug and rubbed heads with her. The ever-untrusting Maude looked love struck at Sparsity. Sparsity waved Birchard through and closed the gates before she jumped back into the wagon, seated herself next to Birchard as if she belonged.

"Are we almost home, Mr. Birchard? I sure need a bath. I smell bad."

"Yes, Sparsity. Now, you must prepare yourself. It has to be Mr. Ward, the owner's decision, if you stay."

"I do not carry a worry, Mr. Birchard. Mr. Ward will keep me."

"My wife's name is Mickey. She's little like me and has beautiful hair, black as the night. Mickey is going to have our baby soon."

Sparsity got so excited she almost fell out of the wagon. "I will take care of Mickey. I can't believe I will get to hold a baby. I was a baby. Is anyone that lives on this exquisite land unkind to babies?"

"No! Sparsity, have you ever been on a horse? If not, I can teach you how to ride."

"Oh, no! Thank you, Mr. Birchard," Sparsity replied. "My feet carry me real good. I prefer to see all the sublime creatures running free in the forests and pastures around me. I would miss too much of the life around me if I was on a horse. Mr. Birchard, I want you to like me enough to let me live where you live."

"Sparsity, I can't promise that. It's all a bit iffy. Everyone's reaction to me bringing home another lost child, there were two more a few years back. We will just have to see. Do you understand?"

"I do," answered Sparsity.

Sparsity asked softly—sometimes her voice was so low, Birchard had to ask her to repeat herself, "Mr. Birchard, please stop. I have to try and reassure that sweet gum tree that no one will cut it down."

Birchard looked at Sparsity with his face full of surprise. "How did you know I had discussed with Mr. Ward about taking that pitiful, misshapen sweet gum down?"

"It called to me, Mr. Birchard. The sweet gum understands that she has no great beauty. That handsome oak named Brutus that pokes his enormous limbs out at her, crowding her space is the reason for her sad shape. But she loves the little hill she stands on and looks out across the pasture. The cows like to take a nap under her because no acorns drop on them and deer stay under the oak. The squirrels play with the sweet gum balls and many, many bees love her nectar in the spring. Lucy is her name." Sparsity hopped off the wagon and crawled under the fence, putting two white, skinny arms around that sweet gum. She called out to Birchard, "Please, talk to Mr. Ward about Lucy. She has a long, full life ahead to give to Protected Earth."

Birchard noticed that Sparsity wore no shoes and realized she was in no way teasing. She believed that tree was asking for her help. Still, how did she know the tree was about to be cut down?

"Come, Sparsity. I am sure we can convince Mr. Ward not to harm Lucy. It's you I am worried about." Birchard had questions in his mind if he did the right thing bringing Sparsity to Protected Earth.

Sparsity released her arms and gave Lucy the tree a kiss, then climbed back up on the wagon seat. Birchard felt that anyone at Protected Earth could handle the situation that was about to be given to them.

The ride into Protected Earth was a lot to take in. Sparsity said, "Mr. Birchard, I am not going to take in any of the beautiful land in case there is a slight possibility Mr. Ward does not let me stay. That way it will not be so painful." Birchard didn't answer. He was wanting to get this situation settled and check on Mickey.

Sparsity had all kinds of thoughts jumping around in her head, thinking about Oak and Pine and the advice they gave her when they were waiting beside the tracks for the train. "Stay quiet, don't talk to anyone, don't eat all of your jam, save some bread, keep your feet dry. Sorry we couldn't get you shoes. God will watch over you." She said to herself, it's odd they never mentioned a God before. But she knew in her heart a great person had created the heavens and the earth. She didn't question. "It's okay, we love you but with Granny gone, we can't take care of you. You deserve better than the two of us."

"I know you both love me." The train slowed almost to a stop on the sharp curve. They literally threw Sparsity onto the boxcar. The images in her head drifted away and she drifted into a sleepy fog.

The wagon rolled into the barn. Lee was unbridling the appaloosa, brown spotted horse after what looked like a long ride. He met Birchard's wagon with a questioning look at the girl seated beside Birchard. Raising his eyebrows and shrugging his shoulders he said, "Who do you have with you, my friend?"

Birchard smiled and said, "Lee, you know all lost children seem to find me. Her name is Sparsity. She hid in my wagon at the train station. But before you hear her story, we need to get her some decent food, a hot bath, then some rest."

Lee saw the girl needed assistance as she tried to stand up. Lee said to Birchard, "Pull the wagon into the barn. Runaway is working the stalls but will empty the supplies while we decide what to do with Sparsity."

Sparsity, only half awake, the world around her did not seem real. Will I awaken and find myself back at the shack with the hounds and the twins? Now becoming more aware of her surroundings, Sparsity looked at Birchard to give her direction.

Lee asked, "Did she carry a letter with explanation in it?"

"No!" said Birchard, "but she has no problem explaining her situation. She is quite proficient with words."

Birchard, anxious to see his wife Mickey, said to Lee, "Do inform Mr. Ward, I am going to check on Mickey, but I will be around later. I am sure he will wish to speak with me."

"Okay, Birchard, I will take Sparsity to the main house."

Runaway, always with keen ears and eyes always open wide for almost anything that concerned Protected Earth and its people who lived on it said, "Mr. Birchard, my daughter is with Mickey. What can I do to help?"

After Birchard thought, he said, "Lee, I will take Sparsity to my house. I believe she will feel more comfortable. I'm sure it will be okay with Mickey."

Lee said, "I will have Runaway saddle our horses and I will ride along with you until all is settled at your place."

Runaway spoke once more, "Mr. Birchard, my chores have kept me busy, so I haven't checked on Mickey, but my daughter is very capable. Anything you need me to do? Like keep an eye on the odd-looking girl."

Lee said to Birchard, "Are you sure Mickey's feeling well enough to take on this young girl?"

Sparsity looked intently as to all the talk going on, mostly about her. She spoke, "Mr. Birchard, is it okay if I walk alongside you? That horse looks mighty high up."

"Trust me a little longer, I promise you will be safe."

"Okay!" With arms to her side, she now stood silent.

Birchard stepped to the top of his striding box then gave instructions to Sparsity to do the same. She did and moved in as close to Birchard as possible. Softly she said, "Mr. Birchard, I feel a bit unnerved, but I trust you."

Lee rode alongside Birchard and Sparsity. On arriving at Mickey's, she came out to greet them, said hello to Lee, asked who the girl was, and touched Birchard's hand. "Hello, my darling. Looks like you have had an interesting day."

Sparsity opened her eyes. She saw Mickey and said, "I promise I will not be a worry to you and Mr. Birchard. You are beautiful like Birchard told me."

Lee expressed his concern and suggested Runaway's daughter stay the night to give any help that was needed. Mickey spoke, "We will take care of Sparsity. Remember, Lee, we have done this before."

Lee smiled, gave Mickey a kiss, and said good night. On his ride through the land that he would one day call his, he thought of that last cold night, and how scared he was, but knowing his brave sister

Azzie, as she held his hand tight, would take care of him. Azzie had never shown him any fear. But Sparsity is alone, looking for a place to call home.

Mr. Ward was waiting on the porch upon Lee's return.

"Lee, you had an extra-long ride today and some excitement, from what Runaway has told me." Mr. Ward had just returned from a few days in Atlanta.

"Hi, Father. It sure is good to have you home."

Mr. Ward rose from his chair. Chase and Talker greeted Lee as if he had been away a long time, blue tick kisses and a hug from his father. Lee was now almost as tall as Mr. Ward, standing side by side, one could observe the pride and love on their faces for each other.

"Come sit, Son. Your concern on your face says you have something on your mind."

"I do, Father," Lee said as he sat. He stretched his long legs out and removed his boots. "Ah, that always feels good. First, how was your trip to Atlanta? Any good news about a doctor for Darnell?"

"No! Very disappointed the man wasn't for our town. But upon arriving today, another post was waiting with an interesting and promising reply from the doc that answered my ad. He's ready to leave tomorrow for Darnell. I will send a wire early tomorrow for him to come. Sounds like the kind of doctor and man we want for our town."

"That's good because Mickey isn't doing so well. Birchard is extremely concerned, along with the rest of us. She is finding each day very arduous."

"Anything else troubling you?"

"Yes. When Birchard picked up supplies today, halfway home a girl about 12 was hiding in his wagon."

"Oh my! And what happened?"

"Birchard brought her home. She is at his house. A very unusual looking girl. All white. White! With white ringlet long hair, very enchanting, says her name is Sparsity and Birchard says she talks non-stop."

"Is Mickey well enough to handle this situation?"

"Well, Runaway let his daughter stay with Mickey to do the chores and she will stay over until we decide what to do. Birchard will bring her by tomorrow to meet you. He seems to think she will be a plus to Protected Earth."

"Son, you know I value Birchard's opinion on most anything. We will see what tomorrow holds and what Mickey and Birchard have to say about the new Sparsity. Now, let's draft a letter to this Doc Francis and get him here as soon as possible, along with a wire in the morning."

Back at Birchard's home, Sparsity was feeling some discernment of her own. But she was enthralled with Birchard and the small, beautiful, and plentiful pregnant Mickey.

Sparsity slept through the night on clean smelling sheets. She was too large for Mickey's clothes but did manage to wear a pair of Birchard's pants and a shirt. Early morning after a good breakfast, Birchard took Sparsity to meet Mr. Ward. He knew Mr. Ward would not turn the girl away, remembering the compassion that he had shown to Lee and Azzie.

"Yes. I trust you and Mickey's decision." Once decided, it didn't take long for Sparsity to become an integral part of Protected Earth. She became indispensable to Mickey. She was quick to catch on and took over a lot of chores and cleaning. Her knowledge of healing herbs and her rare wisdom was welcome by any who lived on Protected Earth and soon most of the community received Sparsity's help.

Mr. Ward had informed the town council he felt sure he had hired the right doctor and he would arrive shortly.

In the meanwhile, the nearest doctor was in Atlanta and as word got around about the exotic, young, healing girl that had successfully treated some of the citizens' ailments, there was a line to Birchard and Mickey's to see Sparsity. The townspeople were in great need for a doctor. But at the moment, the young, girl was welcome with her knowledge of herbs. The wild herbs that grew on Protected Earth, Sparsity was very familiar with, and the healing qualities the wild herbs held within the plants and she used them with great care.

Mr. Ward instructed Lee and Runaway to build a small, stone cottage in the lowlands. When Sparsity gets older, she will have a place of her own. Mr. Ward and Lee enjoyed their privacy and Sparsity did do lots of chores for them. Birchard and Mickey were happy having Sparsity live with them. Exuberant, Sparsity found herself enthusiastically welcomed in her new home.

The stone cottage was started from the numerous piles of stone piled up on Protected Earth. That had been placed when the land had been cleared for grain fields and cattle, goats, and horses. With great patience, Birchard discreetly chipped away at Sparsity's resolve at learning to ride. But, in the meantime, he made a small, hand pulled wagon for her. She painted it purple and adorned it with spirit words. When the fields were plowed or parts of the river dragged, the workmen had made piles of rock. Sparsity would go back and forth pulling her wagon, placing rocks along the path from the main house leading to where, eventually, she would live in her own cottage.

Each day when she had free time, she also planted herbs and wildflowers. Mr. Ward had ordered all kinds of seeds and bulbs, he had let her pick from the many catalogs he received. She asked permission to create a rose garden for him, outside his studio, where he sculpted, painted, cast, and often just relaxed. The side facing open fields, all the way to the river, the studio windows and doors all offered great views. A rose garden would be perfect. She had his okay. Birchard would order anything that was needed for the garden, stone, roses from England… Sparsity was a lightning bolt that hit Protected Earth. Her youth never stopped anything. She could cut wood, trees, have special dirt from the decomposed earth in the forest to make a rich beautiful foundation for Mr. Ward's rose garden.

All who met the strikingly fanciful albino girl were taken with her. A few had doubts about the mysterious Sparsity. One in particular was Cal. For years, Cal had been the one that the locals went to for solving their problems. Also, it was obvious that Cal and Mr. Ward were more than good friends. Cal was unfamiliar with jealousy and hadn't realized she liked her position in Darnell.

Cal called on Mickey to check if she needed anything and expressed her concerns about the young girl. Mickey responded with a laugh. "Cal, I believe Sparsity is beyond grateful for being taken in by Mr. Ward. I don't see any interest from Sparsity toward anyone of the male gender. She wishes with all her heart to settle herself long-term on Protected Earth. She is a child. Not sure of her age. No record of her birth. She is a talent and a quick learner. She is very wise, very into healing and helping all people, animals, and nature. Where she came from is almost an implausible story, but I believe her."

Cal started to sputter. "How ridiculous of me. She is an off looking little thing. Just remember, Mickey, I am here, anytime day or night if you or Birchard need me."

"Yes, Cal, we know what a wonderful friend you are. The glow in Mr. Ward's face when he hears your name gives us thankfulness to you—he deserves all the love you have for him. And no one could replace you. You have been a rock from the day we arrived."

Cal felt reassured that all was good and a rare feeling of silliness for any doubts of her judgments of the girl. "Thanks, Mickey. By the way, remember this weekend our much talked about new Doc Francis arrives. Exciting for our town. Ward says the first one he visits will be you. Thanks for the good, wise talk. See you."

"Oh, by the way," Mickey said to Cal, "Sparsity says I am carrying two babies this time. As you know Cal, I have had two miscarriages. Birchard and I were both concerned about me getting pregnant once more. We waited, in hopes of Darnell getting a permanent Doctor. This wasn't planned. We have watched Darnell growing into a self-sufficient town. Now that a doctor is on his way, should be here in a month or so, I still have a few months before I am due." Mickey waddled her tiny body to give Cal a hug.

Cal pressed her ear next to Mickey's protruded stomach, also her hand. "Sounds and movement seem like Sparsity might be right." Mickey said, "I coo and chat to my baby—now I will change my chats for two babies and will welcome our new Doc Francis. See you, Cal."

Before Cal left, she walked back and asked Mickey, "Why is Sparsity so sure you are going to have two babies?" Cal said in a serious questioning voice.

"She massages my belly with oils each day and says that she can feel each one. I have that same feeling, Cal. Sometimes I don't think I can go on. My body feels stretched to the limit. But I have so many reasons to live."

"Mr. Ward insists that the new doctor comes at once to check on you. We understand the load on your body."

"We will welcome him and any kind of relief. My Birchard is in a state of extreme worry."

Cal gave Mickey another hug and reassured her.

Mickey watched as Cal rode away and said to no one in particular, "That Cal sure looks fine in a saddle." With a small wave, Mickey held her belly and waddled into the house. Cal lifted her hand and rode away.

CHAPTER 11

A Good Doc Comes to Darnell Dr. Francis Charing

Subscriptions of newspapers were systematically laid out on a large carved oak table that sat under a floor to ceiling window. Mr. Ward had been searching for just the right doctor to serve the people of Darnell. He had placed ads in each paper. His goal was to soften the heartaches, or at least lessen their difficulties some. His own health was deteriorating. He was weary of the many treatments that he had sought in Atlanta in secret. Affording the best of care, his goal and focus was not on how long he would live, but on reaching the many goals he had set for the town.

One major thing he realized was that families in small Southern towns routinely came face-to-face with the occurrence of death. By the time a doctor arrived, it was often too late. Sparsity walked in with a steaming fresh pot of coffee, a small pitcher of condensed milk, and even with the loud rustle of her taffeta skirt. Her presence didn't register at all.

Absorbed in his task, he was seated with a pile of discarded newspapers on the floor beside his desk, mixed in with scattered piles of stone chips from a sculpture he was ferociously chiseling on. The lifelike circus sculpture will be placed in the center of Darnell's small park. He divided his time between his newspaper advertisements and the sculpture but, of course, all of the inhabitants of Protected Earth, and his constant love, Cal, was in his heart and mind each day also. Determined to concentrate on his best efforts into his project, he refused any attempts to clear the rubble or straighten the room. Since his usual vitality had slowed, he was particularly careful of his time spent on anything.

Sparsity cleared her throat. No response. She tried again, louder. Mr. Ward continued to write. Finally, Sparsity spoke. "Mr. Ward?"

Mr. Ward raised his head and stared at her. "Yes, Sparsity," he finally responded. "Remember, I asked not to be intruded upon."

"I do remember," she said, standing her ground. "But your lunch is ready. It's time you ate something. I've carried away too many untouched meals. I won't leave this room until you nourish your body."

Mr. Ward sighed and put down his pen. "All right, you win. Place the tray on the porch. I'll wash up and be there shortly."

She raised her white eyebrows at him.

He smiled and sighed at the sassy Sparsity humming as she left the room. Her skirts always swishing a glorious tune. After placing three spoons of condensed milk into the wonderful smell of perked coffee, he drank a few sips and thought, "My, my that first taste is divine."

Mr. Ward stood. The entire morning had passed without his notice. He rubbed the back of his neck and slowly stretched, then picked up the London newspaper to take to the porch.

Sparsity had set the porch table with a pretty, embroidered tablecloth. The tablecloth was ablaze with blue birds, flying this way and that. His meal was placed in his best china. Fresh wildflowers adorning the middle.

He smiled wide at the pretty setting and thought back to when Birchard returned from town, bringing the enchanting girl, her white skin, and white hair fell down to her waist in ringlets. Still not sure of her age, but at that time he was placing it about 12.

He was impressed with her straightforwardness, there was nothing shy about Sparsity. Her voice came out strong. Her long white arms and legs tended to give her a marionette appearance.

Yes, God did well when he sent Sparsity to Protected Earth. All had quickly accepted the quick witted, smart girl, who was honest to a fault.

She amused Mr. Ward, and he depended on her more each day. He sat taking a few more drinks of the sugared coffee, then brought his mind back to the task at hand.

He had contacted a Doc Francis from a large, detailed ad in the London Times that had caught his attention. It stated a Francis Charing M.D. desired a position in America. And the doctor specifically desired a position in a growing Southern town, somewhat remote, where he could learn each patient's name, the children, and even their dogs' names. Some available forested areas where he could mollycoddle his other interests, like long walks, indulge in his penchant for entomology, horseback ride, camping. He also stated he grew up on his grandfather's farm where he learned the art of beekeeping from a child. He was enthralled with American history and admired the spirit and freedom America offered its people.

He had studied the ad closely at the time. Mr. Ward thought out loud, "Sounds like one busy doctor." Ward was surprised he had eaten all of his lunch Sparsity had prepared. Sparsity walked out to check.

She picked up the tray. Ward spoke, "Sparsity, please find Lee. I believe our new doctor is on his way."

Sparsity found Lee in the stables.

Lee turned his attention to Sparsity. "Father sent you, what's up?"

She explained what she knew about the doctor, which wasn't much. Ward only said, "He believes he has found our doctor and has heard from the doctor. He is leaving England for Darnell."

"I haven't seen Mr. Ward this excited in some time. We do need a doctor that can perform operations. I can set a broken arm or leg, but to cut into a person, not sure I could, even with special schooling," continued Sparsity.

Lee said, "Sparsity, the town of Darnell and Protected Earth has relied on your healing knowledge, that won't change."

Lee removed his boots, still dirty from the barn. Excited Mr. Ward gave Lee instructions to read the wire he had received from Dr. Francis Charing. It was the doctor's response, with a complete list of references.

Mr. Ward had meticulously checked credentials, communicated directly with Dr. Charing's professors from medical school. All references had been carefully consulted. The telegrams from both sides of the Atlantic had crossed back and forth.

Satisfied at last, Mr. Ward had sent a contract. Dr. Charing accepted the offer and Mr. Ward made travel arrangements for the doctor. He was to arrive in one month if his travel arrangements went as planned.

Lee knew his father had put his attention on hiring a doctor. He was rushing to get the doctor to Darnell in hope of helping Mickey to have her baby.

After the interminable wait, the day finally dawned for Dr. Charing's arrival. The Hub was brimming at mid-morning with Darnell's citizenry, spilling humanity into the wide front porch, down the stairs, and into the parking lot. People clustered into groups, chatting excitedly, dressed in their Sunday best. Children shouted with laughter as they chased each other. Mr. Ward cracked a smile at the cacophony of unbridled excitement.

Children held small bunches of honeysuckle and handwritten signs welcoming Dr. Francis Charing.

From far off, a train whistle was heard. Everyone pressed into the station's receiving platform. Conversations hushed in the anticipation of the train, billowing steam, as it pulled, hissing, into the station. The steam cleared and the door to the passenger car opened. From the moment that the handsome, stylish Dr. Francis stepped off the train, he was as enthralled with Darnell and its people as they were with him.

Mr. Ward and Lee met him on the platform with their hands outstretched. Lee took his bags to the wagon. Mr. Ward turned to Dr. Charing then followed to the crowd. Spontaneous applause and cheers erupted from the townspeople.

Thoroughly charmed, Dr. Charing bowed and tipped his silk hat to the crowd. Mothers of young ladies silently began to scheme as their daughters gaped at the new handsome doctor. This thirty-something doctor from London, England… his black top hat may as well have been a jeweled crown. The absence of wife or children had the females of Darnell even more excited. Maybe they had visions of riding to Sunday church seated beside the handsome doctor. He was dressed in the most recent fashionable suit from Paris, which, being a doctor, he could surely afford. He was a standout.

Cal went through her usual routine double time inside the Hub, as did the extra helpers that she hired for the occasion. Extra tables were set up. Every single Darnell household was represented at the Hub that day. Mr. Ward introduced his highly valued citizens to Dr. Charing, young and old. The crowd parted to let Mr. Ward, Dr. Charing, and Lee go to the Hub. The smells inside were nothing short of heavenly. Cal seated the three at the best table by the big window and served them personally.

When Mr. Ward introduced Dr. Charing to Cal, he noticed she looked particularly desirable today. But Cal never lost her air of sternness and seriousness. All staff was involved in activity or work, within Cal's sight. The staff felt like Cal was thinking, "You could do it a little better, could you not." Lee noted a glint of interest in Dr. Charing's eyes. Uh oh, thought Lee. Later after the empty plates had been whisked away, Cal set dishes of peach cobbler covered with whipped fresh cream in front of them. Mr. Ward touched her hand as she passed back and forth at their table.

Cal smiled inside knowing this small gesture of Mr. Ward's was to show the handsome doctor this woman was taken. She and Mr. Ward exchanged an agreed look. Cal placed her hand on Mr. Ward's shoulder. "Hope all is fine," she said, then turned to hurry back to the bustling kitchen. The message had been sent, received, and thoroughly understood. The doctor turned his attention to scan the room, seemingly in the search for surpassing feminine beauty.

Later, Mr. Ward took the young doctor to his temporary quarters in the back of the library cabin. The townspeople of Darnell had all pitched in to start to build a house for the new doctor. Each family wanted to be a part of hiring their doctor. Mr. Ward desired them to feel this. Children saved their coins, even though nearly all the young people had school, they also had chores to do at home. They hired out to neighbors to work any irksome task that needed doing. The light and excitement showed from each face. The house was not quite finished, several items that had been ordered hadn't arrived. But in the intermediate, the cabin was a cozy place to live.

Mr. Ward grinned and remarked to Dr. Charing, "You surely never have to worry about Sunday dinner. Your social calendar is certain to be booked by these good folks."

Dr. Charing took it all in, the roaring fire in the fireplace, a small bar set up of fine brandies, scotch, rye, and local lighting. The local white lighting had different flavors of peach, blackberries, plum. They made a colorful row on the table.

To top all of this off, a soft knock sounded at the open door, a lovely red-haired vision stood with a tray of food and an invitation in her eyes. Dr. Francis let his mind wander… a fancy-free female with questionable morals.

A sweet but strong voice said, "Hi, Mr. Ward. Mother sent a tray to the new doctor. Father said, 'Maybe we will see the new doctor in church this Sunday.'"

Mr. Ward was not a churchgoer, but a believer.

Mr. Ward quickly became aware of the glint in Dr. Charing's eyes for the ladies. He felt he should give the doctor some good advice. He wanted him alive and well serving the citizens of Darnell. "A word to the wise, though, stay away from the married or committed ladies, my friend. This is not London. The men in Darnell all possess an arsenal of firearms and are not shy about protecting their own. These are not lame words that I speak, Dr. Charing. Remember them and heed each one."

Dr. Charing reached inside his tweed jacket and pulled out a silver flask. He offered the flask to Mr. Ward, who declined. Dr. Charing downed the aged scotch whiskey and replied, "Thank you for your advice. I'll take heed. The lovely ladies of Darnell are indeed enticing, but I have no wish for trouble."

The soft-spoken lovely girl was still standing with a tray waiting a comment about Sunday's services, and her father's invite to the new doctor.

Mr. Ward answered, "All places could be a good place, on one's knees. But I never question others' beliefs. Janeisse, that's up to Doc Francis. He will make his own decisions."

"Well I'll just place the tray on the table. Nice to make your acquaintance, Dr. Charing." And she gave a warm smile and walked out with the swish of her starched skirt.

Mr. Ward was smiling, "Would it be the preacher's daughter that got your attention?"

Doc Francis replied, "I don't hold any preconceived opinion on that matter, but top notch on your well-furnished library."

"Settle in, Doc. Rest, wander around, if you feel in the mood to explore, Cal said walk back to her barn, and saddle one of her appaloosas if you seek to venture out."

"Just maybe, my favorite horse."

"Tomorrow the town will celebrate once more your arrival at Cal's. See you at 10:00 for breakfast."

He shook Doc's hand and walked toward the door, bending his head forward at the door.

Doc Francis said, "Yes, Mr. Ward at last I feel I am home. I do appreciate the celebrated welcome. But, I wish to pay a call on Mickey before I enjoy anything else. You stated Mickey was a priority."

"Fine, I will have Cal pick you up at 4:00 this afternoon. Pack a few things, I think it's good you have a few days to rest and explore. I have just the spot for you, a nice pond cabin you can stay for privacy. Lee will be happy to show you around, either by foot or horseback. It will be your call."

Mr. Ward said, "We must make the town celebration in the morning, if you feel all is okay with Mickey. See you tonight, Doc." Ward waved his hand in a downward sweep from the elbow. A gesture he did often. A sign that togetherness was over.

Mr. Ward and Lee left. Their faces showed contentment that Darnell had a jewel for a doctor, a new citizen, and both felt sure a potential good friend. Mr. Ward had informed him his new office and living space would soon be completed.

Dr. Francis had responded, "I have a liking for different places to lay my head, but a permanent space would be wonderful to have for my personal belongings such as clothes, an extensive boot collection, and an assortment of magnifying lenses for observation. One of my irresistible interests is in bees."

The entire upstairs floor of the house was to be Dr. Charing's living quarters. Several trunks were to arrive from England, filled with Dr. Charing's personal belongings. Mr. Ward had commissioned a large closet designed for Dr. Charing's extensive boot collection, and also for his collection of lenses for observing insects, bees in particular. All felt Doc Francis would prove to be an excellent doctor.

On Dr. Francis Charing's schedule after he had checked on Mickey was to get to know Darnell, its peoples, and the roads leading to families in the forest. This job was assigned to Lee. "I want to know every road and trail and the fastest way to reach a sick person. A map with this information and including the names of each family member will do just fine." Mr. Ward thought of everything that would make a new doctor not only comfortable in his personal daily life, but whatever he needed to be the most proficient doctor for Darnell citizens.

Cal picked up Doc Francis in the afternoon with two saddled horses and made the ride to Protected Earth with Doctor Francis asking loads of questions about Mickey. He realized the great love all had for Mickey.

Cal was glad the doc asked no personal questions of her life or of her relationship with Mr. Ward. She got the impression the doc let people reveal themselves when they choose.

The ride into Protected Earth was always a feast for the eyes. Doc's comment was, "What a journey I have to look forward to. Beauty creates interest," a trait she liked that does not need a verbal comment.

The two rode up and found Birchard seated on his porch, drink in hand, front door open with a view to Mickey's bed, which had been placed in the room next to the kitchen. After intros, the doc asked Birchard to introduce him to Mickey. The Atlanta doctor that was attending to Mickey stood with a tired worried look on his face.

The room smelled of herbs. Doc noticed a pan steaming on the stove, herbs, and candles on dishes throughout. A long dining table neatly furnished with all the things Doc could ask for was available for when the time came for the baby to be born. The attending doc spoke gently that Mickey had just informed him she felt that there were two babies, one kicks on the right side, then a strong kick on the left.

"I agree with her strongly," he informed Doc Francis of Mickey's up-to-date condition.

"I'm glad to see you, Doc Francis. My understanding is you have performed quite a few cesarean births. I feel Mickey cannot withstand even one baby ripping through her tiny body, much less two."

"May I talk with Mickey?" He asked Birchard's permission, Birchard was now standing by his wife.

"Hi beautiful lady, I am Dr. Francis Charing, I have come all the way from England to be by your side and do what I can to assist you with having these two babies." Doc Francis looked at Birchard, the Atlanta doctor, and Cal. "I would if you all don't mind prefer to have a nice private talk with this lovely lady. Is that okay with you, Mickey?"

Mickey looked at dear Birchard and said, "I would like that. I have some personal questions to ask Doc Francis."

Cal walked over to the stove, picked up the coffee pot and some mugs and said, "We will all be right close, Mickey." They followed Cal to the porch where she poured some strong cups of coffee.

Doc Francis put another pillow behind Mickey's back, reached into the herb water with a cloth, and wiped her face and hands. He took both of her hands in his and said, "Dear, dear lady, tell me what you wish, then I will inform you what I believe our options are."

Doc Francis spent a few hours with Mickey. All waited anxiously for his prognosis. He was impressed with Mickey's intelligence and her outlook in accepting her fate. She told the doc her first wish is that her two babies are healthy. She also confided in the doc that she knew that Birchard's first desire is not for the babies, but for her.

Doc Francis asked, "How much do you wish to disclose to your husband, and the many others that love you?"

"Whatever my fate is, Birchard I know will not want to go on without me. That's why I have asked Sparsity to stay close to Birchard and see that he isn't left alone. All will pitch in and care for Birchard and the babies. Can you give me any hope, Doc Francis?"

Mickey sat up straight, eager to know the doc's answer. "You have given your consent to the cesarean. You know the extreme risk of this. But to put you through trying to have a natural birth of one child, much less two, would be a sure death for you and possibly your babies.

"As long as you remain stable, we can wait a few days. The decision is yours and Birchard's. I wish I could give you a guarantee, lovely Mickey. The best I can give is that I will use all the medical knowledge I have to save your babies and you."

Birchard still seated on the porch but close by hung his head into his hand. "I trust you, Doc Francis." Softly Mickey said, "Please keep a healing eye on my precious Birchard."

Doc gave a wave with his arm, and said, "You can rest well, we will take care of Birchard."

Sparsity had helped the local midwife deliver babies. She had learned a lot, but she knew Mickey needed more and prayed a sigh of relief when Doc Francis burst onto the scene.

The doc gave compliments, making sure Sparsity knew what a great job she was doing. "God bless you, child," along with the doc from Atlanta who had kept close watch over Mickey.

Mickey's skin had an unhealthy gray pallor. Her heart beat fast and too shallow. The twinkle in her eyes had left weeks ago.

Doc said, "I don't believe we can wait. We must go ahead." Doc Francis had let each one re-enter Mickey's room, knowing the urgent situation Mickey was in. After all expressed their love, Doc instructed all out of the room, except Birchard who refused to leave, and Sparsity.

Sparsity was placing pots of hot water close by. The doctor thanked her and repeated his words, "I'm glad you are here. I need you."

A neighbor woman, Judith Harrison arrived, Mrs. Harrison was a mother of eight and the area's midwife. She had experienced her share of births.

Cal, Mr. Ward, and Lee waited on the front porch along with several neighbor women who had set up a constant prayer group.

Cal asked, "What can we do? I feel helpless and don't like this feeling." She paced back and forth on the porch.

Mr. Ward said, "The doctor, midwife and Sparsity will stay by her side. Birchard has refused to budge. All you can do is be here if needed." Cal saw the pain of helplessness on Ward's face. Ward put his arm around Cal. Their eyes followed each other's whereabouts. All knew they were in a devoted love affair.

Mickey was out of her head with pain whenever a contraction gripped her. Sparsity kept up a running stream of encouragement, "Mickey, breathe. That's it. Let it go. You can do this. Breathe deep, good."

Birchard wiped Mickey's face with Sparsity's herbed water. He understood the doctor was using all his skills to save Mickey's life. The doctor moved in to help with the contractions. Doc Francis instructed the midwife to gently keep her hands on Mickey's stomach. Mickey's mind moved in and out of actuality. She could hear Birchard crying and the doctor working over her, trying to keep her tiny body from ripping open. She felt a river surging around her, she wanted her babies, and she now knew there were two inside of her, fighting for their lives. Mrs. Harrison said to Sparsity, "There are two babies." Sparsity went back and forth from the bedroom to the wood stove. The instruments had to be freshly boiled to be sterile. Sparsity new Mickey was in a life-or-death situation. She had seen the same look on Granny Dalia before the Almighty took her away. She silently prayed for the worried Dr. Francis to save Mickey and her babies.

Mickey's travail continued for hours. She weakened with the constant assault on her small, battered body. After each contraction, she shook with violent tremors. Sparsity and Birchard tried their best to hide their despair. But Birchard wept beside his beloved, unaware that he did so. He willed his strength in her, pouring out all he had. His thoughts were, "Why? Why my good, beautiful Mickey?" There was no answer.

Mr. Ward, Cal, Lee, and the neighbor woman paced in the yard. Mr. Ward berating himself for not overriding Mickey's insistence to give birth in her and Birchard's home. But thankful he was able to persuade Doc Francis to come sooner. The Atlanta Doc had been well compensated for any loss he may have incurred to his practice. But he realized Doc Francis was much more qualified to take care of Mickey.

Sparsity, when she was coaching Mickey, murmured a chant that came from deep within. Though she couldn't remember where she had learned it, she felt that the chant had an ancient, healing power. Judith, the midwife, prayed to the Christ of her faith. Mickey was beyond words but strove with all she had to give birth. She had yearned for children throughout her married life. She felt Birchard would make a remarkable father.

Doc Francis consulted with Birchard, the midwife, Mr. Ward, and Sparsity on Mickey's grave condition. "There is little time left."

Birchard spoke, "Do it. Save my Mickey."

Doc Francis requested Mr. Ward have someone take him into Darnell. "I need my equipment. Mickey cannot deliver these babies naturally. I will have to put Mickey into a sleep. Anesthesia I have used to do caesarean birth, all is very risky. With a small person like dear Mickey, it's twofold."

"Make Mickey as comfortable as possible. Lee and I will pick up the med supplies and any equipment I need to try to save Mickey. We will return shortly."

The Atlanta doctor said he would be right at Mickey's side until Doc Francis returned.

Upon Lee and Doc Francis's arrival back from town with Doc's equipment and medicines—the doctors, Sparsity, and the midwife scrubbed their hands with strong lye soap, then poured disinfectant over their hands, including Birchard's. They tied pristine, snowy white cotton cloth around their noses and mouths at the doctor's insistence. The doctor warned each one the most danger would be from severe loss of blood.

The doctor increased the morphine. The doctor's voice rang out as he lifted one boy, handed him to Sparsity, then another. Remarkably Mickey spoke, "My dearest, let me feel my babies next to me, and see their faces." The smell of birth and death filled the room. "Birchard, please rest," Mickey pleaded.

All were in amazement as Mickey continued to speak, while Sparsity cleaned the babies, she slipped pale pink dresses onto the babies and laid them in Birchard's arms.

After the doctor cleaned Mickey's tiny, torn body as best he could, he helped Birchard with the two boys.

He gently laid the babies into Mickey's arms.

Mickey touched each one's delicate fingers and kissed their face.

Sparsity chanted in the background and stirred the herbs she had steaming on the stove, filling the house with her healing potions.

Lee, Mr. Ward, and Cal stayed close by on the porch, ready if needed. "Oh, Ward," Cal said. "I have never been so much in prayer and don't know if anyone can hear my words, but let's pray with the women."

The four went down on their knees. Each speaking their own prayer. They were still there when they realized the sun was beginning to set. Doc Francis opened the door and stepped outside. He was covered in blood. "Mickey's gone," he announced. "The two boys are holding their own." Everyone froze. Stunned. Mickey—gone? Twins?

"Doctor. Can Cal go in?" Ward said.

"Yes. Sparsity and Birchard are drained. I am very worried about Birchard. I would keep someone with him day and night. He said he does not wish to live without Mickey and shows no interest in the two babies. Birchard will not leave his wife. Mickey did get to hold her babies before she passed. She looked into their faces, then looked at Birchard."

Birchard lay with Mickey and the babies, holding her, speaking words of hope and love. But, Mickey had let go and taken her last breath. Sparsity and the doctors took the babies from Mickey's arms.

Birchard was inconsolable. "How can there be a day of sunrise without my beloved Mickey?"

Cal entered the room. Mr. Ward stepped forward and said, "Come, doc. We believe you did all that was possible to save our Mickey. Are the boys healthy? I'll take you to the farmhouse where you can wash up and rest."

"I am sorry," the doctor said. "She was just too far gone. Too small. The damage to her tiny body was extensive. Yes, Mr. Ward, the boys are all right, for now. I'm concerned about that little one, though. I've decided to stay here instead of going back into town. So I can check on the babies and Birchard in the morning, or if they need me tonight. I am worried how the citizens will react to me not being able to save this beloved woman."

"Mickey was his whole world." Mr. Ward spoke, "Do not worry. I will talk with each person that should question. Birchard and the rest of us know you did all in your power to save her."

The doctor opened his bag and took out a bottle of laudanum. "Careful with this. Don't let him take more than I prescribed. Remember, he should not be left alone. He isn't in a good frame of mind."

Lee said, "I will stay with Birchard tonight. Sparsity and Cal will take care of the babies."

Lee took the doc to the main house for rest and to clean up and went back to Birchard's home. Mr. Ward could scarcely believe that beautiful little Mickey was gone. He thought about when he had hired the little couple. After seeing the love and respect that passed between them, for the first time in his life, he believed in true love. Now, many years later, it happened to him. When he met Cal.

Mr. Ward suspected a lot of Birchard's strength was because of Mickey. Her sweet spirit. So kind and gentle, but underneath, was solid steel. Mr. Ward had known her well from all those years with his circus. At times, he didn't know where Birchard stopped, and Mickey began. He knew that the next few hours, days, weeks, and months would be hellish for Birchard to try and rebuild himself after the utter and total devastation.

Mr. Ward, being immersed in his thoughts, didn't realize Lee was back at Birchard's. Lee asked Ward and Judith about the babies and Birchard. Mr. Ward spoke, "Cal is inside, helping with the cleanup. We haven't seen the boys or Birchard." Mr. Ward filled the doorway. Birchard lay beside his wife. He couldn't let her go. Cal and Judith took care of Mickey's body as best they could. The boys were placed on the extra bed that was clean with shiny, white sheets. Each person looked at Birchard and their hearts broke. Mr. Ward tried to push through the numbing fog in his mind and heart, asking himself if there was more he could have done.

Cal had walked out to the porch and said, while resting her hand on Mr. Ward's arm, "Sparsity needs rest. That child is an angel sent to us."

"I will have Lee take her to her cottage." He called Lee's name and he was there.

"Yes, Father? What can I do?"

"Please take Sparsity home. See that she is resting before you leave her. Then, check on the good doctor. We will stay with Birchard." Sparsity stood. She gave Birchard a kiss on the head, and then she left with Lee.

Mr. Ward pulled a chair close by to watch his friend. Birchard seemed not to breathe. It would not have surprised him if Birchard followed Mickey in death. He laid his hand on Birchard's tiny back. He would have done anything to have spared his friend such overwhelming grief. No words were spoken. Mr. Ward sat with his friend throughout the night. He found it hard to believe the lifeless body was their beloved Mickey.

Sparsity returned the next morning, looking surprisingly well rested. She wore her loudest purple skirt. Sparsity informed Mr. Ward the doctor had sent Lee for the undertaker at early morning. He should be arriving shortly.

Birchard finally let go of Mickey at the gentle urging of Mr. Ward and Sparsity.

"Sparsity, would you stay and look after the boys? We need to get Birchard a bath and some food. The doctor will be back soon and go over the instructions as to the welfare of the babies and Birchard. I did get some laudanum down Birchard. It seemed to have quieted him. Lee will help Birchard wash up."

"I plan on being right here," was Sparsity's reply.

The young Sparsity had become the mainstay for Mickey. But the extra help that Cal and some of the neighbor women gave was critical. Sparsity took over care of the boys. She had never cared for the babies of humans, but she often had cared for orphan animals, with great love, care, and know-how. And she had helped Granny when the goats gave birth.

The next few days, Birchard was kept in a drugged state. All pitched in to give Sparsity assistance with the care of the boys. One baby was of normal size and the other boy was a little person with special needs.

The family burial site had been completed for some time. A peaceful spot on top of a high ridge. Large enough for the many loved ones who would follow through the years. It was enclosed with iron fencing. White dogwoods lined the fence.

Mickey's funeral was arranged by Mr. Ward and Cal. Neighbor men took over the duties that had to be done on a working farm. Then they asked, "What's next?" All were willing to help.

Lee showed his capability and took on more responsibility in overseeing the farm. He was still a kid in age but showed himself to be as good as the men. The times he did become overwhelmed with life, he would take a long hike with Chase and Talker and sketch his beloved birds. This would let the heaviness be released from his heart.

Mickey's burial was a celebration of her life. Mr. Ward spoke of her beauty and background as a superior performing artist, her acts of kindness, her wisdom, and the shining light that she was to the world around her. Her father and mother had passed, and any kin were hidden away in another country. Doc Francis was determined to keep Birchard as drugged up as he could to let him have time to heal.

Mr. Ward ordered a white marble headstone with an angel with open wings. He chiseled an epitaph:

Your spirit soars in all the singing seasons
The beloved wife of Birchard and mother of Leeward and Folly

As the boys were named. Birchard agreed on the words.

The graveyard looked out over the fields and forests of Protected Earth. One could see the river that meandered through the property. This truly was the place of peace that Mr. Ward had envisioned.

Birchard withdrew deep within himself. He showed no interest in the children. His grief for Mickey was so into his soul. Mr. Ward worked patiently with his partner and friend to bring him back into their world. He slowly added one thing at a time for Birchard to manage.

It was an organized effort in the weeks that followed to continue to assist Sparsity. The time was moving quickly—and the twins. Under Sparsity's care, Leeward and Folly were also doing well. Folly's personality suited his name. He was a baby full of smiles. Whereas Leeward was far ahead of his age. Leeward was very smart, early to walk, talk, and a loner even as a very young boy, with an aggressive personality.

Life started up once more on Protected Earth. Mickey's death had left a void in a completely spiritless Birchard.

Doc Francis moved into his newly completed office and home.

The new school was already being enlarged and new projects were being added for the continuing building of Darnell.

CHAPTER 12

Mickey's Spirit Lives On

Birchard, Mr. Ward, and Lee kept Mickey's memories alive by sharing stories to a convenient ear. Their goal was for Folly and Leeward to know the beauty of their mother.

It wasn't always easy to retain the boys' attention. The boys, even at this young age, were already showing an extreme difference. Their physical appearance was obvious; one being a little person and the other one a robust sized person. Personality-wise, there was Folly who Doc Francis had named because when he was born, there was a smile on his face. Leeward was named after Lee and Mr. Ward. He was handsome, stern, and talented. They were both growing at an alarming rate under Sparsity's care.

Birchard still remained detached from his children but came alive when he spoke of Mickey. He talked often of her bold spirit and how courageously she fought to live and held her babies in her arms. He would show the drawings Lee had done of Birchard and Mickey on a high wire, depicting their courage and beauty of putting life and limb in peril each time they performed. Lee would repeat often to the boys and Sparsity, who was nearby, the generous hearts of Birchard and Mickey toward him and his sister, Azzie, when their father left them at the circus gate.

Leeward continue to be a robust, healthy, handsome boy, and uncommonly interested in every feature of Protected Earth but looked upon his father and Folly as an embarrassment. Sparsity would say, "That Leeward was born angry." But he was such an extremely hard worker and wished to be a part of and learn everything connected to Protected Earth. Lee could see Leeward, even at a young age, was going to be a huge asset for the land and animals.

Folly was becoming a much-loved person by all the people who lived on Protected Earth or worked there. Folly didn't comprehend it all and lived in his protected world of whimsy. As a small child, he started carving wonderful, small, detailed figures using his imagination. The figures were from the circus that he had heard about. Folly would listen with great interest and asked question after question. What were their legs doing, where were their arms, were they smiling, did Mickey do acrobatics — describe the different acrobatics. Folly would then design the carvings to connect and do the movements. A delight for the eyes and hearts to observe.

When Leeward wasn't in school, he was Lee's shadow. A constant sentence from him was, "When I grow up, I will work and plow the land, cut and plant wheat and oat fields, grow seedlings for all kinds of trees, feed and groom all the animals, gather eggs, milk the cows and goats."

Folly, overhearing his brother, would laugh and say, "Leeward, you are going to be very busy."

Throughout the years, each person on Protected Earth took part in the care and teaching of the boys. Leeward moved ahead in school. He possessed Birchard's smarts, thick head of wavy, brown, shiny hair, strongly and defined face with eyes of Hazel. The difference between Birchard's eyes and Leeward's eyes was Birchard's eyes were soft and kind. Leeward's appeared to see through a person, searching for something.

Folly was winning the hearts of all who came in contact with him.

Folly and Leeward lived most of their time with Sparsity. The two had little relationship with their father Birchard. Sparsity would insist he stop by and spend some time, telling them stories of Mickey. Leeward shot through school and was a graduate at a young age.

Folly spent little time in school and stayed within the shadow of Sparsity.

Leeward took numerous courses on saving and improving the land, water salvage, landscape, and went on to take a course in veterinarian training. But a dark side to Leeward would pop up at times.

He was to marry the lovely Tess, who was an orphan, and worked the local farms. She was indigenous to the area but had no recall of who her parents were. When Leeward asked her to be his wife, she gladly accepted. Mr. Ward had a home built for Leeward, and Tess was no longer a servant. But the wife of the very respected Leeward.

CHAPTER 13

The Circus Statue a Town Celebrates

"Lee, my son," Mr. Ward said as he labored to rise up to a sitting position from his bed, "I feel that there is so much more in me. In five years, we have received the greatest of pleasures from this land. We've walked, worked, played, and feasted our eyes on every inch. Our souls were fed by it all. I've been so committed to give back all that we have gleaned from Protected Earth. So, what does it do? It takes me. But each one of us eventually will return to the Earth." His speech was halted and slow; his once powerful voice no longer echoed throughout the house. But Lee knew, no matter how long he lived, Mr. Ward would always remain deep into all that was Protected Earth and the town of Darnell. But he also knew his father missed his dear friends in the circus. In the corner of his studio stood his tall shiny, patent boots that he wore as ringmaster.

Lee gently eased his father up and propped him with pillows. His father's weakness broke Lee's heart.

"Get upset! Father! Get angry! Fight! Defy the odds and get well!" Lee felt desperation in the depth of his soul. His father was slipping away, and he was powerless to prevent it. Lee held his father's frail hand. That hand that had been so strong, so expressive as it captivated circus audiences with gestures, so giving to people in need. In times of trouble, Lee always felt that things would be alright, if only he could get to the security of his father's hand. And it was.

Gasping for breath now, Mr. Ward spoke, "Bring Chase and Talker to me. I need to see their sweet, wise faces and feel the warmth of their bodies on my bed. In fact, I would like them to stay with me. Do not remove them from my room. Only when they wish to leave." The dogs heard their names and within an instant had their paws up on the side of the bed. Mr. Ward looked at them. "My good boys," he said, "What loyal and amusing companions you both have been. Right by my side every step of the way." He patted the bed and up they jumped and quickly found a comfortable spot and curled up, both facing Mr. Ward.

Daily life continued with the citizens and Mr. Ward's loved ones. People ate breakfast, sent their kids off to school, dressed, and went to work, all appeared as just moving on automatic, their minds and hearts were with the man that had vitalized Darnell.

Cal spent every spare moment by his side. Her customers kept the Hub going, and Liza stayed mostly with Sparsity, and loved being with Birchard's growing boys.

Ward's imposing studio was large, and his bed occupied the center of the room. He could see his beloved land all the way down to the river. On his good days, he took advantage of his energy and the light as he chiseled away on the circus sculpture. The grand sculpture was almost finished. Ward would envision the excitement it would create, the day it would be placed in the small park in the center of town. Cal never grew tired of hearing the stories of each person and animal the sculpture represented. As she sat close to him, she asked, "Ward tell me a story about one of the characters in this sculpture." His face would light up and he would start talking, the stories were endless, loving, tender, and interesting.

His view from his bed was of his beloved land. Beyond on a ridge, pines swayed in tune with the breezes, sweeping fields, grazing horses, cattle, sheep, and goats, lived and ate in harmony. All blended into the horizon beyond the river. Yes! Mr. Ward was a man that planned. But as with daily life, the unexpected always pays a visit. The oaks that surrounded the house were dropping their acorns, making them dance on the roof.

"The deer should be arriving to partake of the acorns," Mr. Ward said to Cal. "They will appear closer to evening or early morning."

"If they don't show, I will go and round each one up and bring them to you," Cal said.

Often during the night, she would hear Ward softly talking in his sleep, not wanting to intrude but desiring to be closer to him, she would quietly get up and lay beside him. She took in his breathing and the heat from his body. There was no odor of sickness in Ward's room. Sparsity searched the fields for flowers and unusual branch shapes to put in vases, attaching dried herbs to them. She also changed the crisp sun-dried white linen on Ward's bed several times a day.

"Birchard is waiting to see you." Lee struggled to maintain control.

"Yes, that Sparsity is insistent I eat. She does bring delicious looking meals, but I just can't seem to muster up an appetite.

"Son, will you and Cal stay with me? I feel like I am back in that trunk. It's difficult to get air." Lee started opening every window in the room.

Dr. Francis sat in a rocker close by, observing his dear friend. Often taking out his silver flask, lifting it high. "Here's to you pal, how are you doing? Are you in any pain?"

"No, Doc. It's nice to have you near," said Mr. Ward. "You aren't neglecting your other patients are you, Doc?"

Doc stood up and smiled. "Seems like the whole town has gotten healthier. Each time I check on someone invariably they say, 'Doc, shouldn't you be with Mr. Ward?' You are a mighty loved man, Ward!"

"Lend me a little support, Doc. I need to get out of bed and do the finishing touches on the sculpture."

Doc said, "Do you feel like a couple swigs of brandy?"

"Don't mind if I do." Surprisingly, Ward stood straight without the Doc's assistance.

Doc poured two brandies from the cut glass container, put them on the small marble table beside the chair, close to the sculpture. The two friends touched glasses and drank the brandy down.

"Pour us another, Doc." And the doctor obliged.

"Ward, tell me something about each person that's included in the awesome sculpture."

Ward never tired of talking about his circus family. Stories were repeated.

"First there is Princess, the white Arabian horse. She was Azzie's horse, a large part of the draw to the circus with the knockout blazing red haired Azzie on her back. I put Azzie beside her horse, so children and adults could sit on Princess, close their eyes, and feel what it was like to ride in the ring. She was a brilliant rider, doing death defying stunts. Birchard and Mickey will be on the tightrope, on their bike.

"One of my favorites is Szabo, the strongman, looking splendid in his one shoulder red and white strongman suit. His muscles are defined and ready to dazzle the audience. The boy seated on his shoulder is Little D, wide eyed and staring at the handsome grand ringmaster in all his finery. That handsome fellow is me."

"You better stick around, Ward, so we can unveil this grand sculpture."

The grand room had taken on an air of gaiety, of drinks and food Sparsity brought in. And the storytelling… the windows were open, a lovely breeze entered the room, all were relaxed at least for the day, the forthcoming sorrow was put aside. Ward, working away on the sculpture, was happy with all his family around him.

"I believe I will, Doc. The men will start moving the sections this weekend, I will be there to direct the placement and the platform is complete."

"Yes, it is impressive. Love the pebbles of washed colors from the streams, mixed into the concrete. How did you achieve the different colors of the costumes and the clothing — amazing."

"With great help from Lee and Sparsity searching the fields, earth, pigments, and garden flowers, fruits, vegetables, greens, berries, tree sap, and soot. They came up with some surprises. And wowed me with the fantastic colors. In fact, Lee believes we can start a paint business for some locals."

"We will start moving the different sections this week, I will watch over these sections to be placed, should be ready by next week to be unveiled. Dinner on the greens. The citizens understand this is to be a reminder that Ward was here, and the history that formed my life and brought me to this place in the great state of Georgia."

Mr. Ward painted the last color and touched up some silver highlights on Princess' headband of feathers. He now reflected a lot. Had it really been only five years? Within these years he had completed most of his goals, not only for building Protected Earth but for the town of Darnell. Yes! He had great support from his son, Lee, his friend and partner, Birchard. And all the new neighbors and friends that had worked alongside him.

He also met the perfect woman for him. Cal was his equal and he felt he couldn't breathe well when she would leave him. He did not have to explain who he was; she knew. This last year they were together most of the time. She still had Liza to raise, and the Hub to run. Good friends ran the Hub and post office. Cal would go into town to prepare the food.

Sparsity was ironing the white linen sheets; the irons opened and were filled with red hot coals from the fireplace. She glided the heavy iron effortlessly along the fresh smelling sheets until every wrinkle was pressed out. Nothing but the best for her friend and boss. Cal walked out of Ward's room to say hello to Sparsity.

"Hi," Cal said. Sparsity rested her iron and gave her attention to Cal. "Just wanted to bring you up on our plans to take Ward into town. He has given all the plans on paper, how these statues are to be positioned. That is taking place with Runaway, Emilio, and some town men and Lee and Birchard tomorrow. All will be placed and covered when Ward arrives at sunrise the next morning. There will be a crowd, everyone near and far to Darnell wishes to be a part of it. We will have plenty of food set up with loads of champagne, sweet tea, and churns of homemade ice cream for the children."

Sparsity put her head in her hands and began to cry. Cal didn't touch her or try to comfort her in any way. Never had anyone that knew Sparsity seen her breakdown, from the time she came to Protected Earth as a child of twelve.

"Excuse me, Miss Cal, just tell me what I am to do. Do you have Mr. Ward ready? But right now, I need a long walk."

"Go! I am here."

Cal poured herself a coffee and thought about the joy and pain of tomorrow.

Doc had seen that Ward was now resting, and said, "Cal, I am going to go back into town. If needed, send for me. See you at sunrise. I will be decked out in my finest clothes for the joyous event, putting that old top hat on once more. Ward said he is wearing his ringmaster suit. Young and old alike will praise him for generations to come."

Doc walked out. Cal moved her chair by Ward's bed. Put her hand on his arm and said softly, "Ward, you have created Protected Earth as close to perfection in all its harmony. Rest well, we will celebrate at sunrise." She once more laid down beside him. "The wagons are prepared."

CHAPTER 14

Gray Clouds Over Protected Earth

The unveiling of the life-size circus statue was a resounding success. And would be talked about and certainly be remembered with future generations.

Children hopped on the statue of Princess, as Birchard and Lee told the crowd stories of the many performances. Birchard seemed happy, a joy that hadn't been seen on his face often since Mickey had died.

A few more adventurous ones stood on her back, as Mr. Ward told of Azzie's feats on Princess. Sure, they may have taken a tumble, and skinned a knee, maybe even a broken collarbone. But they would talk of the daring, due to their friends. Mr. Ward dressed in his ringmasters' clothes, standing tall and regal, but very thin, seemed quite up to the celebration. As the day wore on, dark gray clouds started rolling in over Darnell. Doc requested they take Mr. Ward home, and he would be there shortly. No one knew but Cal that Doc had pumped Mr. Ward full of a stimulant, so Ward would be up to the unveiling of the impressive statue. And it worked; all marveled at how well he appeared.

Lee and Cal accompanied Mr. Ward back to his home. As the buggy stopped at the barn, Mr. Ward said to Lee, "Saddle our horses and let's ride the property, we will stop at the pond house and sit on that sweet porch and have a drink to the glory of life and feel the thrill as we let our imaginations run wild."

And so, they did. Lee jumped out and set the pond house porch up, and the three drinks of Brandy. Lee said, "I think I will take a short walk, while you two talk."

It was a welcome silence for a few minutes. They could hear the soft tunes of nature and paid little attention to the ominous dark sky.

"Wish I could have seen you, Ward, calling out those circus acts. You look mighty handsome in that outfit." Cal moved in close and sat at his feet, he touched her hair. She took his hand and wept.

"I have cried some tears myself, Cal. Are there any answers you need to know before we say goodbye?"

"No."

"Pull off these boots. I want to walk and feel the energy of the earth."

They strolled close to the cabin and rested on the tree stumps at the woodpile.

Lee showed up from his walk, sat and took his boots off. "That sure feels good."

The three sat in silence, knowing each one shared a deep pain that could not be expressed.

They finished the ride through the property. Mr. Ward retired to his room, now looking somewhat exhausted.

Sparsity had laid out his robe and sleep clothes, prepared a warm bath, turned down his freshly made bed, and put large vases of wildflowers in his room, his favorite.

Doc Francis had arrived and was asleep on a day bed in Ward's room.

The curtains were drawn back, so the massive oak that stood in the side yard outside his bedroom would fill his view. He likened his illness to the oak. He could hear a creak and moan from breezes that drifted by and pushed the old oak a little more to its resting place. Lightning had struck the oak a few years back. It stubbornly held its own, still impressive though scarred. Through the years that had followed, the trunk and bark sagged and flayed. Occasionally a branch dropped. As the tree evolved into an entropized state, Mr. Ward knew his health would likewise deteriorate.

Cal lay by his side all night, his arm across her waist, she stayed awake, but Ward slept peacefully. When he awoke, he said, "Good morning. I sure had a nice restful sleep. Think maybe because I had this beautiful woman next to me."

Cal rolled over toward him, and kissed him, his mouth, face, head. She caressed his head, running her fingers through his hair.

"Cal, you get dressed, ask Sparsity to bring us a coffee."

Doc was awake and walked over to Mr. Ward as Cal walked out for coffee. He put pillows behind Ward's head. Doc's feelings were as raw as most anyone in Darnell's. The thought of this man not existing in the world was such a loss.

Mr. Ward reached his hand out to Doc, "How about one of those brandies with me, Doc?"

Doc Francis said, "My thought exactly." Doc poured two brandies from the etched Amber container. Doc turned around as he heard a large crack of lightning, and that 100-year-old oak twisted, sighing as air passed through its branches. The tree plummeted toward the ground. As it fell, its behemoth root system pulled out of the earth and the tree joined Mr. Ward in their final transition into another life.

Doc felt his pulse, then turned the two glasses up and drank them down. "One of the best men on earth just left us."

Now, Mr. Ward was gone. Doc walked out of the room and sat on the trunk of the downed oak. And let his emotions flow out. Doc felt he owed his great contented life to Mr. Ward. The funeral was held in two days. The hilltop was overflowing with the citizens of Darnell. Birchard watched as an increasing wind continued to pile petals from the dogwood blooms onto Mickey's small grave. The growing twins quietly sat beside their mother's grave.

Lee stayed on his knees throughout the service with his face hidden in his hands. Birchard began the eulogy with his hand on Lee's shoulder. "Citizens of Darnell, I will not vaunt about this giant of a man who often likened us all to the oak tree beside his home. He intensely disliked boasting. He never revealed his complete story, and even throughout our long years as friends, he only gave small glimpses into the wounds of his soul. He told me that we are not greater than or less than the oak. No matter what attacks the giant oak, it retains a stillness that is the core of life around us. The oak will live forever in one form or another. It may be a table, a chest, firewood, then ashes that will continue to enrich the earth. In all things, ourselves included, we all started life as a seed. We each carry our own private story. Each of us are impacted by Mr. Ward in some way. How blessed we were to have had him in our lives…" Birchard choked up, composed himself, and continued. "All who loved Mr. Ward has a happy heart. Happy that he fulfilled his dream of a town and a home place that he built and shared with his neighbors and loved ones. He brought so much to Darnell and Protected Earth. One of the greatest gifts Darnell gave him was the love of his life, Cal. There are not enough words that I can add to show my personal love and friendship he gave to my beloved Mickey and me." Birchard could not go on. So, he stepped aside.

By his own request, Mr. Ward's ashes were mixed with logs from the old oak; the man and parts of the tree were committed to the earth. "Ashes to ashes, dust to dust." Sparsity came forward and knelt to place flowers into the open space where his ashes were to be put. She lowered her forehead to the spot for a moment, then rose and walked away. Chase and Talker lay down together on the fresh dirt. There the dogs remained for a few days. On days that Lee would miss them, he knew where to find Chase and Talker.

Up there on the ridge, a gray flannel sky accepted the column of smoke that swirled upward, slanting east. Down below, the bottom field of oats moved as waves by the whipping wind. The people standing around drifted into smaller groups. The service was over, but few left, despite the threat of the storm brewing. One cluster of townspeople became quite animated and pulled others over to the group. Plans were being made. The group grew in number. "Let's discuss this with Lee and Birchard later," one said. "Look at the sky. We'd better get moving."

Cal turned to where Lee still knelt silently with Birchard's hand on his shoulder. Neither one had moved. "I'm available whenever you need me," was all Cal said. She touched Lee's hair.

Birchard answered Cal, "I need you to take the boys for a few days. Sparsity can manage the house, goats, and the cheese making. There's a stack of notes on the kitchen table from neighbors offering to help. Get in touch with them. I need a few days to get Lee and myself moving forward."

"I'll take the boys," Cal said, "glad to have a specific task I can tackle." Cal's grief went deep, but it would have to wait. "And there is enough food in the house to feed an army. Everybody brought food. That's one less thing to worry about. We'll pitch in Birchard. Don't give it another thought," said Cal.

Lee stood, hollow-eyed. He walked over to the dogwood and sagged against it. Birchard softly told Cal, "Lee helped his father plant each tree."

Cal made a movement to go to Lee, but Birchard stopped her. "Let him be, Cal. He will find his own peace."

At that moment, Lee took off running across the ridge toward a thicket of tall pines. Birchard called the boys over and softly talked to them. "You're going to go with Cal for a while. Be good." Their high, innocent voices soothed his sore spirit. Cal left with the children in tow. Birchard spoke with a few friends. The weather looked worse with every passing minute. People were leaving in earnest now.

With all the turmoil in his heart, the prospect of bad weather didn't bother Birchard. He made his way toward a special place by the river where he and Mickey had often visited for some quiet time. He needed her just then. Somehow, he knew he would meet up with Sparsity along the way. Sparsity and Birchard often sought out the same spot when they needed solitude. The two entered the oat field. Only the movement of the top of the oats marked Birchard's passage. Sparsity's blondness blended into the field as they headed towards the river trail.

Lee ran until he could run no more. Once in the pines, he climbed the tallest one, desperate to flee from his overwhelming anguish. When he had almost reached the top, a bolt of lightning cracked the sky open. He held on. Quickly the sudden storm grew fierce. The pine swayed with the fuming upheaval in the sky.

His father had always told him that human beings have a link with all nature that is far beyond understanding. We can grasp the five senses, but there may be a sixth sense we are not quite getting. Lee was sure he was right, and Sparsity and Doc Francis also felt the same. Lee let his mind recall the many times that he and his father would climb the tall pines just before a storm, then tie themselves securely to the trunk. The first time, Mr. Ward had shouted over to him, "Close your eyes, my son. Take in the pulse of the tree. Now open your eyes and delight in the joy of living!" The experience had always thrilled and illuminated him. He'd savored the fear that made his skin prickle, the crash of lightning that he could feel through the tree and from the air, and the stinging pelt of driving rain like bullets on his skin.

The first time that a windy rainstorm caught him and his father high in a pine, Lee had been almost paralyzed with fear. As the storm, the wind, and the rain had loosed itself, his fear had been suspended by pure, wild exhilaration. This was what he now sought—to be carried beyond himself.

When the storm unleashed its full, raging power, he heard his father's voice. "Lee, my son, you will live out your dreams. Now go. Be safe. I will forever be in the air you breathe and in the earth that you walk on. My love and blessings are upon you."

Lee let the wind take his despair and scatter it into the storm. The tree violently rocked him to and fro. He thought of his sister Monterey and how she had held him as a child and rocked him to ease his distress in their highly charged house. The same sense of peace and protection pervaded his spirit. He felt perfectly safe, though lightning and thunder crashed around him. There was no safety rope securing him to the tree this time. Though his father was no longer there… 'Oh, yes he is,' Lee thought. 'He will always be with me.'

Lee rode out the storm until it was fully spent. The tree grew still as the driving rain gentled. The message had been received. All was right. Drenched to the skin and aching now from head to toe, Lee descended the tree. He walked about and gazed at the vastness in the perfect grandness of the oat and hay fields with the river winding through it all. The goats, cattle, and horses had left their usual grazing places, but he visualized them clearly. The newly washed landscape looked like a Vermeer painting with stark fluffs of white clouds starting to appear against the edges of the dark thicket.

Once more he took off at a run. He bolted over the wet grass to the river, then solemnly strode onto the swift-running water, giving himself a baptism of sorts, a rite of passage. Lee knew even at his young age that he was ready for his approaching manhood with its great responsibility of being the caretaker of Protected Earth and taking a leadership role in the town of Darnell. His age was irrelevant to his duties and trustworthy care for Protected Earth and the town of Darnell. Yes, the job may be huge, but his father felt he was ready to take it all on.

Within a few weeks, a smaller, simpler version of the log cabin library was built for visitation beside the little graveyard on the ridge. Large, amber-colored cushions on the floor were reminiscent of Mr. Ward's practice of meditating, inviting any visitor to relax. Lanterns hung off hooks on the porch, ready to be lit. Stained-glass windows which had long been designed by Mr. Ward and built by Birchard that now stood in his studio, were to be installed in the meditating cabin. The windows will illuminate the serene cabin from all sides.

There had been no shortage of volunteers for labor or materials in building and furnishing the cabin. The men of Darnell honored Mr. Ward in the way they knew best.

Lee had made a message box during Mr. Ward's illness. Visitors could leave notes when they dropped by during times that Mr. Ward was resting or too ill to receive well-wishers. The box had sat on the table beside the farmhouse door. Lee now moved the message box to the meditating cabin, as they called it, so that anyone who wished to leave a message could do so.

The women and children of Darnell contributed the planting of flowers from their own gardens. The flowers, the surrounding fields, and soft lowing of distant cattle made the cabin next to the graveyard of Protected Earth a place of peace.

Lee missed his father with an ache that he felt would never go away. He welcomed the friendship that Doc Francis freely offered. Lee would always have a special bond with Birchard, but Birchard had increasingly withdrawn since Mickey's death and even more so after the passing of Mr. Ward. Lee felt isolated. But he had a renewed hope that his sister Monterey had been found. And any day he may receive the joyous news. She would be contacting him. Thanks to Mr. Ward's steadfastness in the pursuit of his sisters.

Today he had a need to talk. So, he paid a call to his good friend Doc Francis. He sat in Doc Francis' waiting room, shoulder to shoulder with neighbors needing Doc's care. He felt honored to have such a huge responsibility to carry on his father's dreams, though frankly terrified at the thought of trying to fill his father's shoes.

"How are you doing, Lee?" asked the farmer seated next to him. The man's boots smelled of manure. He held a pale sick child in his arms. Lee appreciated the fact that, even with his own child sick, the neighbor expressed concern.

Lee mumbled a reply, trying to choke back the emotion rising in his throat. The man nodded with understanding. "If you need anything, just let me know. I'll be there." Lee knew his neighbor spoke the truth. Through the years, he'd seen the man do just that.

The door to the examining room opened. Doc looked around the room. "Give me a few minutes with Lee, folks. I'll be right with you." The people seated on the benches mumbled their assent.

The farmer said, "It's okay. My child is sleeping soundly, we can wait, no problem."

The doc walked over and put his hand on the child's forehead. "No fever. Be with you shortly."

"Thanks, Doc."

Lee glanced around and saw a variety of needs. He said, "Thanks. I won't be long." Doc Francis put a protective arm around Lee's shoulder and drew him into the examining room. Lee sat in the chair in front of Doc's desk. Doc Francis pulled his desk chair around to where Lee sat, grabbed the arm of Lee's chair, and pulled the chair around to face his. He sat knee to knee with Lee.

Doc Francis spoke. "Lee, your father had total faith in you and Birchard to manage your lives, care for the land, and contribute to the town. That's why he pushed you so hard, look at what he accomplished for the people of Darnell. You will carry on his good works." The pervasive smell of disinfectant filled Lee's nose. Light-headed for a moment, he thought he would pass out in the chair.

Doc Francis rose and walked to a cabinet behind the desk. He took out a bottle of blackberry Brandy and poured a small glass for Lee. Doc held out the glass to Lee, "Compliments of the Browns, after I delivered their fourth baby. Mighty good stuff. Drink this right now. Doctor's orders." Lee welcomed the burn that spread down his throat. Relieved for a chance to express his fear that was looming.

He looked around the room of Doc Francis's office. Fresh flowers sat in a large blue vase, a small, short brown vase held wildflowers. Old prints of bees, butterflies, and insects adorned the walls. A beautiful oriental rug filled the room. Candles of various sizes flickered in a silver tray. Lee thought Doc was a great, kind, well-informed doctor—who knows how to live his life.

Lee spoke, "I understand why my father aggressively apprenticed me into many different roles. Because of father, I've learned surveying, mapmaking, and road building. I know how to cultivate and manage the lands and waterways that run through the property. He taught me how to make the land productive while maintaining its integrity and beauty."

"Father often said, 'Son, it's extremely important that you build a well-rounded life. Your knowledge must come not only from books, but also from hands on, until it becomes a part of you. Push your boundaries, then give to others the knowledge and abilities that you have gained. The good book tells us that we are our brother's keeper. We shall also include our sisters. You will gain the respect of others, but more importantly, of yourself. You will be able to meet these hard-working people on the road and look them in the eye. Everyone must play his part in this life.'"

Lee broke down and sobbed. He was poised on the brink of manhood, but in many ways, still a child. The present circumstances in his life seemed to propel him headlong into full manhood and a leadership role. It had come so natural to his father, taking the reins, making things happen, and fixing problems, making things better. He wished to do the same.

Lee felt utterly overwhelmed.

Doc Francis understood. "Lee, I'm not much of a role model. I drink too much, have too much sex—maybe pushed my advantage with lonely widows—but I carry no meanness in me. I am here because your father reached out to me. Because of him, Darnell is my home. Now, I want nothing more than to live and die here. Because of your father, I found a life of incredible contentment. I am deeply grateful."

"After all this time, you have come to know me and all my eccentricities. I am a paradox even to myself. I treat patients all week, then I take my field glasses and magnifying glass and head to the field and forest to seek out tiny creatures to study and wait impatiently for the first yellow jonquil to appear in spring."

"You asked me recently did I think you had missed a lot by not going away to college. I honestly don't see how you could possibly get a better education sitting in a classroom than staying here in this miraculous place. Look around you! Take it from someone who spent many long years in classrooms. You can learn more here than you ever could by leaving. Extraordinary people surround you here, ready to help you. You've only to ask. Your father saw that you had the best of books, tutors if needed."

Lee had now taken control of himself and said, "I believe I will have another of Mr. Brown's BlackBerry Brandy." Doc smiled, poured the Brandy, then continued, "My advice is to decide what you want from this life, then reach out to lots of folks that can help you get there. All of us want to support you. Don't model yourself after me. A much better paradigm for you would be to look back on all your own father taught you. Understand me, though. Nobody expects you to step into his role. They desire for you to come into your own and be the man that your father taught you to be by example. You don't have to do everything by yourself, Lee."

Lee had heard it all. Each word had been a lifeline to him. Doc Francis was a godsend. Lee now knew he could face whatever came. His father, instead of being someone impossible to emulate, became instead a powerful ally. Lee knew how blessed he was to have had such a father. "And even somewhere in my blood, there must have been some good that came from Mr. Darnell."

He shook Doc Francis' hand, thanked him, and left the examining room with his head held high.

He gave a nod to his neighbors seated in Doc Francis's office hallway. They smiled and gave him a nod back of okay. Lee was ready to become a man and take all responsibility of what was needed of him.

CHAPTER 15

Big Sister: Monterey

Cal went about sorting the mail, in between her many chores at the bustling hub. She caught an interesting return address on a letter to Lee. It was from a strange detective agency. Her heart did a little flutter, maybe it might be great news. Maybe that detective has found the location of Lee's sisters. She quickly asked a regular customer to watch the Hub until she returns. "I must take this mail to Lee Darnell." Cal left and hitched up the buggy and off she went, urging the horse along.

She hadn't visited in a while on Protected Earth. Not that Cal needed a reason. She knew there existed an open invitation. Besides, Lee had repeatedly tried to talk her into moving onto Protected Earth. Ward's spirit still penetrated every inch of the land. No. She was no longer that strong. It all hit her heart heavy, his voice ringing out through the fields, the smell of the lands, up all her senses, she wanted to run away and head back to her cabin and drink until she felt numb.

It was late in the afternoon when Cal arrived. Lee was seated on the porch, boots off, bare feet and legs stretched out. Even in such a relaxing looking position, Cal thought Lee has had an old soul from early childhood. Chase and Talker and the cats were all beside him. Rest for all at the end of the day. When Cal's buggy rolled up, Lee's face changed to a huge welcoming smile for one of his favorite people. He walked beside her buggy and reached for her long skinny calloused hand. He then tied her horse to the rail. Lee thought isn't it odd—that love brings such joy, then can drain a person's spirit. Lee felt his father would not want Cal to be so unhappy. The main thing Mr. Ward adored about Cal was her passion for life each day, and how she took it on by herself.

Lee said, "Great to see you, Cal, we have missed you. Come, my friend, and sit. Could we be so blessed that you will stay for supper."

"Sorry Lee, I have to get back and close the restaurant. This letter came for you. It's from a detective agency in Atlanta. I must admit my fingers were burning to open it. Sure hope it's good news. My instinctive feeling says it is good."

Cal turned to see Sparsity as she walked up and spoke, "How have you been, Cal? May I get you and Lee a drink?"

"All's fine, Sparsity. I believe I will have that drink."

Lee noticed how much Cal had aged, her hands trembled, and she was skinny as a pole bean. Cal handed Lee his mail; the letter from the detective was on top. Sparsity was quick as a bee and placed a tray of drinks with a full decanter on the round wicker table. "Would you care for some cheese and rolls. You look like you could use a good dinner," Sparsity asked, shaking her head.

Lee spoke, "What about bringing Cal a tray with some goodies on it." Cal didn't object. She picked up her glass, brushed it against Lee's, and said, "May this be news you have waited for over a long time."

Each emptied their glass. Lee reached and poured another round. "Now let's end this anticipation." Lee gently opened the letter, even though his excitement was great, he read in silence. Tears rolled down his face, then came a heartbreaking cry. "All these years, Cal! Monterey, my big sister, will arrive tomorrow on the noon train."

Cal stood, put her hand on his strong, plaid flannelled covered shoulder, "I am so happy for you, does the letter state where she has been?"

"Sit, Cal, let me read this to you. Sis writes, we will sit and talk and talk some more." Lee spoke, in a breaking voice. "I was in Atlanta so many times. I may have walked right by where she was working or living."

"You can't think about that. She will be here soon. That is what's important. Lee, my love is with you." The two friends stood. Cal gave him a hug—then left. As she left, she thought if only Mr. Ward could see this reunion. But it wasn't to be. She reached under the seat of the buggy for her flask.

Lee went into the kitchen and put on a pot of coffee. Sparsity was preparing a tray.

She said, "Cal left?"

"She did. It's very difficult for her to be here," said Lee. "I understand her pain. It's hard but life goes on. What choice do we have?"

Sparsity said, "I understand. She brought great news."

"Sparsity, my big sister, Monterey, will be here tomorrow. Right here in Darnell. Often, I thought this day would never come. But here it is."

Sparsity took over the coffee and covered the tray she had prepared.

Birchard tapped the door with his cane. No answer came through the screen door. He decided not to sit. His painful joints tightened even more when he sat. He felt at home just to walk in. He started, calling out to Lee or Sparsity.

Lee was seated in the large sunny kitchen. Sparsity poured Lee's special coffee. Very black and hot, hot, two tablespoons of condensed milk, and vanilla. Lee lifted himself up straight and said, "Oh! Sorry pal! Didn't hear you come in. Just rehashing all the years. Thinking about my sisters. How are you feeling? Sorry I didn't stop by. Sparsity said she would take care of you."

"I passed Cal on my way in, great news your older sister Monterey has been found. What a great day? Any idea that she may know where Azzie is. I pray for Azzie."

"Birchard, my friend. Sure wish father was here to enjoy this happiness. He wanted to find all my sisters for me. Enough about my good news. I have been concerned about your health. Doc Francis says he needs you to stop by his office."

"Lee, you just get that room ready for your sister. Right now, your sister is the most important person on our list. I am so excited for you. I am fine. Don't worry." Birchard waved his hand, as if to brush away the worries of Lee.

"Sparsity came with her black bag of magic and got my legs moving once more. She had me wrapped up like a mummy. I have never regretted letting Sparsity stay in our wagon. She has been a healer for so many bodies and souls. She says she plans to live forever. She arrived a mysterious child, with loads of cleverness wrapped in a great compassion for all soul's… animal, man, trees, and plants."

Sparsity said, "Birchard, may I prepare a coffee for you?"

"No, thank you. Had a few cups today."

"Come, pal. We have much to talk about. Monterey will arrive on the noon train. I want you to take the ride with me," said Lee.

"No, Lee. This is your day. Not only is it your birthday, and what a present! Your sister. I believe one day we will also be blessed with Azzie's return."

"It will be nice to have you with me."

"Ok, I am in."

"Sparsity is cooking up a big dinner tonight. We will expect you and the twins."

The good friends shook hands. Birchard said, "We'll be here. Pick me up at Sparsity's. I need to change clothes; want to look sharp for Monterey."

Lee watched his dear Birchard limp away. Lee's heart choked up. It was painful to see Birchard pushing himself through each small step. Lee didn't want to even put a thought in his head of Birchard leaving this earth. Birchard, from the start, had supported him every step of his journey.

Birchard looked over at Lee, the boy he had rescued had stepped up at such a young age to be a man; a man with huge responsibility for the people who lived and worked on Protected Earth. But Lee had always stepped up. If he made mistakes, he took credit for those and tried to right them.

Lee spoke, "Birchard, my friend, I never tire of this ride into Darnell."

* * *

As Monterey's train moved across the countryside, her many thoughts were interrupted by the conductor informing the passengers what the next stop would be.

"Can one even imagine? I am headed for a town named after Little D," Monterey said out loud. Rain was coming down hard and blurred her view as she strained to see the countryside. She was wanting to see the town of Darnell, to plant every detail in her memory. "Nothing can dim this day," she said aloud, with no care what the people around her thought.

She thought about Azzie and Dessie and what they might be doing at this very moment. "If I could holler loud enough, to reach across the States, wherever they may reside and share this joy with them."

She had hired a detective to search for them, to no avail. But she knew she would never give up hope, just as Little D didn't. He found her through a lovely twist of fate. After the detective had died, his son had taken over his practice and found Lee's records. He took the search up.

Monterey opened her black clutch bag and took out the worn picture she held dear of her two sisters holding Little D. The children had held a special bond until their sinister father separated them, robbing the siblings of all these lost years. The silver frame was now tarnished but treasured. Many a night, she had held it close to her heart.

Monterey spoke, "Well, a town in the honor of Darnell. Seeing his name on the town rail station. Her first thought was—our father did make it after all, to be held in esteem. A town named Darnell. There he was Little D, all grown up. A man."

The years Lee Darnell had waited for words from his sister Monterey, and now they were coming to a close. Chase and Talker were barking at the train that just rolled in. "Hush," Lee said as he petted each blue tic on their quivering bodies. Lee thought how animals seem to always anticipate a happening.

The death of her husband and his family in a horrific fire left her alone. When his will was read, he left all his holdings to Monterey. The lawyer found a letter in his papers that revealed the whereabout of a detective that wrote he had found her brother, and an address. Her husband never told her about the letter.

She quickly wrote a letter to the detective. No response came. The letter came back stating no address existed.

So, she proceeded to go on with her life, having taken courses through the mail to be a teacher. She applied to a women's school in Atlanta and was accepted. Thanking her kind neighbors for taking her in after the disastrous fire, and the neighbor lady for a shopping spree for a new wardrobe to wear for her new job in Atlanta.

The train snorted out its last growl and came to a stop. The passengers were stirring about inside, ready to embark.

A uniformed steward appeared and unfolded the steps. Lee walked in closer. Dressed all in black with a red rose at the neckline, her black hair pulled back tightly into a braided bun at the nape of her neck, dark clear eyes piercing as Lee remembered. A soft full mouth broke into a wide smile. Lee hollered, "Big sis come, did you have a comfortable trip?"

She dropped two canvas bags, stuck out her arms, Lee reached out and brother and sister embraced. Monterey pulled away and spoke, as she touched her brothers face.

"Little D, how handsome and a grand looking man you have become."

Directing Monterey by her elbow, he asked, "Do you have any more luggage?"

"Only what I am carrying. It feels good to leave the old things behind me. To answer your earlier question, the train ride was a delight. A cattleman and his new younger mail order bride kept me entertained. They were graciously interested in my story and gave me their address." What Monterey didn't disclose was there was another young woman on the train that had been a student at the Atlanta Girls Academy where Monterey was a teacher. She thought she would check out Lee's status first to see if the woman was of interest.

Two blue tic hounds were seated in the back of the buggy. They bounded over the side upon seeing Lee.

"These wonderful creatures are Chase and Talker," said Lee as he watched his big sis.

Monterey bent down into a squatted position and took their faces in her hands. "I know we will be the best of pals."

Birchard had been standing off to the side, until Lee called out to him. "Birchard, come meet my big sister."

Lee was overcome with emotion, he sat on the stations waiting bench, his body shook, Monterey kept her hand on his shoulder.

She stuck out her hand to Birchard. "I know you have been a dear friend. I don't need words, I see all in your face, dear Birchard. We have so many stories to share."

"What a glorious day this is, Miss Monterey?"

The sky had turned dark, and lightning ran across the sky. The sky burst open, and rain came with a fury. The three moved back under the train station shelter.

Monterey said, "Little D, remember how terrified you were of rainstorms as a child?"

"Yes! I would look for a hiding place. Then one of my sisters would find me and hold me close until the weather cleared. And here you are, Sis, once more. I must say, I still don't care for rain and lightning storms."

Lee sat her baggage behind the seat. "Shall I leave the carriage top up?" He asked as he touched her arm to assist her step up.

"Since the rain seems to have taken a pause, let's roll the top back and enjoy the air. And your fancy rig. How beautiful it will be in the mist. Darnell looks charming."

Monterey paused, "I want to drink in the atmosphere, the ducks in the stream, the soft buzz of the people. I'm loving each moment. Your beard is admirable." She reached down to pick up a tiny bluebird's feather. Reaching down, she pulled her black skirt up, using her petticoat, she gently pressed the feather between the fabric until it was dry. Then said, "Miss blue bird lost a piece of her clothing." Monterey ran her finger along the vein of the feather and rubbed it across her cheek.

"Lee, are you still an ardent devotee of birds, as I have remained?"

Lee said, "Big Sis, you still have an impulsive mind that jumps and turns. How hungry my soul has been for my family. Yes. I have catalogued and drawn many breeds. It's extremely hard to choose a favorite. They are all so beautiful and interesting."

"I am most anxious to share them with you. I often take my earlier tablets out to read and view. It lets me live that day over. I have sat for hours slowly getting close to experience the birds. Now when a bird lights in my view, I don't need to be up close. I know how the wind ruffles its feathers. I understand its calls in distress or when it's happy when a lady bird has found just the right spot for her nest."

Monterey smiled and placed the small feather into her braid. "Lee, most of my students call me Crow because of my black eyes, hair, and clothes. I like it. Please call me Crow."

Crow sat beside her brother, the two displayed a bond of love that years were not able to rob.

Lee snapped the reins and said, "Maude, take us to Protected Earth.

Crow has come home." He never tired of the sound of the hoofs on the stone bridge.

The ride home was of a relaxed, satisfied nature. Monterey was feeling very big sisterly, "Are you happy with your life, Lee?"

"I can assure you, I am. Father could not have given me a better gift than leaving me at the circus. The huge pain of being separated from my sisters could have ruined my life. Monterey, the man that took sister Azzie and me in became my father. You will learn all about him. He is the reason for the growth of this lovely town, along with its many great citizens."

"Did he legally adopt you and Azzie?"

"He did me, Azzie didn't want it. She was an amazing star, but she became more and more confused in her head. She was loved and admired by so many."

Monterey was pleased greatly with all her eyes landed upon; the clean flowing creeks, pine forest, hundred-year-old oaks, magnolia trees that touched the ground with their evergreen waxy leaves, and each thing that jumped into her view, including the two blue tick hounds that kept pushing her with their paws.

Birchard answered and said, "I will look forward to a great friendship with you, Miss Crow."

"And Birchard, you have been with Lee from his start at the circus."

As the buggy approached the main house, Crow asked her brother to stop. "How wonderful, we know a God is present. Let me take it all in."

Crow adjusted well to her brother's life and quickly found her position of honor. She became a dear part of the Protected Earth family. Each evening found Lee and Crow seated on the porch with much talk and a little too much sweet tea topped off with local moonshine. Cal stopped by more often to hear Crow's stories of her lost years without her family.

Sparsity was overjoyed to see the happiness in Lee's face since

Crow had joined the family. Sparsity could now spend more time at her own cottage and herb garden.

Crow stated, "I can easily take care of the duties of the house." But she gave Sparsity assurances of how important Sparsity was to Lee and the entire farm.

Lee said, "Yes, Crow, there's hardly a citizen in this town that hasn't called on Sparsity with their health issues and a few she has brought back from death's door."

Sparsity swished around. Her colorful layers of skirts sang a song with each of her movements. "Not so much now, since the good doctor has come to Darnell."

"Lee, Folly hasn't been up to par as of late. Poor little darling, maybe Dr. Francis should check on him. Each time I mention the doctor, Folly starts to panic. But I'm concerned."

"Thanks, Sparsity, Crow and I will stop by tomorrow. I will be showing Crow the property and we will check on him and have Dr. Francis meet us there."

Crow was delighted with the dapper, intelligent, caring Doc Francis. "The town is blessed to have such a man as the good Doctor," Crow would repeat often.

"Folly is an innocent soul, a child of the stars to be protected and cared for," Monterey said to Lee after meeting Folly and hearing his story.

The farmhouse overflowed with Crow's efficacious ways. She was precise and stern on all she undertook. The linens shined fresh after being hung on the clothesline and ironed to perfection. Canning preserves, berries, and vegetable for the winter months, fireplaces filled with vases of flowers in spring, music flowed out from the new crank Victrola.

Lee would do his special jig, somewhere between the Irish and a southern clog dance. It was a time of joyful feelings.

But there was no children's laughter or Lee getting all dressed up because he was excited about a woman. Plenty of neighbors stopped by with extra kills of rabbits, cleaned and ready for stew or dumplings, or just to have Lee's advice on a matter. But this home cried out for more life. Crow wasn't ready to sit back and not make sure Lee carried on his bloodline. Crow got out her pen and ink and paper and wrote a letter to the beautiful young artist maverick woman whom she had known from the girls' school where she had been a much loved teacher.

After graduation, the young woman had applied for the art teacher's position. The school found her to be a little showy in appearance and manner. But Crow found her to be of interest and sought to help her find a job. Crow believed it was more than just a chance occurrence that the girl was on the same train. It was fate.

Her name was Garrison Anne Polly. Crow had composed a letter for her to a more liberal girl's school in Savannah. Garrison, after once more seeing Crow on the train, gave Crow an address where she received mail. She told Crow she had been sick and placed in a sanatorium for a while. But she was ready for travel and new adventures.

"Please write me for any reason. I am very grateful for your kindness," wrote the uncommon beauty.

Crow said to herself Garrison just might spice things up a bit with a visit to Protected Earth. Crow knew her brother was mighty handsome, and believed he fulfilled his desires by visiting the ladies of the night in Atlanta and other out of town trips when he purchased cattle, farm equipment, and the many supplies that a farm required. Why had he never been in love—or married? She aimed to find out. The brother and sister talked and just let the words flow and their thoughts jump around.

"I often think about what Mr. Ward said, 'Little D and Azzie as sad and unhappy as your father's deeds were, I do hope that some day you both will see the deed was a fortunate abandonment.'"

Crow spoke, "Lee when my husband died, I felt sorrow, but I must say, God forgive me, there was a relief from the drudgery of household duties, the care of him almost around the clock, and his children. Now being unified once more with you, the phenomenal world you have created on Protected Earth. All 5'10" of me sings with joy each day. Just living in a household of consideration and laughter, I can't wait to open my eyes each morning. By the way, where are Chase and Talker today? They didn't greet me this morning. I miss those two when they are not close by."

"I understand. I like them nearby. I believe Sparsity has them. She was checking out herbs by the river. She likes for them to accompany her. It can get risky on those soft banks. Sparsity has had a horror of running into quicksand. No one has ever come across any, but she says it's there somewhere, and most likely it is—if Sparsity believes it." Crow got up and poured another drink.

"Anyway, let's talk about why you have never taken a wife." They both took a few more sips of their drinks.

Lee said, "Now Crow, you think these blackberry wonders are going to loosen my tongue to reveal my inner secrets."

Crow looked at her beloved brother as he uncrossed his bare feet, finished his drink, and gave a roaring laugh. Crow let the soft breeze blowing through the screens wash over her. She thought how inconceivable all the magic the earth is. She put her attention back to Lee.

"Crow, the years have passed like a whirlwind since Mr. Ward died. I only wish you could have known him. I was young. Even though he did his best to teach me all that he believed I needed to manage this land and give back to the town and live a respected life, I would sit here on this porch each night and ask myself; can I really meet this challenge? But with my cherished friend, and second father Birchard, we did it and well. Birchard and I had years of Mr. Ward's impeccability when looking for an answer to a problem. He would say, 'Lee, leave no stone unturned, keep an open mind' and that's what I have lived my life by."

"Lee, don't dodge my question, why have you not married? You're such an imposing figure. I must tell you, I have been sending my energies out for you a woman." Crow was right. Years of hard labor had only favored Lee. His strong muscular body that moved as if he was ready to pounce. The ladies of the town had not given up, he was much sought after. But no one turned on his inner generator.

"It has not been a goal for me—women are amazing—but, I have not been lonely for a wife."

"Are you sorry that you have never married or had children?" asked Crow. The brother and sister continued their talk, the woodland sounds filled the air. It was a peaceful scene of contentment as the two drank and opened their hearts.

"No! I do not feel deprived in any part of my life. I have shared my bed with many, but I've never been in love, even for a night. Crow, I feel I have many years left." Lee seldom offered up explanations, especially about his personal life. But he felt this was Monterey asking.

"Just because I give my time, however limited, to a woman, doesn't mean I have to possess her in marriage."

"Well! Well!" said Crow, "We will see. My intuition tells me someone special is on the horizon."

"Sis, now what have you been up to? You are sounding like Birchard. He keeps pushing me to settle in with a wife. I don't believe it's in my future to marry. I somehow just know that for certain."

Birchard rode up on his special bike. Lee noticed each day the decline in Birchard's health. He moved slower because of his painful joints now ridden with arthritis. "Hi, you two! Feeling those spirits, I see? Lee, I need to pick up some supplies in town, could use some company today. Can you take a ride with me?"

"Sure!" Lee had pretty much decided not to go back to the fields today. "Crow and I did a wonderful job on this pitcher of her special drinks. I'll go hitch up the wagon. Meet you in the barn!"

Crow spoke up. "Think I will come along, mind a third party?"

"Of course not, Miss Crow! Your company is a pleasant welcome," Birchard said.

Lee and Crow often took afternoon breaks from life's responsibilities and used the time for some front porch talks catching up on all the years they missed. As Lee would say, "What's a better pleasure and more of a treat for the soul than just sitting and talking." Today Lee mixed up their special drink, blackberry juice, moonshine, and crème. Lee removed his shoes, turned his rocker toward the sun where Crow sat, and said, "Here's to the lifting and soothing of our spirits."

The brother and sister clinked glasses, drank and talk began. First, about the enjoyment of the simple things; a breeze, some cluster of soft clouds hanging in the sky, the different sounds each heard, as they closed their eyes for a few minutes, and then on with talk.

Crow was quick to say, "Lee, the years apart, we were both living a full life, but always with the part of life that was removed by our father. It's a mystery as to where we would have ended up if father had kept us."

Birchard's spirits were also lifted since Crow moved in, he would often fall asleep in the porch swing, Crow would tuck a cover over him, and he would sleep through the night.

Crow changed her mind about going into town and decided she would enjoy the lovely day doing exactly as she wished.

Crow liked to sit in the newest addition to the porch, her bright red swing Birchard had gifted to her, sat waiting with a cozy quilt to cover one's legs on a chilly day. Sparsity dropped by with an armload of wild and domestic flowers. She refreshed not only the large vase that greeted each one in the main hall entrance but also throughout the happy house. Sparsity also hung fresh pine branches and placed baskets of pinecones mixed with a medley of dried herbs and unknown things she suspected to be of the mysticism nature. This morning, she was carrying two carpet bags.

Crow said as Sparsity walked out onto the porch, "Dear, when I see you, I feel like a colorful exotic bird has landed on our porch."

Sparsity laughed a small, silly laugh.

After arranging all the flowers throughout the house, Sparsity started opening the bags she had sat on the porch. She removed colorful spools of cotton threads. "Today, I teach Crow to crochet." Crow took to it quickly. She began making bedspreads, shawls, and skirts. Sparsity loved the stylish crocheted garments. She wore the skirts over purple and red taffeta. The beds throughout the house now wore the exquisite spreads.

Birchard and Crow formed a special friendship. Birchard called out to Crow. "Here my friend, the kitchen," Crow answered. Crow emerged in her usual black. Her apron carried an array of indications of delicious food being cooked.

On Protected Earth, it was a rarity if the day was bland. Something always turned up to either touch one's heart or give your face a large smile of delight.

Birchard said, "Miss Crow, I have those bluebird houses completed as you requested, seventy-five for future homes. Also, I wanted to check with you and Lee. Sparsity and I are cooking catfish by the pond tonight. Like to join us." Birchard now used two canes for support and stepped onto the two-tier steps Lee had made for him. He had developed a nervous habit of swinging his legs back and forth when seated. When Crow asked Birchard about this habit he said, "Sparsity says I should keep my legs moving, for circulation. Otherwise, they may freeze up."

Crow was smiling at this glorious little man. He had a giant love for all around him, but sad lonely eyes. Crow said, "She does have some smart ideas, and they all seem to work."

Crow was cooking lemon pies and sending that heavenly smell throughout the house.

Birchard said, "Great looking pies. One sure would taste good along with those fried catfish."

Crow smiled, "The pond it is. We will be there along with the pie. Now, how about a glass of Lee's blackberry wine? We can check on Lee. He is busy chiseling away on a marble statue."

Birchard spoke, "Let's take a look."

"Lee says when completed, it will grace a spot at the top of pine ridge. It's a statue fit for a Paris gallery."

Crow spoke, "Lee gets his talent from our mother."

Birchard said, "Our dear Azzie. Oh, how I still wonder about her. What a daredevil. You should have seen her, Crow. How beautiful she was." Birchard choked up and wiped his tear-stained face. "Got so silly."

"It tugs at all of our hearts, Birchard, the sadness of the passing of all these rare people. I never saw Azzie perform in the circus. But she gave outstanding performances on the street corners as a child. How utterly brave she was. She was beautiful then, Birchard. But there were signs of her illness. We ignored them, because of our love for her. I still believe she will come home one day."

Both let the subject of their dear Azzie rest for a moment.

Life on Protected Earth continued at a rapid pace. The bonds of its inhabitants ran deep. Birchard grew more ill. But he was still able to get around on a special three-wheel bike with some kind of mechanism of a motor that Lee had made for him. His son, Leeward, was capable of taking over all of Birchard's duties. But Leeward was showing concerned flaws in his character. Leeward was extremely clever, brilliant, he had built his own house, designed water systems for the Protected Earth lands, and had recently married a young, beautiful girl indigent from town. He was jealous of his new wife's every move. She was now with child.

Lee Darnell needed Leeward since Birchard had lost his health. Lee felt he could handle Leeward maybe now that he was married, and his new wife was expecting.

Lee continued in his search for Azzie and Dessie. Crow had

brought a few treasured pictures of the sisters when they were children. Lee and Crow often sat, and Crow would answer Lee's many questions about their childhood. Looking the pictures over with a magnifying glass, he would ask, "Where is this taken? What kind of day? Were we happy?" The questions went on and on. Crow answered as best she could recall. Crow still felt an overpowering feeling to protect her little brother's feelings. In one picture, Little Darnell appeared to be holding something in his hand. His three sisters were in the background, playing on a large boulder. Lee held the picture in his hands. Excited, he yelled, "Crow! Crow! Crow! I remember! My memory is coming back. I had blocked most of it out and could not recall all the years."

Crow had had a little too much blackberry wine. "Sorry Lee, my own sorrow was so great, I lost my soul. You gained Mr. Ward. But go on. What do you remember of that day?"

"I had found a small stone. You told me move it around in your hand. Close your eyes and feel it against your skin. Smell it. Look at its layers. Now that you know it, let's go up the hill and sit on the huge boulder. You will feel all the energy the little stone had to give. And I recall the warmth of the huge boulder on my body and the tiny stone in my hand."

They turned off the lanterns and walked into the house.

Lee said, "A heart full of red hearts." Lee had given one of his carved hearts to Crow and one to Birchard to show his care and love. They knew how he cherished each one. A gift from his beloved sister, Azzie.

CHAPTER 16

Folly

The years that followed Mickey's death were a painful push for Birchard to carry on. He moved through his days—sunup to sundown—and he carried his depression. Mr. Ward's concern for his partner and dear friend led him to keep someone by Birchard's side. He still took care of his responsibilities. Being a highly moral person, he would not slack off.

Sparsity suggested Mr. Ward build onto her cottage and let Birchard move in with her. This was done.

Sparsity felt a special duty towards Birchard. He had saved her from an almost sure street life, or worse. She would say, "Mr. Birchard could have just as easily left me in town. I will, until the day I die, be beholden to Birchard."

Her care of the boys had helped to relieve some of Birchard's troubles and the guilt he must have hidden in his heart because he felt so detached of emotion towards the boys.

As the boys grew, so did their relationships have a prolonged struggle. Leeward grew into a handsome, smart adult. But he never outwardly accepted that his parents were little people, and he carried the same anger toward Folly.

With Leeward now building a family, Folly also wished to be on his own. He voiced his desire to Sparsity, "Miss Sparsity, you know that little cabin in the wildflower field?"

"Yes! What about it, Folly?" asked Sparsity.

"I am a man now, like Leeward. Could I live there?"

"Folly, right now I need you here. Your father is not well. You are needed to be here while I am at the main house. Birchard can't be left alone."

"Okay, Miss Sparsity. Will you still ask Lee?"

"I will ask. Are you unhappy here with us?" asked Sparsity.

Folly sat in his chair and started swaying back and forth. Under any kind of stress, he would start. But he then stood and said to Sparsity, "Is my father going to die? I don't want him to die."

"I don't know, Folly. All I know is he has lost all interest in living."

"I will stay strong. Sorry. You will ask Lee?"

"Yes."

At one time, when Mr. Ward was alive, he found a doctor in Atlanta that he felt could help Folly. The doctor spent hours with Folly, talking and a-head-to-toe exam. The doctor felt Folly was doing quite well. He appeared healthy and lived in a well-off environment of love and care. The doctor said Folly did express that one day he would love to live on his own. "It's my opinion that he can someday, but only to be semi-independent. He mentioned he was afraid of horses but repeated often he was a fine worker and all the animals on Protected Earth he loved caring for, especially the goats." When the doctor had finished his opinion and evaluation of Folly, Birchard and Mr. Ward were satisfied.

Folly was jubilant at the thought of someday having his own place.

The detailed figures he carved of mostly circus performers could be attached to his special bike. As Folly peddled, the figures went through a series of performances, such as a figure of Szabo the strong man in one shouldered leotard and red and white tights, holding a lion over his head; the lion went up and down and Szabo lifted it. A sight to behold.

Folly became somewhat of a celebrity and loved the attention, especially when the children met him on the road into town. They would holler with delight at seeing all the circus acrobats. Wherever Folly biked, his circus came with him. He was happy. The bike gave him freedom to ride the trails and to go back and forth to town and he would have his lunch at his and Pal's, his dog who stayed right beside him, special spot on the creek.

Folly was still leery of all strangers, comfortable with the close family on Protected Earth, and maintained his special bond with Sparsity. He had relied on her from the time he was a small child.

Folly's morning routine was to feed Pal, eat his own breakfast, clean up, put on the appropriate clothes for whatever the weather called for. "Come, Pal, let's go check on those sweet goats." Folly loved the goats. He took his life on Protected Earth seriously. He would give instructions to Pal to check for sick or disabled goats, or ones that had drifted away from the flock and were now in a panic. As long as it wasn't sick or hurt, Folly would first console the goat's disturbed concern with soft talk. Folly and Pal managed to return it to the flock. Pal would round up the remaining goats, ready to head for home before the sun went down.

When one of the goats became sick, Folly was uncontrollably excited. Sparsity would say, "Folly, go get Leeward. He will know what the goat needs to get well."

Folly would shake his head, grind his hands together, "Oh my, no! Leeward doesn't love the goats enough. They need hugs and kisses. Leeward will just give them a shot and make them cry. I will take the goat to Doc Francis." He would attach his small wagon to his bike, wrap the goat in a blanket, and off he would go looking for Doc Francis.

Arriving at Doc's office in a frantic state, it was hard to understand him as he jabbered away. No matter how many times Lee told Folly, "Doc is not an animal doctor," it didn't matter. Folly felt only Doc Francis could cure the goat.

It was not easy to say no to the diminutive Folly. Unless Doc was in surgery or out in the far country taking care of someone, he would take care of Folly. Doc felt Folly was a person that had to be treated kindly in every phase of his days. His whole system could not tolerate anyone being displeased with him. Dixie, Doc's nurse, would calm Folly. "The Doc will be along shortly; he is just about five miles away at Mrs. Jones' house. She just had a baby. Where is Leeward? Can't he help?"

Folly would shake his head and start to walk away, then remember his manners, turn quickly, and say, "Miss Dixie," ever so softly, "thank you," lay the little goat on the waiting bench, and take off his leather bag on his back that Lee had made for him. He wanted to always be aware as to where that bag was and not out of his sight. He took out a tiny carved duck and handed it to Dixie.

"Oh my! Is this for me?" She asked while excessively blinking her eyes, a habit she had carried since a head accident. "How pretty. I will treasure this gift as I do the others." She placed it on her desk with numerous carvings Folly had gifted to her.

Folly would beg, "Please Miss Dixie, tell Doc Francis I have a sick goat and I need him. He must come. Gotta go." Pal was sitting close by panting away. "Pal, my dog, needs water. He ran all the way alongside my bike. Pal isn't so young anymore. Gap says we should get a pup to keep Pal company."

Folly picked up the goat. Pal followed. The three left, headed back toward Protected Earth.

Dixie thought, most likely he will meet up with Doc along the road.

He met up with Doc, Doc checked the goat out and figured the goat had most likely eaten too many wild onions. He poured some harmless herb tonic that Sparsity had conjured up down the goat. Folly was once more the happy little shepherd of Protected Earth.

Folly didn't like change of any kind. He had a special table at the Hub. When he would go in and someone was eating at that table, he would just stand there until Liza would explain to the customer who Folly was. Most everyone understood. Folly always had chicken and dumplings. Liza would suggest a new dish. "Oh no, I can't eat cow. I love them too much. Those mean chickens chase me and peck at me when Crow has to gather their eggs." Liza smiled. She would tell him to go home before dark.

Folly came in a few days without Pal. Liza asked about his dog. Folly said, "Pal's mad at me. He is at Lee's. I locked him out."

Liza said to Folly, "Well, I don't blame him. That wasn't nice. Pal's a good, loyal dog. Now, go before dark, pick-up Pal, and make up with him."

"I will. I am off." Liza saw him pedaling as fast as his small legs would work.

Lee had purchased some small pails for Folly. He loved picking berries, plums, and apples, even pretty rocks from his special spot on the creek. He would leave these gifts at people's doors. All knew it was from Folly.

On rare times, Lee would give Folly a ride on a horse. "Now, hold on tight, Folly. We will ride like the wind." He could feel his small arms tighten around him when he gave his horse a nudge to take off.

Folly didn't feel comfortable around his brother. "Leeward has a mean voice. Maybe he isn't very nice, but he is my brother."

Sparsity would often walk and find a good spot to sit and observe Folly with the goats. "There isn't a more precious sight on this earth than viewing the hills or valleys with the goats grazing, Pal alongside Folly. Sometimes the grass can cover Folly up to his neck, then out he walks with his shepherd's stick, a funny little cap on his head. The vibrations of his dear soul and his love of all things around him is a blessing to experience," she would say to Lee.

Once, when Pal showed up at Lee's door in the middle of the night, Sparsity happened to be at Lee's. After giving Pal water and a meal, the two set out to find Folly, Sparsity with her bag of herbs and riding behind Lee on his horse. Sparsity said, "I am mighty happy it's a clear night and I realize, Lee, you know every inch of this land. Can we take the trail without crossing Kudzu creek?"

Kudzu Creek was overgrown with Kudzu. Lee kept the Kudzu trimmed over the years so that now it created a tunnel one had to walk or ride through. It was quite dark and shadowy in the daytime but at night, even with a full moon, one couldn't find their way through. Not many things could spook Sparsity like Kudzu Creek. She avoided it when possible. Lee had sent one of the workers to get Doc Francis and meet them at Sparsity's.

The two's worry for Folly didn't let them enjoy the moon filled night or the lovely soft, wet air that caressed their faces. Pal ran ahead. They found him along a trail to Sparsity's. He was having a difficult time breathing. Sparsity asked Folly what happened. "I got very tired, and my legs just would not go. I sent Pal to get Lee."

Sparsity got to work giving quick directions to Lee. "Lee take him to my house and get a fire roaring. I will need hot water. Folly has a fever, and it sounds like his lung ailment is back. Doc Francis most likely will be there waiting for us. I am sure Runaway located him." Upon arrival at her house, Sparsity started treatment on Folly. Doc Francis had not arrived. She took out a muslin cloth and mustard for a chest patch. "I will sit out the night with Folly. You go and hurry Doc Francis along. Let him know this is serious."

Lee stopped outside and quickly loaded an armful of wood that he took into Sparsity. She was busy mixing herbs. Her cottage was consumed by a mist of herbs. The odors hit Lee's face; he cleared his lungs. "Hey, Sparsity. That's some powerful drugs. I'm off."

For years, Sparsity had believed she would cure Folly's lung ailments. His health had improved, and his joints seemed stronger, but at certain times, his lungs would still become congested.

Lee sent another worker into town to find Doc Francis and was going back to check on Folly. Crow saw a little worry on Lee's face for Folly. "Go, Lee, hitch up the buggy. I will ride with you. I wish to see Folly also."

Doc Francis met them on the wagon trail and checked on the sick Folly. Sparsity was correct on all accounts; the chest congestion was back. He left instructions and some medicine for Sparsity to give to Folly every three hours. Soon Folly was back to his happy self.

CHAPTER 17

Garrison Anne Polly, The Woman With All First Names

Crow had been working tirelessly to make contact with Garrison Anne Polly. She saw signs of loneliness in Lee that she felt only a woman could fulfill, otherwise his life was a full and happy one. After all, I am the older sister that looks after him. And then it happened, walking by the large ornate round table that sat in the foyer. She stopped and admired the outstanding vase of flowers and tree branches Sparsity had arranged and placed in the center of the table. The mail was placed in a wood tray Birchard had made. The edge of a pale pink envelope caught her eye. Garrison Anne Polly's name stood out on the back of the envelope, but no return address. The handwriting was unconventional, all the letters slanted to the right, with swirls of hearts and flowers attached to some letters. She stuck the letter in her apron pocket, giving it a pat of hope that Garrison was taking her up on the offer to come to Protected Earth. Crow felt she had covered all the bases to entice this wandering beautiful woman.

The coffee smelled good as Crow took a big whiff. She said with satisfaction, "That morning cup of coffee, my my so delicious. Black, very hot, just right." She positioned herself on the porch swing and opened the letter.

Dear Madame Crow,
I have received all of your correspondence. But have only now been in a state of mind and physically well enough to respond. Yes, I accept your offer to visit this place you paint such a beautiful and contented picture of.
I have made all of my travel arrangements, and I hope this date rings good to your ears. There is no promise from me how long I will stay, could be a day, months, or forever. Only my innermost self can dictate the time. You can expect me to arrive on the 9th of June, all should be in bloom.
P.S. Arriving with hope and anticipation of some adventure. I will bring all my painting supplies and work clothes, of which I hope to pay my way, as money is always for me, the means to have a few grand outfits, and if I need to get some place, oh and some fancy but comfortable boots, that suit the occasion.

Garrison Anne Polly
The woman with all first names.

Garrison was only sixteen when she graduated from the Atlanta Women's College. Any correspondence she said, "My dearest Madame Crow, never lose contact with me. I check in with a friend at this address. You have been such a great influence on my life," Garrison walked away with honors.

Crow's letter to Garrison was of great interest, Garrison was delighted that her teacher had not forgotten her. Crow wrote how she had connected with her brother. How peaceful her present life was, and the description of the place where she now lived, called Protected Earth. This information drew Garrison to want to know more. And the man that owned it all, Lee Darnell.

In Crow's letter she stated Garrison would have freedom without judgement, paint to your soul's contentment, horses available for long enchanting rides. There are a thousand acres to explore, and an extremely exciting man to get to know, my brother. Crow saw that Lee was not interested in local women. He needed some fire to shake him up. So, her mind had gone to Garrison.

Garrison Anne Polly was a woman interested in adventure. She could not be purchased. She brought her thoughts back to the present. At this moment all life seemed to stand frozen in time. As if God said, "Hush! People on the streets were stationary, their mouths open, hands in the air, dogs didn't bark, even the water in the creek stopped its flow," then God nodded, and life resumed around her. This was not unusual for Garrison to close her eyes and become totally from her present surroundings.

Garrison stepped onto the platform. All eyes were on this young woman, in red. Garrison saw Crow, black hair slicked back with two braids, rolled and pinned close to the nape of her neck. That had not changed. Her students had named her Madame Crow. There was no missing her past teacher. She was extremely interested to hear all about Crow's life. She had always found her to be a fascinating person. Madame Crow had never revealed her past life to her students. But she had asked Garrison to keep in touch. And by a turn of fate, she had once more met Madame Crow, on a train trip. Madame was going to meet a long-lost brother named Lee. And here she was, ready to start a new life. She assumed the tall handsome tan faced grey bearded man with her was Lee Darnell.

He looked older than she expected with premature grey hair and beard. But he was of interest and the town carried his name.

Garrison's thoughts were flying. Why am I here? I am not reliable under any circumstances. Why did Madame Crow believe Lee Darnell would be interested in me? My mind is in a constant state of pandemonium, yes people accept my crazy behavior, mainly because I am an artist, an exceptional one, and I have been blessed with beauty. But I do believe all actions have a consequence.

When Garrison had received Crow's letter, she was excited to hear from her favorite teacher. A friendship had formed between teacher and student. Crow knew Garrison had a great talent, a brilliant mind, but needed direction.

"There she is Lee, outstanding as ever." Crow called out, "Over here Garrison Anne Polly." Crow walked out in front of Lee to greet the young woman.

Lee Darnell would have noticed the young woman in red velvet. She stood apart from all the rest. Tall, posture beautiful.

Garrison greeted Crow with a kiss on each cheek. "My, my, Madame Crow, you are a pleasing sight. How I have missed our exploring conversations about almost everything."

"And you, dear. So delighted you came." Lee's attention was livened at the tall honeyed haired woman standing before him. Her hair was pulled softly back into a bun. No jewelry, her red dress sported three ruffles along the hemline. Her pattern lace-up boots sported a green leather tassel. Her large, brocaded travel bag was frayed. It had seen many an adventure. He was intrigued.

Crow spoke, "Garrison, my brother Lee."

"Yes, I gathered from your detailed description."

As Lee reached for her hand, she removed her brown fringed leather glove. Lee said, "Welcome to Darnell." Her thin long fingered hand had a strong grip and sent an excitement through his body, which he had not let himself indulge in for some time.

He reached and got her travel bag. "What's in the jar that you were drinking from?" she asked.

"Blackberry moonshine," answered Lee.

"Sounds like a lovely drink and I am curious, or have you cleared the bottom?"

Before Lee could answer, Garrison had moved on to other talk.

"How are we traveling?" she asked.

"Right this way. Do you have any more luggage? Your carriage awaits." He motioned with a wave of his hand.

"No, I travel light."

Crow stood close by, holding back a smile of gladness, things seemed to be going well.

Garrison spoke, with a voice that fulfilled Lee's expectations. Lee thought, I never realized how much I love a good, clear, well-spoken voice — direct, but soft, while eyes make contact.

They walked to the two-horse carriage. Crow sat in the rear and Lee and Garrison sat in the front. As they crossed over the stone bridge — Garrison said, "Is there another jar of that special blackberry shine?" Lee quickly handed a jar to Garrison, noticing her jar had emptied fast.

She unscrewed the top and turned toward Crow, "Madame Crow, will you celebrate with us."

Crow said, "My pleasure," and took the jar and downed a large swallow. The jar was passed back and forth among the three. All now had cheerfulness, excitement of being in this discovery of things to come. Maybe the blackberry moonshine assisted in the excitement of each. But the character was certainly interesting enough.

Garrison was full of questions. "Lee… Crow stated in her letter, Protected Earth might have an employment position for me. I sit fine in the saddle, good at most physical labor, I am an artist deserving of respect, paint in oils, and can also paint a whole farmhouse inside and out if needed. I need to earn some money and don't mind if I squeeze some new adventure into my life while I am doing it."

Lee replied, "That's quite a determined mouthful." He gave a rich welcoming laugh, "Yes, Garrison, we can always use another hand."

Crow was amused at the obvious intimacy between her brother and Garrison. She had been right. It would take an unusual woman to perk Lee's interest.

"You will make quite an imposing new hire," he said as he admired Garrison intently.

The ride home was of lively chatter. They finished two jars of blackberry moonshine. Enough to loosen any tongue.

Upon arrival, Crow saw Garrison was pleased. She was standing in the wagon, pointing to the blooming azalea bushes, a profusion of colors. But Crow also saw another side of the woman, it was an intense wild look in her eyes. Crow thought 'I will just make a mental note'.

Lee spoke, "Crow, Garrison can live in my studio, please have Sparsity prepare the day bed, and anything else Garrison feels she may need. She can use the entrance onto the rock patio and can come and go as she chooses for her privacy. I will drop you both off at the main house—Sparsity can show Garrison the main kitchen, and the studio, I will take care of rubbing the horses down, I will look forward to seeing all for breakfast." Crow looked surprised.

"Are you saying goodnight, Lee?" Garrison said as she reached for his arm.

"Yes, Sparsity will welcome you at dinner—and see that all of your needs are met. Sleep well, you are a delightful surprise." Lee took her hand as she stepped out of the carriage, his hand lingered, then he turned to assist his beloved sister Crow. He gave Crow a kiss on the cheek and said, "Thanks." And turned the carriage toward the barn.

Garrison felt it was a little off—that Lee was not too eager to spend the first night getting to know her better. But she felt such strong chemistry between them. Oh well.

Sparsity greeted Crow and Garrison in the foyer, introduced herself, always as with all things and all people with a questioning eye. Sparsity was extremely protective of each one and everything on Protected Earth.

Garrison was curious about Sparsity, as almost everyone was when they first met her. Taken back by her white skin, white lashes that adorned such pale blue eyes, color almost didn't exist, her colorful clothes, a sunflower color skirt, a purple blouse, her white gold flecked hair braided to the side.

After showing Garrison the studio and laying out her bed, Sparsity had not said a word of personal nature to Garrison. She finally spoke, "Supper will be on the table in one hour. Is that time alright with you?" Not receiving a fast answer, Sparsity turned, taffeta skirt swishing away and started for the door.

"All looks fine, Sparsity. Thanks for the lovely flowers. If you don't mind, ask Madame Crow if she would be insulted if I have my meal in this beautiful room tonight. Hopefully she will not think me rude."

Sparsity left the room to prepare Garrison's meal and relay Garrison's message to Crow.

Garrison showed up after her meal and found Crow on the porch. She asked if she could use some of Lee's oils and canvas. Crow said, "I am sure it will be fine, or else Lee would not have so generously given you his studio, knowing you are a painter"

Garrison asked, "Madame Crow, do you think Sparsity would sit for me? I would love to capture that interesting creature on canvas."

Crow replied, "That will be entirely up to Sparsity. I agree she is a sight and should be put on a forever canvas. I will ask. A thought, she is at her best in the fields or forest, gathering herbs, flowers, odd bits of nature. Not sure how she will feel, seeing herself on a canvas."

Garrison walked away with no response.

Sparsity gave Crow a questioning look as she came back into the room but had taken care to set up Garrison's easel and paints in the studio. She noticed the food had been picked at. Sparsity thought I will ask if she would like anything special.

Sparsity said, "Madame Crow, I believe I will stay here tonight, instead of going to my cottage. Will Mr. Lee be having a late dinner tonight?"

"Not sure, Sparsity you may as well clean up. I will retire early, and brother said he would see us at breakfast. That seems to be his plan."

Sparsity tidied up, then went on the porch and fell asleep in the swing. Her last thoughts before sleep was—odd Chase and Talker didn't come around and check out the stranger. Something feels off with the beautiful Garrison Lady.

Sparsity was restless and slept off and on throughout the night. She had dreams of Granny Dahlia and Granny always saying, "Listen to your gut." Lee and the dogs never showed up. But Lee was known to build a small campfire and sleep out with the dogs on a hillside or by the pond. He had built lean to's throughout the property and he could stay at the pond cabin. So, Sparsity wasn't worried. Sure that he was pondering the beauty of the houseguest. Lee was a thinker.

At daybreak, Sparsity left a note for Crow that she had gone to her cottage. The walk in the early morning bathed her mind. Her favorite time of day. She would say, "The earth blinks and the day and night change."

Garrison also arose early, dressed in work clothes and a determination. Making herself at home in the kitchen, she fired up the cook stove, made coffee, put out a breakfast of eggs, cheese, and grits. She sat to have her coffee on the porch, waiting for daylight to show itself.

She decided to take a walk toward the barn, hoping to meet up with Lee, still a puzzlement that he fled the night. Maybe he took an early ride. Meeting no one, she stopped at the wood pile. The axe was in the chop block, along with the splitter. She began to split and chop like a pro. Singing all the while, moving the axe in a furious manner.

Lee came riding up, along with Chase and Talker. He was somewhat surprised to see Garrison splitting logs, and even stranger that Chase and Talker didn't run to investigate the new person. The dogs went and laid down in front of the barn.

Garrison still did not look up, she kept right on chopping.

Lee called out her name, so as not to startle her by riding up unexpected. Upon hearing her name, she stopped, but still held the axe. "I need to get all of these logs split."

Lee got down from his horse, gave it a pat—motioned it toward the barn.

"Right now, I must check this situation out," he said to himself.

Lee reached and took the axe and moved Garrison away from the wood pile. "It's okay, Garrison, thank you, that is more than enough wood for our needs."

"Why don't we go get some breakfast, I am starved."

She put her arm through his and said, "I made food for us. I take it you had a restful night. Did you spend the night under the stars, they were sparkling a plenty last night?"

"Yes! It was a special beauty of a night. Maybe to celebrate the beauty that graced Protected Earth yesterday. How nice. You cooked breakfast and made yourself at home. Was Sparsity not around?"

No answer from Garrison. Garrison was a beautiful woman. Lee felt his interest moving.

"Where did you go last night? Were you running away from me?" She said in that sexy voice.

"I don't always know why, Garrison; I just followed my feelings—and needed the time to think about us. Crow had good intentions. And you are extraordinary. Let's just go along—you are welcome to stay, you are free to paint, work, but go a little slower on the wood chopping."

They both laughed.

"Will you show me your land? And I would like to paint, I don't know for how long, Lee. I am a traveler. It's plain to see you are a good honorable man. I have no need of a relationship, especially long term. I can always earn dollars, enough to keep moving. I am not after wealth or stability. I earn money to finance my travel. And all that Madame wrote about, it sounded much too great not to take a look at."

When they reached the house, Lee stopped, put his hands on Garrison's waist, lifted her up and sat her on the rail fence that was close by. "Garrison, you are an intoxicating woman. I will honor your desires. If you change your mind and wish to build a life here, with no financial worries. At this moment, I don't see a problem. But my gut tells me there is great turmoil going on in you. I have seen this pain before with my sister Azzie—it destroyed her and was extremely painful for those that loved her."

Garrison said loudly in a desperate voice, "Lee! Lee! There is so much insaneness in my head, I have been in sanatoriums in this country and Switzerland. There have been doctors and other men who have tried to help. It's never worked out. When Madame Crow's letters did reach me, I had been desperate for some time—I needed a place, so I came. My respect for Madame Crow is great. If I see my life is starting to spiral out of control—you have my promise, I will leave. I did not come to create a situation of difficulty for anyone."

"Garrison, my beloved sister, Azzie, has been missing for years, she lives with mental problems, as I said. I understand some of the torture that you may face each day."

"Ok, I will stay—let's go somewhere, is there a spot on Protected Earth?"

"What about the lovely breakfast you laid out," said Lee.

"Can we go now? Saddle a horse for me and point the way—food holds no interest for me, but you do."

Crow presided over the household from the moment she had put foot inside the screen door of Protected Earth. Lee liked it that way. He rested easy knowing all was in order, even if he disappeared for days sometimes isolating in the forest. Sparsity was delighted with

Crow's arrival. Sparsity's duties were lightened, and she adored and respected Crow.

Lee did as Garrison asked. He assumed she was a good rider as he led her horse out of the barn. As she started to put her foot in the stirrup, Lee and Garrison kissed. It was a deep very sexual pent-up kiss. He finally pushed her away, gave her directions to the pond cabin and said, "I will bring your things and also art supplies. Is there anything else you wish me to bring?"

"I am sure you will see that our needs are taken care of." She guided her horse around and rode in a gallop toward the pond cabin as Lee had directed.

Lee noticed how upright she sat on the horse. Her build was slender, with noticeably large breasts, which by the judge of her clothes, she tried to hide.

It had been sometime since Lee had such a desire for a woman. Today is as far as I will think, he told himself. Lee retrieved Garrison's things and left word with Crow to send the art supplies that Sparsity has expertly arranged in his studio to the pond house. He then rode furiously toward his desired destination—he knew there was no turning back. Whatever the outcome.

Garrison reached the pond cabin as if she had traveled the path hundreds of times. Of course she had not, it was a first.

She wiped her horse down, guided him to the fenced in area by the cabin, then entered and looked around. She noticed a tub of rainwater sat outside. She explored the charming place. A few plush robes hung on some hangers. She removed her clothes, found the liquor cabinet, poured a large brandy for herself, then said, "Lee will be along shortly." She reached for a glass and poured another brandy for Lee. She walked outside, placed Lee's brandy on a small log table, let her robe slide off and eased herself into the warm rainwater. She closed her eyes and let the glass of brandy and peaceful setting overtake her.

When Lee rode up to the pond cabin, Garrison was seated on a log, brandy in her hand, robe wrapped around her, looking extraordinary. Her wet hair was framing her perfect face.

Never to forget the care of his horse, he rubbed his horse down and released him into the corral.

"Believe I will partake of that tub," and so he did. Garrison handed Lee the brandy. There was no holding back, their passion satisfied, then resparked, over and over.

It had now been one week since Lee and Garrison rode to the pond cabin. Lee knew all would run smoothly without him. And they would find him if needed.

Lee mostly listened to Garrison's rambling. She spoke of animals and her beliefs that the animals send people signals. "If we would only listen. Each living thing has a voice. It may not sound like us, but why would God not give all of life that he created a say."

Lee listened and watched Garrison as she picked at her food, taking tiny bites, and he had not heard her comment even one time on how her food tasted. She cared not if it was hot or cold.

She wanted to sleep on the open porch. Lee moved the mattress to the porch, kept the open fire in the nearby fire pit going. There were all kinds of animals that would come around to investigate. The fire made them keep a distance from the cabin. He was accustomed to often sleeping in the open air and understood its appeal.

Just as fast and furious as their passion came, it left the same way. Lee awoke to find Garrison once more splitting wood and talking incoherent. He made coffee and some breakfast but did not approach Garrison, but let her come around when she was ready.

She sat on the stump, drank some black coffee, and said, "Lee would it be possible for me to move in with Sparsity? I am going to need someone to look after me."

"Why do you feel this way? Do you feel ill? We can call Doc Francis."

"Lee, I am ill and soon my illness will put me in bed. I never know for how long. It could be a week, months, or a year. Plus, I know we conceived a child last night. You will see. Most likely the reason I was sent here was to give you a daughter."

Lee believed her. He felt she just knew. Even if only one week had passed.

"Garrison, I will honor all your wishes. I am sure Sparsity will look after you. Are you sure you don't want Doc Francis? He is a kind, well informed doctor."

"No!" said Garrison. "I prefer that Sparsity takes care of me. Do you want this child, Lee?"

"Of course, and I will build a house for you and a studio for your beautiful paintings. What do you see in the future for yourself and this child you say will arrive?"

Garrison said, "Would you take a walk with me? I would like to sit by the river."

"First answer my question."

Lee gently took her by the arm and led her inside the cabin. Both sat at the table. Garrison spoke, "Lee, I have no intentions of being married. As I stated, I am a traveler. As soon as this baby is born, I'll move on. I don't want anything from you. I know in my heart you are a good decent man, and you will see that all goes well. But I have no need of wealth. I should not be bringing a child into the world. Doctors have said I could pass my mental disorder down to a child. But the doctors also say my disorder will most likely pass over a generation. But here we are, and I know we had no control over my being here. I was destined to give you a child."

"You are an intoxicating woman, a great artist, you can have your freedom with no financial worries. Maybe after the baby arrives, you will change your mind. Here I am talking, after a week, that you are carrying my child. It has happened too fast. But in my gut, I know it's true."

Garrison got up and walked outside and started her rhythmical wood cutting.

She stopped as Lee walked onto the porch. Garrison said, "Have my belongings sent to Sparsity's cottage, including my art supplies and if I may have a horse for my use. I love the brown and white appaloosa I rode to the cabin if that's okay."

Lee, not often shaken by life, felt this life experience. He was used to controlling his world. But he sure wasn't prepared for Garrison. Lee said, "Still wish to take that river walk, it's a beautiful sunny day?" He felt excitement inside that was almost not containable at the thoughts of his child. He knew he could not put any reins on this woman, come what may.

Sparsity was more than happy to do Lee a favor of caring for Garrison. Sparsity was now a midwife, who had delivered lots of babies in Darnell. Many depended on her when they got sick. Her healing herbs had cured a loved one of most families. Doc Francis was the first to praise Sparsity's knowledge. When others considered her to be strange, the citizens of Darnell had grown to respect her and love her.

Garrison was an excellent worker, very smart, and aware of the smallest detail in nature and in people. The eight months Garrison lived with Sparsity, she painted several lovely paintings of Sparsity that aroused one's curiosity, fascinating indeed. She requested that certain paintings be sent to one particular gallery in New York. Lee assured her the request would be honored.

Sparsity gave Garrison run of her cottage. Birchard, who now lived at Sparsity's, moved to the main house. Garrison liked sleeping on the open porch. She assisted Sparsity and tended the herb garden. Sparsity enjoyed the strangeness and beauty of Garrison, she lived in a different space on Earth, but so did Sparsity. There were days where Garrison was bed ridden. Sparsity kept herbs boiling on the stove, put fresh white dry lined and ironed linens on Garrison's bed each day. Every comfort Sparsity could think of for Garrison and the baby to be.

Garrison gave Lee the blessing of a unique, extraordinary, beautiful baby girl. Lee desperately wanted to take care of Garrison. Garrison didn't have an easy birth, but Crow, Doc Francis, Lee, and Sparsity took turns sitting holding her hand. She was a woman possessed.

The baby girl was remarkable, perfect. Lee could not take his eyes off his new daughter. She smiled and was happy from her first breath.

Garrison showed no interest in her beautiful baby. She would keep asking Doc and Sparsity, "When will I be well enough to travel? My journey here is complete."

Lee left money with Sparsity, just to make sure Garrison didn't leave without the means to get started, wherever she landed. Sparsity placed the money in Garrison Anne Polly's carpet bag with an open long letter from Lee. It was of the utmost importance that Garrison knew that if she was in trouble or need, or wished to know about her daughter, all was favorable for her to contact anyone on Protected Earth.

Garrison did make one request. "Do name the baby my name? I like GAP—Garrison Anne Polly."

"That's a long name for a baby, Garrison." Sparsity said while holding the smiling baby close to her. "But Lee has told us to try and meet any wishes you may have, so Gap it is."

Garrison circled the room. Then walked out to the herb garden, picked a few herbs, rubbed them through her hands, gently letting the herbs drop into the garden, walked inside, walked over to Sparsity and Lee. She gave Lee a passionate kiss and said, "I have given you a gift like no other."

Lee stood and said, "It will be a pleasure, Gap she is. I like it and she will also. I will tell her about her extraordinary mother. Garrison, you know where we are. Protected Earth is also your home—everyone on Protected Earth knows this."

After a couple of weeks of rest, Doc Francis gave her the okay to travel.

"I feel good, would you have Leeward take me to the train station? I will stop by the main house and talk with Madame Crow."

"Okay and he will take the fancy carriage. The mother of Gap should ride like a queen." When Leeward arrived at the station, he asked Garrison if she wished for him to wait with her. She did not respond. He could not help but notice how people stared at Garrison. She wore the same red outfit she arrived in.

Leeward walked over to Cal's porch and waited and listened for the train. Once it arrived and Garrison was on it, he left for home to report to Lee. Only a few words had passed between Garrison and Leeward.

He met Lee and told him he had waited until the train left the station and Garrison didn't even look back.

Lee felt there wasn't anything he could offer Garrison that would entice her to make Protected Earth her home. She said, "Lee, I feel soon my mental illness will overtake me completely. This is not a part of me I wish to share. I will be far away from here. Gap, I know will have the best of life. Could a mother ask more?" That was the first and only time that Garrison warmed in any way toward her child.

Garrison knew Lee had left a brown envelope with Sparsity. She accepted his gift, because she knew she would need money for the hospital that she was checking into—far away in a mountainous location in landlocked Switzerland.

The train left Darnell. All who had partaken and participated in Garrison's stay on Protected Earth wondered; would they ever hear from the lovely lady in red? The lady who left a beautiful baby girl behind named GAP. A baby girl with three first names.

CHAPTER 18

Growing

Protected Earth's pathways, roads, fields, and forest were kept noticeable by the use of the inhabitants that wandered, animal and human. The wild mushrooms, herbs, and wildflowers that grew along the many trails were gathered. They were hung and dried to be placed in baskets that hung throughout the main house, also on fences and trees. Bags of mixed dried petals and spices were placed in old china bowls, to perfume rooms throughout.

It was not unusual to be on a walk and come upon a delightful large container of wildflowers placed on a stump or rock, or a basket of acorns placed for deer or small creatures to enjoy. Sparsity often had

Gap with her, papoose style, but as Gap grew, she wanted to be next to her father.

Mr. Ward, when he was alive, would say what a pleasure to sit quietly in an inconspicuous spot and observe Sparsity interacting with the earth around her. She was a rare creature that lit the spaces she occupied. At one with it all… her white hair and colorful clothing making an exit from a dark part of the forest, or rising out of a kudzu covered creek.

But, Gap could never be enticed by Sparsity or her papa to enter the dark edge of the forest. As a small child the thick forest looked gnarled and unfriendly, "Besides Papa, from deep inside I hear mutterings."

Today as Papa and Gap explored a pathway, they met up with Sparsity. Out of the forest she walked. Barefoot, leather pouches dangling from her waist, each one overflowing with herbs. Herbs that have and can heal a sick body. A pack on her back, adorned with colorful stones and ink artwork. Moss, seeds, and rocks pushed the pack to its limits, a present from Leeward. A thank you from Leeward to her for the cure of a bad infection on his feet. She mixed up a foot soak and a salve to keep on his feet during the day. Sparsity was surprised by the wonderful gift he had made just for her. Leeward was not known for a generosity toward people. And Sparsity held some resentment because of his lack of love toward Folly and Birchard, she adored both of them.

Singing softly, Gap called out, "Sparsity want to share some lunch?"

What would have startled anyone, with a voice coming unexpectedly from the forest, didn't even phase Sparsity. "Yes, that will be nice!"

They sat talking with the warmth of friendship and the sweetness that Protected Earth provided.

Gap eyed some mushrooms nearby, knowing Papa loved them. She knew Sparsity had the knowledge of the wild treats of the land.

"We want to stay away from those called scaly ink cap, they can make one very sick. Let's check under our native trees, the white ash. I am sure we can spot some nice chanterelle," said Sparsity.

Lee had fallen asleep against a tree after their lunch.

"I stay away from all mushrooms, let the fairies and the frogs play among them," said Gap.

Sparsity gave a snicker.

That made Gap smile.

"Feel like a canoe ride down the river?" Gap asked Sparsity. "We can wake Papa, he is always up for a canoe ride."

"Now, Miss Gap, you know I like my bare feet on solid ground. You enjoy, I'm headed home, with my nice supply."

As Sparsity walked away, and she woke her Papa, Gap threw up her hand that is all well and headed toward the river, holding tight to her Papa's hand, asking question after question. "Papa can we stop under the big oak tree."

Gap grew at lightning speed. Wanting to work alongside her daddy. Copying his every gesture and work habits. Today Chase and Talker streaked through the woods, zipping in front of the wagon, then circling behind and sprinting in front again. Maude, the mule, was long-since conditioned to the dogs' habits. If they miscalculated their split-second timing and got stepped on by a one-thousand-pound hoof, it was nothing to her. She wagged her ears and continued her steady pace.

This Maude was second generation to the original. Birchard had bartered the stud services of a neighbor's donkey with a Protected Earth mare to get this Maude. More than satisfactory in every regard, she was hardy, even tempered, and could outwork any horse on the place, and Maude knew her value. And it looked as if the mule was going to live forever.

Gap and Papa watched as the dogs raced around, each jockeying to be first. Gap with endless questions, thinking her Papa always knew the reason for stuff. "Papa, why are the dogs running like that? They look like they're chasing something. What are they in pursuit of?"

Papa replied, "Sparsity and Crow believe generations of restless spirits are moving about in these pine thickets and oak groves. The spirits are stuck in time. Most likely Indian spirits. Others still fight the same battles over and over, or else endlessly repeat the business of their unsettled lives from when they lived before. Sis Crow believes Chase and Talker can see them and if we opened our hearts and minds to them, when they try to make contact with us. We would see maybe they are coming forth to protect us. Crow says we make contact and don't even realize it. With Chase and Talker around, those spirits get no rest."

Wide-eyed, Gap swiveled this way and that, trying to keep the dogs in sight. She reasoned, "Now I know why you named them Chase and Talker—Chase rounds up the spirits and Talker communicates with them. Is that right, Papa?"

"That's right, honey." Papa responded. "The blue ticks love the spirits that died happy, because they can frolic and play with them."

"Papa, do you remember when I told you that sometimes when I go for my walks with Chase and Talker I would hear a buzz, and then see a shadow? Once I could smell lemons all about." Gap used her hands to help explain and maybe it gave her words more meaning.

"Yes, my dear one, Crow says that our mother Fancy smelled like lemons. She believes Mother's spirit watches over Protected Earth. And Crow says Mother's spirit touched her arm or head. Tingles run up and down her and the lemon fragrance is all around her."

"My grandmother's spirit. Oh! Papa," said Gap, barely able to contain herself, "that must have been grandmother that day on my walk."

The wagon rolled along at a nice pace. Gap had moved closer to Papa, it wasn't that she was afraid, thinking spirits are all around. She just felt more comfortable when her Papa was close.

Lee fondly recalled the Original Chase and Talker from his childhood. This pair carried their same bloodline.

Intrigued, Gap shivered. Her imagination soared, and she could almost make out the layers of spirits from different times in the past inhabiting the forest. She was relieved to have such talented guardians as Chase and Talker to escort Papa and herself home. And she was now doubly glad they slept on her bed every night.

Papa guided Maude around the last curve before the farmhouse. The road crossed right through the creek. When the wagon reached the shallow shoals in the middle of the creek bed, Papa called out, "Whoa, Maude," and softly pulled the reins. "Thirsty, girl?"

Maude dipped her head to the water. The dogs waded through the water, lapping as they walked. Gap hopped off the wagon.

"Chase! Talker!" Gap called the dogs to her side with a new appreciation of their unique abilities. They yipped their greetings a few times, received her hugs and responded with messy blue tick kisses. "You haven't brought me any treasures in a while, but I forgive you." Their last gift had been a small hand-held mirror that they had dug up in the woods. It was caked with dirt. After washing it in the stream, she saw it was decorated with pretty blue beads. Gap often thought of all kinds of stories and reasons why a child's hand-held mirror would be buried in the woods. Maybe the little girl was kidnapped or just wandered away one night from a wagon train, never to be seen again. But it just might be, she is living with the wild animals, and is now an old woman, roaming the woods, searching for her belongings. Gap splashed over to a deeper area, the dogs at her side. Gap often tripped into a story. But quickly returned her thoughts and observations back to the present. "Come on, boys. You could use a bath."

Gap sat in the water, which came up to her shoulders. She and the dogs let the refreshing water run over and around them. Then she turned her head to see whether her Papa was watching her. He was. She grinned at him and waved. Gap craved her Papa's praise, and constantly did things contrived to receive it.

Papa gazed at her with a happy heart. He adored his beautiful, fearless daughter. She had her mother's beauty and his unrelenting curiosity, and the Darnell eyes, a velvet brow just like his mother.

While Gap played in the water with the dogs, Papa Lee closed his eyes and let his mind wander into thoughts of his mother. He could feel her frail arms holding him, and a soft floral scent entered his nose. She spoke softly, "Know you are deeply loved by me and your sisters." He knew his mother only held him next to her heart a short time. Then she was gone. But he felt she was always with him.

Lee folded his notebook and called out to Gap, "Let's get you home and out of those wet clothes. Crow will be upset with us."

Out of the blue, Gap said, "Papa you need me on Protected Earth. I can learn discipline right here." Gap had never before been anything but wild and free. "Papa, I love you beyond all words, but, if you send me away to school, I won't have a choice but to run away. Wherever you send me, I will head straight back to Protected Earth."

"Yes! I know," Papa said. He couldn't help but smile. Inside he was ashamed of his selfish feelings. The thought of being away from his daughter so many hours was not pleasant. But he knew she needed school. And the interplay with other children.

Maude quickened her pace as the wagon rounded the curve to home.

Papa reached for his sketch book, which rarely left his side, pulling out his mother's picture. Her soft, gentle looking brown eyes, fringed with long lashes, looked at him. He raised his eyes from his mother's picture and looked at Gap. He could see his mother in Gap's eyes; his mother was a great beauty brought down from the era she was born by the scurrilous treatment by her husband.

Gap, feeling her Papa's sadness, his head down, said, "Papa, you miss your mother," as she reached out for his hand.

"I miss never seeing her, but life is what it is. Do you miss not knowing your mother?" Papa said.

"No," said Gap and that was that and Papa knew she meant it.

Wanting to know why to everything he did throughout his day and night. In truth, she pestered everyone on Protected Earth as to the why of their knowledge. All adored the spirited child.

True to her word, she ran away every day when he registered her in public school.

"But Papa, why can't you teach me all I need to know? And Aunt Crow can give me my lessons."

"Gap, I will consider it. We will sit with Sis Crow and see how she feels about home school."

Papa said with a sigh as he rubbed his forehead, "You can't add too much knowledge. You will just store it on a little shelf in there until one day you will need it. That's why you can't skip over the things you aren't interested in. Curiosity is a great, exciting thing for a person to have and, my dear one, you have it. We will talk with Crow tonight."

"Papa, who will be beside you… handing you a tool, pointing out the many bird sightings that you may have not seen, and listening to their songs. Its better I stay right here." Lee felt a laugh coming forward from the words Gap spoke.

Papa held education dear to his heart. "Honey, it's not just about learning from books," he responded. "As I have previously told you, it's good for you to be with other children, their diverse personalities, and different points of view. You have to learn to get along with others and learn the discipline of something you might not want to do, but it'll enrich you in ways you can't see until much later in your life. When you're ready for college, you will spend a year at the Women's School for Higher Education in Atlanta. Then, we'll see. Wouldn't it be exciting to go to a big university?"

Gap set her chin and tapped her foot on the ground, "No, Papa, I won't go! You need me on Protected Earth. Why should I go off somewhere to try and get what I can get here?" Papa could see that Gap had her back up.

Gap was silent. She already regretted the wasted time that she would have to spend away from her home. Protected Earth was sacred ground to her. She couldn't bear the thought of being away from the people and things she dearly loved.

Gap continued to cast a spell, not only on her Daddy, but anyone who met her. Since she started walking and talking, her gestures and speech confirmed her eagerness to put in motion her life. Most of her words ended with a question mark. Therefore, she loved receiving answers. The more she could take in, the more delighted her day became.

Lee relished greatly in watching his daughter grow, she was rarely out of his sight. At night, she slept in Crow's room, but come daybreak, she first crawled, then walked in her daddy's shadow. When Lee lifted his morning coffee cup, Gap would arrive at the table. "I am ready, Papa." She carried the face of wonder for what the days were to hold. Lee took her on almost every chore. As she grew, she worked alongside her daddy. And was excited to learn and to physically do each chore that she could possibly do.

Protected Earth was endowed with all kinds of entrancements. Lee, from a young child, had explored every inch of the property and still marveled in the many way's nature changed every day. He wanted Gap to see and learn every day and not to miss anything. In his daughter, he found a willing student.

Birchard had gifted Gap with a small field magnifying glass. She treasured it. Once, she forgot and left it in the wildflower field. It had been a particular strenuous day of walking. Gap, being only five and growing, fell asleep early, but during the night she awoke and missed it. Hollering, "Aunt Crow, please wake Papa, I can't find my seeing glass." Crow knew there was no amount of sustained effort that would convince Gap to wait until daybreak. She went with her Papa, and ran right to the spot, Papa shining his flashlight.

"Oh, Papa, thank you. I love you. I promise to place more value on my things." And she did.

Crow would say to Lee, "Why do you give in to that child's every whim? She is going to be spoiled."

"Maybe so! But I don't believe that will happen, not with Gap.

Even from a toddler, Crow, you know how levelheaded she has always been—determined, yes. She will be fine."

On what Gap called her "seeing walks," the questions would start. "Papa, come see this big seed that this tiny ant is moving." Getting as close as possible, she would bring her interests into detail with her magnifier. "Papa, come look. This ant has brown eyes. Where is the ant taking the seed?" To Lee's delight, she never stopped asking questions. He wanted Gap to understand the importance that insects had on earth so he would go into great detail, no matter her age.

"Gap, remember we can never take nature for granted. Let's sit and rest."

"Put your magnifier in your pack and take out your notepad. We will record our experiences, someday we will want to remember all of our happenings. You know how much you love to hear about when your Papa grew up. One day, you will read to your child how you grew up."

Lee watched his daughter with fullness of heart. Gap did not relate well to other children. She had little curiosity in them. Her mind was not in the same place as most girls and boys her age. Gap interrupted his thoughts, "Papa, would you help me draw a brown eyed ant?" She handed her notepad toward him.

"No! You try. I will look at your completed drawing, then together we will decide if it needs work. Darling, you are going to be a great artist. Better than your Papa."

Gap laughed and continued to draw their walks and rides, which were taken under most every weather condition.

Gap was extremely upset to leave her home and go to school. She refused to eat her breakfast. She wasn't forced and Lee had the wagon waiting for the ride into town.

Gap talked non-stop about all the things she was needed for.

"Surely, Papa, you know that Leeward says I am a huge help with the baby goats. He most certainly could use me today."

Lee let her jabbering continue and the wagon got closer to the school.

Carrying a long, sad face, Gap kissed and hugged her daddy several times.

"Leeward will pick you up today. Your papa has other business that must be taken care of. You are brave. It will be okay."

Gap found town school not to her liking. One boy pulled her braid. When she smacked him, the teacher made her come to the front of the class and tell the class she was sorry for fighting. She refused and tried to explain why. "Your father will be told about your bad conduct, young lady," the teacher said, shaking her finger at Gap.

"My Papa teaches me to defend myself. He won't be upset," Gap said in defiance.

"We will see about that," the teacher said.

When the teacher rang the bell for recess, Gap headed for home. The determined little girl walked all seven miles. She knew all the little pathways—the shortcuts in and out off the main road. Papa patiently returned her to school over and over and was distressed to see her tears. She cried throughout her days and nights, even in her sleep.

Rather than adapting to the school, Gap began to withdraw into despondence. Papa, seeing the loss of her laughter, found that in the end, he valued her happiness over his insistence that she attend the school in town. Lee decided to ask Crow how she felt about educating Gap at home.

Crow leaned against the kitchen sink and heard her brother out. She still thought of him as Little D. Though Lee had long grown well into manhood, all started calling the young Lee Papa, some felt for such a young person he took on great responsibility. Lee had an old soul. So, Papa Lee stuck. He took on fulfilling Mr. Ward's dreams of building Darnell into a town the citizen's loved and were proud of. Crow carefully listened to every word; her hands covered in flour.

When she heard his last word, she said, "It will be one of my greatest joys to teach my niece. We can get started just as soon as I put these biscuits in the oven."

Papa had been wound up for the necessity of defending his argument. He was prepared to go on for hours. Crow's assent took him by surprise.

"Well," she spoke in her prim school-marm voice, "You might know that I am well qualified. Many others have been most pleased to have me teach their girls." After one look at Lee's face, Crow's laughter rang throughout the house. "Of course, I'll do it. Anything for you, Little D." She slid the pan of biscuits into the hot oven.

"Mind you," she continued on a somber note as she turned back to him, "I will have order in my schoolhouse of one. No countermanding me for rides through the woods and fields during school hours. No nonsense, Lee. No matter how hard she tries to convince you otherwise. And I must admit, she is very smart with her reasoning. I won't have my niece growing up without a proper education, not on my watch. Understand?"

Lee humbly answered, "Yes, ma'am — and I plan on bringing in tutors for her advanced history, astronomy, and science since you will have a lot to cope with. Sparsity can teach Gap on cooking, sewing, and herbs.

Crow kicked into gear. "I'll need you to order a blackboard and some chalk, along with some other things. I'll make a list. We will begin tomorrow, even without the blackboard. She already has a week of catch-up work to do." Crow reached for paper and pencil. The list was underway. "I'll take the small drawing room for our schoolroom."

Crow was ready to pull out the books. She would also find out the level of education that was being taught at the local school. Gap was smart, but she had been raised in this utopian place.

Crow would teach her that there were places in America and Darnell where women and girls were not given the respect as they are given in her daddy's world. Especially when men feel a woman trespasses on their turf. Crow's head was spinning with ideas. Her mind went back to her dear mother and the awful oppression she endured. But how remarkable a woman she was to still give her children loving care, even up to her last breath.

Crow stood in front of the open window, taking in some fresh air. She looked out and thought, there is some form of beauty no matter where my eyes roam. The pines were lifting their branches with movements that were perfect.

Lee broke into her thoughts. He answered again, this time with a smile. "Yes, ma'am." His heart gave a tingle—remembering when he and his sisters sat at attention under Monterey's tutorial sessions. What a godsend! His daughter could experience Crow as he had.

Crow smelled the biscuits, "Oh my" and ran to the oven, they came out golden brown.

They told Gap just after supper. She was ecstatic. She ran from Papa to Crow, to the dogs, then back to Papa and Crow, hugging them and thanking them all. "Yes! Yes! Yes! Thank you, Papa! Thank you, Aunt Crow. You'll see how good I'll study! I'll work so hard! I'll make you proud of me! Oh, Papa, let's go out tomorrow for a picnic to celebrate! We can play hide and seek in the corn rows. This is one of the happiest days of my life."

Papa and Crow looked at each other over Gap's head. Crow raised an eyebrow at him. Papa said, "Alright, honey. We'll do that, just as soon as your lessons are over, and you've completed your assignments. We want to start out by Crow's rules, or she could change her mind." Papa gave Crow a wink.

Gap had not expected this response. She looked up at her Aunt Crow, incredulous that school would supersede their celebratory outing. Crow told her, "Just as soon as you get finished, Little Miss. I'll make the sandwiches."

Gap looked at them both, round-eyed. Then, she slowly nodded her head. "Yes, ma'am." All of them had won.

But Gap wasn't without bad behavior. Like most children, they can be cruel. Losing her temper one day, she jumped on a frog, and crushed it. The incident caused a deep talk from Lee and crying from Gap. She could not come up with a reason for doing such a bad thing.

"What do you think your punishment should be?" Papa asked of the distraught child. After a few minutes, her crying stopped. She said, "Papa, I will stay all night by the frog pond and let the frogs know how sorry I am."

Lee smiled inside. Knowing his daughter, that would not be a punishment, but an adventure she wants all along. Just like Brer Rabbit and the briar patch.

"I will sleep on that and I will decide tomorrow."

She ran into his arms. "Papa, I will never hurt anything again ever. I promise to protect each one." The next morning, after her studies were completed, she asked to take a walk. One of her favorite games was just around the bend. "Papa, can we play just around the bend? It would do my heart good—and yours."

Lee walked out in front of Gap to a distance where he couldn't be seen. Winding roads and paths ran throughout Protected Earth. A person could easily disappear for a moment. Gap felt a tug at her heart when she couldn't see Papa. Then she would start running toward the bend in the path or road as fast as her growing legs would get her there.

A resounding voice came from the forest. "Gap, I am just around the bend." Her face lit up and she ran into his outstretched arms. Then they reversed and off Gap ran.

Lee could see his daughter growing at an alarming rate. She learned how to work hard digging, cutting, and sawing trees for firewood, working in the barns, but there was one area: the bees. Gap never overcame her fear of being stung. She loved honey but feared the honey makers. After being homeschooled by Crow until out of high school, Lee wanted her to go to Paris for one year to study painting and learn another language. He desired for her to experience a broader life experience. She refused.

"Papa, all I want is here in Darnell. I want to paint. I believe I am good. Not a talent as you are, Papa, but I will be one day. I'll help run the cheese-making business. My heart would be too lonely away from you, Crow, the animals, the land, Sparsity, Birchard, Leeward, and Folly."

Gap's teenage years took flight and here she was: sixteen. She had been raised and educated as if she had no gender by Crow, Lee, Birchard, Leeward, Sparsity, and the town of Darnell. Lee did bring in special tutors for many subjects and as her Papa and Aunt Crow, she loved books and learning. She would often say, "Oh, how glorious it is when my brain and senses are sparked with a new idea. There is no feeling like it for me."

He expected to convince Gap to finish her education in Paris. She continued to refuse. "Papa, I do have the Darnell indomitable spirit. I have no longings to be anywhere but Georgia, but I will never shirk work. I want to live to be very old and right here with my family."

Gap was an individual. She possessed a more then ordinary enthusiasm for all things that engrossed her. She did not like to deprive herself.

Gap stayed on Protected Earth and worked as hard or harder than anyone. She saw how her Papa went all out for whatever he took on and she never wanted to disappoint him. She watched how he gave instructions, always in a kind, soft voice, but he showed a strong demeanor when needed.

She had freedom with little constraints, losing her purity at around sixteen. She revealed this fact to Crow and Sparsity. They didn't inquire as to who the boy or man was; it was an unspoken word in this family to let a person reveal of themselves on their own accord, what they wanted to share of a personal nature and as it happened, most were very open with each other. There were no present marriages in the Darnell family except Crow, and she had been sold into an arranged marriage for money.

The citizens of Darnell, especially the good churchgoers, may have whispered under their breath at the freedom Lee raised his daughter with, but all steered clear of ever having voiced their opinions… at least to persons close to Lee or Gap.

Their daughters were kept close at home and married young. Gap did not seek out any females for friends. Cal's daughter, Liza, had returned to take over the Hub and enjoyed a friendship with Gap. Gap put challenges on herself. Living was Gap's passion, but horses were her priority.

She was scandalous as seen through society views, but she didn't seek their approval of her life, as her Papa never did.

From age fourteen, she would take her tent and go on long horse rides into the county. Papa felt she knew how to use the rifle she carried on the side of her horse and the pistol in her saddle bag. He had taught her the skills to survive in the wild. She was no ordinary young woman.

When things were taken care of on Protected Earth, crops were harvested, cheese-making was completed and ready for market, Gap met with Papa and he confirmed all was okay. He expected her to take off on extended hikes and rides, packing just the necessities, warm sweaters, maps, canteens, and off she would go, leaving the security of her family. If the trek was on horseback, she slept in barns, not wishing to abandon her beloved horse overnight in strange areas. Often, Chase and Talker would accompany her on her adventures. When she returned, she was a welcomed sight.

Crow didn't always approve of the freedom Papa gave the young girl, but felt Gap was strong and understood her wanderlust.

Gap was turning seventeen. She didn't desire a party, a special dinner with her family was the best of her life. She had not been exposed to romantic love—but that was soon to change.

CHAPTER 19

Lee's Mornings

Lee was called Papa after Mr. Ward died. He became head of Protected Earth at the age of seventeen. He carried an old soul in a young body. So Papa Lee it was. And he lived up to his position.

Mornings were a favorite time, not that he didn't treasure them all. He loved the music of the mornings when the birds synchronized. First a lone one, then another, until all had joined the music of the morning.

It was also the time of day when he missed Mr. Ward the most. Many days, Mr. Ward would say when Lee would hear him strongly humming, "Humming keeps my voice strong, vibrant, and my belly flat. Another day to live, build, plant, and watch nature waking up."

Lee had taken on a lot of Mr. Ward's habits. He laid on the hard plank floor and did pushups, and deep breathing. His thoughts always ran as to why? Ward with his great attitude, strong body, and mind fell to an illness so quickly. But Lee knew as life goes, there are things we never know the answers to.

He reached for his starched white shirt, one of the many that hung in his closet, pressed perfect by Sparsity. His overalls neatly folded on a chair, with his treasured ivory handle pocketknife, given to him as a boy by Mr. Ward. Every boy should reach into his pocket and let his fingers feel the warmth and smoothness of a pocketknife. Lee would say, "I have never felt young. A strong sense of duty lives inside me." His early morning rides were not to just take in the many usual delights throughout the property, but also to check on a large productive working farm. His over-searer, Leeward, would meet up with him along the way. The two would discuss not only the day's work, but also any future plans. Lee had total confidence in Leeward's abilities. He did a fine job of taking care of any problems that arose such as, sick animals, farm equipment, cheese-making production, the trees, and farm production in general.

Leeward was born with problems to be dealt with. Some he had put aside, and others had increased. But no person is all good or all bad. And Lee felt Leeward had a lot more good than bad. There were things that tore at Leeward's heart that no amount of prayers would change.

After checking with all the workers throughout Protected Earth. Lee would continue his ride, often stopping to view different birds and letting his thoughts run at random. The wonder of their day-to-day survival. One's imagination should be tested each day. How can I make a contribution to this world? One day I will complete a book on birds. He would close his sketch book, lie back against a large rock or log and be in complete harmony with his life.

Did he miss the company of a companion? Suppose when he stretched out his arm at night. He often felt the absence of a special someone in that vacant space. But it wasn't something that stayed in him. He had given of himself to hard outside work, some social talk, the giving of care to the town and his loved ones.

There were daily matters to take care of, sick animals, trees to check for pine beetles, hire of new workers, the beaver dams routing the creek in a different direction, and on and on. But today he walked for the joy of being on this Earth. As he walked the fields, he was reminded of the clearing of the fields, the rocks that now were stacked along the edge of the fields, how beautiful, and they will withstand time. Each one was carefully placed to form the stacked walls.

Yes, there were struggles along the way, but what great rewards were reaped. In the beginning, there were strained and even broken arms and legs from accidents, families of the men who worked the land were getting sick. But when Mr. Ward hired Doc Francis, all had changed in the small town. The citizens had a healer and a friend in Doc Francis. Not only did he put casts on many broken bones, but also, he listened to their woes.

He came upon Doc today, as Doc was checking on his bees. Lee still had not mastered the art of the honey makers. Throwing his hand up to Doc, he kept going with a huge warm feeling in his heart. Yes, Doc, he thought, may you live long, we need you, our town will always need you. Doc had talked with Lee about a young man in town that wanted to go to med school. Doc had hired the boy after his woman assist retired. "I believe Lee, he will be the perfect person to take my place."

So, it was done. Lee agreed to take care of all expenses for the boy. The money was there, Mr. Ward had seen to that. Doc Francis desired for the boy to go to a med school that Doc chose. Lee told Doc, "You take care and train him. Let him know we expect commitment from him in Darnell."

Today was a day of picking up memories. He visited the resting place, as Gap referred to the cemetery. It was always an emotional time, no matter how many times he was there. Lee lit some candles, spread a quilt on the floor, but not just any quilt from the stack, the quilts were made by Crow. Lee picked out one with a beautiful tall, long haired pine on it, gently gave Crow some praise for the many hours put in to create each one. He propped some pillows behind his back, removed his boots, and put himself into a day's meditation. He would enjoy his goat cheese and bacon biscuit later.

Gap had been occupied with school and had adjusted well with Crow as her teacher. Crow was extremely strict and her sole student lived up to all her rules.

Lee had more free time, and Birchard still accepted lots of the responsibilities of running Protected Earth. This week, Lee would make time to spend with Doc Francis, Leeward, Folly, and Birchard and pay a call on some new neighbors. Doc had just delivered a new baby and mentioned the family looked like they could use a few things. Lee usually took Sparsity along; she would often even stay a few days until the lady of the house was up and about. Doc Francis loved birthing babies. He held very strong beliefs of how a baby should enter the world. He would repeat often, "A baby should only have kind hands welcoming it."

He didn't mind getting involved in the families if needed to create the right environment when a baby was due. He held meetings with the fathers, which was not always an easy task. The men worked hard and raw, and the women alongside them. Doctor Francis tried to educate them on seeing that the mother's health be protected so she could deliver a healthy, happy baby.

Doc's beliefs were strong and his tenacity even stronger. His charm of words, handsomeness, intelligence, and his overall attraction did change the people of Darnell's views—in good ways. Mr. Ward had brought them a jewel of a doctor and man.

Lee was awakened by Doc Francis.

"Hi there, Lee. Won't interfere with your dreaming time, just wanted to check and make sure you pay that new family a visit."

"Sure thing, on my list to stop by tomorrow, taking Sparsity."

Lee stood up; the men hugged.

"See you, Lee. Looking to run upon Leeward, see if he has some spare time next week to help me with the honey."

Doc raised his arm goodbye and continued on his way.

Lee said his goodbyes to the dear ones, left a small stone on each grave. He stood arms outstretched, taking in the beauty of the days. And looking forward to his walk home. He would inform Sparsity about Doc willing to take her into Atlanta.

CHAPTER 20

Walks with Doc

Doc Francis was a welcome sight as his red fringed fancy equipped carriage rolled into Protected Earth's front yard.

Mr. Ward, before he passed away, saw that Doc had the best of equipment in his office and lab. He could do extensive operations, if needed. Why, he could have opened you up and easily removed your appendix right there, on the side of that red dirt road. The small twenty-bed hospital was now being completed in Darnell. It was to be named after Mickey, in honor of her struggle to give birth; too many women died along with their newborns from lack of care. Our citizens will know they will receive the best we can give them. Mr. Ward had felt if Doc Francis had only arrived sooner, Mickey would have not died. But Doc tried to reassure him all was done that was possible. Taking a day off for the doc was a most welcome time. The doors of Protected Earth were unlocked, Doc gave a soft knock, and stepped inside the welcoming entrance. Fresh flowers welcomed anyone who entered.

"Hi Doc, good to see you, just felt you might be by today. Have a seat on the porch, help yourself to the bar, or coffee on the stove. I will join you shortly." Lee reached out and shook Doc's hand, then the two gave a hug.

"Sure thing."

Doc let his eyes roam his surroundings and let his thoughts wander as he poured a sherry into an oversize brandy sniffer. How a person ends up on the very spot they are on this very moment, he found this kind of asking always fascinating. Maybe there is a reasonable explanation that I took the first step to arrive here.

"Deep in thought there, Doc," Lee said as he walked to the table and poured a sherry for himself.

"This mind of mine is running uncontrollable when I find free moments."

Lee smiled, "Yes, I have somewhat the same situation. I feel it's that first step that can lead one across the room into facing a huge new life experience."

"Let's finish this sherry and head for the hills." Doc stood and picked up his backpack and stick.

The two friends whistled, and the pleasure of friendship was all around them. The walk today started with Doc Francis' pontification on bees. "The blooms from the many trees and the wildflowers, know when they send off this pleasantly perfumed smell, those are just invitations to the passing bees. And if we are lucky, we get a sniff or two that can linger in our memory forever. And years down life's path, we can smell that perfumed smell and that brings forth a memory that we treasure. It's all so exciting… nature."

Lee said, "Sparsity claims she can hear the trees when something is up with them. She will hold her head down and press her ear against the earth, close in on a tree to see if she could hear a cracking root."

Doc answers and smiles, "Well, I must say, I most likely will believe anything Sparsity informs me about. She does know and has a special relationship with the forest that most humans don't possess."

Lee smiled at Doc and the men continued their hike around the property and along the riverbank. It was a perfect day, blue, blue sky, warm soothing sun, a small, sweet breeze that came around a corner ever so often. What is more pleasant than feeling the warmth of the sun, a lovely little breeze caressing you along a walk with a dear friend. Where conversation flows without thought. And an unexpected word or observation can stimulate the mind and senses.

"Where is that daughter of yours this morning? Surprised she wasn't close by, packed and ready to hit the trails."

"Gap spent the night with Sparsity last night. Sparsity has a list of chores for her to do in the herb garden. And I like for her to be around Birchard, as you well know. I don't believe Birchard will be with us much longer, Doc."

Birchard had recently had a checkup from Doc. Doc felt Birchard didn't have much interest in going on with his life. But nothing major with his health… some stiff joints in his knees and shoulders, but he told Doc, "Sparsity makes hot towels of herbs and wraps my legs. Loosens me up. Yes, Doc, that woman knows her stuff. She has kept me alive, not that all of Protected Earth hasn't, but Sparsity just reads a person's moods, knows how to handle each one."

Doc once more confirmed that he was excited about accompanying Sparsity on an Atlanta tour.

"Sure, that will be great. But don't let her go exploring on her own. The city folks may have never seen anyone that looks like Sparsity. She might possibly get harassed by someone. She is used to being stared at, but not sure how she would handle harassment."

"Consider it done." Doc and Lee ended up at the pond cabin talking through the night. Lee inquired if Doc missed England, or anything in particular, about his life he left behind.

Doc, "No! I was searching for a new way of life, and upon reading Mr. Ward's ad, all sounded perfect. I have not been disappointed, my love and respect grows each day. I have a great admiration for the citizens of Darnell, my life is full beyond my expectations. I may be considering marriage in the near future."

Lee left Doc relaxing on the cabin's porch and headed back toward home. If anyone needed the Doc, they would likely contact me, Lee thought, as he walked, looking forward to each day on Protected Earth, watching nature, and the people of Darnell raising families, building businesses, making Darnell a place where people never wish to leave.

CHAPTER 21

Gap Captures Hearts

P rotected Earth—all thousand acres surrounded the beautiful, happy energetic baby girl. From the time she was born and Lee picked her up and looked into her perfect face, she was in her Papa's shadow. He had her on horseback as he rode the property. If he stopped to check on the cheese making, she hugged the goats, tasted the cheese, was passed among the workers, to be held and loved. There was no shyness in Gap. She was swimming in the pond before she could walk or stand alone. She crawled among the grass and reeds, and in Sparsity's herb garden, as Sparsity hoed and hung herbs to dry.

Seated on the tractor was giggle time as her Papa plowed the fields and various jobs that required the tractor.

As she grew up, Lee did not want Gap to be inhibited because of any culture or socialization because she was a girl. Her mother, the phenomenal Garrison Anne Polly, carried uncommon traits such as fearless adventure, changeable, prepared to do anything, no bother of social convention, but there were also traits he didn't wish for his daughter that Garrison had. She held no bother for others feelings, and lived her life with no care of the consequences of her behavior. And above all, she must be kind.

And Gap didn't disappoint. To Lee's delight, she understood and was rapidly growing into the kind of human to be admired.

Gap loved daily chores and was strong. She could be seen, even as a small child, cleaning barn stalls with Birchard and Leeward. She understood the stalls had to be cleaned and sanitized to keep the horses, mules, and donkeys healthy. Chicken cages cleaned, baby chicks to admire and carry in her pockets. A practice a mother hen would become annoyed at. After a few encounters with an upset mother hen, she understood and stopped.

Gap was in the midst of it all. And was overjoyed to be there. One of her favorite things to do were tree walks. On the walks, her questions were nonstop with her Papa or Sparsity. "Can we go on a tree walk, Papa, today Papa, not tomorrow, today." Lee found it almost impossible to say no to his daughter. Her enthusiasm for learning made Lee keep up on nature. In teaching Gap, he also learned.

Sparsity would say, "All trees deserve a second look."

Leeward was the most scientific and checked on the trees for their health, mossy growths, exposed roots, how they were leaning, and on and on.

Gap took all the knowledge in and never seemed to get enough. She was taught the wonders of the trees.

As she grew into adulthood, the tree walks remained a special time in her life.

Often the two would walk upon a wind-blown tree that might also be reaching one way or another for some light. This tree made them linger to observe it, or maybe Papa would bring out his pad and pencil to sketch it. The special trees required one to give more than just a quick look. Maybe a sweet taste lunch under it, or at least close by. Lee would say, "Such happiness… to lie under the shattering arms of a tree." The walks usually ended up at the shade pond for a cool dip or just to soak their feet and give arms and face a cool splash.

Gap would pretend the water striders were ice dancers and marvel at their performance as they glided across the pond.

Gap had never really played with other children. She would play marbles with Sparsity; even as grownups the two still enjoyed the fun game. Gap treasured her special Aggie marble. The winner got to keep the marbles called (keepsies). Gap had collected jars of the pretty aesthetic colors that sat along her windowsill.

Gap was a worrier, "Papa we need to check on the baby goats. The baby chicks are about to hatch, the blue birdhouses need to be cleaned and checked that the playing squirrels haven't robbed their nest." On and on she would go as to the work to be done.

Lee assured her, "We have people that can take care of those needed chores, so you don't have to worry."

CHAPTER 22

Today Just Feels Different

Crow's arrival this morning in the barn was a surprise, but a welcomed one. Birchard would often say, "One gets this overall feeling that all is okay when Madame Crow is nearby." Always a fresh flower stuck in one of her rolled braids. Maybe a pink rose, as no red grew in the Gardens, a large double petal chrysanthemum, depending on what was in bloom. Birchard greeted her, "Madame Crow, what brings you out today? Something exceptional happening?"

Birchard stopped rubbing down one of the horses and walked toward her. It was rare for Crow to be anywhere near the barn. The reason was the barn housed horses. It wasn't that she disliked horses. In fact, she admired their beauty, grace, and power. But they made her anxious. She did undertake a dare from Darnell once to ride a horse. "Once was enough, the horse felt as petrified as I was. That I was on her back. No! I will admire them from a distance."

"I am not sure, Birchard, I woke up this morning with a strong feeling of urgency. Seems silly but I feel the urge to make myself a new dress," Crow adjusted her waistline. "Maybe even buy some red fabric. Would it interfere with your day to take me into town?"

"My pleasure, I'll have Runaway get the buggy ready." Birchard smiled and answered, "Maybe you will become a red bird instead of a crow."

Crow gave a small laugh, "Probably not. One day, Birchard, would you show me how to guide the mule and wagon? It's time I took control of this silly fear!"

When Runaway finished rigging, Birchard standing nearby smiled and then said, "Why not today? You said today feels different. So let's do it. Maude is in a sweet mood today, so she will behave. What do you say, Madame Crow?" Birchard extended his hand. Crow climbed up into the driver's side. Birchard handed her the reins. She wrapped her fingers around the reins very confidently. "Sure feels good. My heart is beating fast, I am ready, Birchard. Thank you, Runaway."

"Anytime, Madame Crow." Birchard climbed up beside her. Maude sounded her approval that she was ready. Maude was one of the family and knew her place was special.

"Maude knows the road well, she is extremely smart and will guide you." Birchard finished with detailed instruction for Crow. "Once you master this, Crow, I will teach you to rig the buggy. Then you won't have to wait to be driven, I predict you'll be on these roads, exploring the countryside, soon and all by yourself. Even get into a race when you meet up with Doc. Maude can move when she chooses to." The two had a good laugh at that picture.

Crow was surprised she felt a powerful rush of emotion, a surging movement of freedom had entered her head. "Thank you, Birchard. This morning while drinking my coffee, a voice said, 'Monterey, enjoy this day, seek a new adventure.' Since most of my life has been filled with duty, how about we have lunch today at the Hub after I thoroughly take pleasure in a stroll through town and linger at Mr. Ward's imposing & noble circus statue: And try and coach some good emotional stories from you. My dear Birchard, as you know, I can sit hour after hour and listen to your stories, of when Little D and Azzie arrived at Mr. Ward's circus.

"I envision you and Mickey on the high wire. As the crowd held their breath, silence except for a random gasp as you pedal across that skinny wire. Maybe we can have our lunch beside the circus statue. Tell me more of Mickey spinning over your head. Oh! How beautiful you two must have been. I have seen the posters in Mr. Ward's room, but oh! To have been there live. Never do I forget a gratitude prayer, for you taking in my Little D and Azzie. Birchard, I have a little shopping to do, if you would pick up our lunch."

Birchard's thoughts were soaring, thinking how good it felt to hear Madam Crow so excited about enjoying herself. She mostly took care of others. Birchard said with a large smile on his handsome, aging face, "Some new red material for that dress!" Birchard reached over and put his hand on Crow's.

Crow picked up quickly, in fact, she seemed as if she had been driving the wagon all her life, and she made a friend in Maude. Each person had to go out of their way to win Maude over. A warm soft sun and a delicious breeze stayed with Birchard and Crow on the ride into Darnell. Upon reaching town, Birchard said, "Crow, I need a few supplies and Maude needs to be watered; she also likes a quick rubdown. Plus, you need to let her know how much you appreciate that she let you guide the wagon. She is extremely sensitive about who guides her reins. I will pick up our lunch."

Crow spent a few minutes talking softly close to Maude's ear. The mule was quite extraordinary. Maude gave Crow a nuzzle. A new friendship was born.

Crow walked away, feeling taller, and a smile on her face.

After her purchase of several different fabrics, one fabric in a particular red velvet with gold threads running through it with a few yards of gold-colored velvet ribbon for trim. She also spied some fancy bone buttons. Crow thought, 'I know this is way too much to spend, but they will look just right on this dress.' She considered it strange, why was she drawn to purchase something so outlandish. The feeling was too strong not to do it.

She strolled the stone sidewalks. Upon noticing her reflection in a store window, a shiver washed over her. She felt somewhat guilty for this indulgence. She thought of her beautiful mother, and the sacrifices she gave for her children. Emotions Crow felt that had been gone from her heart were returning: passion, singing, argument, and most of all touch. She wanted to hug each person that strolled by her, but the people nodded as they passed. But no one stopped to chat. Crow didn't give off an approachable demeanor. She certainly painted a person of interest, tall straight spine, hair black as the blackest crow, pulled taught from her face, a strong caring face, few lines, still with her authoritarian air. A person that walked too close may have felt they intruded on her space. The norm of Darnell's citizens were the opposite.

When Crow reached the steps of the Hub, she felt short-winded, her legs went weak, her overall feelings went beyond anxious. Her first thought was, 'God don't take me now. I want to take that buggy out by myself. And ride these country roads, breathe in the fresh air, give a sign to Maude to go a little faster. I may even undo these braids, and let the wind move my hair, flying free like some wild bird. No! Not now. I am not ready to leave this place.'

"Big sis Monterey," Crow's insides moved about, and chills attacked her spine. She stood, yes! It was the voice of her precious sister Azzie, here, in front of her.

For a moment, Crow was transported back when the two had stood in the stinging cold, singing for a few coins to purchase food for the family and Azzie doing backflips, her red shiny hair, flinging about.

Azzie was an undaunted fiery redhead child that would say, "Big sis, do you think we have enough coins? I could do more flips." How I have missed my fearless little sis.

Crow turned to look into the face of a woman who held a few characteristic qualities of her beloved Azzie.

Her hair was hennaed a brass red, her purple dress was frayed but stylish, a front tooth was missing, the once perfect round deliciously beautiful freckled face was worn with sadness beyond belief. Azzie dragged her right leg, the limp didn't pull her shoulders down—she still stood tall, and very thin. Her tiny waist was cinched with a gold cord. Her voice was a perfect pitch, it seemed to have stayed 12 years old. She carried a small cage, with a hairless dog—that she had dressed regal, exactly as Lee had described "Princess Attire" that of Azzie's show horse. A tiny beaded harness was around the dog's neck, feathered plumage rested on its tiny head, and a little coat covered its back.

Monterey said, "How miraculous you found me."

"No Monterey, you found me. A detective you hired followed me through my performances for kings and queens all over the world, and some small towns. A terrible accident happened. You know I never performed with the safety rope and after my fall, no one believed I would live." Azzie lifted her fringed dress to show Crow her mangled leg.

"After my body started to heal, I was put into a sanitarium. The voices that often entered my head returned. Later I was told that a detective had visited. But since the disturbances of my mind came and went, I didn't remember him. My doctors informed me that I had extensive conversations with the detective. Convinced that I was one of the Darnell children. He kept in contact with one of those strong-hearted doctors, along with money to be used for my welfare. He said the money was from an amount Mr. Ward had left with him, in case he found Little D's sisters. How about that? I thought he was still mad at me."

Tears ran down her weathered cheeks. Monterey reached into her pocket, pulling out a lovely embroidered white handkerchief and wiped Azzie's tears. Azzie stopped her talking and started looking around. Her head and eyes moving as if she had lost something. "Where is Little D? Let's find him. That precious boy can find the most adventurous places to hide. You don't think he climbed up into the top of the main circus tent?"

Monterey stared at her beloved sister, taking in her appearance. Azzie's lips were painted red as the reddest apple. Remembering red was her favorite color. The lipstick seeped into the lines around her once lovely, soft wide lips. Oh! If only Lee could have found Azzie earlier. Maybe she could have been helped with loving care. But according to Birchard's account of the early years, Mickey and Birchard gave Azzie great love and care. Also, Mr. Ward searched for all kinds of doctors to help Azzie. It wasn't to be. She ran away.

Azzie sensing Monterey was upset, spoke, "Big sister, my dear, dear, sister. I was respected and admired for my extraordinary horsemanship, more so than my beauty."

Monterey realized her once talented beautiful Azzie was mentally unbalanced. But one moment she was back in time, the next lucid, her intelligence shining from her face and words.

Crow said, "Come here." She motioned with her arms, Azzie walked into a hug so strong, with all the love and anguish her big sister had to give. The pain of life had taken its toll on both sisters. But at this moment, the years were swept away and nothing but peace and love engulfed the sisters.

The two sisters stood outside the Hub. Crow was excited to a frenzy, at the same time crestfallen. Would Azzie know Lee and Birchard?

A small crowd was gathering around. Crow, being completely lost in her thoughts, didn't realize Azzie had taken a few small colored rings from her carpet bag—and her dog princess was doing tricks. The small white dog was jumping and circling, stopping to stand on two back paws, enjoying the crowd's applause.

"What happens here, when Birchard appears?" Crow said to no one in particular.

Azzie, even with her injuries, stood right at six feet. The sisters were still eye-catching, Crow in all black, and Azzie in purple. The two slowed the passersby's, to stop to look, wonder, and join the people now gathered around them.

Crow shouted, "It's miraculous, I knew this day was going to be different, but never did I dream how much. I have missed you every day of my life."

"I know," said Azzie, "I'll tell you everything." Azzie released Crow's arm and let out a scream. "Birchard, my dear, dear Birchard. It's really you, have you forgiven me? Where is Mickey? Do you have any babies?" She asked questions as though it had only been a few years and moved towards the small dog. "Come, Princess, time to rest." After she put Princess in her small carry case, she once more turned her attention to Birchard.

Crow replied, "Mickey died in childbirth."

Azzie spoke, "Not radiant Mickey… she deserved to live, her goodness touched all." Azzie collapsed onto the steps. "Birchard," she moaned, "Birchard you now know how sick I was and am, otherwise I never would have caused you or Mickey pain, I was in a bad mental state, those voices coming and going in my head. Telling me to do terrible mean stuff. Please tell me that Mickey forgave me?" Azzie covered her still long, graceful hands. Her crying shook her body.

Birchard spoke, his voice emotional, "We all understood how

messed up you were, so there was never anything to forgive, we loved and adored you. So how could we not have been pained at you leaving us? The hardest part was the heartache of Little D, as he was called then."

People continued to stop and ask their good friend, Birchard, if all was okay, "Can we be of help, anything?" Birchard was loved by all who knew him.

"No, please. Thank you."

Birchard said, "Crow, why don't we head home, how can we keep Lee waiting. Azzie, Lee speaks of you every day."

"Is Little D mad at me? Maybe he will not wish to see me."

Crow took hold of her sister's arm, leading her toward the wagon.

"Why are you called Crow, my dear Monterey?"

"When I lost all my siblings and my new family was destroyed, I have since dressed in black. The girls where I taught school said I looked like a crow. I like the name and have stuck with it."

Birchard thought, "How did she ever reach here in her mental state?" His thoughts were disrupted by Azzie's questions. "Birchard, do you have children?

Crow answered for him. "Dear Azzie, as I told you before, Mickey died in childbirth. There are two boys, Leeward and Folly. They work on Protected Earth."

Showing no interest in Crow's answer, Azzie said, "I wish you could have seen me in my prime, I was respected, was I not, Birchard?"

"Yes! You were the star attraction, but you broke my Mickey's heart." Birchard thought, 'I should not say these things, Azzie is so sick, but I still hurt at the heartache it caused my Mickey.'

Azzie kept right on talking, "Mickey—she will be expecting me, she does worry. I am bad. Mickey will forgive me. Where is Mickey?"

Crow thought—should I continue to bring her back to the present? Crow repeated and said to her ill sister—once more "My dear one, Mickey died giving birth to two boys."

Azzie lost interest in the painful subject. Her mind jumped from past to present. She didn't realize what Birchard had said, or that she ran away so long ago.

"Big sis Monterey, where is Little D and Dessie?"

Birchard walked away, struggling with his walk, with a look of disbelief on his face, to bring the carriage closer. He picked up Azzie's carpet bag that had circus clowns on it.

"Azzie my dear, what kind of accident happened to your leg?" asked Crow.

"My attachment broke that held my legs. I was dragged by a horse I wasn't familiar with. My leg wasn't set properly, but it's okay. My life could have ended that day, had it not been I was strong and fit, the doctor told me."

"That detective had traced you to the girls' school in Atlanta. And how could I believe Little D was grown and you had moved to a town named Darnell. I can't believe a town named after us Darnell's — that S.B. of a Daddy — finally received his status."

Birchard had been hurt so deeply, even though long years had passed. His memory of how painful Lee and Mickey suffered when Azzie up and left in the night. His high values toward loyalty would not let him be so free as to embrace her. She had caused so much worry and pain to the persons he loved so deeply.

Crow asked Birchard to please pause at the fabric shop. Birchard surmised from the look of Azzie's frayed dressage, he knew what Crow intended, a new frock for her sister.

Crow put her arm around her sister, "It's all okay. Soon — very soon. Birchard will take us home, home is Protected Earth. But first, come — I want you to see something beautiful."

Crow said, "Can we let Birchard lookout for Princess? We'll be right back, and she will be safe."

"Birchard's mad at me. Maybe he doesn't like Princess?" Azzie had tears streaming down her face.

She held onto the cage. Crow and Azzie walked over to see the circus statue of Mr. Ward, regal in his top hat as the ringmaster. Azzie standing beside Princess, Birchard, and Mickey on the high wire bike. A separate statue of a boy of about seven. Looking spellbound at the circus act. All done in bronze life-size. The statue sat in the center of the small park that ran along the creek. Before Crow could stop her, Azzie sat Princess down. Threw her leg over the statue of the horse, her crippled leg shaking as she tried to stand up on the horse's back holding on to the statue of herself at seventeen. There she stood, in her mind, back at the circus.

"Close your eyes, big sis, you can go to the circus with me, Princess and I are the star attraction, The Amazing Blaze. Do you see us, and hear the thundering applause? I am whirling tumblers on my horse." Azzie was teetering on top of the bronze statue. Crow reached out to steady her. Azzie was fast, she came out of the fall by giving a backflip. Her dress flying, showing black French undergarments. She landed and hooked her arms through her sisters.

Crow put her head back and gave a big hearty laugh, "That was a glorious sight for my eyes to take in. You are still a star."

Crow looked around at the faces of the gathering audience. She saw that Azzie was indifferent as to what the citizens of Darnell thought. Azzie was for the moment a star once more. Her small dog, dressed in its costume, was her incredible white horse, Princess. When Princess pranced into the Big Top, she took the audience's breath away.

The people now gathered around Azzie, looking upon her as an oddity. But Crow found her to be an astonishing, whimsical character, carrying no hate. She loved her to the edge of the earth, as she did her brother and sis Dessie.

Birchard sat behind the reins on the way home. Maude didn't need directions, but she did seem in somewhat of a hurry today. Something was different. Azzie had fallen asleep with her head in Crow's lap.

Azzie wasn't the least bit interested in the tree-lined drive or the lush rolling hills laced with cattle, goats, and mares showing off their colts.

Azzie spoke, "Where is Little D? I thought maybe Mr. Ward would ride out with Little D to meet me."

Crow put her hand on Azzie's arm and spoke softly, "Azzie, dear Mr. Ward is dead, he passed away, he created this beautiful place, he worked so hard. Lee has been running everything, along with Birchard, since he was seventeen."

Azzie looked towards Crow in disbelief. She said nothing. Princess, her dog, arose and moved in close to Azzie.

Crow reached into her bag and brought out a silver flask. Reaching under her seat, she pulled out a small black bag that contained some silver shot cups. She poured a brandy and handed it to Azzie, then one to Birchard and herself. Birchard stopped the wagon at the creek that ran across the road. While Maude helped herself to some cold, refreshing water, Crow toasted, "My precious beautiful little sister. What a most beloved day this is, you are back in our lives. I love you and pray you never leave us again."

Azzie had tears rolling down her face, "I won't," and the three drank.

"That was nice," said Birchard. "How about another?" After the second brandy, all felt more relaxed. A verbal sign to Maude to move on.

The rest of the ride home was quiet. Azzie fell asleep with her head in Monterey's lap. Monterey soothed her brow as she spoke to Birchard, "Birchard, you must not hate our dear Azzie. She has been ill for some time, I am sure. Did you not witness this, even when she first came to Mr. Ward's circus at such a young age?"

Birchard answered, "Madame Crow, you are correct. She was an ill-fated talented beauty. I am trying hard not to remember the pain."

Crow wondered, how has Azzie survived in this state of mind. Remarkably she was quite well-groomed for being so out of touch with reality. The signs of her mental illness seemed to come and go. How long a period was difficult to know. Crow knew, if possible, she was going to take care of Azzie, and that Lee would feel the same.

Azzie awoke when the buggy came to a stop at the barn. Lee had just been for a ride and was walking out of the barn. He stopped, then ran the few steps to the wagon. If ever there was a greeting between two people that showed their love for one another, it was Azzie and Lee.

Azzie saw Little D, the baby brother she had protected, and told beautiful stories to at night, about their siblings to soothe his breaking heart at being separated from them. She did not see the handsome man, large mustache, tan-lined face, with the Darnell dark eyes moving toward her. The two hugged and cried. The years had vanished.

Lee motioned for Crow to step forward into the embrace, the three were locked in years of pain.

Crow spoke, "We must take Azzie to Doc Francis for a check-up, as soon as possible."

Darnell now had a small hospital; Doc Francis was involved in every part of Darnell's citizens' care. He was training a local boy who had just returned to Darnell with a doctor's degree, thanks to the funds that Mr. Ward left for college fees for the locals. Doc Francis often thought how pleased Mr. Ward would be, resting in heaven knowing that so many young people were coming back to their roots, and starting their own business, getting married, having children, and settling in.

That was Mr. Ward's main goal, to make Darnell such a town, that the young people did not wish to leave.

"Yes! My friend, you succeeded," Doc Francis would say often.

Lee asked, "Azzie, are you well?"

Azzie knew it was Little D but kept staring at him puzzled.

Lee thought he would lighten the air around them. "How about we take a ride and show Azzie Protected Earth?"

Crow softly spoke, "Count me out. Lee, you will not get me on a horse again." From the barn, Crow could see Sparsity and Gap looking toward them from the main house.

Birchard was very tired. "Lee, I am afraid I can't make it, I need some rest. It's been a busy day. Azzie dear, I will see you at breakfast. Good evening."

"Well sis, Azzie, it's just the two of us."

When Lee started to put the saddle on Azzie's horse, she said, "No brother—bareback is fine." She walked to the horse—put her cheek against his head, whispered in his ears, ran her hand along his back to his hindquarters—took hold of his main and scaled onto his back—off she rode, moving on the horse like a spinning top—she stopped—turned him, and rode back to where Lee was standing.

Lee was spellbound, staring with his mouth hanging open. Lee, looking at Gap and Sparsity who had walked into the barn, spoke, "Now you know why she was the star attraction, a shining diamond."

Gap said, "Papa can it be, it's really Aunt Azzie? How did she ever find us? Oh! Papa how wonderful! This is a grand day!"

Gap didn't wait for Azzie to descend her horse, she was right there. "Aunt Azzie, you are so fantastic. I feel I know you from all of Papa's stories. Papa and Crow have kept you with us through their beautiful memories, they are always able to reach out and grasp one."

Azzie wasn't finished; she did her backflip dismount, shaky when she hit the ground. Her bad leg was wobbly. It was a brave show she gave, and her dress be damned. Gap spoke, "Papa, I will help put the horses away. Take Aunt Azzie to the house. I will be along shortly."

Sparsity stood on the side, "Never have I ever seen anything so amazing and beautiful. She is here, right here with us."

Lee put his arm around his sister. He spoke softly, "I want you to love it here, all will be okay, you are home."

Azzie turned to face her little brother, "I never left you. Where's Princess? And Birchard, is he still mad at me?" she did not ask who Gap and Sparsity were.

"Princess is with Crow, she will take care of her."

"Lee, my dear, dear brother, you do know that the voices still follow me and take over my life. Can I stay with you and big sister? At least for a short while and then I will be moving on."

A soft rain had started to fall. Lee's lips quivered, his heart was full, he thought dear Azzie is really here, he answered, "You will never leave Protected Earth, there is so much love for you here. And riding every day as you wish. Sparsity will help heal your leg with special herbs and love and care from all of us. Our local Doc Francis may possibly be able to fix your leg."

Princess, her small dog, now slept in her arms. If only Azzie will find the same contentment.

Azzie enjoyed only a few months living on Protected Earth. Not only was her mind shattered, but she also had a weak heart.

Lee had taken her for an exam with Doc Francis. Doc felt her heart was only operating at about thirty percent. She slept most days.

One morning she came to join Lee and Crow for breakfast, dressed, with luggage in hand, and stated she was going back to the circus.

She laid her head onto her folded arms and went to sleep forever. No struggle. She was buried in the family plot, where Mr. Ward, Mickey, and Cal were laid to rest.

All felt extremely blessed they had been given the gift of Azzie, for the time she had to give.

Gap cried, "Oh Papa, it breaks my heart to think we almost missed her."

CHAPTER 23

Sparsity's Walk

Today Sparsity's walk was to make a list for Lee, to give to Leeward. Her list was to be of any trees on Protected Earth that needed some attention. Also, on her last walk, as she headed toward home she noticed the property could use more native plants in certain areas. She knew Lee and Leeward understood this need to keep the wildlife provided with shrubs, trees, and perennials so all may flourish.

Today her list was long and in detail. She asked herself, "How have I missed all of this need?" There are native pachysandra, woodland phlox, wild ginger. More spaces for these and the ever-wonderful piedmont azalea, (Rhododendrons), Gap's most loved plant. Leeward may have personality faults, but he is well informed on the environment and has great interests in preserving it.

Over the years, she requested and Lee planted many, many understory trees, such as the pink dogwoods. They help to add layers to the landscapes and what a complete feast for the eyes when in bloom.

All who knew Sparsity knew she marched to a different drummer. She was not easily intimidated by anyone's view of her. Sparsity was always in the pursuit of something—could be a herb, or flower. With no formal schooling, she was amazingly up on most things. Sparsity loved books, and the joy of learning. She felt better alone, which could frustrate others. Much respected by the citizens, they knew she was there for them wherever needed.

Her main contentment was her lone walks and her love of trees. If anyone thought of her as strange, they may have judged her because of how she talked to the trees and carried a special friendship with the woods. Lee purchased books and courses for Sparsity. She read and studied. She learned that the African Acacia tree would release a chemical into the air when the tree felt a threat, such as an animal eating its bark. Her excitement was that she had always believed that trees have their own communication.

Lee had seen an advertisement in the Times—For Sale, Small Tables made from recycled African Acacia Trees—he ordered one for Sparsity. She treasured it and placed it in its own special place in her cottage.

Today she came upon a patch of honeysuckle taking the life out of young trees. The vine has sweet lily-type blooms but can distort young trees into odd shapes. Sparsity made a note and would give Lee full details to have Leeward take care of it.

She tucked her notes away, stopped by the pond, and had her lunch. She took a small rolled quilt out of her pack, spread it on a nice moss area, and took a nap.

Awakened by a wet nose, it was Chase and Talker, with Gap. Gap spoke, "Sorry for the intrusion, we thought a cool dip in the pond, after our long hike, would seal a lovely day."

"Oh! All's okay. I should be up and on my way." Shaking off a few leaves, she quickly packed up, and said goodbye.

Gap, took off her clothes, hung them over a limb and she and the dogs had a nice cool off swim.

CHAPTER 24

Gap and Starling

G ap expected her days to be glorious. Papa would remind her, "Don't get too full of yourself." When she felt herself becoming self-absorbed, she turned to hard physical labor. Labor was easy to be had on Protected Earth. There were always available chores, such as clearing beetle-infested pines, planting beloved Azaleas throughout the property, goats to milk, cheese to make; the list was endless, and she loved every moment.

But first comes coffee, then a long walk. She stretched her muscular arms out to the aging blue ticks that were snuggled in close to her. The two never missed a chance to receive or show affection. Gap wiped a tear away, just thinking of Chase and Talker no longer on this earth.

"Seems only a short time ago when you two would already be out in the forest on some adventure."

Their old bones were tired and probably full of ache. Upon hearing their names, Chase and Talker turned their heads sideways, but within a flash, they were fast asleep. Gap smiled and wiped away a few more tears. Chase and Talker's loyalty to the Darnell family was unscathed. The long gold framed mirror that hung between two floor-to-ceiling windows gave a beautiful image of Gap. She stared at herself and a thought came to her about her mother. As of late, Gap took to wondering about the strange, mysterious young woman that had given birth to her. Crow described Garrison as a real showstopper. Papa told his daughter, "If you have questions about your mother, I can answer very little. She was not a woman that revealed herself. One could see that she had talent as an artist, she could sleep for days, and also stay awake for nights. There was nothing ordinary about Garrison. She would go to the pond and swim nude until she collapsed on the soft moss. She ate very little, drank coffee and brandy when she painted, and rarely gave an opinion on anything. She read any book that came into her sight, and not once did she discuss anything she absorbed or felt about the book."

Papa showed no emotion when he spoke of Garrison Anne Polly. Her self-portrait was extraordinary. It was life-sized and rested against a wall in Papa's room. Every so often, Gap would go into her Papa's room and study the painting. Yes! She had her mother's beauty, but she wanted to see and understand more about the spirit of her mother.

Gap knew how her Papa felt about interference in another's decision. Garrison Anne Polly had chosen to walk away forever, leaving her newborn daughter. As far as anyone knew, Papa Lee never sought to go after her. He once told Crow he felt Garrison Anne Polly was a wonder of an angel that delivered his incredible daughter into his life. "Why was I so blessed? Only a higher power knows."

Papa told Gap that he would have gladly built Garrison a house, taken care of her finances, and opened a studio for her if she had desired. But she wanted nothing from him.

Gap knew her Papa would be there if she was in danger of any kind. He had taught Gap to think before your act. She was responsible for her actions. Papa was empathetic when it came to holding a person back. "If a person wishes to go, it's wrong to ask that person to stay. It doesn't mean you can't state your feelings on their choice, but in the end, it is their decision."

"Hey," Gap said to no one. "I am here, and I plan on living a long time. I dearly love and feel connected to all my Protected Earth family. I may wander, but I will always come home to Protected Earth."

A knock at her door broke into her conversation with herself. She knew Papa's knock. Papa walked in, filling up the doorway. "Morning, Papa." She gave him the strongest hug.

"Sounded like you were talking to someone."

"No! Just questioning myself about stuff." She reached down and pulled on her boots, tucking her pant leg into the boots. He would always be concerned for her happiness.

"Want to share anything with your Papa?"

"Yes, but later. I have some deliveries to take cheeses to the Hub, along with a few paintings that are overdue to a New York gallery."

"Need some assistance? Since it is your birthday. Why don't you take Emilio?"

"Okay, Papa. Sounds good. Looking forward to dinner tonight. Sparsity says she is making all our favorites. Dinner on the porch with lanterns. We can chat about my meandering thoughts this morning. I love you heaven and earth, Papa. See you tonight."

Chase and Talker came alive and jumped off the bed like young pups. The thought of Gap leaving without them was too much.

"Okay, come boys. Let's go find Emilio."

Emilio was piling fresh hay in a small wagon for Folly to pick up to feed his much-loved goats. He glanced towards Gap. Emilio was happy with his life on Protected Earth with his wife and three children. He was doing what he loved, along with Runaway, training and caring for horses. He wasn't about to do anything that would endanger his employment. Besides, Lee Darnell was the smartest and kindest man he had ever known. Lee had given him a job. He understood he was to be working and learning alongside Leeward. One had only to look around and know the depth of Leeward's accomplishments. A home, free-range of the land, and a safe place to raise his children. No! He would not do anything to hurt Mr. Lee or his family. Emilio was a handsome, sexy man. Braided black hair surrounded his dark, finely defined golden-colored face. He was Cherokee and Spanish. A proud one.

"Morning, Miss Gap, going for a ride?" Emilio asked.

"No, but I do need your assistance today. Everyone else is committed to other things. I have to deliver cheese to the Hub and pack some art to be sent out."

"Do Markita and Sparsity have the cheese packed? And should I go pick that up? Also, I can inform Folly his hay for the goats is ready, he can hook the pony up to his wagon."

"Sounds good. Pick me up at Papa's studio doors."

Gap walked away, well aware of the sexual tension between her and Emilio. Emilio returned and Gap noticed he had changed his shirt. After loading the art onto the wagon, Gap pointed out, "I'll take the reins into Darnell." First, she gave Maude a few kisses, rubs, and some appreciation talk. The proud reliable mule ate it up.

Emilio chattered non-stop about his love of Appaloosa horses, the long races his father had won. Gap smiled.

Gap was extremely adventurous to seize life when she glimpsed it. She thought about seducing Emilio, but only a delicious thought. She liked that he desired her, and fantasy never hurt anyone. She gave a small pull on the reins and Maude moved a little faster. Chase and Talker slept peacefully in the wagon bed.

The rest of the ride into town, Gap mostly listened to Emilio chatting away about horses and his father's heroics. Besides, she turned seventeen today, and was looking forward to celebrating.

Liza had seen Gap roll up in her wagon with Emilio. She wanted to engage Gap's attention before she spotted the handsome stranger. She need not have concerned herself. Gap already spotted the new traveler.

Gap called out to Liza, "Morning, I'll eat breakfast on the porch. Emilio will return after he takes care of some other business and help unload the paintings. Which he will also crate and wrap for mailing."

Gap wasn't the kind of girl who thought about her looks, she didn't have to, she had it all. Tall, almost six feet, perfect flawless tan skin, golden blonde hair that always seemed to shine and smell nice. Her long legs and body were muscular from the heavy farm work she did most every day. Her chocolate amber flecked eyes met each person face-to-face. She preferred the company of men and liked working alongside them outdoors where she held her own. She respected strength, physique, and all the women she knew were exceptional; Crow, Sparsity, Liza, and all the ones that had gone before her. She knew them well from Papa's stories and often asked him to repeat.

Sam, a long-time citizen, could be found most anytime seated either in the Hub or on a rocker on the porch of the Hub. Just in case he might be needed for anything. Sam was a quiet man who sat and observed his surroundings. And one supposed went back into his memories of his beloved Cal. He was getting on up in age.

Sam said, "Gap, I'll water and rub down Maude and freshen some water for Chase and Talker."

"Thanks, Sam," Gap said. Gap knew the lonesomeness that Sam carried around since Cal died. And the heartache he had endured when Cal fell hard for Mr. Ward. Sam was one of the most trustworthy people on earth and was dearly loved by the citizens of Darnell. He will be missed when he passes on.

When Gap was in town, she would often share lunch and a drink with Sam, Dr. Francis, or Liza. Liza now ran the Hub. Doc Francis said it was amazing Cal had lived so long. She was skin and bones and rarely had a drink out of her hand after Mr. Ward died. Gap knew the love between Cal and Mr. Ward. Papa Lee noted, "Ward took her heartbeat, her laughter, and her desire. In truth, he was Cal's only love, nothing was ever the same after Ward died. Cal had expected to live out her life with Mr. Ward, but for whatever the reason, God saw different."

Sam moving a little slower each year, he proceeded to take care of Maude and the blue ticks. Gap started into the Hub when Liza walked through the door. Gap put her arm around Liza's shoulder, moving close into her ear, and said, "Any information on the new man in town?"

"Don't know too much, seems to be a loner, eats alone, walks alone. He leaves early mornings for the woods and hills. Says he is a gemologist, heavy backpack, shovel, and pics. Comes in late, sometimes not until the next morning. I have found him seated on the steps when I come in early to open the Hub. If interested, Gap, he also sleeps alone."

Gap sat on the steps and considered the information about the mysterious newcomer. She took a large drink from the mason jar Liza had just handed her. She felt his presence before she saw him walk up. He removed the backpack and untied his blue-neck scarf. He wet it in the mules and horses watering trough and walked over to Maude and started to wipe down Maude's haunches. Maude, who didn't take kindly to strangers, was reveling in this man's attention.

Sam had given Maude a light rub down, but she loved the rub downs.

Gap was thinking, can't blame Maude for that, everything about him was good to look at. He was at least 6'3", chiseled tan face, and a body that moved well in every direction.

Gap said, "I like action, kindness, something I would do for someone."

He looked at her, she knew, and he knew, this is what is called love at first sight.

He walked up the steps, tying the wet scarf back around his neck. He nodded as he stepped in closer. "I am Starling, your mule looked tired and hot. I know how good it feels to have a cool cloth after a long walk or rough day. Your dogs are taking a swim in the creek."

Gap liked the familiar way he talked, and he was looking out for her animals. She stood at six feet, and Starling surpassed her by at least three inches. She put her hand out, "I am Gap Darnell."

He reached for her hand, her strong grip made him smile and shiver right down to his spine. His thoughts were, I am in trouble here, and she is young. To compose himself he asked, "Is that Darnell, like in this charming town?"

Gap pulled her hand away reluctantly, thinking this feels right. "Yes! That's my daddy. Any last name for you?"

"Okay! But no laughing. Starling Songster."

"Well, Starling Songster, do you ride? Or do you walk everywhere you go?"

"Yes, but I prefer my two feet on the ground."

Starling took his eyes away to stare at Chase and Talker running toward Gap, stopping ever so often, to shake and water shower whoever was nearby. The dogs approached and gave Starling some questionable looks, observing the situation. Gap patted her leg for the two to come in close, and added, "This is Starling, boys. He looks friendly enough."

"Are they alright with me?" asked Starling.

"You would already know it if they didn't trust you," boasted Gap. Gap was bold when she desired something, and this ranked high. She thought, 'he isn't asking my age.'

Starling looked as if he was walking away, but paused in a familiar way, and put his backpack in Gap's wagon. Emilio walked up. Emilio noticed Maude gave the man a nuzzle as he walked near her. Extremely odd for the cantankerous Maude.

"Miss Gap, sorry I was delayed. All the supplies are ready to be loaded." Emilio was still eyeing the stranger. He knew Lee Darnell expected him to protect his one child at any cost. Not that it was an easy task. Gap had a mind of her own.

"Oh! No problem, Emilio. Would you mind borrowing a horse from Liza? I don't believe I am going straight home. Tell Papa I am fine, and something has come up. I will finish loading the wagon, is there anything that needs to be unloaded today?"

"No, as long as you are good. Remember your papa expects me to protect you."

Gap smiled at Emilio's concern, "I am fine — tell Papa I will be at the wildflower cabin overnight."

"Sure thing, Miss Gap." Emilio walked towards the Hub. He kept looking back. Not one hundred percent certain he was doing the right thing, leaving Gap with a stranger.

Starling had returned with some rolled-up clothes and stuffed them into his pack.

"Hey. I didn't pay for my breakfast, got a bit distracted."

Chase and Talker lingered close by waiting for a signal from Gap to indicate their direction.

Liza was standing on the Hub porch, curious as to what was taking place. Starling took out a worn leather pouch to pay Liza. She pushed his hand away. Starling explained, "Thanks, I like the people and the town with each passing minute. This means I owe you, Liza, find a chore for me to take care of." All the time, his eyes were on Gap.

Gap gave a high sigh to Chase and Talker, "Going with us, boys?" The dogs stayed close as the two walked to the wagon.

In the meantime, a couple of locals loaded up the supplies onto the wagon that Emilio had placed close by. Starling climbed onto the seat next to Gap. Gap signaled Maude and the wagon headed toward home.

Gap and Starling sat silent. Almost a mile down the road, Gap broke the silence. "Starling, what brings you to our part of the world?"

"I was commissioned by a Mr. O'Shay to check for gems on his farm. Besides, I like being on the road, keeps me more of a sound mind. Does not always work. I can still become insufferable to myself and others. Some even say unbalanced."

"Sounds a bit tangled. Tell me more."

"No! You might run the other way. Can we just let it be for now?"

"Sure." Gap's mind was rainy, along with her lust for this man.

Even with two interesting persons, the wagon ride was not filled with talk.

They reached the entrance to Protected Earth. She stopped Maude and jumped out to open the gates. Maude walked on through without Gap's direction. She had been through those gates' countless times. Gap waited and closed the gate. She felt Starling's eyes on her every move and could feel him studying her. Most likely, he was concerned about my age, what kind of abilities I possess. Gap thought, oh well, he will know soon know. He is a Yankee. Northerners, from her limited experience, were skeptical about most everything.

Heading toward the cabin instead of the drive to the main house, Starling spoke, "Appears to be a perfect world we have entered." He had moved to take over the reins. He stopped the wagon and was enjoying the lovely sight of a group of Lady Slippers on a hillside now blooming. They covered the hillside that ended in a small stream that ran along the side of the road. "So far, all is gratifying to the eye."

Gap thought, I sure do like that he isn't full of empty talk.

They reached the cabin. Starling quickly jumped out. "I will unhitch Maude and wipe her down."

Chase and Talker had been taken with this character right away. The dogs ran to the cabin door, jumped, and pushed the door open.

Gap said, "I'll make some coffee after I build a fire and heat some water for our bath. You start filling the tub on the porch from the rain barrels on the side of the cabin. A bath for me brings a new light to my day, no matter the time."

Starling reached for her hand and turned her toward him and said, "You are the most astounding person. Are you sure I am awake?"

Gap went into his arms. "I want to mesh into your skin," she said. They kissed and she moved away and walked into the cabin. Gap opened a jar of blackberry cobbler, poured it into a fry pan. The fire was quickly going. She heated it alongside the bathwater. She put a tablecloth on the table, set out cups of hot, bubbly cobbler with canned crème and two brandy glasses. Starling had walked outside and was standing by the well. Gap called out, "Our bath water is ready, there's a robe on the hook next to the tub."

Starling added the hot water to the tub.

Gap got undressed and put a robe on and waited until she heard Starling get into the tub.

She removed the blanket from the bed, exposing crisp, white linen, all the while drinking her coffee and brandy. Starling came inside, "Believe I'll have another. How old are you, Gap?"

She knew that question was coming, "Seventeen today, and I am not a virgin."

Starling looked around the cabin, books were stacked in piles, dried wildflowers and herbs were abundant in baskets that hung on the walls, mason jars of canned goods made a colorful display on shelves that included tomatoes, cherries, peppers, okra, peaches, blackberries, plums, and on and on.

"Gap, you should know I am a mentally unstable man. You are so young. If you wish to stop this right now, I can walk away. No, I can't, but I am not ready for your daddy to come after me with a shotgun."

Gap stood and removed her robe. "Starling, I will never marry. My life is here on Protected Earth. I will never leave Papa, the land, and its people, the animals, and all the things this land has given me. If we only have today, it's okay. I don't like a lot of words or exclamations. My papa knows I can take care of myself. He trusts me not to take dangerous chances."

They moved to the bed, moving their faces close. Exploring each other with a sweetness of passion. He lowered his body over her and entered her slowly. Afterward, she touched his face and said, "I am happy, and I love you."

"Gap, I have said 'I love you' to many a mountain, an ocean, on moonlit nights alone by a campfire, but this is my first to tell a woman I love her." They fell asleep.

When Gap awoke, the sun was going down. She woke Starling and said, "I have to take the wagon home and see my Papa. You are welcome to join me or stay in the cabin. I'll return at daybreak. I am to have dinner with my Papa. He was expecting me for my birthday. But he will understand."

"You go, I'll stay." He pulled her toward him and once more they made love without words, just the way Gap liked. She kissed him. "Want to help me hitch the wagon back up?"

"Yes."

"Will you be okay? If you get lonely, follow the trail to the first turn off, you will come to the main house. The front screen porch is open. You can sleep on the porch."

Starling said, "I'll be fine. And miss you every moment, as I would miss the air I breathe."

Starling watched the wagon pull away as darkness started coming in.

Papa and Crow were on the porch. Gap took Maude and the wagon to the barn. Chase and Talker ran to the house ahead of Gap.

"You had a long day, daughter. Is all, okay? Emilio stopped by and said he left you in town. You were very involved in conversation with a handsome gentleman."

"Papa, you aren't starting to worry about me, are you?"

"I have never stopped from the day you were laid in my arms. But I know you can handle most any occurrences."

"The handsome gentleman is named Starling. He is at the pond cabin."

Crow gave Gap a hug and said, "It shows all over you. Want to talk about him?"

"No." She kissed them and said, "Any of that special dinner left? I won't be having breakfast with my two-favorite people, but I am here now. Let's celebrate my birthday." Gap was with the two people she loved most, but her whole body was yearning for Starling.

"We understand, but you know if a man hurts you, he will see his Maker all too soon," said Papa—as he pretended to draw his six-shooter.

"I know, Papa, and I adore you for your ever-vigilant watch over me." Gap walked inside, smiling, feeling elated about her day and every fiber of her longed for Starling. She had champagne and cake with Papa, Crow, and Sparsity. Afterward, Gap saddled two horses. She knew she wanted the spotted Appaloosa for Starling. With Appaloosa in tow, she rode toward the cabin.

During the ride to the cabin, she realized her mind was focused completely on Starling. One of the few times she didn't take in what was happening along the way. Starling was chopping wood when she rode up. She thought, what selfish joy I am feeling from the sight of him.

"Hey!" She hollered. "That's my job. I brought fresh eggs and the most luscious goat cheese you will ever taste, made right here on Protected Earth." She held out her saddlebags. Starling went on cutting wood.

Gap thought for a second, I believe I saw in that face a touch of insanity—but she pushed it aside and wondered, why would I have such a thought?

She released the horses to graze, put the saddles on the porch, and went inside.

Coffee aroma filled the room along with bacon. Starling had not disappointed.

Starling walked in. She handed him a coffee. "Let's talk," he firmly declared.

"I am listening, but it isn't necessary. Starling, yes! I am only seventeen, but I know my mind and my heart, I am willing to give my time to you and do not wish to waste a moment of it. What do you wish to talk about? There isn't any need for any kind of obligation that is going to restrict your freedom or mine. I understand you have lived your life free, and so have I."

"Gap, I am a traveler and a bit insane at times. So often, when I feel the insanity come on, I head to the hills. Deep into the wilderness. This isn't to scare you or an excuse to walk away. But I know what I had with you yesterday rarely comes along in anyone's lifetime, that's why I am telling you who I am."

"Let's walk after we eat," she said softly. "Starling, I can't think too deeply about what you just told me. I am ecstatic about being in love and so full of desire. How can I possibly have any discerning thoughts?"

Gap picked up a quilt and they headed out. A red-tail hawk soared over their heads, field mice moved through the tall grass. The air had turned a bit cool, but the warm sun heated their faces.

There was between them a galvanic force. Upon reaching the pond, Starling laid the quilt on a moss-covered spot by a large oak.

Gap removed her clothes. Starling joined her. He sat against the tree and pulled her onto him. Once more they consumed each other without any words exchanged.

Starling spoke, "Gap, you are ravishing as is all of this place. My eyes can't take in enough. I feel like I wandered into a magical place."

"Ditto to you," as she moved her face along his skin. "All is fine. Why don't we have dinner with my Papa and Aunt Crow. We will pick up your belongings from the library guest house in the village. I will leave you a horse at the wildflower cabin. You can come and go as you please with your work. I do need to inform Papa Lee that you will be living in the cabin for whatever amount of time you choose. There are others that live on Protected Earth; you will meet each one."

"Let's go get my things." Starling lifted Gap up to a standing position.

For three months, their love affair was intense. Starling lived in the cabin. He kept his commitment to his client. Gap often accompanied him on his long walks to complete his gemology report.

Papa Lee found Starling of interest, but Starling worried him. He understood his daughter's interest. He had felt that desire for her mother. Papa and Crow both felt the romance between Gap and Starling could not be interfered with. Her disappointment would be huge if they showed they didn't trust her.

The early morning mist hovered over Gap and Starling as they sat on wet tree logs, their passion, as they talked, filled the air around them. Spring was budding out; all kinds of lyrical noises came out of the forest. A coyote and her three pups crossed over the path toward the river. Crows teased a red tail hawk. Bluebirds were busy on a nest in a fence post.

Morning lingered. Gap thought, why can't this wrap around Starling and me? She looked into his face. All in her felt numb. Her head was saying, "Let him go." Her heart was saying, "How can this be that he will be able to walk away?"

Starling went into the cabin and returned with two steaming cups of coffee. He handed one to Gap. The warmth of the cup felt comforting. Gap said, "I understand you will leave." Starling sat his cup down, reached for her shoulders, and directed her up beside him. He pulled her in close.

In his beautiful voice he said, "Gap, there will never nor has there been another love as I feel for you. This burden that I carry that attacks my mind isn't a curable illness. There are voices yelling in my head. I can't bring your blessed soul into this pain. I feel I am losing my fight with this insanity. Us wanting it to be different won't make it so. My decay into madness is inevitable."

"I have a small understanding, because my Papa's dear sister Azzie was possessed at times with madness. Of course, I only know the pain that was caused to her and the people around her that loved her. She ran away to spare them pain — Papa has missed her every day. She was the star attraction in Ward's circus. But Papa says her mental illness was stronger than any kind of reason.

"Starling, I can handle anything that concerns you. Papa will build you a cabin in the forest. You can have all the isolation you need, and you can come and go as you please. At least there will be a part of you I can hold sometimes. Will you consider the idea?"

"No," he said. "Gap, I can't give you all the reasons why I am the way I am. It's complicated. I never even suspected a love such as you would enter my crazy life. My emotions are in the physical and manifest into adventure. If I cause you fear or pain, I will be sorry for that but it's not about us or you. It's me. And these crazy, smart voices that stay in my head often rule my life."

Gap didn't like the lump in her chest or the sweat running between her shoulder blades. Should she tell him that she is carrying his child? His hand on her stomach. Maybe he knew. But the thought of being a daddy was so far from Starling's thoughts.

She chose not to inform him. Maybe it would make him stay, but that's not how Gap wanted him. They walked toward the cabin; smoke softly floated out from the chimney. The double-sized washtub sat steaming on the porch.

Starling sat his pack down, Gap went inside and returned with mason jars of Crow's canned peaches and a bottle of vodka. She poured the vodka into the peaches and handed a spoon and the jar to

Starling. Removing her clothes, she flawlessly got into the tub, waiting for Starling to join her.

The steam from the hot bath water filled the brisk air around them. Neither was much for words. With such a physical desire, words were not necessary. Starling didn't answer. He looked into her perfect, anguished face. "Hold me."

Starling took her into his arms and languished in their love and desire. They went into the cabin and made love to depletion. When Starling awoke, his head was pounding. He touched Gap's shoulder. Chase and Talker were barking to be let into the cabin. The dogs were confused; never had Gap locked them out of anywhere. Gap let the dogs in.

Gap sat on the bed, her dogs beside her with questioning looks on their faces. The three watched Starling dress. She gave Chase and Talker a reassuring hug.

Starling spoke, "I have to go alone. The madness in my head is stronger." The voices of insanity were starting to return more frequently to Starling. He was with all his strength trying to subdue the turmoil and wanting to spare Gap of seeing him all messed up.

In a wise voice, Gap spoke, "I know. I will watch for you every day of my life, maybe you will come riding over the ridge, standing at the pond, or cutting wood." She decided to tell him. "Starling, I believe I am with child. My body feels different. May it be true. There will never be another man for me." She outlined his face with her fingers, smelled his sexiness, and moved so close into his body she could hardly breathe. Starling was starting to leave on hikes where he disappeared for days. Gap would be in a state of panic until he returned. She knew he needed to have unrestricted choices. Will this news add to his pain? But she felt it was right for him to know. Each time, upon his return, she would say, "Soon, there will be no you."

"Take the Appaloosa, he is yours. Papa has approved. Galway has intelligence, he's strong, he will take care of you. He does like company so camp out or sleep in a barn so he can stay with you. Be extra careful if you decide to cross water—he is nervous with any water, especially if it flows fast."

"Thank you to your Papa. I will take care of Galway, you have my promise. Tell our child about the love she was conceived in, and if it comes to be true that I gave my child a terrible burden to carry, forgive me. Please Gap, don't wait outside and watch me disappear each time I leave. I am not going away from you; I just have to go."

"You said she, how do you know the baby will be a girl?"

"The baby will be a girl," Starling nodded.

"I won't watch." She knew in all her being today was the day he would ride away forever.

When Starling felt confined, all his confusion came in to haunt him. He asked Gap to forgive him, "My dear, dear Gap, my turmoil has reached the unbearable."

Gap would find him on the floor, cuddled in a corner, talking angrily for the voices to leave.

Gap, who as far back as she could remember, always looked forward to her mornings. But now, she never knew what to expect. Will I once more see his handsome face, or will there be an empty space?

Starling saddled Galway and rode away, but returned shortly. Gap ran toward him. He swept her up, they kissed. He gently returned her to solid ground.

He wanted Gap and the love and life she offered, but he knew it could never be.

Her body was starting to change with a baby on the way. It had been raining for five days. "Please God, keep him safe," she would scream into the night.

Papa showed up to check on his beloved daughter. Father and daughter sat and talked through the night. Before he left, he asked Gap, "Do you wish to go to Europe for a while? Anything you need?"

"No, Papa. I will stay here at the cabin. For now, I need to be here.

I love you." Papa hugged her, his heart was being ripped out seeing his child in such emotional pain and he felt helpless to end it.

"Do you want Sparsity to bring you anything?"

"Papa, Chase and Talker will stay with me. I will send them to get you if I need anything."

Gap longed to go looking for Starling when he left for weeks at a time. Papa discouraged this, keeping a close watch on his daughter. He still tried to give her hope, Starling would return.

Her pain was high, with feeling so very helpless to help the only man she knew she would love forever.

Gap awoke, she checked outside, maybe Starling had returned. She had never felt such fear overtake her. The river was over its banks. She knew Starling was not in a good state of mind when he left. When he was in a good state of mind, he preferred to walk.

Leeward happened to stop by the cabin. She told him to go get Papa. "We need to ride out and look for Starling. I don't have a good feeling. Thanks, Leeward."

Leeward knew it wasn't any good to tell Gap to wait, she already had her horse saddled. The rain kept up its pelting of Earth. It would be difficult riding; the hillsides were soft and some of the trails could be washed away. Gap knew if anyone could pick up on Starling's trail, Leeward could.

"Tell Papa I am going to start looking up on the pine ridge. Starling loved it there."

Gap rode out in a fury. She searched the woods and trails. After hours, she headed back to the cabin. She saw Papa and Leeward's horses along the lower pasture, but Starling's Appaloosa wasn't anywhere in sight. Papa met her on the porch. Gap knew by the dead look on Papa's face that it was not good news and, in her heart, she was already feeling the pain of hearing the words he was about to speak.

"Gap, the men found Starling's body a few miles down river. Looks like he drowned. He tried to cross that raging river. Galway's tracks led into the river. Something could have spooked Galway but the Appaloosa has never liked the river. I am so sorry, my darling."

"Papa, do you believe Starling killed himself?"

"Gap, we have no way of knowing. When Leeward met him on the pine thicket trail the last time he left, Leeward said Starling's mental state was frightful. Leeward tried to bring him back to the cabin but he refused. Starling asked Leeward to let him be. He would be okay in a few days, then he would return."

Gap's eyes were so full of pain. Her usually tan face was void of color.

Papa wanted to take his daughter's pain away but was helpless. He sent Leeward after Doc Francis. Gap was in shock.

With glazed-over eyes, she said, "Papa, Starling was and forever will be my only love and he's the daddy of your grandchild I am carrying."

"I know, dear child. Crow told me. What can I do? Do you wish to go to Atlanta or Savannah? Any place."

"Oh no, Papa. I want to stay here in the cabin."

"Can I send Sparsity to watch over you? I would feel much better. I don't like you being alone in this state of mind."

"Okay. Yes, it's okay. Papa, Starling asked me if he died, would I give him an Indian ceremonial."

"Yes, of course. Anything you wish. You know this. Why was this discussed."

"I am sure with his illness, he felt he would never live to an old age," groaned Gap.

"Was Starling part Indian?" Papa asked.

"I don't know, Daddy. He was skilled in the wilderness, fearless, and an expert archer. He just finished a beautiful bow for me. I was learning. He was a striking sight to watch him shoot the bow and arrow."

"Did you tell him you were carrying his child?"

"Yes!"

Papa searched for anything, "I am going to check out the leather bag he left. Maybe he had kinfolks somewhere. I believe he had an accident. He had no desire to be away from you. You must know that. He was trying to run away from that awful mental pain as my dear sister Azzie tried. There was no escape except death."

Papa Lee laid out each piece of clothing, which was the minimum. There were four journals: one personal, two concerning his gemology findings and a fourth on plants, mostly unknowns, at least, none Lee had ever heard of, which surprised him greatly. Lee felt he knew every plant on his Protected Earth. No information to indicate Starling knew or was connected to another living soul. He did have a roll of money. Papa suggested, "Put it into an account for his child. That way he will have a contribution to her welfare."

"I will notify the gentleman he was commissioned by. He just might have more information for us."

"Papa, should I read his personal notes?"

"Not yet. The pain is too raw in your heart. Give yourself some time. You have grieving and care for yourself and your baby. Of course, it's your decision."

"I'll wait. At least until after his ceremonial. Papa, may I confer with the Indian families that live on the property to help with Starling's ceremony?"

"No need. I will arrange everything."

Sparsity arrived at the cabin with bags of healing herbs and her take-charge kind of love. "I'll take care of Gap. Crow was in the garden. I left a note for her. She will still be worried. She treats Gap as a child. Go, Mr. Lee Darnell, Gap will be okay," said Sparsity.

Papa said, "Gap, be assured I will stop by and ask Barefoot Charlie to stop by this evening to see you, if that would make you feel better, to go over the burial customs."

"Thanks, Papa. I would like that."

Papa hugged his daughter and left to check on the many chores that were required to run Protected Earth. His face told of his concern for his daughter's pain.

Barefoot Charlie and his extended families picked the burial site for Starling. Much to all's surprise, the Indian families knew Starling well, since his stay in the cabin. He often visited with them, ate with them, smoked, and turned over to them Indian artifacts he had found on his many digs. The Indians were happy to be part of their friend's burial rites.

They asked permission to build a wood shelter over Starling's rock grave. "This will be to house the spirit of your beloved, Miss Gap."

"Yes! Of course," replied Gap happily. "I am full of happiness that Starling knew your families as friends. I thank you, Barefoot Charlie."

And so it was done. Starling Songster would forever be a part of Protected Earth. The wooden shelter and stone grave, resting at a rocky point off the pine ridge looking down onto the fields of wheat and the river that took his life. A few gemstones that had been gifted to Barefoot Charlie had been put onto his grave mound. When the sun's light hit the mound, the different colored stones sparkled, sending rays of light toward the heavens.

Now that Gap was having a child, she understood the tremendous care of a child. Her father, Sparsity, and Crow would be right beside her, as they had always been.

They had given her a strong sense of life. Her choices were conscious and not merely a reaction. But she understood how blessed a life she lives, with all the love and acceptance. They were a family of little guilt, one makes a decision and lives by it.

Gap remained in the pond cabin for weeks after Starling drowned in the river. She would sit on the small porch, staring at the cutting stump, the axe placed deep in the middle where Starling had left it. Newly fresh-smelling wood was neatly stacked, ready for the fireplace and wood-cooking stove. She had sat close by, watching his beautiful movements as he raised the axe over his head. Watching and hearing the sound of the wood split as he brought the axe down, Gap had a rambling talk going with herself. "Starling, I knew so little about you, but knowing you more would not have changed anything," she said to a man who was no longer present. She heard a swish of wings scooping down as a red-tailed hawk picked off a bluebird that had stopped to treat itself to a blackberry.

Gap jumped up at the sighting. She hollered, "I am not in the mood for another death." She ran into the cabin for her gun, aiming it at the hawk, but she could not bring herself to pull the trigger. Then a death would be at her hands.

"Out of here, go away. Enough." The hawk held the quivering bluebird in its talons and flew to a tall dead pine close by. For some reason, the hawk released the bird. It was so frozen with fright; it was free falling from the tall pine tree. Gap sprinted toward the tree, but a few inches from the Earth it flew free.

Gap fell to her knees and put her head in her hands. She thanked a God she rarely prayed to but believed in.

"For whatever the reason, I give you honor and thankfulness for the bluebird's life, and I am sure, God, the bluebird is in the deepest gratitude. I, for the short time I had Starling with me. Now, I carry his child."

Gap asked herself after the death of Starling, "Will I ever feel completely alive again? How does one endure the unendurable? Starling made me feel there was limitless time, but there wasn't."

After Starling died, Gap went back to take her long hikes, sometimes overnight and often days. She took downtime to have her baby. Starling would visit Gap's mind, racing through her head and tugging at her young heart. Her baby girl, now called Monty, was on her back and would grow by her side, or her Papa's.

The swimming hole especially held endeared memories of when she learned how to swim, Papa showing her every stroke of an arm or leg. She would swim to the other side quickly. Papa would make her wait while he ran around the moist path by the pool and praised her for a great swim. I did become a great swimmer.

Monty was born in the swim hole with Sparsity and Papa holding Gap's hands and back. Monty came forward from my body, into the water. Monty would tell me often that she remembered when she was born, the cool water, the loving hands holding her and laughter around her, joy. The fire pit by the pond was made from river stones. Even in warm weather, the family would often have picnics and even sleep in the open, under the stars.

Gap's thoughts drifted to the time when Starling had been moving a new mattress to the small cabin. He wanted the bed to be higher from the floor. We stopped by the swim pond to cool off from the hot, mucky day. Starling removed the mattress from the truck bed. He kept walking around with it on his back to find the perfect spot. Finally, he placed it in the tall reeds, pressing them all down. We had a bar of Sparsity's homemade mixed herbed soap and had a nice bath in the cool water. Neither Starling nor I were verbal lovers. He was the sexiest, sweetest smelling man. Not a finger-pinch of fat on a long, tan, lean body. His foreplay started from the moment he said, "Hello."

Each time Starling left on a long walk, I would watch him walk away and think, embrace this pleasure. He would stop and look back at me. A choice is being made here; I would think. But he would turn and walk away, leaving me with a huge knot in my chest. A sure sign of pleasure walked away with him, and pain stayed. But how can I believe any time spent with Starling wasn't good? He gave me my magical child, Monty.

CHAPTER 25

A Forever Goodbye

Talks inside the house just don't seem to warm up the soul the same way front porch talks do. Lee, Crow, Gap, Monty, and often Birchard would head for the porch after supper to mull things over, tell stories, or be silent to take in all the night sounds. Sparsity was a rarity in groups, she would excuse herself. It wasn't that she didn't love each one, but her time spent alone, observing nature, was best with no second interpretations of the animal or plant she was focused on. Sparsity went by what Granny Dalia and the twins had taught her. Work hard to keep your human motives and emotions out of what you are observing. Not an easy thing to do. But all on Protected Earth understood Sparsity—and felt no slight on her aloneness. She was always promptly by your side when needed. Their after-dinner banter was an observance of the day and on occasion carried over to daybreak with all falling asleep.

Gap would assist her child, Monty, to catch fireflies, both would enjoy the twinkling dances in the night. The captive fireflies would be put into mason jars with air holed lids. Sometimes, Monty put the jars in a circle, or arranged them on the porch. The fireflies would later be released to be fruitful and multiply. Monty sat with her eyes glued to the sky, in case, just by chance, a shooting star showed its dazzling display. "I need to make a special wish," Monty would say but invariably, Monty was the first to fall asleep, reluctantly curling on the quilt between Chase and Talker.

Each person would tell a story, it could be whatever anybody wanted to say. Sometimes it was a tall tale, sometimes not.

Papa was a marvelous storyteller. His narratives held his listeners spellbound; it didn't matter how often they were repeated or maybe even a little stretched. It never took much effort to get him to tell one of his circus stories.

But today he wished to hear from Crow, "Sister Crow," Papa said.

Crow looked around her with love shining on her face, grateful to be with her brother. She took a sip of Brandy and let it flow down her throat, then she started to speak slowly and deliberately. She began, "Mother was a beautiful soul. She had always been delicate, and then father's way of life beat her down. He berated her night and day until he utterly broke her spirit. His resentment for her was high. He got a beautiful wife but none of the riches he believed would come by his marriage. Weakened, she tried her best, but she wasn't strong enough to keep up with the physical or expense demands of running the house. When mother died, I naturally, being the oldest, stepped into mother's role. The girls cared for the baby. Between us we managed to buy a milk cow from a neighbor. Azzie was the bartering person, she managed to get a shed built in the garden for Nell, our heaven-sent cow.

Nell kept us supplied with milk for Little D, buttermilk for the family, and sweet butter which we put into beautiful carved butter molds of flowers, birds, and bees that came out on the butter. Almost too pretty to cut into it, but we managed, and the taste on a hot biscuit or sweet potato has me licking my lips. "Oh my! How we loved Nell. We would exchange butter for eggs from our neighbor. The neighbor had a small pasture and would let Azzie bring Nell for a few hours. Azzie would watch over Nell as she enjoyed the grass and some play time. Azzie would tell us how Nell would even take off at a run, then returned to have Azzie pet her. Nell was a treasure. I was the protector whenever father was home. I did my best to stay between him and the others. We hated his belt. He was vicious when he was drunk.

"Constantly, we tried to come up with new ways to bring money into the household. We had to fend for ourselves. The money that we earned was well hidden. We held our own, barely, but at least we had each other. As Little D grew into a precious but beautiful boy, he gave us such great joy. Then my world shattered. I carried a knot of longing and despair in my chest when Father sold me to Mr. Andrews. Leaving my home and family tore my soul apart. The cries of Azzie, Dessie, and Little D haunt me to this day.

"But I am thankful I am here with my beloved Lee, his beautiful Gap, and all who live on Protected Earth."

Aunt Crow composed herself and then continued as she wiped away tears and reached for her BlackBerry Brandy glass.

"Mr. Andrews was an older man, a politician. He'd recently been made a widower and needed a wife to take care of his five children. So, at sixteen years old, I married a complete stranger and went to Charleston with him. I kept his house and his family and entertained his many acquaintances. I did what I had to do, with whatever was left of me. Mr. Andrews was kind to me, at least I had that. I learned to fake being a happy fulfilled wife. I yearned for my own life, my own family, but kept it to myself.

"By no means did I lead a blissful life. Women were not allowed to have grievances, so I never complained. I cooked, cleaned, ironed, learned bookkeeping, tended to the children, and did more than wifely duties. Late in the evenings, after all my chores were done, I would sneak down the hall to the guest room. Everyone in the house was asleep, so I could drop all the pretense. I lost myself in books, English History, classic novels, anything I could get my hands on. It made my life bearable, knowing that I could escape for a while. The man kept a good Library."

Crow paused, she sat silent, then spoke.

"Gone. They were all gone. I'd warned my husband only the night before about smoking his cigars in bed. I hadn't dared to insist too stringently. How many times have I had to darn the sheets from tobacco burns? That night I hadn't been there to remove the still burning cigar from his fingers after he drifted off to sleep. And now the fire."

Crow's voice thickened. "I hadn't been there! Now they were all gone, except for me. I was numb. Someone put a shawl around my shoulders and eased me onto a garden bench. Funny, the bench was all I had left. I passed out."

"I woke up alone in a strange room. The odor of smoke clung to my hair and skin, I knew, it wasn't all just a bad dream. The following days I moved in a fog, with my husband's good friend at my side. I was staying in the Davis's house. Katie's oldest daughter brought my meals on silver trays. I couldn't face the kind people who came to offer their condolences.

"It was my good fortune that Mr. Davis was also a banker, well able to negotiate through the business of the funerals, my husband's will, and such practical matters. My husband had been well pleased with me all those years, it turned out. He left me his entire estate. Mr. Davis took charge of my finances and hauled me into the shops in town. He gave instructions to the lady's dress shop owner to outfit me with a present stylish wardrobe. The Davis' saw that I had everything I needed. Mostly, I felt comfortable in black, still do.

"When you're in shock, it's not a good time to make major decisions about your life. Here again, those wonderful people stepped right up and guided me through every step. My anchor to that place was gone. Mr. Davis suggested maybe I would like to go back and check out my old home place, maybe one of my sisters had had some luck with their life. 'Was father dead?' I asked myself. I didn't have the will to go back. It felt like I was just floating around with no purpose. The one thing I knew for sure was I wanted to return to my studies and become a teacher. I decided to go to Atlanta.

"My husband's friends put me on a train with a new trunk packed with mostly stylish black clothes. Also, most important, they gave me a letter of introduction after making contact with a new and excellent detective firm. I was determined to find my family... And they also got me into a well-established private institute for young ladies and paid my fees out of the money Mr. Andrews had left for me.

"I said to Mr. and Mrs. Davis, 'How can I ever thank you both for your kindness.' Mr. Davis put his strong supportive arm around my shoulder and said, 'Monterey, it will be thanks enough knowing you are doing something with your skills and courage. You have the strength. There may be mistakes, but we know you will reach your goal, and become a great and kind teacher.'

"Later, in a box that somehow did not burn in the fire, Mr. Davis sent me a letter from a detective agency that they had found my brother. But no one answered and the letter was returned. The new firm would start a new search.

"I settled in at the Atlanta school for women and threw myself into my studies with wild abandon. Education was my lifeline, and I knew it. I graduated with honors and received my teaching degree. The school was pleased with me and I'm sure Mr. and Mrs. Davis' recommendation was taken in. They offered me a position, which I accepted.

"A neighbor decided he would check out the old Darnell home place. And maybe, if Father was still alive, he could tell me where my sisters and Little D were.

"The neighbor did some great detective work and found out the rich widow Father had hoped to marry found him out to be the scoundrel he was. She walked away. Father lost all his worldly possessions, including his mind. He was committed to an asylum.

"Mr. Davis felt compelled to visit the asylum, he found Father was in the gravest of health with only a few days left to live. But, when questioned as to what he did with his children, he had no remembrance of anyone or anything. Which in some ways was a blessing to him." Crow was now standing, animated with her hands and arms moving about.

Lee spoke, "Sister, I can only feel extreme pity for father."

Crow continued, "My other aim in life was to find my sisters and you, Lee. I kept the detective agency motivated." Her voice cracked. She sighed deeply and raised a shaking hand to her brow. In the moonlight, we saw that Crow's face was distorted with painful memories.

"One day when leaving the school, a man approached me. He simply said, 'Miss Monterey Darnell?'

"I replied, 'Yes, I am Monterey.' I stood staring, waiting for more as to why he was inquiring.

"'I am a detective, hired by your brother, Lee Darnell.' he spoke matter-of-factly. His lips barely opened.

"I went weak. My knees buckled and I sank onto the steps. I asked, 'Is my brother okay?'

"Very much so. I have been searching for years. I was hired by Mr. Ward. When he passed on, he left more than enough money to pay for my services. This would be a proud day for him. I haven't contacted your brother with the news. This time I wanted to be sure.

"I stood, my mouth hanging open, wondering who was this Mr. Ward.

"What about my two sisters?"

"No, over the years—some leads, but I got there too late and they had moved on. I have left letters at these places of interest—how Lee and I can be contacted. But here you are. This is truly a great day! I will get word to your brother. Do you need me to accompany you?"

"No, but thanks for the offer. I am profoundly curious who Mr. Ward was."

"The detective answered, 'Why not let your brother explain all when you meet with him, I assume that will be soon.'"

Papa Lee was hurting, seeing how deeply Crow's own story was still affecting her. No one had been prepared for this accounting of what all she'd been through. She had never spoken in such detail of these things before. Papa gently interjected, "Crow." She looked at him with tears streaming down her face. Papa got up from his rocker, pulled her to her feet, and wrapped his arms around her. He softly said, "Enough stories for tonight." He spoke to Birchard over the top of Crow's head, "Sing one of your happy songs for us."

Birchard reached for his ukulele and played. He got all of them laughing. The lighthearted music lifted their spirits. Even Crow smiled. Now and then, all started smothering yawns. Gap picked up the soundly sleeping Monty and carefully handed her to Papa, then shooed the dogs off the quilt and picked it up. She tossed the quilt on the porch swing. Papa carried the sleeping child to her room to be put to bed and tucked in.

"Good night, all," Gap told everyone. Just as she was turning to go inside, a shooting star flamed across the sky in a wide arc. Everyone, including Chase, Talker, and the cats, had already gone inside except Birchard, Gap, and Crow. Gap and Crow stood close together at the top of the steps, watching the sky even after the star had glittered out. "Aunt Crow," Gap said softly, "let's make our wish." And so, they did.

After Gap and Crow went inside, Birchard released the fireflies, and then cocooned himself in the still warm quilt. He fell asleep on the porch swing to the songs of the crickets.

Birchard awoke before daylight. Folly's dog, Pal, had been locked out once more, and was pawing on the screen to be let in. Folly's hearing was bad, and he often forgot Pal was outside. Pal would head across the field to Papa Lee's. He jumped onto the swing with Birchard, frenzied in actions to see Birchard. Birchard would go for walks when the moon was bright and Pal would follow him step by small step and now, extremely slow ones for Birchard.

Birchard was deemed a member of the family and was never treated otherwise. He knew he could have slept in the house but preferred the porch and the music of the night. His bones did pain him, and he felt his body was giving up the fight.

After Mickey died, his responsibilities kept him in a busy state between raising two boys, even though he had little to do with the boys. Sparsity was the one the boys went to, and she had taken upon herself their care. She had promised Mickey on her dying bed she would. Sparsity was a person of her word. The boys were complex. Birchard lived the rest of his life in grief for Mickey. Could it really be — so many years ago? Sparsity became the person Birchard called on in all hours of the day and night. If there was any intimacy between them, no one knew and never pried into the state of their friendship.

When Birchard's feeling overwhelmed him, he would stop by Sparsity's cottage.

Sparsity listened.

Birchard often said he was glad his Mickey never knew the troubled twin boys. "It would have been heart wrenching for her gentle soul."

"I understand, but I can't say I agree. Mickey was the wisest of people. I am sure she would have handled any dilemma," said Sparsity.

Birchard knew he was a marvel and had long-lived a life that all doctors said that most little people were never expected to reach. But he felt his wintertime was soon to be when he would lie beside his beloved.

Crow had loved every moment of her coming home to her brother Lee. She had educated Gap, watched her fall in love at such a young age. And been beside her when Gap's heart was full of pain at the loss of Starling. But she saw Gap's beloved wonderful child Monty born—and now, Crow rested her head for the night and took the pills Doc had insisted she take for her heart. She knew Doc had not approved of her keeping her bad health a secret, but he kept his word.

Within a few weeks, Crow went to bed one night and never woke up.

Lee had two of his sisters return, from which he has been forever grateful. And now once more he had to say goodbye forever to Crow and lay her to rest by Azzie and his father, Ward. Only the family of Protected Earth said goodbye to Crow. Crow did not frequent town often. She wanted her time with her brother, Gap, Monty, Birchard, and Sparsity. And once more Protected Earth had taken a loved one.

***

Monty came into the world a beloved child. She carried all the beauty of Gap and Starling.

A magical child, all who knew her would say. But there were early childhood signs that were read, not as a problem, but only that Monty was different. Gap often thought of Starlings words, "May our child not carry my demons."

Lee worried the most, he had seen the same signs in his sister Azzie, and also in Monty's father Starling. It was the genes she was dealt. Lee had lived through the pain of seeing his sister deteriorate almost into madness. Could this be the path his exceptional grandchild was headed? He prayed he was wrong. Monty had an unusual sensitivity to stimuli, such as noise or light. Even Birchard's banjo-picking could send her into a disturbed mood. She could quickly change from stubborn to peaceful and then back again.

As Monty grew, more often did her mental problems show. Sometimes her symptoms returned. She would return to a full functioning person. And life in and around Protected Earth was once again happy.

Monty felt her illness was beginning to diffuse into the environment of Protected Earth. Her fulfilling walks and rides were now filled with shadows, unfriendly to her every move. Even when her adored mother and grandfather joined her, their aura wasn't strong enough to change the undercurrent around her. She had descended from hours seated or asleep on the porch swing to now being almost bedridden. For the past few weeks, her mind and body had recessed into a dark, dispirited place.

Tonight, however, her head cleared enough for a coherent thought. Monty sat on the porch with Gap. She looked all around her with a full heart. tainting this glorious place was not to be borne. She knew that she had to leave. She knew for sure she was pregnant, she didn't remember the night it happened but felt sure it was the hiker she met when she had disappeared for two days, after leaving for a long alone hike. Lee and Gap didn't worry, it was common for Monty.

Memories race through her mind — seventeen years of experience, her love affair with this land, of the faithful dogs that shadowed her every move, of her loving family. Monty knew that she had now chosen to walk away from a huge piece of her soul.

The hanging blue kerosene lanterns that Papa had lit on the porch overhang cast a soft glow. Moths fluttered around the low lights. As a small child, Monty had loved to stand under the lanterns, giddy with joy as the moths lit on her hair and flew back and forth in a beautiful dance. Sometimes her mood changed in an instant. Monty could see the moths as eerie creatures ready to turn and devour them all. Then she would recognize the onset separation from rationality and pull her thoughts back by sheer force of will.

Crow had made Monty a set of wings when she was a child. The wings were in colors of pale yellow, dotted with soft mauve, amber tips, blended into the yellow. Different textures of material were infused that made the wings real looking. They tied at her wrist and spread out when Monty lifted her arms.

"Mama Gap," Monty said to reconnect with the world, "this gift is my favorite that Crow made. I miss our Crow. Sparsity says she sees Crow up on Pine Ridge picking blackberries. Do you believe in spirits, Mama? Do you think a person's spirit comes back to visit Earth? I feel her presence but it sure would be good to see her face and hear her singing one of her sweet songs as she served up her blackberry cobbler to our delight."

The porch swing always held one of Crow's lovely quilts on it.

Monty rubbed her fingers over the stitching, feeling empathy with Crow's needle outlining the birds and flowers. In, out. Slender, silver, sharp ended, the needle moved from darkness to light — in, out, in, out. Thousands and millions of times, traveling slowly over the universe of what ended up being a lovely quilt. Again, feeling the pull of an alternate reality, Monty wrenched herself from the needle and brought herself back to the present situation. She had Gap untie the wings and laid down on the quilt.

Papa Lee rocked. He carefully checked on the whereabouts of the aging Chase and Talker before he set the rocking chair in motion. Lee would often say, "This would be a better world if each person had a rocker. A rocker keeps pace with one's heart and soothes the core of a person."

Once assured of the dogs' position away from the rockers, he gently placed his bare feet on their backs and caressed them with his toes. Each dog grunted with pleasure and thumped the floor a few times with their wagging tails, then sighed deeply and settled in for a snooze.

Papa Lee thought about the first rambunctious Bluetick pups that

Cal had given to his father. Each successive generation of pups had a pair which carried the names Chase and Talker.

He was keenly attuned to his beautiful granddaughter's eccentricities. When Monty told of hearing birds, bees, and flowers that spoke to her, most folks deemed her behavior bizarre. He and Gap rejected outright the term "hallucinations" and considered their occurrence as miracles. That didn't mean they lived in denial about the seriousness of Monty's state of mind. The two would have moved Heaven and Earth to help their Monty. Grandfather and mother had watched their lovely Monty grow into a gorgeous young woman.

Even so, Papa felt a sucking darkness about the night that had precipitated her collapse. When Monty's cherished horse died of unknown causes, Monty whirled into a tailspin of increasingly irrational conduct. One fateful evening, she got up in the middle of the night and took the new truck. Her Papas much loved 1925 model T Roadster runabout. Seamus, one of Papa's hard-working dedicated Irish farm hands had heard the truck and gone outside to check. Trucks didn't just roam around the place in the middle of the night. He saw the truck's headlights approach erratically from around the curve. The farm animals and wildlife had awakened at the strange lights moving about the property. The different sounds put Seamus in a state of alarm.

"It's all over the road," he protested in alarm. "No!"

More pragmatic than Papa Lee and Gap where Monty was concerned, Seamus didn't see Monty's eccentricities as charming and miraculous. He'd kept his mouth shut and his eyes open. He had somewhat expected this. The truck barreled past, headed for the bridge. Seamus started to run towards the river.

The truck growled to Monty to drive into the river. Monty obeyed.

Thoroughly jolted by the truck hitting the water and sinking, Monty thought, disconnected, how curious, the headlights are still on. The cab immediately filled with bone-chilling river water through the open window. From the bridge above, the headlights shone a beacon under the surface of the black water. With no thought of his own safety, Seamus dove into the treacherous river. Seamus was awash with adrenaline.

"Miss Monty! Miss Monty!" Seamus shook her shoulders. Monty was stunned, saying nothing, looking around in a daze.

Seamus didn't bother to be delicate. He slung her over his shoulders and hurried back to his cottage. He whistled for his horse. There was no time for the saddle. After draping Monty over the horse's withers, Seamus hoisted himself over the horse's back. Clutching the unresponsive Monty, he galloped his horse towards Papa Lee's. By the time they arrived at the farmhouse, Monty was raving incoherently. Seamus carried her to the porch and laid her gently on the porch swing. He pounded on the door with his fists. Lee and Gap arrived at the door at the same time. Quickly, Seamus gave them what information he knew about the situation.

"Go, Seamus, and fetch Doc Francis."

"I am on my way," Seamus replied.

And he was. Seamus had lost his own family in a horrible fire. Seamus had lived in the Library Cabin in Darnell after his heart-rendering family loss. Before Lee brought him to Protected Earth, he had been a loyal, exceedingly hard worker and he still was. Even Leeward learned from Seamus.

Papa Lee and Gap refused to leave Monty's bedside. They took turns bathing her face with cool cloths soaked in herbal infusions prepared by Sparsity and talking to her constantly. The dogs posted themselves on each side of her.

Sparsity left her cottage and moved into the main house full-time to take care of the wounded Monty. She kept up with her meals, burning mixed herbs, the aromas spread throughout the house. Friends and neighbors came and went, wanting to give something back to the Darnell's for all their many generosities.

Papa and Gap thanked them profusely and said their goodbyes at Monty's door.

Sparsity saw to each neighbor. She had been a part of the Darnell family for so long, their pain was her own.

Papa and Gap coaxed Monty with stories and songs from childhood. They read to her from her favorite books.

Sparsity and Gap continued to bathe her in warm herb water, then brushed her long, blonde hair to assure that it didn't mat or knot. Papa Lee waited patiently outside the bedroom door until he could re-enter.

Days, then weeks, then a full month passed with excruciating slowness. The doctor told Lee and Gap there wasn't anything he could do to improve Monty's psychotic state. He could only help with her physical ills.

At long last, Monty came to herself and spoke with Papa and Gap for brief moments. Little by little, Monty slowly came back to them from wherever it was she had been.

Lee and Gap's hearts were in disaster mode. They felt their Monty had slipped away. Monty possessed all life's energies, beauty, wisdom, smarts, and great common sense, but she could not outrun the outsiders that picked at her brain and confused her brilliant, innocent soul.

Just when Gap and Lee thought maybe Monty had returned to them, she would relapse into delusions or go into a deep sleep for days on end. She at times became so lethargic she couldn't hold the reins on a horse. She could feel the ankus probing her. Now, it broke her even more to say to her Papa, "Papa, forgive me. I don't feel strong enough to ride."

On one fateful day, when she did take a horse out, she met up with a lone handsome hiker. Acting out a casual innocence of her curiosity, she had sex with the stranger. After the occurrence, on the ride home, a voice said, "You have sealed your faith." She just knew she was going to have a child.

Monty started falling asleep on the porch. Since she had unusual waking hours, she was not disturbed. This general pattern had gone on for about three months. Gap or Papa would check on her throughout the night.

Half asleep, she felt Gap cover her with extra quilts and kiss her forehead. She took in the clean smell of her mother's soft hair as it brushed her face. She knew today was the day—she made the decision of her life. She awakened close to four in the early morning.

She arose from the swing. Chase and Talker stirred and moved in close to her legs. Both dogs accepted their responsibility to protect Gap's child. She knelt and spoke to her beloved dogs, "Hi, my sweet things. All is okay." They carried a concerned look on their faces, moving in even closer. Holding their faces close, she sat on the floor between them. "I am once more going to take Mama's truck, but I'll leave it at the station." She took the key off the small wooden hook at the screen door.

The dogs turned their heads inquiringly at Monty. Sorrowfully, she kissed them. Monty's life choice didn't come easy. The moral conflict, along with the alien person in her head, went back and forth.

"Stay," she told Chase and Talker as she walked out the screen door. She retrieved her bag, earlier placed behind the large oak outside her bedroom window. Never again will I sit on its branch and view the world from a special place. She knew every spot on Protected Earth,

She guided the truck slowly out of the main area. Monty had ample time to catch the early morning train. She hoped to avoid any close neighbors. Monty had confined her plans to Liza, knowing Liza would not break her trust.

This was a decision she was sure of. She had been homeschooled by Gap and Papa Lee. They tried sending her to public school but, like her mama, she would leave and walk home. They eventually gave in. She lived a bewitching life, free of any guile.

The truck was softly running as Monty stopped at the old iron gates. She thought that river ride didn't hurt this Ford Model T at all.

She had opened and closed the gates so often. Her pace was quick and efficacious. Soon, she was out of the sight of the two giant pines that welcomed each person into Protected Earth.

The large, handsome leather bag that rested on the seat beside her, Papa had made for her sixteenth birthday. Each stone that adorned it was set in a bed of silver. The stones Papa had shaped and sanded to perfection. Never! Never! Would she part with it. It felt comfortable having the bag so close.

She reached the station but didn't remember the drive. For a few minutes, she sat on the station bench. Forgetting, she asked herself, "What am I doing here?"

The voices in her head were back, causing confusion. "Go away! Go away," she cried, putting her hands over her ears. She dropped the truck key. It jolted her. Alone at the station, she took the key and laid it inside the truck. She thought, "Darnell's citizens move slow in their mornings. They awake with a slow, stretching yawn, brewing coffee, eat a bit of breakfast, some conversation, then they are ready to start their day. She managed a smile of approval for Darnell. The sounds of the night carried over and she listened to some very vocal owls. This sent her memory back to when she had been on a walk with Gap. Owls were making such a noise answering each other, back and forth. They kept walking and came upon a blooded, dead golden horned rim owl. She helped her mother give the majestic owl a proper burial. They placed a field stone for a marker. She was deep in a memory and startled when the train pulled in. The steward dropped the steps as he exited. "Alone, miss?" he asked.

"No, sir. I am never alone."

He smiled and asked for a ticket and any baggage to be checked. "No, sir." The train made a few rumbles and she boarded.

Monty looked around, observing the other passengers scattered throughout. Most were sleeping. Suddenly, she felt hungry. The cheese, fruit, and biscuits were going to be welcomed. She ate, then drifted off to sleep. Night passed into day, small towns and farmlands were left behind as the train continued on. Her thoughts moved about but mostly on what she had left behind. The letter she left on the hall entrance table, Gap and Papa would miss her at breakfast, most likely thinking she was out for an early walk. No! Chase and Talker would be scratching on the door or barking to inform them of the situation.

The train continued its stops. Somewhere, she got off and had to continue on a bus for a good while until she reached a train connector that finally was to end her excursion into New York City. The trip was mostly a blur. She thought to herself, I can't remember if I told Papa and Gap that I was going to have a baby. But anyway, nothing would have changed my decision. The large, stained-glass clock welcomed an exceptionally beautiful seventeen-year-old Georgia girl, to Grand Central Station.

Monty's Letter

Few words passed between Papa and Gap upon finding and reading Monty's letter. The two energetic people sagged; part of their heart was gone. Gap walked to the barn and saddled the horses.

Papa approached, put out his arms to Gap, his body spasmodic with emotion.

"Papa it's her choice, we taught her to be independent, we must honor her decision. She is strong, even in her darkest times, enough strength comes through. Monty will do whatever is needed, her temerity will carry her."

The two pained souls turned their horses toward the open range. Papa and Gap were silent, the morning air was damp. It was one of the few times they didn't observe the countryside. The horses headed for the resting place of their departed loved ones. The words didn't have to be said, they just knew in their hearts they would never see Monty again.

Upon reaching the meditation shed, father and daughter walked inside, lit a lantern, and sat down. The spirits of Mr. Ward, Crow, Azzie, Mickey, and all the beloved animals surrounded them. They settled in on some overstuffed cushions.

Papa spoke, "Do you think we could have loved her more?"

"No Papa, we gave all to Monty." They sat in private thoughts for a while. Then Gap stood, walked outside, and whistled for the horses. The horses had wandered to graze.

They rode the land for hours, the knot of pain still in their bellies. They met up with Sparsity on the trail, searching and filling her basket with many findings. Stopping for a chat, Sparsity spoke her wise voice. She touched Gap's leg as she stood by her horse.

"Papa Lee, Gap, go heal your heart, Monty will make another life for herself. It's out of our hands." Sparsity walked between the horses, reached out for Papa and Gap's hands. She closed her eyes, as if seeing the future. It's okay, all is okay. The two rode back toward home. But neither felt life would ever feel okay again.

"Gap, you go to the house, I will take care of the horses. Emilio will be around shortly. Set us up some coffee and a fat brandy, I need a few. Then I want you to read Monty's letter to me once more, then we will put it away."

"Papa," Gap started to say something, she didn't know what, but nothing came out but, "I love you; you have always been the best daddy and friend any human could possibly want. See you on the porch."

The two finished off a few coffees and brandy, Papa took the letter from his overall pocket and handed it to Gap. She read.

My dear beautiful souls, each night I ask the infinite spirit to reach my heart and head, that I am doing what my soul is telling me to do. May you erase any slight doubt that may enter your thoughts on my reasons for leaving this enchanted life. I just know, Mama Gap and Papa, your understanding will be clear. Who is to judge the time on earth we have with a loved one?

Be it seventeen years or eighty, not a day will pass. I will continue to see you both in the sun's rays, a shooting star, rain on my face, a laugh that echoes your voices calling my name. Always know you will never be far from me, no matter where my life leads. The love and knowledge you both have given me lives in my cells, as does your blood genes run through my body.

The wretchedness that haunts me— night and day, tells me to find my own way to deal with them as you both clearly see the voices are becoming more frequent and my torment greater after Papa found me rolled into a ball, in the corner of the barn stall, banging my head against the wall. If Papa hadn't found me, who knows how bad my head would have been gashed in; and Papa, the pain on your face for me breaks my heart each time. My heart isn't that strong to bring you and Mama Gap down with me. The same sun, moon, and stars that give our Protected Earth life, will always be over me and you both. As I know your spirits will be my guardian. My blessed talent that you passed on to me, each time my brush strokes touch the canvas, you will be with me.

Papa, your honesty, value of friendship, unconditional love, to think beyond the situation, and survive on my own in the woods. I am at every moment aware of my love for Protected Earth.

The mental illness as you both have seen seesaws my life and touches everything close to me. I know, Mama Gap, you and Papa would have turned the heavens and earth to find a cure or help me in my pain. But how far can we keep going—and enjoy this magnitude of agony with no hope in sight. The voices are coming into my head almost every day. My ordeal is almost too much to bear when I see what I'm bringing into your lives. Another big reason for my farewell is I am going to have a baby. I have such a fright that my child will be born with my illness. Down the road I am sure your grandchild will be with you, in Georgia, someday. I can't see the future but this I am sure of.

I know my life will be short. How many years I have, that I do not know. There will come a day that I will send my child to you.

Papa said last night as he kissed me good night, "Life works itself out, that's just the way it is. You are worthwhile, as the whole of you. You are perfect with flaws. Your papa always shines over you. Sweet dreams my dear, dear, Monty girl."

His love can't keep the many voices out of my divided head. I want to be brave and gutsy and be more powerful than them, but they are stronger.

When Monty wrote the letter, she had knelt by the swing, the two lanterns gave shadows that danced on the porch. She laid down her pencil. She felt the air and nature spirits around her. It took all her energy to block the voices attacking her brain for a moment of peace and a connection of love of the land and every person, animal, insect, or flower who ever lived on it. She once more started to write.

Gap continued to read:

Your truck, Mama, is something special. It survived my drive into the river. This will probably be the last time I will ever drive. When you find my letter, I will be headed toward another life. Unknown. Papa, I took the cash from our cash box. Don't worry, I can always earn a living with my art. So, I will be fine.

When you all awake, I can see Chase, Talker, and the new pups waiting by the door, in anticipation of me returning. I know you will be sensing something is wrong, you'll walk out into the morning and see your wonderful new truck is missing. Mama you will turn, Papa will be right there. He will say she's gone, and we will never see our Monty's face again.

Papa, you will saddle up and ride for hours, and Mama, I know you will be beside Papa, very sad but looking beautiful as always. Papa will say, "Gap, where do you believe our Monty is, and should I move Heaven and Earth to find her?"

"No, dear papa." Mama will say, "she most likely picked New York because of the extreme difference of her comfortable safe life here on Protected Earth."

See you in the Stars. My love every movement.

Your child forever
Monty

CHAPTER 26

Monty Arrives at Grand Central

Grand Central was loaded with people scurrying about. Monty said softly to herself, "Like a gigantic ant hill, it is." She took a seat on a bench to take it all in. An unknown phase of her life had begun and she was determined to meet it head on. A poem kept jumping into her head that Papa would repeat when a new situation arose.

> Tender-handed stroke a nettle,
> And it stings you for your pains.
> Grasp it like a man of mettle,
> And it soft as silk remains.
> *Poem author — Unknown*

"As Papa would say," Monty softly said as she looked around the immense building, "grasp the nettle." This was exactly what she intended to do.

Monty had enough money to sustain herself for a while. She knew that she would have no problem earning a living; her artist's skills were solid, and as natural to her as breathing. A grandiose stained-glass clock struck midday. She put her hand to her head, as if to help her and spoke aloud to herself. "I will not have my baby in a hospital. And the clock just told me that I should come back and have the baby right here in the glorious Grand Central Station. Okay, then." Confident and smiling now, she arose and walked out into the waning sunshine, carrying one bag.

She found a small quaint hotel close by.

Her bag was made of brown leather adorned with semi-precious stones, each secured in silver. Papa had made the bag. She'd watched those strong hands make every stitch. Over several years, they had gathered each one of those stones from Protected Earth. Many had been dug from the Earth itself that she had grown up on. Papa and Monty were constantly on the lookout for special stones. Whenever one was found, they showed their excitement to each other with unbridled glee.

When at last their special rock bucket was full, Papa and Monty tumbled them in the tumbling machine that he bought her. Processing the stones in stages with progressively finer grit had taken months, but the final step using granulated polish had rendered their little stones into jewels. Papa had carefully secured the stones on the finished bag, he had given her the one-of-a-kind bag for her birthday. Monty hadn't known that Papa was doing it all for her. The gift had nearly broken her heart—it was as though he had given her a piece of his soul. It was her greatest treasure.

Her needs were few. The bag contained her wallet, two pairs of jeans, two white linen shirts and one sage colored shirt, a long gypsy skirt, black laced vest, a fringed suede jacket, underclothes, toothbrush, hairbrush, a small bag of toiletries, paintbrushes, notepad and pen, two treasured books, and a few tubes of oil paints. There were also two gold-framed photographs, one of Papa barefooted, seated in his rocker with Monty seated beside him on a milking stool and holding a baby goat. The other photo showed her mother on horseback, Chase and Talker standing alongside with tongues lolling.

Monty quickly dressed in her skirt, a sage colored shirt and vest, checked out of the hotel, then walked in the direction of the park. Her stomach reminded her that it had been a long time since she had eaten. Cafes seemed to be everywhere, so she had a wide range of choices. She selected a pleasant looking coffee shop which seemed to welcome her with wide, multi-paned windows. Poppy red geraniums in large terracotta pots flanked the bright green door. This one will do nicely, she thought.

Seventeen-year-old Monty entered the coffee shop, mildly unaware of the stares that she attracted. She had long, straight hair the color of moonlight, her large brown eyes ringed with lush black lashes. Tall and slender at five feet ten with exquisitely sculpted features, Monty could have graced any runway in New York's High Fashion District. Her poise and deportment bellied her origins on a working farm in Georgia.

Scanning the chalk-written menu on the blackboard, she asked the young man behind the counter, "No biscuits today?"

"Biscuits? No, we never have biscuits. Would you like a croissant or bagel? We have them made fresh daily."

No biscuits, ever? Well she'd adapt then. Smiling, she ordered a coffee and a croissant and made her way to a booth.

Sipping the last of her coffee with her bag at her feet, Monty noticed the admiring gaze of an attractive man — mid-to-late twenties, she guessed. She gave him a half-smile just as several laughing people came into the shop and made their way to his table. They made themselves at home at his table. Nope, she thought. If three's a crowd, that group's a right mob. She popped the last bite of croissant in her mouth, drained her coffee mug, picked up her bag, and walked out of the shop, amused by the man's dismayed expression.

Monty walked for what seemed to be miles and came across an older hotel, somewhat seedy, but she was tired. The sign in the window said "Vacancy". She rented a room for one night, making shelter her top priority for tomorrow. For now, though, her room was clean, mostly, and her hot shower felt like heaven. She washed her top and undies in the sink, spread them on the shower rod to dry, and crawled up on the aging little bed with visions of horses running through green pastures. She slept unhindered by the sounds of the street on the other side of the windowpane.

Monty woke shortly before the sun came up. For a second or two, she didn't know where she was, and felt around on her bed for Chase and Talker. As her brain fog cleared, she remembered the train ride and her first hours in New York. The sounds of morning traffic finally registered in her awareness. She liked the feel of the city and felt very much at home. Today, she would find a better place to stay. Too bad there's not a barn around, she thought to herself.

The room that she had rented for the night may have lacked style, but again the water was nice and hot. She stood in the shower and let the hot water pelt her into the new day and her new life.

Brushing her hair dry, she decided that her ankle-length gypsy skirt suited her mood perfectly. The neighborhood that she'd been in for coffee was definitely preferable to this one, Monty thought as she tossed her things into her bag. She kissed her two framed photographs, then wrapped them in her clean clothes and placed them in her bag with great care. On the way out, she asked the desk attendant where the closest art supply store was, then retraced her steps block by block to the quaint little neighborhood just down from Central Park.

The coffee shop was bustling at this early hour. As she waited her turn to order, Monty decided to dash off to the park, take her breakfast with her, and do some painting. Just a quick one, she promised herself. Painting would help her to get her center in this strange place. When she started a painting, she usually didn't stop until it was finished. that might be a couple of hours, or days. She ordered three coffees and two fried eggs on whatever kind of bread was available.

She then stopped by the art supply store, which was just a bit down the street. A short while later, she emerged with canvas and a new collapsible easel, along with a bag of sundry painting supplies. She worked to navigate her food and supplies. She stepped into the river of humanity flowing quickly down the sidewalk, then crossed the busy street and entered Central Park.

After walking around a while, Monty found a small, secluded field circled with trees. This hidden treasure reminded Monty of Protective Earth, so she set up her easel with a practiced eye for light and shadow. A bench sat beside the winding trail. Perfect. Gotta paint fast to get this light, she thought. Monty took off her boots and vigorously trampled the grass. Ah, the sweet smell of grass. This grass may be New York grass, but it smelled and felt just like the grass of Protected Earth. The smell of home grounded her like nothing else could. She quickly laid into her canvas, expertly squirting onto the palette both the new paints that she had just purchased and the ones that she carried from home. Monty loved the feeling of entering the world of her art. She lost track of time.

After meeting a man in the park named Jazzy—her life took another turn. Jazzy felt himself sinking like a stone. Intuitively, he sensed that there would be a point of no return with this one. And she agreed to have coffee with him. So they headed toward the coffee shop chatting as they strolled.

"I'm Monty. Just arrived yesterday on the train. And you are…?"

"Jazzy. I'm a musician. So… what do you think of Manhattan so far?"

Monty looked around her. "It's a long way from Darnell, Georgia. It feels like home here too, only a different home."

Jazzy was charmed. He couldn't think of a delicate way to ask, but he had to know. "How old are you, Monty?"

She stopped walking and turned to him. Looking up and meeting his eyes, she said, "I'm seventeen. Papa Lee and Mama Gap, they won't look for me. They understand why I left. I mailed them a postcard during the trip. I won't be going back. And Jazzy, I'm four months pregnant." She hesitated, then added, "and I've been told that I'm a bit psychotic."

The bottom dropped out of Jazzy's world in that instant. Even so, a fierce desire to protect her bloomed in his chest and surprised him. He gently changed the subject; he needed to digest this. He realized that his whole future could pivot on minute choices in this very conversation. He wanted to slow things down and navigate this with great care.

They continued to chat lightly all the way to the coffee shop. Jazzy was careful not to push. Jazzy ordered some late lunch. Monty excused herself to go to the ladies' room. Jazzy's thoughts soared, swooped, and dived. What am I thinking? This girl is a runaway and only seventeen! I could end up behind bars. But if she ends up with someone else, she could be in danger. How could I stand that? And her condition…! She needs help. This girl needs… me. Maybe I need her too. Jazzy conquered his runaway thoughts. His desire to shelter and protect this girl overwhelmed him. But…!

Monty returned to the table and sat across from him. He watched her as she spoke. So graceful. She appeared strong, stubborn, proud, and troubled, all at once. Innocent. experience. Lovely. Flawed. Study in opposites, and intriguing. Her depth of perception, her immense talent, her soft southern drawl, and her beauty defeated him. He wanted this girl in his life. God help me, he thought. He did his best to sound casual, "Where are you staying?"

She told him about the rundown hotel where she'd stayed the

night before. "I need a safe place to live. Do you know of such a place where I can go?"

After her question, Jazzy actually felt dizzy. In a twinkling, he made a decision, took a deep breath, and dived in. "I have a loft not too far from here. I'm a good cook and keep the place clean. I've just had my thirtieth birthday. Single. I've had one serious relationship. I do chin-ups on the doorsill and one hundred push-ups every day, plus, I walk everywhere. My teeth are good. I don't smoke, which is amazing for a musician. My income depends on my lung power, so I take care of it. I work nights. My income is reliable since there's a huge demand for jazz around here. I live with two cats and the best dog in the whole world."

He covered her hands with his own. "Stay with me until you can find a good place. I'll take the couch—you can have the bed. You'll be safe. I would never hurt you or allow anyone else to. You set the boundaries, and I'll respect them. Your call, Monty. Will you come home with me?"

Monty didn't miss a beat. She asked him, "What hours do you work?"

Jazzy took Monty to his loft. She loved the spacious feel and the view. And meeting Jazzy's pets was a love fest for Monty. They all vied for her attention. "Hey guys, I'm here too," Jazzy teased.

The first night, Jazzy had left Monty napping when he'd gone to work at the club. He played every single song for her. His saxophone channeled his longing for her, the fleeting expressions across her face, and even her southern drawl. He played from his soul that night. After the last customer had left, the boys in the band turned and stood gaping at him while he quickly put his sax in its case. "I've got to get home, guys. See you tomorrow," he tossed over his shoulder, moving more quickly than they'd ever seen him go. They'd always headed en masse to another club to wind down after their final set.

"Oh my," the bass player said. "Our Jazzy is certainly eager to get home. Wonder what she looks like." Wild speculation followed. Jazzy hadn't heard a single word of it, he was already gone.

When Jazzy opened his door, he'd called out softly so he wouldn't frighten her. Monty called him over to the bed. He kissed her softly, and they talked awhile, then Jazzy moved to leave her for the sofa. She pulled him back, and they'd fallen asleep holding each other.

Jazzy kept his word. He and Monty made their way through the golden days that followed in a sweet, though platonic time of "getting to know you." Finding much common ground in their interest, they fell easily into harmony. Jazzy taught Monty how to play cards. They took long walks in the park and in the city. Monty said to Jazzy, "There is so much you don't see, Jazzy. You only look at the obvious—my papa taught me to look beyond."

"Teach me," said Jazzy. "I want to know what you see." The walk back to Jazzy's loft was both pointing things out to each other.

Seated at the kitchen table, Monty told Jazzy all about the voices. "Make no mistake," she told him. "I am not a victim of my illness. For whatever reason, it's part of who I am. I alone know that fine line that separates me from the darkness inside."

"You must never patronize me." Their coffee mugs jumped when Monty thumped her fist on the kitchen table when she said the word 'never'. "I was strong enough to leave a home that was part of my soul—I left the people of my own blood who loved me. And Jazzy, I will leave you, should the voices ever tell me to leave. My very survival depends on that strength. Compromising that would be the end of me."

Jazzy understood for the first time the delicate balance of Monty's mental state and his role in her stability. He knew that he must never smother her with his natural inclination to overprotect. She needed plenty of room, and he must give it. Jazzy accepted Monty on her terms. It would require a great deal of adjustment on his part. So be it. Jazzy made a trip to the library and came back loaded down with books. He required information. In supporting her from the distance that she established, he was determined to be competent and up to the task of whatever she needed of him. He knew something of mental illness and his bloodline.

When he broached the subject of her pregnancy and raising her baby, she put up walls. "I'm not ready for that yet," was all she said as she began to withdraw. Jazzy had dropped the subject. Her boundaries were harder on him than he'd expected. He desired to know more of her past. He was in love.

In addition to his music, Jazzy owned half interest in a small bookshop. He spent three days a week working there. The shop was his heaven, where he knew exactly what his role was, the routine was fixed, and where he was in control.

While Jazzy was at the book shop, Monty painted in Central Park. She bought additional easels and had set them up at varying heights to market her paintings as she worked. The park inspired her. She loved the feeling of the park and also the deep satisfaction in the appreciation of her paintings by the art savvy New Yorkers. Jazzy cleared a corner in the bookshop to further market her paintings. He was concerned for her safety in the park. Arrangements were made with a messenger service to stop by daily to bring her lunch and take the money from painting sales for deposit into a bank account that he helped her to set up.

For Monty, it was all about creating beauty on canvas, interacting with her buyers, and being outside where she could take her shoes off, feel the grass, smell the air. She produced paintings at a dizzying rate.

Monty asked Jazzy to go with her to experience the Statue of Liberty.

Taking the ferry to the Statue of Liberty, Monty was overcome with emotion to actually be at the feet of Lady Liberty. The torch the lady held had long symbolized the hard triumph of light over darkness in a way that was deeply and irrevocably personal. Jazzy stood behind

Monty with his arms around her, his hands on her belly, her hands on top of his. Secretly, he fantasized that her baby was his.

Monty and Jazzy loved being together, watching each other. Jazzy was like an open book, but Monty was a different story. Jazzy was amazed to find the depth of his love. He didn't think of himself as single anymore—he was now half an "us". He pushed away his persistent intuition of an encroaching predator. He controlled, with tremendous effort, his instinctive inclination to take charge over the looming danger to his loved one. Monty's internal battle made him ready to fight the foe to death and save her.

This was a battle he could not win. Jazzy carefully and with great subtlety worked at grounding Monty with ordinary things. When she started talking out of her head, he would begin to question her on money matters, and her supply of paints. Usually, with patience, he could pull her back into his world.

Monty transitioned into her part of the "us" more gradually. She had instantly loved his pets, now her pets too. She thought of the loft as her home. Her work fulfilled her. And the night came when Jazzy returned home from work and she knew. She understood that her unique needs would be hard on any man. But Jazzy wasn't just anyone, he was extraordinary in all ways. Monty looked at Jazzy and knew at her core—he was right.

She simply walked up to him, pulled his face down to hers, and kissed him with all the feeling in her heart, and with the heart of desire. She said, "I love you, Jazzy." He scooped her up and took her to the bed. They had been sharing the bed since their first night together. He never did sleep on the sofa; Monty wouldn't have it. They shared soft kisses and holding each other all night. That boundary had been set, not by Monty, but by Jazzy. He wanted her to know her own heart and mind. Waiting for her had been excruciating, but necessary. He hadn't wanted convenience with this woman. She carried no age. Wise and smart beyond any woman he had ever known.

Monty had no guile. She simply acted and her body was changing to accommodate The growing child inside. She often experienced discomfort. Monty felt conflicted. She wanted nothing more than to make love with Jazzy. But her body was no longer exclusively her own. It was a strange feeling, no longer being sovereign in one's own skin.

Jazzy's hands shook as he took her face between them. "I've loved you since the first moment that I saw you in the coffee shop. I don't want to hurt you, though, or the baby. I can wait." With all the two had to contend with on a moment-by-moment basis, there was an overload of cares and concerns. Neither of them wished to wait.

Jazzy learned he could not pressure Monty for answers. But his heart hangs heavy with concerns. She did tell him, "I will not keep my child. I'm not asking you to understand my reasons."

His reply was always to let her know, he would take care of her and the child.

"Please, dear Jazzy. I know this. But it's my life. You must honor that."

And he saw, no matter how he longed to care and protect Monty, she was not going to be swayed from her will. If he pressed her, he would surely lose her.

CHAPTER 27

Monty and Jazzy

On awakening, Monty said, "Come take a bath with me. Is there a place we can find a cold pond?"

"There's Central Park, but I don't think we can use the lake for a bath, but we can take a canoe out and take a carriage through the park for a ride if you feel it. Or the stable has some fine horses."

"Jazzy, that sounds wonderful. Up for the bath first."

She noticed his look and said as he was looking at her belly, protruding a little.

"I am about four months. No cause to worry. The ride will be good for me."

"Monty, you are exquisite," he said and took her by the hand.

"Got my mama's looks and my Papa Lee's strength, my father's mixed-up head, and my Great Aunt Azzie's odd ways. I promise you, Jazzy, I only hurt myself. This divided brain is not enjoyable to live with."

"Monty, do you have any thoughts on what your life will be like after your child is born? What direction do you wish to go?"

"Yes, I can take care of my obligations. Will you respect my wishes and not ask any more questions on the subject? You may not approve of mine and the grand clock's plan."

"You have my support. It's soon in our relationship but I feel we have known each other somewhere else in time."

For certain, Monty was a Darnell and a person could only get information out of her if she chose to give it.

The days moved swiftly into weeks and months. Monty resumed her painting and quickly sold them. She liked painting on the streets and in the park. Jazzy played several nights in a club. He also worked part-time in his bookstore. The bookshop carried old books and new books of art, fiction, poetry, music, and children's books. He spent a few days a week in the shop. A section was made to display Monty's art. But the peaceful life the two were living soon turned to concern. Monty didn't come home one night. Even though Jazzy had started to notice symptoms of which Monty had informed him would happen, he still was not prepared for his susceptibility. After checking the park, hospitals, and local law enforcers, he went home. On the steps of the brownstone were her art supplies, his heart beat fast, gathering the materials, he quickly went in. No Monty!

He moved drone-like through the next few days. Each morning, he headed for the park and streets. By chance, a homeless person in the park had gotten to know Monty. He suggested Jazzy should inquire at the mental hospital. "That's the place they take us when we become unhinged."

"Thank you," and then he pressed some money into the man's hand and left the park.

He left his dog with a security guard and entered the hospital. Monty was there.

The nurse said, "Your young friend is in a comatose state. She may not respond. Be prepared."

The long hallway was gloomy, and the walls were gray to fit the mood. Some rooms were locked with tiny, bare windows to look out. Noises of whimpers, wailing, and mixed up loud and soft voices filled the suffocating place. Monty lay alone, her hair was matted and dirty. One foot was uncovered, her foot swollen, cuts with dried blood and dirt on it.

Jazzy was overcome with emotion. He asked the overburdened nurse, "What do you think happened to her shoes? Can't she have a bath?"

The nurse saw his pain in seeing the beautiful girl in such a bad state. She said, "I tried to get her into the bath, but her emotional state only increased. She kept screaming for Gap. Do you know who this Gap is?"

"No, but if you could get me a pan of warm water, I believe she will let me gently clean her up a little. I can't bear to see her this way." Jazzy looked around the room. No chairs were in her room. Jazzy touched her hand; it was bruised badly.

The nurse said, "Are you related to the girl?"

"No, I am a close friend. She lives with me. Where was she found? Is she hurt badly?"

"Doesn't seem so. So far, she hasn't spoken. The police picked her up in the village; a person had covered her with a blanket in the doorway of an empty building."

Jazzy could see the nurse was kind, by the softness in her voice and the gentle way she pulled the cover off Monty's feet. He thanked the nurse for her caring. He said in a trembling voice, "She did inform me of her mental condition and said it's possible she could go off the deep end. She hears voices. This is a first time for me to see her this way." Jazzy broke down into deep crying.

The nurse put her hands on his arm. "Would you like to stay with her? She may come out of the catatonic stage."

He thought of his dog outside, kept with a stranger. "I have my dog outside with the guard." Jazzy had happened upon a nurse with a kind heart.

"If you like, I will check on your dog. The guard is on for the night. I will see to it that your dog has food and water. Nick is the guard—he's a real sucker for animals."

Jazzy could not express his gratitude enough. "May many blessings be with you."

The nurse started to leave the room, walked back to the door, and said, "They will be assigning a social worker to the girl. I have a good friend—her name is June Light. I'll see that your girl is in her care."

"The girl's name is Monty Darnell," Jazzy said.

"See that she carries a card with your name and address. June will help. She always knows what to do. Hope your love brings her around. And you do know she is pregnant. Is it your child?"

"No, ma'am. But I will take care of her."

Jazzy washed her face, arms, and feet. Monty awakened as if she was a beautiful butterfly, coming from a cocoon, and Jazzy welcomed the morning with joy in his heart.

June Light arrived early. Jazzy left her with Monty while he checked on his dog. When he returned to Monty's room, June had seen that Monty had a bath and had even somehow got a dress for her to wear.

Jazzy said, "You think she is okay to go home, Mrs. Light?"

"Yes! Sorry, I don't have any shoes for her."

How could she look so beautiful? After her condition last night. Her blonde hair was shining, her slender, perfect feet stood out from the long dress.

Monty spoke, "Oh, it's fine! I go barefoot most of the time, like my Papa."

The three people smiled. June gave Monty and Jazzy a hug. "Monty, I need to meet with you in two days at your home. Okay? We are releasing you into Jazzy's care. The doctors have medicine for you to take."

Monty said, "Ms. Light, I can't take any meds because of my condition. Please understand it isn't that I don't give thanks for the doctors' care, but the meds may harm my baby." June wanted to ask Monty's plans for the coming baby but thought it can wait.

Jazzy said, "We will welcome you. Bless you, and please thank the compassionate nurse for us; we are both so grateful for her."

June the social worker stood looking at the couple, in love. Jazzy handsome in a crème color, turtleneck sweater, and grey slacks. His protective arm around the lovely mixed up girl.

"I'll be sure she knows. See you in two days."

Jazzy could not believe it. Monty looked as if she had not been knocking on death's door only 24 hours ago and now, in a soft, pale, blue shirtdress she was a head-turner.

"Let's go home. I am starved," said Monty as she slipped her hand in Jazzy's. The guard was now off duty but waited with Jazzy's dog — now pulling at his leash with happiness at seeing Jazzy and Monty. Jazzy offered some money to the guard, but the guard pushed his hand away. "Hey, I have to help a fellow out now and then."

Once more thanking the man profusely, the couple walked out the gate. The large, iron gates made a terrible growl as they shut.

Jazzy thought, may we never return here.

After Monty came home from the mental hospital, she would birth her daughter in Grand Central Station only a few months later.

Jazzy had not left Monty's side for three days, except for brief walks with his dog.

Her thin body quivered. Jazzy kept talking in a soft, soothing voice, "Monty you are going to get better. We miss you; the cats, Charlie and Chaplin, will not eat and my dog rushes back from his walks to be with you."

Jazzy thought about the deep, unspoken knowing when you see a loved one endure the emotional, physical, and mental pain that Monty lived with. The long, torturous days seemed to go on forever. His dog stood up quickly and walked to Monty's bed and barked. He kept barking. Jazzy tried to shush him but Temple seemed unshakable. He stopped barking long enough to take Monty's hand in his mouth. He gently tried to rouse her.

There was movement. Her other hand came over and touched the dog's head. He was jubilant, his tail was moving, he quivered and cried for joy.

"You did it, I gave up, but you were persistent," said Jazzy in a grateful voice. Monty spoke, "Jazzy, do you have an R.C. Cola, very cold?"

"It's my great pleasure. I'll have one with you." He supported her back with extra pillows, his hand felt her bones. There was just skin covering her body. He closed his eyes and took some breaths. He tried not to let his heartache show in his face. He said, "It sure is good to have you back with us. Monty, have you thought any more about your baby?" She didn't answer.

He kept the closet stacked with R.C. Colas since Monty moved in. Monty sat up in bed with a weak and very welcoming smile, then drank the complete cola down. Then with a weakened voice, she said, "Jazzy, thank you. I know you are here for me. I also feel you would want my baby, also. But I have made my choice from the time I arrived in Grand Central Station."

"I respect your decisions. I don't have to understand them so you will not be pressured by me. All that you share of yourself, I receive wholeheartedly." He massaged her feet gently. Her skin was uttermost sensitive after a psychotic occurrence.

A knock at the door caused Temple to jump off the bed. His sweet nature now turned to being protective. Jazzy opened the door to welcome a friend who was also a doctor.

"Thanks so much, we do appreciate you coming by." Jazzy shook his hand. The doc asked Jazzy, " If you would, take your dog for a walk. I need to check Monty."

"Remember, my friend, I adore this girl. I will feel lost with Monty not in my life. Thanks, Doc."

The doctor asked Monty where she was planning the birth of her baby. "Monty, I just need to know about your health and what kind of pain you are in." After the exam, he felt she needed meds to ward off any infection in such a weakened state, and some good food to get her strong.

"Monty, do you remember June Light, your social worker? She is also a friend of mine. She knows how to reach me, along with Jazzy. I am sorry I can't help more."

Jazzy's re-entrance brought a wide smile to Monty's face. Her voice sounded clearer as she spoke. "Hi. I missed you. Doc fixed me up. I want to thank him with a painting."

"That isn't called for. I am a friend!" said the doctor.

"It will make me feel good. Please accept."

Jazzy motioned with a back sweep of his hand to the canvas's lining the wall. The doctor picked up a small painting of a Central Park rock bridge with a homeless woman having tea, lifting a china teacup to her lips.

"Great choice. A favorite. The lady is named Hanna, the city has tried to give her housing, but she said, 'My home is here, in the park.'"

"Hanna has really great style," said Monty. Jazzy wrapped the painting.

"Good night, remember, I am close by, anytime, any hour. I'll do my best to be here for you both. See you at the jazz club, Jazzy."

Monty, the cats, and the dog all fell asleep as if sedated. Jazzy poured himself a glass of wine, sat on a small spring green velvet sofa that had been his mother's, and let his mind drift into unanswerable thoughts.

Will there be a cure for Monty's psychosis? The doctor had informed Jazzy of the harmful effects that had happened to her heart, lungs, and kidneys. Another bout in freezing cold on the streets overnight, I do not wish to say the results.

His dog awoke and came over, seemingly to bolster Jazzy. "Hi, buddy." His ears perked back, he laid his trusting, loyal head in Jazzy's lap.

Jazzy didn't wait to let a thought such as the doctor's last words even enter his head; so he turned his thoughts back to when he first met Monty and said a prayer for their future together.

VOLUME III
Plaid Patience

CHAPTER 28

Grand Central Welcomes Plaid Patience

Seventeen-year-old Monty Darnell had often helped her Papa Darnell and her mother Gap deliver numerous babies for the farm animals. Most of the little ones came into the world with no complication. With slight direction, they were standing and searching for a first meal. But once in a while, the mother and the baby, be it cow, horse, goat, or puppies, would be fighting for their lives during a difficult birth.

Gap would massage the animal's stomach as Papa would stick his strong, caring, and skilled arm inside the cow, and turn the baby to the right position. Out would come one of God's wonders. Monty would ask, almost breathless from excitement, "Papa, can I help cut the cord, please, please?" Papa's heart was gratified to observe his daughter, and now his granddaughter was giving such kindness. Monty knew well the scent and blessing of a newborn.

Monty would have tears rolling down her cheeks. Papa said, "Monty, there's a time for tears, but now this animal needs us to be strong." Monty would pick up her wash pan of cool water and gently start to wipe the animal down.

Even at an early age, Monty would say that the animals talked to her. "She wants me to cover her, Papa. She's cold." "I think I'd better sleep in the barn with the baby. It needs me." "Papa, the mama's exhausted. She would like for me to wash her baby. Is it okay, Papa?"

Papa usually answered, "We will go with what its mama does. If it's okay with her, sure." Monty would lovingly clean it, then she would cry herself to sleep in the barn. Gap would give her daughter a loving look and smile with pride and say, "Would it be okay with the new mother if I stayed with you?"

"That would make us both very happy, Monty."

It was a sparkling time when she and Gap slept in the barn with the sickly mother and her baby to make sure they knew someone was there for them throughout the night.

When Monty arrived in Grand Central Station only seven months ago, the formidable stained-glass clock that dominated Grand Central told her to have her baby in the station. So here she was, in unbelievable circumstances, but one that she felt her life on the farm had prepared her for. The clock showed the time coming up on 2:00 AM. She was having this baby in Grand Central Station, New York, only neither her mother nor Papa was with her to cut the birth cord or to bathe her face with a cool cloth. "I can't question my decision to be here," she said out loud to no one. Now she had Jazzy, who was with her every step she took if wanted. It was Monty not letting him in close to all her tribulations. She had laid out who she was, scars and all. He understood and Jazzy didn't push or go back on his word to her.

Monty's contractions were coming often. She opened her bag and managed a smile at how prepared she was. "I got my prepared aptitude from you, Papa and Mother Gap. Even in my state o' mind, your strong teachings stay with me and help guide me." Her present thoughts were of the idealistic life she had lived on Protected Earth. At times it seemed so long ago, but only seven months had disappeared since she sat on her much loved screened-in porch for her last front porch talks.

Crow, Birchard, Papa, Gap, and Monty—had eaten, played guitar, and sang songs on the porch. It had been a moonlit night with a soft breeze that swayed the lanterns that hung from the soffit, in turn casting shadows that danced across their faces.

She was curled up in her mother's arms on the worn, cozy wooden red swing. Dear Aunt Crow's peony-laden quilt had been tucked around them. The smells that were cast in Monty's memory were Papa's whiskey, dried herbs, Chase's and Talker's subtle odors that they carried from the woods on their coats, and fresh coconut cake. Memories that she knew would never leave her heart. She pictured the strong memory of her Papa as he had stroked the three cats positioned on him, his bare feet resting between Chase and Talker. He would lead into story; his robust storyteller's voice always perked the ears around him. I always leaned in closer to clearly hear each word. How I loved when Papa would pause with a self-appreciative chortle.

Monty brought herself back to the present. The cold marble bench sent a chill through her clothing. Her thoughts also ran to Jazzy and his worry about her. The contractions came closer together, she felt secure and strangely not alone. She was familiar with each interval of childbirth. Monty felt she remembered her own peaceful birth. As a child, she would ask Gap to repeat her birth and never tired of hearing it, "Mama Gap, tell me the story of my birth." Each time, her mother had repeated every detail of when she had been born. She seemed to remember new details of the swimming pond on Protected Earth. Monty put her hands on her large, round belly and started telling her child the same story that Gap had told to her all those years ago. The baby was kicking at life, eager to be born. Monty began.

"Papa and Sparsity were holding your grandmother's hands. I was kicking to be born, just as you are now. Strong contractions almost made her cry out." Monty closed her eyes and let herself sink into the soft memory of Gap's voice and was taken away by it. She continued, "My baby, I felt the cool pond water touch my head and it surrounded me as I left the warm softness of my mother's body. My long, gangly arms and legs flailed without delay against the water.

"My feet touched the bottom of the soft, marshy pond. I lay there feeling safe like I had in my mother's womb. Then, softly I rose to the top, gathering garlands of pond grass, and a small fish nibbled on my legs, then Mama Gap's strong, muscular hands lifted me out of the water and Sparsity cut the cord. For a moment, I felt my heart stop, then beat and then... freedom, and I breathed in the air of Protected Earth.

"Sparsity wrapped a soft blanket around me and put me in the arms of your grandfather. I felt my face against the wetness of his beard, he kissed my head, and I knew complete love. Someday you will understand. The voices tell me that you will be safe, and you will eventually know the love of all the people on Protected Earth. And carry with you the exhilarating excitement of a big city."

Monty's child was about to have her own extraordinary birth. Monty would put down each detail in writing so that one day her child could relive its birth and she will tell Gap and Papa.

Monty reached for clean towels and diapers, Papa Lee's purple flannel shirt was laid to the side to cover the baby, antiseptic to clean the newborn and herself, also a pair of surgical scissors that she had taken from her last hospital visit, to cut the cord. She knew that she could do this. Closing her eyes once more, she sent thoughts to Mama

Gap and Papa Lee to watch over her and their grandchild that was to be born right here in Grand Central Station.

Monty could hear the rollers of the cleaning woman's supply cart as she moved it across the marble floor. The cavernous station caused an echo of sounds. Monty did find some comfort in the fact that someone was close by, in case she had a problem giving birth and cried out. The woman came into view. She was colorfully dressed—a long, silk sari wrapped around her. The silk swished as she walked. Monty remembered having read that a city of homeless people lived under Grand Central, the city that never sleeps. But this woman looked regal and beautiful.

The hands on the huge stained-glass clock moved. A lone train pulled into the station. The hiss of the brakes carried her mind back to the small train station in Darnell, where she used to wait with her Papa and Gap for the train to arrive, bringing supplies. Monty gave an energetic push, perfectly timed.

Monty busied herself with cleaning the baby girl, a white fuzz of hair, dark eyes, pouty lips, and perfect, tiny fingers that closed around one of Monty's as she cleaned each one. She brushed her lips against the white hair, so soft. The infant had flawless feet, a long body, and long legs. The baby let out a funny little cry, it became louder, and then recoiled into soft breathing.

She was beyond anything that Monty had experienced. Monty cut the cord and said, "My precious girl, you will never be disjoined from my soul. Someday, my fervent hope is that you will comprehend what I believe is rational reasoning, in my wanting you to experience some years of disappointments, different nationalities, street people, and circumstances where you will meet with resistance, so all these experiences will give you a point of view that few will have at any time in their life. My magical child, I will keep watch over you and at the right time, return you to your rightful home in Georgia."

Monty felt, and often expressed to her boyfriend Jazzy, "No one could possibly understand why I am giving up my child." From the deepest part of Monty, she felt no guilt, so she was not encumbered to carry it. Jazzy expressed his desire for her to keep the child—"I give you my word I will always take care of the two of you."

Monty expressed herself, forcibly and clearly, "No! Plaid will someday be going to her folks in Georgia." Monty wrapped the baby warmly, then buttoned Papa Lee's purple flannel shirt around her and tucked it over her feet.

The baby was starting to fret. "After all," Monty told her, "you are a Darnell, and they all love food." Monty had worn Papa's shirt the night she left Protected Earth. Taking out the leather and tiny multi-stone bracelet that Gap had made with love for her, she slipped it around her own daughter's tiny ankle and pulled the slip knot. "You will be protected by the spirit and energy of the people whose blood is running through your veins." Monty busied herself with the towels and disposed of the afterbirth in the trash. Now feeling some dizziness, she closed her eyes and asked for strength. She thought of Jazzy. Back at the apartment, pacing and stopping to pet the animals, talking to them of his worry for her. Please know, Jazzy, I am okay and I feel your love. The exhausted Monty, sometimes mature beyond her seventeen years, drew a surge of power.

The cleaning woman had often seen the stunning, tall young blonde with her paints and easel late at night at Grand Central Station. Tonight, the blonde girl smiled at her, walked around the station, and then disappeared from view. In fact, she had hoped to see the girl and give her a proper thank you for the lovely painting the girl had gifted her with one night. The painting was of herself eating her dinner of curry, rice, yogurt, fruit, and a cup of tea, all spread on a small, colorful silk scarf. The scarf had been a gift from her son in India. Her son promptly wrote to her that he treasured the painting. And was soon to join his mother in New York.

Thoughts of the girl slipped out of the woman's head and she continued to roll the cart across the floor to the other end of the long station, where she paused to check out what she believed to be a parcel someone had left on a bench. When a soft cry and movement came from the bundle, she saw that it was a newborn baby. Picking the baby up, she thought about her children still in India, when she had held them in her arms for the first time. Then her thoughts went to the girl. The girl was the only person she had seen in the station for the past few hours. She went to find the security guard to report the abandoned baby.

Monty had positioned herself so as to have a full view of her baby and the brown-skinned cleaning woman with the kind face. She observed the woman picking up her baby and talking to the police as they arrived. Monty felt that she must get herself to the hospital and somehow let Jazzy know she was alive and well. She walked into the clear, starry night. Lucky to hail a taxi right away, she was now in great pain. She gave the driver instructions to drive her to the hospital and paid him upfront to deliver a letter to Jazzy. Monty woke up two days later in a hospital with a newspaper lying on her bed. The headlines read of a beautiful baby girl found in Grand Central Station.

The hospital nurses had named her Plaid Patience because she was wrapped in a purple plaid flannel shirt and had such patience for a hungry baby. The tiny stone and leather bracelet on the child's leg spelled out "Darnell". No one had come forward to claim the baby. Offers were pouring in to adopt her.

June Light, Monty's assigned social worker, stood beside the hospital bed where Monty lay sleeping. "I have seen the downward spiral of this precious girl," June murmured to the night nurse, "the demons of mental illness eating her intellect and health."

June had been Monty's social worker for three months and had taken the Georgia girl home with her several times, going against state protocol. Monty had nicknamed her June Bug. The first time Monty was found walking down the street, she had no shoes, her clothes were torn, and she had been dirty from her own vomit. She was drinking straight whiskey to kill the voices in her head. Jazzy had been searching the streets, hospitals, and shelters for her. Jazzy's phone number and address were in Monty's leather artist's bag. June called Jazzy to inform him of Monty's condition and asked him about their relationship. Monty was often in and out of delirium, sometimes days or weeks. Jazzy was beside her as often as possible.

Jazzy wasn't a stranger in dealing with mental illness. His mother was eventually confined because of numerous suicide attempts. The embarrassment and pain that he endured throughout his childhood followed him. When he finished high school, his father sent him to New York to live with an uncle. Jazzy felt it odd to live in a normal household but grew to welcome the calming love and care in his uncle's home.

New York pushed all his buttons. Jazzy felt alive as never before. One afternoon, he decided on a whim to stroll in Central Park. A bench dappled with sunlight and shade invited him to sit down and rest. He hadn't noticed the artist further back. When he stood to continue his walk, a beautiful blonde ran up to him and put her hand on his arm. "Please, is there any way you could sit back down for a bit? I've already started roughing you in." Her hands and shirt sported streaks of oil paint. A canvas on an easel several yards behind the bench revealed a work in progress.

This was the same girl that had smiled at him in the coffee shop the day before! He'd been about to go over to the girl when his friends had descended on his table. She stood and left before he had the chance to disentangle himself from his buddies. Now, here she was with her hand on his arm! Thanks to my God… it's fate and meant to be.

Jazzy was dazzled. He asked to see her painting, and sure enough, she had roughed him into the scene. He obliged her by sitting back down; he was scarcely able to breathe anyway. They went to a nearby café. From there, they went to the jazz club where he worked, and to his loft apartment. They were still together. His heart was committed for better or for worse. The "worse" had soon become apparent.

He had fallen in love with this lovely young psychotic girl from the deep south. It was too late; he didn't want to walk away. He knew that there would always be a crisis, but his father had stayed devoted to his mother and had loved her to the end. Jazzy sat holding Monty's hand. Monty asked, "Why did you send Papa away? My horse was at my window and told me that Papa was here."

Jazzy didn't try to dissuade Monty from her delusions—for her, they were real. He was by her side most times during the spells of her "dark nights of the soul." He would try to steer the conversation in another direction, such as, "Talk to me, Monty, about the early morning rides on Protected Earth. What were they like?" He knew that Monty was exceptionally talented and smart. He was so grateful that June understood, and that Monty was blessed to have June Bug as her social worker. June was someone who wasn't afraid to step outside the box when the situation called for it.

June knew that Monty was connected to the baby that had been found in Grand Central Station; after all, Monty was pregnant one day, then not pregnant the very next day that the baby appeared. June knowing the hell Monty had put her body through, how blessed that her baby appeared to be perfect. Having been with New York Social Services for many years, June felt that she was aware of the ins and outs of getting special favors for her cases from the city, and also how to get herself assigned to the baby girl, now called Plaid Patience. June was more sympathetic to Monty after hearing her story. She had uncharacteristically decided not to report Monty's situation.

Monty was trusting June more with each visit. June felt that she was right in not being above board on her reports to the city. Her gut feeling was guiding her. She was not budging on either Plaid Patience or Monty. This time, she was determined to follow her heart and not any set rules. When Monty improved, June felt that she would find out all the unbroken truth to Monty's life.

Jazzy seemed to be the girl's only friend. Monty spoke of no family members to June. Jazzy told June that it was up to Monty to supply any information that she chose to share. He knew Monty's story but was totally loyal to her. Jazzy was an out-of-the-ordinary guy. Monty was lucky to have him in her corner. Jazzy asked June to call him and he would pick up Monty when she was to be released from the hospital, and that she would be in his care. Jazzy didn't question Monty's decisions. It would not have changed anything. She was strong-willed.

He knew that Plaid Patience was Monty's baby. He also knew the hell that she lived with every day and understood that there was no recovery from her illness. Hers was an illness that slowly would eat away her mind, beauty, and immeasurable talent. But within all of her pain, there was an inner focus to her strength that could not be explained. Monty's decisions came from a place that no one intruded on. Anyone allowed into her life became dedicated to her. June Light was now one of those people. Monty trusted June with her care and asked to be kept informed about Plaid. June did much more. She was devoted and protective of all cases in her care. Monty's health and mind stayed on a rollercoaster. The months and years stayed pretty much the same.

June juggled decisions about Plaid and kept Monty informed as to where she was being fostered. June knew that Monty would never sign for any adoption. Monty confided in June that Plaid would be going to her "Grandmother Gap's" in Georgia at some time. June would not break Monty's trust and had grown to understand why she wanted Plaid to have these experiences. Plaid was growing up, and there was no doubt whose child she was. She looked like a miniature of her mother. Jazzy and June had letters from Monty giving them specific plans for Plaid, should anything happen to her.

CHAPTER 29

Monty's Letter Sent to Papa and Gap

Monty admired the elegant stationery she held in her thin, opaline hand. Beautiful writing paper is a treasure, she thought. Papa and Gap had passed along a taste for quality. The beige linen sheets were embossed at the top with a spider writing in green and lavender. Weaving her intricate web through the spokes of a bike.

An art shop owner had equally bartered Monty's somewhat idealized painting of his shop for the expensive stationery. Today, Monty was resting. She broke down often. At times, her body was too weak to function.

The morning was dark with rain. Jazzy piled pillows behind her and straightened the comforter, then positioned her lap desk as Monty requested. Jazzy spoke with worry, "Promise me you will not venture outdoors." She did not reply. The voices in her head often gave her bad directions, knowing when she was too fragile to defeat them. Jazzy understood this.

"Jazzy, today the voices are active. I feel extremely weak, but I will be getting a letter written to Gap and Papa Lee." Jazzy once more adjusted the pillows behind her and kissed the top of her head with a silent prayer that she was strong enough to maintain control. Each time he left the apartment, his thoughts were of Monty. He often hurried his day to get back to check on her.

Monty picked up the pen and pursed her lips. She organized her thoughts and, with a deep sigh began to write:

My dear, dear hearts,

I am dying. As I see the words on paper, it hits my soul even harder. Even in my last days, I can't always control my divided mind. The voice shouts incessantly, everything from sheer nonsense to distorted memories. My memories of Protected Earth get all mixed up. I see Plaid riding a horse with Gap. I understand my brain is scrambled, and as my optic nerve enters my brain, maybe even God only knows what might come out.

Papa, you are standing to the side with your head thrown back. Laughing with unrestrained joy to see your eight-year-old granddaughter's blonde braids flying out behind her. Then the voices move back into my chest and become silent for a while. Yes, you two splendid souls have a granddaughter.

Gap, she looks exactly like me, as I look like you. I was always so proud to hear folks say that I looked just like you. You are the most beautiful woman I've ever seen. So now you have another little mirror image. When you look at her, you will see yourself. You will see me.

Monty glanced at the clock. Startled, she saw that it had taken over an hour to write this mere beginning. Jazzy returned shortly, laden with grocery bags. Monty laid down her pen and smiled at him. Suddenly, she felt her body start to quicken. The extremes in her physical state did not surprise Jazzy or her anymore. It was now the so-called "normal" for them. She softly spoke, "You look happy. Anything you wish to tell me?"

Jazzy put the bags on the table and came straight to her. He moved her lap desk to the chair, then sat on the edge of the bed and laid his head on her lap. Monty reached out and caressed his hair. She noticed it was starting to thin on top. He reached up to touch her hands. She brought it up to her cheek. "Your gentle, loving hands. I love your hands, your goodness, and your smell."

Jazzy looked up into her face, feeling that he couldn't get enough of her. "Monty, do you feel strong enough to take a buggy ride through the park? The rain has stopped, and the sun is trying to peek through. I thought that it would be nice to go through the park together. Maybe even stop at the bench where you painted so often and where you first entered my life." He added, "Did you finish your letter?"

"No, but I got it started. That's okay, I still have time. I have to get it right. Since you came in, I feel stronger." Her snappy movements had disappeared, but her eyes were clear and bright. Today was free of shadows. His Monty was back. She surprised him, "Let's make love."

Jazzy was conflicted. Monty was frail and weak. He wanted to ask her if she was up to it but she was already unbuttoning her nightshirt. His hesitation amused her. "Are you deciding, my knight-errant?"

He smiled at her. "Have I ever said no to you?" He squelched his concern and closed the shutters, then lit every candle in the room.

As Jazzy began to remove his clothes, Monty's admiring eyes took in every inch of him. "You always make it so special, like the first time." He carefully lay beside her and took her in his arms. With his whole heart, Jazzy made love to her. He took his time. He then surrendered himself to the moment and stopped thinking. There was nothing but her and his mind and heart. She was his world.

Thoroughly satiated, they lay in each other's arms. Monty put her hand over his heart. Caressing him with every whispered word, she told Jazzy of her love for him.

Monty kissed his hair. "Now, let's go for that buggy ride."

Later that afternoon, they returned from their buggy ride through the park. The rain had washed the air clean and made the park sparkle. The ride had been magical and bittersweet for them both. They held each other close as they stood looking at the now clear blue sky. Monty whispered, "Jazzy, don't you love the many moods of the sky? It can change drastically all in a moment, the way I do."

"Never looked at the sky as having moods, but I sure agree with your view of it." He took her hands and they walked toward home.

Jazzy took the dog for a walk. When he got back, he dressed for work at the Jazz Club and turned to her just before he left. "Monty, you are with me every moment."

"Play something for me tonight." Monty always asked him for a special song. He smiled at her, then picked up his sax case and left.

Monty felt stronger. The day had been extraordinary. She made an espresso, got comfortable, and once more picked up her pen.

Plaid Patience is your granddaughter and what a prize she is. She has never lived with me and knows nothing about me or my condition. Also, she knows nothing of her background. Plaid is watched over by a dear friend who tells me that Plaid is absolutely fearless and that she is full of desire for adventure. Sound familiar?

My ability to carry on, with the villain that invades my mind and body, is soon to end. It has robbed me of my life. The doctors at the mental hospital want me to have shock treatment. I fear that it will take my memories. I will not have you all taken from me ever again.

I want you two to know that your pictures have always been by my side. Every moment of my life since I left Protected Earth, you have been right there with me. Never doubt that. Has it really just been seven years? It seems I am so old.

I don't know how much time is left. Days and weeks are lost to me now. I am often in a catatonic state and know that one day. I will not recover.

The darkness within had even begun to surface in my painting. I refuse to give the darkness expression through my precious gift, so dear to me, so much a part of me. So, of course, I have packed away my paints and brushes. That part of me has died. I miss the smell and feel of the paint and the brush in my hand. The wondrous feeling of being one with my own creation. I grieve for that part of me that is lost. But June has shown me some of Plaid's drawings, so I feel the talent you gave me is now passed down to her.

I am blessed to have Jazzy in my life. He is my friend and lover, my mensch, to use his word, and my caregiver. June Light is my social worker and a dear friend. She goes above and beyond (and often against) her job on my behalf. Mama Gap and Papa, you would approve of them if you knew them, and you would love them as I do. Maybe one day the two can visit Plaid on Protected Earth.

My appetite has gone. Jazzy is always trying to find a new dish that will entice me to eat a healthy meal. In my dreams, though, I still taste the hot cheese grits, big, fluffy, browned, crunchy biscuits, and warm gravy made with milk. Mama, I really miss you and Sparsity's superb southern cooking.

Jazzy tries undeterred. He is a jazz musician, you probably guess. He is full of spirit, kind-hearted even through the extreme, and devoted to me. He never hesitated—he took me into his heart from the beginning. I have never felt judged or rejected in any way. He never burdened me with expectations.

Jazzy became my business manager of sorts. I painted in Central Park every sunny day and found an appreciative clientele in these artsy New Yorkers. He took care of me on all levels. Your problematic girl has been in caring hands.

Coming to New York was the hardest thing I ever did, next to leaving Plaid, but it is my highest hope that you two understand why I left. It was my principled choice to leave. Mama, you gave me life, and then you both showed me the way to live with high standards and appreciate all living things. To have been your child, Mama, and Papa, your granddaughter—how could anyone have been more blessed? And how could I have asked you to watch me fall apart?

The memories that I cherish will continue to sustain me. Papa, do you remember when a beautiful writing spider made her web in the spokes of my bicycle? You instructed me, "She has taken the wheel as her home and labored hard. We will not destroy it." You bought me a new bike and Lady Spider lived happily. You are my hero. And there is no one on earth like you, Papa.

Do you remember the three of us at the swimming hole with Chase and Talker, the wet, musty, smell of the dogs, and all of us falling asleep on the carpet of moss? Papa, you had a fire in the stone pit that you had made with smooth river rocks. Your antique carved rocker... That rocker went with us almost everywhere. I felt so loved with you watching over me. I love to be barefoot, like you. My paintings were all produced with my bare feet on the ground. Remember how I would pile small stones and acorns for you to pick up with your toes?

Papa, I loved when you would carry me on your shoulders. I felt like I was flying up with the birds. Remember when Crow made my angel wings? I jumped out of the viewing Nest, high up in the pine tree. I think I did fly a bit. That magnificent feeling was well worth the pain of my broken ankle.

I know that the viewing platform will be one of Plaid's favorite places in the world. Tell Plaid how the three of us would fall asleep on the platform and you built a harness to pull Chase and Talker up, otherwise, the two would sit under the tree and howl to be with us. Then see how many different birds we could see. Papa, you would look in your treasured sketchbook to see if you had drawn it. How glorious they were, even the ones from your childhood. June Light gave me a sketch Plaid did of a little Finch. I treasure it and must look at it 20 times a day.

Remember, Papa, when you were carrying me on your shoulders, and I would grab a piece of Evergreen as we walked by? I held it up to my nose and inhaled the scent of pine with the smell of your orange lifebuoy soap that you bathe with every day. I would bury my head in your protective shoulders, thinking, I will miss this ride when I get too big for papa to carry me.

Papa, I copied your every gesture. Once, when I was running along one of the Forest Trails and got a large thorn stuck in my foot. How it hurt! I trusted you when you told me, it has to come out. My faith in you was complete and I let you take the thorn out. I recall seeing you get your Swiss knife. Sometimes you would let me carry that knife in my pocket. I would put my hand in my pocket to hold your knife, determined not to use it.

You took out a match and burned the ends of the tweezers. When you pulled out the thorn, you said, "Let's keep this, Monty. Put it in your treasure box to remind you of how Brave you are." I shed no tears. We gave complete trust to each other.

I remember saying, 'Oh Papa, I love, love, love, love you.' You then lifted me up on your shoulders and we went to look for the horses that we had let run and graze. I felt so much love, I didn't know how to express it. I bit down hard on your shoulder.

Startled, you stopped like an animal stops in the wild when they hear a sound. You placed me on the ground in front of you. You kept my face in your large, wonderful hands and asked, "Monty, my precious one, why did you bite Papa?"

"I wanted you to really feel my love, Papa." Tears filled my eyes. I was ashamed.

You answered and your sweet voice, so loving, I understand. 'Let's go home so I can wash this love bite.' Then you laughed up to the heavens. Your laughter fell on the Hills and Valleys and landed on everything and on me. I still carry it with me every day.

Mama, your beautiful face is before me as I close my eyes every night. I say your name to hear the sound of it before I fall asleep.

Do you know that within my soul, I know that you and Papa did everything possible for my health on all levels? I simply could not bear the thought of putting you through the rigors of my illness. You always protected me from harm. Now I felt I could protect you.

I know this. I love you too much to have you care for me as I literally fight from moment to moment to hold onto lucidity. I won't describe these episodes to you, and have you tormented by the memories of my suffering.

Mama, I have drawn on your strength more times than you will ever know. Now, I will be strong for you. Bless you, for your goodness, generosity, and your shining beautiful spirit. I love you.

Our Plaid is a wonderful child. When I left Protected Earth, I was four months pregnant and terrified that my child would inherit my illness. I felt that it was my responsibility to leave.

Enclosed, you will find newspaper clippings about Plaid. She became a celebrity. She was born in Grand Central Station. Her birth was easy. I cut the cord, cleaned her up, wrapped her in Papa's Plaid purple shirt. You, Sparsity, and Crow taught me well. Mama, she has our eyes, our hair, and Papa's wide, full smile. Leaving her on the bench took every bit of strength that I possessed, I hid and watched her until she was found. I know my head was all messed up but somehow, I knew all would be okay and she would be in the right hands.

June Light has kept me informed of all Plaid's foster parents. June knew that Plaid was not to be adopted by anyone. She had to fight for that, bless her loyal heart. I had this far-reaching dream that I could be cured and take custody of my daughter someday. I so wanted us to return to Protected Earth — with Jazzy, too. It was a beautiful dream.

June Light and Jazzy know how to contact each other when I am gone, I have arranged for Plaid to be brought to Georgia. Jazzy and June both wanted her, but Plaid's place is with you. Plaid is now eight years old and at present, lives in a foster home with wonderful people. They are retired teachers and are marvelously kind. June really outdid herself in finding them.

June understands that, with my life in such disorder, how could I possibly subject Plaid to this life.

I know that my decision was a selfish nature not to have sent her to you and Papa sooner. My reason for doing this was that I wanted Plaid to have different experiences than the Charmed Life she will have on Protected Earth. Now, she knows some of the hard realities of life. She's tough, my daughter, a real Survivor, and the pride of my life.

To tell you something of her character, June tells me that Plaid is a wonderful Storyteller. So, I know she will have a lot to tell you.

Plaid brings with her many hard lessons. With you, she will now experience exuberant freedom and, for the first time in her young life, real Security in a loving home with those of her own blood. Someday, she will understand my reason for what I chose for her.

The decision to send her to you now has been made for me. I haven't many days left. Mama, Jazzy will be with me, holding my hand.

One bright spot, most unexpected, happened yesterday. June let me sit close by and observe her meeting with Plaid. She is all that you could wish for in your granddaughter— beautiful, independent, talented, intelligent, and she loves everything in nature.

How staggering—when Plaid and June walked past, I was nervous, I dropped my notepads. Plaid saw this and came over to pick it up for me, her hand touched mine! She smiled at me! How Blissful was that? I have no words to describe it.

It is my wish to be cremated. Jazzy will send my ashes to you. I want to rest beside Papa's sisters in the little graveyard on the ridge. Mr. Ward's pocket watch that Papa gave me, I would like Plaid to have. Also, for Plaid my paints and brushes are in that beautiful bag Papa made with such love. The bracelets that we made together will stay with me.

Jazzy will also crate my paintings and send them to you, minus the three that I promised June. My paintings sold while in New York and actually, my paintings kept me financially quite comfortable. Jazzy will send you a check for all of my savings. Plaid may spend it as she wishes.

My prayer is that Plaid gets to spend many years with you both. Her memories with you will be rich with love and will give her the life that she was born to live. The years in New York will give her the strength to stand where others may fall.

My spirit will be ever abiding in protective Earth. Chase and Talker will be with me as my spirit runs through the Wildflower Meadow. Papa's sisters will be gathering herbs with me. Birchard, Mickey, and Mr. Ward will be there with me. I am ready to come home.

With all that I am, I love you both. Let Plaid know that we share the same sun, moon, and stars, and are part of Protected Earth. I know Mama and Papa Lee, you will let me live through your story Plaid will learn from you and the rest of the beautiful people who live on Protected Earth.

Blessings always, my heart, my love, my light. See you in the raindrops. Kisses all of life. Remember how much you are loved by your baby girl.

Your child, your grandchild,
Monty

CHAPTER 30

The Right Foster Home

"June Bug, I need to see Plaid now." June did not like the anguish in her friend's voice. Her sense of obligation to Monty had grown. June loved both Monty and Plaid. She really hadn't let the thought of losing them both at the same time submerge into her heart.

June gripped the phone so hard, her hands cramped. She realized that she hadn't answered Monty. "Monty, are you well enough to meet me across from Plaid's school and the little park?"

"Yes, I'll be there. What time?"

"Are you sure that you are okay? If not, I can send a friend to accompany you." June didn't like the inescapable lump in her chest, as she listened to Monty's voice. "Why don't I just send a friend to pick you up?"

"All right, June Bug. That would be better. I'll be waiting outside. Thank you." Monty thought, how could I ever repay this woman? She is always watching my back.

June watched a fragile Monty approaching, holding on to the arm of June's friend. Monty had lost more weight. Her 5'11" frame had vanquished all her muscle tone. Her terrific face was too sad to be beautiful anymore. But miraculously, it was framed with a head full of long, shining blonde hair. June stood from her seat on the park bench and walked to greet Monty. Monty managed to smile as she reached for June's shoulder for support. "June bug, you are always a healing sight." June thanked the man for bringing Monty to her. He then left.

As June watched her friend struggle just to stand, she remembered when Monty had once said, "I left Georgia because life was too comfortable."

As the two sat on the park bench, June watched Monty, but Monty's eyes were raptly seeking a glimpse of her daughter.

June asked softly, "Monty, how could comfort have created such discomfort that you would just up and leave such loving and kind people you tell me your grandfather and mother are?" Monty was so intent on looking for Plaid, she didn't even hear the question. If she did, she let it pass. June sighed and let it drop. She found it difficult to accept explanations. They were not something Monty tended to give anyway. June smiled to herself and thought, 'Well yes, Plaid has the same trait.'

When June had become involved with Monty and Plaid, she had for the first time, stepped outside the detailed criteria outlined in her job description. She broke many rules. She knew that it was too late to change tactics. There was simply no way she could maintain objectivity on decisions involving either.

June's extraordinary attachment to these special people had begun from the moment Monty was put on her caseload. Now, her commitment to Monty was like Huck Finn and Tom Sawyer; they had made an unspoken Blood Oath.

For months, then years, June had assured Monty that she was working wholeheartedly to find the right foster parents for Plaid. June put herself in Monty's shoes. She often asked herself, could I make this kind of sacrifice? Can anyone really know another's heart? She knew for certain that she would continue to inform Monty about Plaid's life. And on occasion, she would help Monty—like today—see her daughter from afar, never knowing if it might be Monty's last time.

Monty would bombard June with questions such as "Does Plaid wake up happy? Will she stand up for herself? Can she draw? Does she love nature?" June answered Monty's questions with as much certainty as she could about knowing Plaids likes and dislikes. This was not easy, as her answer always generated more questions.

Monty treasured even the smallest information about Plaid. So why didn't she just come forward and claim her daughter?

June informed Monty of the uniqueness of Plaid. "I believe Plaid can cope with most any situation." But Monty felt that her illness was a great burden for her little girl. Monty's face would show such pain, her hands trembled at the thought. She also knew that soon she would send Plaid to Gap and Papa Lee.

Her health was continuing to make a downward spiral. She would often say to Jazzy, "I believe winter will come early to me. But not... just... yet.

Each stolen moment watching her daughter sustained her. Monty felt that without Plaid to anchor her, she would quickly disappear into madness. The thought of living beyond the veil, never to see Plaid again, was unbearable. Yes, she would wait as long as she could. She would fight moment by moment to hold back the abyss that yawned before her. She even had thoughts, I'm tearing up the letter to Gap and Papa, if there was even a remote possibility, that she could overcome this last huddle. And Plaid, Jazzy, and I can all go back to Georgia. In seven years, she had not even considered it even in the realm of possibility.

She nervously rubs her long-fingered hands back and forth. She picked at the skin on her fingers until they bled and rubbed her hand off on her sweater. Monty stared at her hands and nails. She said, "All colors of the rainbow are under my nails."

Reaching into her handbag for a Band-Aid, June, said "Looks like you've been painting." No reply. Monty had a curious habit of not replying to conversational questions. She simply wasn't interested in small talk.

June brought out two Band-Aids. Reaching out for Monty's hand she put the Band-Aids on Monty's torn fingers.

Monty's voice sounded clear. "June, Jazzy has paintings of mine. He knows that most are for Plaid. But I want you to pick out three paintings. I could never repay you for all your understanding and compassion, putting your job on the line for me and Plaid, and for caring for us from your heart. I am so beholden to you."

June felt her throat tighten. "I will choose my three. Thank you. Plaid is your child, Monty. She will one day understand the reason behind your decisions. Your truth is too harsh for most folks, but it won't be for Plaid."

Monty looks down. "And June…" She hesitated. "Jazzy has my letter to Papa Lee and Mama Gap. I want you to mail it to them after my death."

Monty's words hung in the air between them. June didn't want to accept something so dire, even though she had long witnessed Monty's decline. The despair of it all made a knot in her chest. June knew that her heart was breaking for Monty and Plaid, and for Jazzy and herself too.

The signs of fall filled the air as golden leaves floated from the trees that lined the street, then danced around their feet. June drew in a deep breath. "I believe I found Plaid the perfect foster parents. Plaid doesn't look at change like most children. She welcomes it. There's a huge dissimilarity between Plaid and the other children her age. She possesses a keenness for adventure—she craves it. Of course, these very traits keep her in hot water, not only with her teachers and foster parents, but also with children her age."

Monty pulled out a smile "I am thankful for it's a good signal, that her individuality is in check."

June continued, "Plaid likes making decisions and doesn't like it when decisions affecting her are made by someone else. As we know, adults have to take this liberty with children. With all the other homes that I have placed Plaid in, I could expect to be notified shortly to pick her up. Not everyone would commit to a child that they considered difficult, or sometimes even just different. They wish their child to blend in. But my prayers have been answered—I really believe that they have. Mr. And Mrs. Millhouse have expressed their interest in Plaid. They're both retired teachers, educated in England. They have two children in college, but at this time in their lives, they want the stimulation of helping an exceptional child. Plaid is perfect for them, and they are for her. I believe we have a match."

It was difficult for anyone or anything to hold Monty's attention for long. But when June talked about Plaid, Monty's ears were wide open.

As June kept talking, Monty had reached out and taken hold of June's wrist. June felt the pressure of Monty's grip. She realized how painful this scene was for Monty. June's compassion ran high. As June saw Plaid exit the school. Monty started to tremble. In a low almost whisper, Monty said, "There she is June. My beautiful daughter."

"I know, Monty. She is your image."

Plaid sat down on the school steps. She quickly opened her backpack. Took out a pad and started doodling, her head down. As the leaves fell onto the steps, Plaid would pick one up, and study it; run her fingers over it, and then place the leaf into her pad.

June said to Monty as she guided her to a park bench close by, "Monty, please sit. My friend will be here shortly to take you home."

"June, watching Plaid play is like going back in time — to my childhood. I know exactly what she is thinking and feeling when she picks up each leaf. I would sit with my mama and hold her hands. The veins on her hands, I would slowly trace, they seemed so like the veins of the leaf. Mama would go into an interesting explanation, how humans and nature are connected."

The street vents blew steam into the air, mixing dust, leaves, and odd bits of trash into swirls around the two women.

June released Monty's hands from her wrist and crossed to the opposite side of the street to meet Plaid.

June asked, "Plaid, would you want to get a hot dog with an old friend?"

Plaid looked up and gave June a big smile. June's heart gave a funny little hop as she saw a younger version of the once breathtaking Monty. Plaid's resemblance to her mother was uncanny. June couldn't help but wonder whether Plaid got the chromosomes for her mother's illness as well. "Please God, no," she pleaded under her breath.

Plaid was clearly delighted. "I'm always good for a hot dog!" She adored June and often told her so. June made her feel protected. But Plaid also felt that someone else watched over her. Plaid had by this time gone through several foster mothers. She had never stayed with one long enough to feel much of anything one way or another, "Miss June, I just know my very own mother is close by. Sometimes I can feel her."

June felt like saying, "Yes, Plaid! She's right here! Run to her!" But she could not break her pledge to Monty.

June waited while Plaid packed her books. The chattering child made her think of her own family. June McGill Light's parents came to New York from Ireland. As her family settled into their new home, her father had worked his way up from fireman to chief. Her mother had cleaned homes and raised seven children under difficult circumstances. June's parent's goal was that each of their children would have a college education.

As a child, June was dark-haired, robust, and freckled faced. She grew to be a woman with a roar of a laugh that lifted a person's spirit. June did not disappoint her parents. She even earned a master's degree in child development, was respected by her peers, and held a lot of clout with Social Services. The mayor of New York City often called on June with challenging cases.

June was single and devoted to her family, job, and the people under her care. When her friends and family made reference to wedding bells, she would just say, "I just don't fancy having a man in my life right now. That would pull my focus from my real love—the people who look to me for help and support. Love and marriage can wait. For now, there is simply no time for that sort of thing. I'm doing what I was meant to do."

Plaid and June approached the bench where Monty sat. June did not look at Monty, but walked straight past her toward the train station. Plaid noticed that June seem to be distressed. "I believe I see a new freckle, Miss June," Plaid giggled, trying to make June laugh. They laughed and joked at each other. Plaid was in heaven. She loved being with June. They stopped at a street vendor for hot dogs and then ate them on the way to the train.

Monty, in the meantime, was met by June's friend and escorted back to Jazzy's apartment. Once back at Jazzy's, Monty had several drinks to try and nullify her pain. This was a common occurrence after being so close to her daughter. When Jazzy returned, he found her passed out.

When Plaid and June reached the train station, it was a hub of activity. "Like an anthill," Plaid said. They boarded the train and made their way to a seat. It was a process, Plaid was always careful to search out the cleanest seats in the best condition.

June would often say to Plaid, "You are seeking perfection."

June observed that Plaid quieted down and that she had become pensive. She waited for Plaid to open up to her. A couple miles later, Plaid asked, "Miss June, why don't you just adopt me? Am I too much trouble? I'll be good and not ask so many questions. I'll keep my opinions to myself and study hard—I do anyway—and I will make you proud of me." Plaid's big brown eyes conveyed her heart's cry.

"Plaid, if only I could, I'd take you home in a minute." June spoke deliberately. "I would be so proud to be your mother. You must know that I promise that someday you'll understand why I can't. I'm so sorry, Plaid. I'm sad for both of us."

Seeing that June was upset, Plaid said softly, "It's okay." June could see that Plaid was going to be okay in her daily life—once Plaid had said it was okay, she let it go and it was okay.

Plaid always got charged up on trains, watching all the different people. She liked to try and read their eyes, old, young, different nationalities—they all fascinated her. She marveled at how each was holding secrets. Plaid often took out her pad and sketched the people who caught her eye. Later she would turn her imagination loose and write fictionalized short stories about each one. Her sketch pads and notebooks were full of carefully noted dates and places. June was one of the few people who saw her art and writings and she marveled at Plaid's talent. Can it really be this child is only seven. Of course, I know that, I have held her as a baby.

Plaid's pencil character sketches were enthralling. Today she sketched a very rotund, cherubic, red-faced old lady dressed in yellow from her hat to her shoes. The woman carried silk yellow pansies in a basket. Pansies were pinned to her hair and dress. From the front of the railway car, the lady held up a bunch of flowers and sang a little song. Her song delighted Plaid.

I sell my flowers
To gentlemen so swell
Heroes or cowards
A little time will tell
Pocket change I will take
So what if
My pansies are fake
A maiden will welcome
Them
After all, that's what the gentleman brought

People began to make their way down the aisle to purchase her flowers. June thought to herself about how one single person could turn a train ride into a party. Many passengers' faces that she observed had changed from guarded to lighthearted enjoyment. As they purchase flowers from the colorful woman.

Plaid said, "Miss June, it would be so wonderful if people felt joyful enough to break into dance."

"Yes, Plaid. How delightful it would be to come upon a person in the middle of an inopportune dance."

Plaid sketched away and chatted to June. June listened, and then said, "You're so talented. I absolutely believe you will be famous." Plaid put her sketch pad back into her backpack.

Now that June had Plaid's undivided attention, she picked up her hand and said, "Plaid, I have found the ideal foster parents for you."

Plaid's eyes went round. "What are they like? Where do they live? Are they looking forward to meeting me?"

June smiled at Plaid's eagerness. "Yes," she responded, "very much so. They have the most wonderful voices—I know how much voices affect you. They are retired teachers, no children in the home."

June continued, pleased that Plaid was excited. "Today we break the rules. You spend the night with me. Tomorrow, we'll pick up your belongings and meet with your new foster parents, Mr. and Mrs. Millhouse."

The train slowed to a stop. Plaid and June got off. Where are all the people going? Plaid wondered. They passed the old woman in yellow. She was already working the crowd milling around the station. The colorful character left smiles in her wake. On a whim, June turned around. They went back and June bought a flower for Plaid. The sweet old lady's eyes twinkled as she watched June present the silk flower to Plaid as the old lady pocketed June's bills.

"Plaid, how about I cook dinner for us tonight? In the morning, we'll have a nice breakfast and then go out and buy you some new clothes."

"Sounds good to me. Thanks. I'd like that. Could we maybe buy some warm gloves for Hanna? She's my friend who lives in Central Park."

June smiled She never knew what Plaid was going to come up with. "Sure, it will be my pleasure. I would like to meet your friend Hanna." June wondered whether Hanna needed other things as well. She would look into it; this person who lived in the park might need some help.

"I don't know, Miss June," Plaid answered slowly. "Hanna doesn't like to meet new people, but I'll ask." She turned their conversation back to her new foster home. Plaid rapidly fired off a stream of questions about the Millhouses. June was hard-pressed to keep up.

The next day, June and Plaid stood in the foyer of the Millhouses' apartment building. The doorman rang up to announce their arrival. Plaid sported a new outfit and braids. She held June's hand. June detected a slight tremor and squeezed Plaid's hand to reassure her. The door opened. The first thing Plaid noticed was the warm smiles and open arms. She walked around the main entrance room, she asked Mrs. Millhouse, "May I touch things, I always get a better feel for my surroundings when I can get energy from things."

June was right. A few days later, Plaid luxuriated in having a room of her own. The room was very feminine; it had been the Millhouses' daughter's room. There were posters of movie stars and high fashion drawings attached to the walls. The daughter was now living in France studying fashion design.

The Millhouse's had offered to move the books out, but Plaid had asked, "Okay, but may I read them first?"

What Plaid wanted to know about was France. The high fashion models featured in the books posed indifferently in front of the glorious French architecture, French statuary, and the very, very French Eiffel tower. When they offered Spanish language in her school, she asked "May I learn French instead, nothing against Spanish, but I do hope to visit France someday, and it would be really nice to speak their language." The teacher made an exception and let her take French with a higher class.

Had she but known it, she had a flair for being unique in not only her mode of dress and hair, but also in her interests and point of view. She dressed in layers. "Bohemian Chic," said Mrs. Millhouse, and encouraged her.

On her visits, June would tease her and say, "Plaid I think that you try and wear every piece of clothing you own at one time." Silently she added in her mind... just like Monty.

Plaid liked living with the Millhouses. They gave her a lot of freedom around the house. Plaid spent pleasurable time in their terrace garden. She was fascinated with the many insects that visited each day. She categorized them. She had been given permission to use Mr. Millhouse's garden. Plaid felt it was a fortunate happening to share the garden with all the insects, birds, and any visitor that happened to join in. The bees particularly held her interest. She would sit and watch a bee work on flower after flower. Once, she got stung. She calmly got up and went to Mrs. Millhouse for first aid. "I annoyed it by getting too close," she told Mrs. Millhouse. "Poor bee. It'll die now. I'm sorry. I just wanted to observe it."

One evening as Mrs. Millhouse came up behind Plaid, she gasped with astonishment. Plaid was drawing a series of different bees that visited the garden. "Plaid! What talent you have! Do you have other sketches?" The drawings were so warm and life-like, from the tiniest tentacle to the most expressive eye.

"Oh yes." Plaid responded, still sketching her bees. "My other sketches are mostly of riders on the train." Plaid put down her pencil and looked up at Mrs. Millhouse. "Would you like to see?" This was huge. Plaid didn't make this offer to just anyone.

Plaid gave her consent with a quiet sense of having been acknowledged. It felt good, the feeling of being validated by someone she respected. Of course, June had done this too, but Plaid knew in her soul that she and June had a heart-link. Mrs. Millhouse was in a place to be much more objective. Plaid glowed all the way down to her toes.

Plaid felt herself opening up to her fosters. For as long as she could remember, she had felt the need to protect herself from... what?... from the nebulous, free-floating cloud of anxiety that hovered somewhere just beyond the periphery. Plaid relaxed into the security of a home with caring people, and her own room.

Mr. Millhouse was impressed as well, in his quiet, understated fashion. He had an air of wisdom about him, Plaid thought, an old soul like I feel inside.

Closing the sketchpad, Mr. Millhouse reflected for a quiet moment "Plaid," he said, "How do you feel about being schooled at home?"

"Well, I don't know. You and Mrs. Millhouse are so smart and nice. It certainly isn't that I love public school so much. But I do love the ride on the train and walking through Central Park. If I was home all day long, day after day, I don't think I'd be happy." Plaid didn't want to hurt Mr. Millhouse's feelings. She added, "I'll do whatever you think is best though."

Mr. Millhouse passed the book back to her and said, "Very impressive. The level of work is well beyond your years. We'll have to look into art tutorage, whether you are home-schooled or not." He stood up to retrieve his pipe from the bookshelf. Beside the chair, Mr. Millhouse stood 6'2". He looked very commanding, Plaid thought as he turned back to her. He said with authority, "I'm not sure it's a good idea for you to be walking through the park alone. It can be a dangerous place, especially for a young girl."

Plaid looked at him and thought fleetingly that it must be wonderful to view the world from that high up. Maybe, just maybe, I'll be nice and tall when I grow up. I want to see all that I can see from there! She was careful not to sound whiney in her response; she had cut her teeth on foster parents from way back and knew the ropes. "But Mr. Millhouse, I have a friend that lives in the park. We visit when I walk through the park after school. Her name is Hanna McCray. She is a good person and knows all kinds of interesting stuff. I would be sad not to see Hanna anymore."

Mr. Millhouse exchanged a look with his wife. "We'll discuss this together with June and make a decision before we go to the park to meet Hanna. For now, though, select a book from the shelf and read to me." Plaid loved reading aloud, to hear beautiful words spoken was so pleasing for her heart. This became a special time for Plaid and Mr. Millhouse. He explained words and new concepts to her when she hit upon difficulties. She felt a little guilty, sometimes she would pretend not to understand, just to enjoy Mr. Millhouse with his expert knowledge, give the meaning and history of a word. Plaid chose a book about birds. The book was written by one of Mr. Millhouse's favorite authors, John Burroughs.

"Great choice," approved Mr. Millhouse. "You love the outdoors, don't you?"

"Oh my! Yes sir! I think I could live outside with the animals."

Plaid began reading, "People who have not made friends with the birds do not know how much they miss. Especially to one living in the country, of strong local attachments and an observing turn of mind, does an acquaintance with the birds form a close and valuable tie?" Plaid stopped and asked Mr. Millhouse, "Please explain more to me exactly what you believe the author Mr. Burroughs is thinking here."

"Bring the dictionary to me. Let's read some of the definitions of his words first. Then we will discuss more." Mr. Millhouse was in his element. Plaid's eager mind readied for ideas that were beyond her understanding. She loved learning as much as Mr. Millhouse loved teaching.

Plaid was a godsend for the Millhouses. They loved having her in their life and in their home. The Millhouses met Hanna, who introduced herself as Dame Hanna McCray. June and the Millhouses gave their blessings to Plaid being friends with Hanna. Hanna promised to watch over Plaid's safety when Plaid visited her in the park. The park policemen, regular walkers, and the priest from the local church all kept a close eye on Hanna, her welfare, and the beautiful blonde child that visited Hanna. The decision was made, after careful deliberation, that Plaid would go to public school and could take short walks through the park. Rules were established for time requirements and areas to avoid in the park.

As of late, Hanna had been ill and weak in body. The Millhouses' had a doctor friend check on Hanna because Plaid was so worried about her. He left medicine and a health tonic for Hanna. Hanna was as excited as Plaid was that Plaid loved her new foster parents. Plaid Patience just couldn't imagine how her life could possibly get any better. But after one year with the Millhouses, her adventurous spirit got her into trouble with the Millhouses and very soon, her life would change forever.

CHAPTER 31

Plaid and Hanna

Plaid Patience preferred the company of grown-ups. She liked doing things and rarely ever participated in the children's constructed games. Her likes were books, drawing, learning history, and people. She would ask questions and learn from their answers. In nature, and any place outside, she said made her happy all over.

Plaid would seek any place that had a bit of nature. After her first walk in Central Park with June Light, the park stayed on her mind. She would lie in bed at night, and long for the feel of the grass and smell of the open air, with its many aromas. One of her favorite things to do was lie under a tree, and look through the tree limbs at the sky. The tree limbs formed a continuous changing picture, a large Hawk, tiny birds, larger birds, pigeons, jays, blackbirds, cloud formations. School was of interest, but Plaid felt herself hurrying through her paperwork, not that the teacher would let her leave early. But she could use that extra time to imagine her adventures in Central Park.

As her train neared her stop, her heart and head would race. People looked at her with her long blonde braids, she was a beauty. She thought, "I bet they hear my heart beating. They think maybe it's a little drum in my chest, but of course that's silly."

Entering the park, she removed her shoes, putting them in her backpack. "Oh my!" she said aloud. Wiggling her toes against the sweet texture of the grass, then pressing her feet into the grass hard enough to feel the dirt underneath. She then closed her eyes, letting her mind soar. "I am running through meadows, insects salute as I disturb their rest. I stop and roll down a grassy knoll, it seems I pick up speed and all the world is whizzing past me as I go faster and faster."

"Hi Miss Plaid, doing some daydreaming?"

It was her friend Hanna. Plaid opened her eyes. Hanna was pulling a wagon—piled high with stuff. She had rails on the side to hold her stuff tight.

"Yes, I suppose I am. My foster parents have now given me permission to cut through the park."

"Are you sad, Plaid?" Hanna said. "We talked briefly of your being abandoned by your mother. Is that the reason you look sad?"

"Oh no! Dame Hanna McCray, I know my mama must have had the best of reasons to have abandoned me. Someday I will unite with my beloved folks. In the meantime, I don't have much time and my goal today is to smell the sweet fragrant grass, maybe lie under the giant oak, look up to the sky, and enjoy the extraordinary sun's rays as they find their way through the limbs to touch the earth. Then I need to scatter some cookies I saved for the crows and birds to share."

"Come Plaid, I have a surprise. The priest from a close by church had a carpenter build me a small shelter." As Plaid followed, they came upon the shelter. Hidden behind some bushes and a huge rock, it was off the ground, dry and warm. On extremely cold nights, the kind, young priest let Hanna and others sleep in the church, gave them hot meals, and then partake of a very welcome bath.

"How wonderful," Plaid said and clapped her hands.

Hanna gave a smile, showing traces of once beautiful teeth, now stained and broken down from life.

After checking out Hanna's new shelter, Plaid laid back on a large boulder, taking notice of each word Hanna spoke. Plaid started to jump down from the rock, right smack into a small mud puddle. Hanna let out a little holler, "Oh please, Miss Plaid. Watch for the mud people." Plaid looked around, but saw nothing.

"Where, Hanna?"

Hanna showed a slight exasperation, shaking her head along with a sucking sound through her teeth that her extremely bright new friend could not see the mud people.

"Plaid, most folks, I don't mean to sound like I am including you in the masses, have never been informed about the dear mud people. Oh! The mud people are so precious, kind, smart, and protective of good. They say the fairies ousted them because they live in the mud."

Plaid's interest was perked. "Hanna, when can I meet the mud people?"

"You may not, unless you are in need of protection. Some folks ponder about U.F.O.'s. Do they exist? Possible. But I believe in the mud people and forest creatures."

Plaid had a mind of her own. Hanna knew she would not be swayed when people tried to convince her there were no mud people.

"Hanna, I always learn something new when I am in your company. Thanks. I have to go. June Bug is coming by today, she said to tell me something really big. I'll let you know." Plaid never tried to hug Hanna because Hanna did not like to be touched. Plaid had seen her go into a wild fit if someone tried to touch her.

Plaid stopped and looked back at her friend, knowing Hanna watched her until she was out of sight. Plaid raised her hand, then touched her heart to remind Hanna, her heart was with her.

Plaid could not quit thinking about Hanna, the park lady. How did Hanna wind up living in the park?

One day, Plaid had a plan. School was released early, and Plaid headed straight for the park. She had made two ham and cheese sandwiches with lots of sweet butter on the bread. She used part of her allowance to buy two of her favorite candy bars, Zero's, a delicious combination of caramel, peanuts, and almond nougat covered with a layer of white fudge. She was going to ask the park lady to share lunch with her, but Hanna did not show. She ate her sandwich and pinched the other into little pieces and left it for the animals.

It was a few days before she could visit the park, taking care of a few chores and homework. She put Hanna in her nightly prayers.

Plaid had informed her foster parents of her trips to the park; they now approved of limited time in the park. She was happy now that she didn't have to hold a secret.

Plaid continued her trips to the park and found out about Hanna's life in the park. Hanna was not a person who was ashamed or apologized for her life. "I'm not homeless, Plaid. Look at my home, what person has all this beauty surrounding them? When the weather becomes unbearable, the kind, generous minister in the church across the street takes me in. He has set up cots and a bathroom. I can wash up and sleep out of the freezing cold. The minister is understanding of not only the way I choose to live, but others as well. Now you stop that smart, pretty head of yours from worry."

Today the two sat under the oak with the warm sun shining through its limbs and enjoyed a feast of candy bars that Plaid had purchased with a five-dollar bill she found on the street.

Hanna had spread a small lace curtain she had found in a discarded trunk. The two laughed as they made a decision which candy bar to eat next.

"How delightful to have choices of these lovely treats. You should go first, Plaid Patience, since it's your gift."

The two friends made quite a picture on the grass. Plaid's white braids with green ribbons intertwined in them, her beautiful face shining with excitement and Hanna, layers of clothes, a mid-calf purple coat, tightened with an orange wide belt, a red soft silk dress hung in soft tattered folds around her ankles, green army boots covered her feet, beads of various lengths were numerous around her neck, a flowered silk scarf wrapped around her head. Her hands were always covered with a pair of tight kid's gloves, given to her by a church lady. When Plaid asked Hanna why she never took the gloves off, Hanna said, "My fingers, which at one time were long and slender and quite beautiful, are now knotted with arthritic knots and not a pleasing sight." Plaid reached out with her small hands and held Hanna's.

Plaid and Hanna McCray made many delightful memories in the park. Plaid would carry these with her, dear to her heart.

On occasion a rider would stop by to water their horse in the small spring that ran through the park. Once when Plaid got to pet a horse, the rider even let her sit on the horse. "Oh my, this is the most beautiful animal in the world, I bet," said Plaid. Plaid was trembling from excitement. She thanked the rider profusely. "May I draw a quick sketch of your horse? I will be very fast." Before the lady rider could answer, Plaid was taking out her sketch pad. "What kind of horse is he?"

"He is an Appaloosa."

Plaid's pencil could not move fast enough, his head, front legs and back legs were a dark chestnut, his girth a lighter chestnut. White encircled his eyes, the mane, and tail. "One day I vow I will own an Appaloosa horse exactly like your horse. Once more and many, many thank yous for giving me this unexpected joy. I will never forget it."

The rider mounted and rode away. Hanna looked on as Plaid took the sketch of the horse and wrote DREAM on it.

"Hanna, the grass under my bare feet makes me feel more of

everything. The birds are chirping extra music, the people in the park look happier, the world took on more joy today." Plaid stuck out her arms and spun around and around like a twirling dervish. She became dizzy until she fell down.

Hanna started calling her name, she opened her eyes and said, "Oh Hanna, I'm fine. Just so excited I could fly around the moon."

"Okay, little one. It's time for you to head home. You don't wish to worry those nice folks you are living with."

Plaid picked up her backpack, said goodbye to Hanna, and ran for home, all kinds of dreams running through her head.

Plaid would lie in bed at night and think of exciting and magical things.

Plaid told, "One day, Hanna, someone will leave a book on a park bench. You will pick it up, you will smile as you read the authors name, dust the bench off and have a seat, open your thermos of hot tea, and start reading, smiling all the while and knowing this author can write really well, she is my friend Plaid."

Hanna replied, "Have no doubt, your dream will come true. You have a story to be written about."

June kept in touch with Monty and brought her up to date on Plaid.

After June told Monty how much Plaid loved birds, Monty purchased a pocket-sized book of birds from the New York area. Plaid had listed over 200 bird's species she had viewed and jotted them down in her very handy notebook.

She had drawn a picture of a hooded warbler seated on a small, broken off tree limb with spring leaves just bursting forth, and recorded over ten different warbler species. She had gifted the drawing to June. June passed it on to Monty. Monty treasured it like no other gift in her life. She must have viewed it a hundred times a day.

CHAPTER 32

Monty Lets Go

June felt Monty was having misgivings about her decisions of leaving Georgia and of being separated from Plaid. She was becoming more aggressive for June to arrange for her to view more of Plaid's daily life. Plaid was growing at a rapid rate, and Monty felt her own health was in a fast decline. She wanted to take in as much as possible of her daughter's life.

June told Monty that Plaid was a strong and independent child. If Monty wished to disclose to Plaid that she was her mother, Plaid could handle the situation. But Monty was unshakable, Plaid was not to be told, or was Gap or Papa Lee to be notified until after her death, of which she had put her final wishes in a letter that Jazzy held. She felt confident Jazzy and June would honor her requests. Soon, Monty was back in the hospital fighting for her life.

Jazzy had taken leave from both his jobs to be near and care for Monty. He got down on his knees begging her to marry him. "I am with you all the way please, Monty. We can take care of Plaid. We will move back to Georgia. let me contact your mother Gap and your Papa Lee."

Monty had responded, "Jazzy, I love you, and you of all people know how sick I am, mental and physical. I beg of you to continue to respect my decisions on my life and Plaids. Plaid has been so happy the past two years with the Millhouses. I see it in her perfect face, and June informs me she has also mastered her studies."

But Jazzy knew on most things Monty's manner could change in an instant, and anytime or night she could be right back on the streets and end up in a catatonic state once again. Jazzy and June were in great torment on keeping their promise to Monty and not notifying her Mother and Grandfather. But, they both knew if they betrayed her, she would not forgive.

This illness would destroy this highly intelligent, talented woman.

When Monty would not come home, Jazzy would start his search. He always first checked the mental hospital where she was taken if found on the street. Once more, Monty would either be in a catatonic state, or total delirium. The knot in his chest was growing tighter. He knew that fateful day may not be far away.

Today was one of those days. He had walked the dog, the phone was ringing as he walked in. He felt bad vibrations even before he picked up the phone. "Hi June... Yes, I'll be there shortly. Do you think the hospital will release Monty into my care?"

June responded, "I don't know. Please hurry. I don't have lots of hope. This time feels different."

Jazzy had been to this hospital often in going on eight years that he had been with Monty. Since the security guard knew him, Jazzy would take his dog with him. The guard let Jazzy tie his dog inside the fence, and he would watch over him, at least until his shift was up. Jazzy left dog food with the guard and a watering pan.

The guard asked Jazzy, "And how is your love?" A virtual stranger cared.

"I am hopeful that there will come some good news during the night. I'll be by her bedside." Jazzy reached down and reassured his dog that he would return. Since one of his dogs had died from a bad heart, he felt a little overprotected.

The guard offered, "I could keep your dog a few days. A sweet, nice dog, this one is. Be happy to help you out."

"Thanks for the offer, but he would be unhappy away from us."

Jazzy felt frightened. Life without Monty was unthinkable. He made his way to her room and entered. June Light was holding Monty's lifeless hand and talking to her as if she was fully aware.

June said, "The doctor feels she will come out of this, as she has so many times before." Jazzy looked down at Monty. Something really is different this time, he thought. He kissed her forehead. Her lips were swollen as she had bitten through her lip and tongue. Jazzy pulled a chair over to her bed and took her hand. He saw marks on her wrist from being restrained.

"June, I will stay the night, or until she comes around. I hope to take her home tomorrow." Jazzy had an odd thought as he looked around the room and down the hall at the gray painted walls. Maybe when Monty is well, she can paint some flowers or trees, clouds, a sunrise on the walls. The disinfected smell of pine sol consumed one's nose.

June put her arm on Jazzy's shoulder, "You need someone with you," she said.

The hours passed with no response from Monty. Jazzy thought about the many times over the past few years when all had seemed hopeless. Often, he had left for coffee, only to return and find Monty standing and asking, "Where are my clothes? I am leaving this place."

Jazzy told June he was going to check on his dog for a few minutes and get some air and ask the guard for a cigarette. He had not smoked for years, but under extreme stress, smoke still calmed his nerves.

When Jazzy returned, June met him in the hallway. She softly said, "Monty has let go."

Unable to accept June's words, Jazzy collapsed into a heap and moaned. How can life be so cruel? June did not try to touch him. She stood by. In the nurse's station, the clock's hand was at 2:00.

A passing doctor asked if Jazzy was alright. "Yes," said June. "Our loss is overwhelming. We were not granted a goodbye. Thank you, Doctor, I will stay with him tonight. She is to be cremated. I'll be back to take care of everything. How easily a life leaves." The doctor didn't have an answer and walked away.

June's eyes were still on Jazzy as he pulled himself up by the railing attached to the wall.

She noticed he held onto the rail for support. "Jazzy, would you like to sit with her?"

"No. She is gone."

June understood his anguish. "I'll go sign some release papers." The doctor did not like the way Jazzy looked, so she had returned to check on him. June asked the doctor, "Could you stay with him? Please?"

"Yes, I will be here."

Jazzy felt the joy of living replaced by unbearable pain. He knew that memories of the most interesting person he had ever known would be relived forever. Could there really be no more life in my precious Monty. His insides roamed. This pain, I can't endure this. How does one endure the unendurable, he did not know.

He felt a familiar hand on his shoulder. He said, "June, I can't stand, my legs won't lift me."

"You must, Jazzy, Monty is depending on us to take care of her wishes."

Jazzy and June had to arrange a meeting with Plaid's present foster parents, the Millhouses.

The Millhouses had been wishing to adopt Plaid. Now this information that Plaids real mother had been alive all along. And had just died. Her will stated that Plaid Patience had a grandmother and great grandfather living in Darnell, Georgia.

June asked Jazzy, "Have you known from the start that there was a family in a small town?"

"Yes," Jazzy softly murmured, "I didn't like Monty's decisions, but it was her life."

June put her arm around Jazzy and said, "I understand the burden you carried, for I kept Monty's secret also, and went against all rules to keep her and Plaid safe. In all my being, I wanted Monty to regain her health, but I am so grateful you came into her life."

"So am I. I know I will never love this much ever again. These years have been the best and the most unbearable pain at times—but I would not trade my time with Monty for anything."

"June, her wishes are that we send her ashes with her letter to her mother and Grandfather right away. Then we can meet with the Millhouses. What kind of people are they. Are they going to give us a difficult time about taking Plaid?"

"I don't think so. They love and want only the very best for Plaid. I am going to impose on them to drive Plaid back to Georgia. I believe it will be the right way for Plaid to take all of this in and give these wonderful people a chance to say goodbye—and also meet Plaid's family. I know this will be of concern for them."

"I agree," said Jazzy. "You tell me when and I'll be there. Now I am going to the park."

Jazzy gave June a strong hug and thanked her profusely for all her many kindnesses to Monty.

He stopped and purchased a bottle of vodka. As he walked down the path in Central Park, the pain of longing was so intense he found it difficult to get air into his lungs. When he reached the bench, he stopped and stared at the spot. The sun was shining on the bench where he had first met Monty—highlighting it. Inviting him to sit. Usually, his dog was excited to run and play or chase a squirrel up a tree. But today, he lay down at the bench and looked up at Jazzy.

"I know I must go on, but never did I know there was this much heartache." He just turned the vodka up and drank it down, until he almost lost his breath. He closed his eyes and put his face to the sun. *How many times will I relive this fateful day when my life changed forever?* He took another long drink. His dog moved in closer to him. Jazzy passed out. And was awakened in the dark by his dog licking his face.

"Ok. Buddy, we will go home and let tomorrow show up."

* * *

Tomorrow showed up in a huge way, with World War looming, and hard times starting to hit the U.S.

After Monty's death, life didn't hold much for Jazzy. He went through the motions of his days. His doctor friend who had been there during Monty's worse times, was now very concerned for his good friend Jazzy. He stopped by often. The doctor wanted Jazzy to know that he had enlisted in the army. Both men had purchased liberty bonds, but the doctor felt he wasn't giving enough.

"Jazzy, Germany has invaded Poland and the Nazi Party is gaining power. It looks as if this homicidal maniac, Adolf Hitler, has set his goal to take over the world and rid the world of all the Jews," the doctor was emotional. He sat with his head in his hands.

Jazzy was mostly in the dark, because of his pain at losing Monty. But the doctor's heartfelt words convinced him he also must enlist. He called June Light and asked if she would take his animals. He would box up his small belongings to be stored.

She was more than happy to help her friend. The two had grown closer and spent more and more time consoling their pain of losing Monty.

Franklin D. Roosevelt would be re-elected to an unprecedented third term as president. Most of the US felt Roosevelt would get the people through the hard times ahead! On his public broadcasts, he assured the people that their welfare and the US was his priority. This proved to be true.

All changed even more when Japan bombed Pearl Harbor on December 7, 1941. The next day, with a unanimous vote of both houses of Congress, President Roosevelt declared war on both Japan and Germany.

Jazzy was deployed and participated in Operation Torch, the Allies invasion of North Africa in November 1942. He was wounded and sent home to recover. Later learning his close friend, the doctor had been killed, this added greatly to his sorrow. June, who had exchanged many letters with Jazzy after he had joined the Army, had met his ship. Having made no plans, Jazzy moved in with her.

She helped him gain back his good health, and he even felt well enough to play Jazz at the USO for the troops. The war lasted until May 8, 1945 in Europe and until September 2, 1945 in Japan, after two atomic bombs had been dropped on Japan.

Jazzy and June often received letters from Plaid Patience, writing long well written stories of her family and daily life. They had a standing invitation to visit Georgia and Protected Earth.

CHAPTER 33

Notice of Plaid Patience

"Hello there, Liza, a million thanks for sending out the whole kit 'n caboodle of paintings."

Gap appreciated her friend. Liza and Gap had become extremely close.

"With that talk, you create the beauty, I do the shop work. Besides I love having the paintings but mixed emotions when they leave."

The two women stood on the porch of the Hub, as they had done so many times before. But today felt different. Both seemed a bit edgy. Gap sat on the steps, her long jean-covered legs stretched out. She gave a long sigh, not knowing why.

Liza standing alongside exclaimed, "By the way a package came for you and Papa from New York. Sure looks like your handwriting." It had only been a few weeks, since the ashes of her beloved Monty arrived and was put to rest on Protected Earth. Gap and Papa had honored Monty's wishes as she had stated. Monty had written, "Please Mama and Papa Lee, I do not want a big farewell, or anyone talking over me, except the two of you and Sparsity. If my dear friends, Jazzy and June Bug could be there, it would be okay. But as you and Papa will find out, there are more important matters that must be taken care of. I know you both will honor my wishes."

Gap and Papa knew they had a granddaughter. Monty did mention her, also that her name was Plaid. They were anxious to receive more information on Plaid.

"Bring it right out," Gap said, a little too sharp. Liza thought, sometimes the lightness of my actions surprise even me. The old screen door never failed to make a mournful cry as it closed. Gap knew the package was from Monty. Liza handed Gap the package.

"Sorry, Gap, for being so casual."

"I am a little on edge lately, with putting Monty to rest and all. And knowing I have a granddaughter in New York. We are friends, not that sensitive. See ya!" And she headed toward her horse, tied under the shade tree.

She opened the saddle bag and ran her fingers over the stone on the clasp. "Monty had dug the stone out of the creek bank when she was five. Papa polished it for a gift for Monty, but she gave the stone to Gap. Gap changed her mind and didn't put the package in her saddle bag. She walked over to the statue in the town square and sat on a bench. She ran her fingers over the package, once more changed her mind, and decided to wait to open it.

Just as she stood, Liza walked up with a sandwich and a lemonade. Gap was glad for the interruption and the smell of Liza's egg salad on crusty brown biscuits. Well, who could pass that up.

"Thanks, Liza, my emotions are running high. Thinking about my Monty sure can cut into a reserve."

Liza leaned down and kissed the top of Gap's sun-kissed blond head. "I know I don't have to say it, but I am here anytime day or night."

"I know."

Liza walked back toward the busy hub. Gap remembered Chase and Talker had accompanied her into town. These younger pups were not as well trained as the previous Chase and Talker. They would sit eyeing a person, as if you had done something wrong by keeping the food all to yourself.

Not feeling she could get even Liza's delicious sandwich down, she divided it between the dogs. They sat on the grass and slowly ate the sandwich. Gap forced herself to rise and head toward home. She felt it was the right thing to do… open the package when she and Papa were together.

On Gap's return, the package was opened.

"Papa, can you believe we have this priceless gift—Monty's daughter 'Plaid Patience' is coming into our life." Papa was standing by the large, white enamel trimmed, iron wood-burning cook stove pouring a large cup of strong-smelling coffee. Gap reached and got a cup and moved it toward Papa, he filled her cup.

Gap brought the cup up to her nose and took in the aroma. "Papa, you make the best coffee in the world. I sure am happy Cal was far ahead, bringing to our town all the different coffee beans from other countries. So many reminders of Cal and all our dear ones. Plaid will most likely take over the task of grinding the old brass coffee mill. Monty loved grinding coffee for our breakfast."

"Yes," Papa sighed, "and often with sleepy eyes as Monty would say as she came out to the porch, knowing I would be there to welcome my mornings. She would put her sweet little hand in mine, pulling me back into the house.

"I can hear that sweet voice so excited saying, 'Now, Papa, Now! Your coffee beans are ground and smelling so-ooooo good. Ready for some perking.' Pulling her stool up close to the stove, she waited for the first perk. staring at this same old speckled pot. She would clap her hands with delight and do a little dance, still seated, moving her shoulders up and down, right and left. What a joy that child was."

Papa walked to the round table in the foyer and picked up an empty treasure box he had made. Different shapes and colors of polished stones adorned the top. He walked towards his daughter and said, "Dear, dear Gap. There isn't a day that passes when I walk into this kitchen, that I don't see Monty standing, smiling. I know she is gone." He choked up; his chest and shoulders moving in emotion. "But I always felt that someday she would come back to Protected Earth, and not as a vase of ashes."

"Papa," Gap gasped as she moved closer and gave him a hug, "Monty is sending her most treasured to us, her daughter?"

Gap reached out and ran her hand over the wood box. "Plaid will love the treasure box. Especially after she knows the wood came from your old woodshed. Interesting you made it, not sure who would be the happy recipient of such a treasure."

"Here, you take it," said Papa. "It will be nice to hand her a welcome gift."

The large oak table also held a jar of mixed, dried colorful flowers. Gap and Monty's treasure boxes also held a prized place on the table. Papa and Gap took the boxes out to the porch. As they took each treasure out, it would stimulate a memory to be talked about. This was a special time. Gap, ready and anxious to pick up Plaid, put her arm on her Daddy's shoulder. He opened Monty's box and took out a bunch of feathers tied with a green cord that had been used for green beans to climb on in the garden.

Lee held the feathers, his voice once more breaking. He said, "That day Monty and I walked for hours trying to spot and pick up bird feathers. Each time she found one, her excitement erupted. 'Look, Papa, Look!' She would yell. 'A cardinal feather, so red. Think, Papa, how happy God must have been when he saw his red bird fly across a blue sky. Maybe it circled a big pine then came back and lit on his knee. What do you think, Papa?'"

"Monty always wanted my opinion."

Lee handed the feathers to Gap, who was wiping away tears.

Gap said, "Papa, so do I. So what was your answer?"

"As close as I remember, I babbled, 'Monty, let's close our eyes and imagine our divine creator alone in the world with his precious animals. God puts his hand to his ear and thinks… the Earth needs a pulse. How about a concerto of trills, beeps, hoots, tweets, chirps, barks, and all the small noises from the millions of insects joining in the concert? There will be birds of the sky, land, and rushing water to give the ears a treat with its sounds.' God took a dab of blue sky and a bit of brown soil and created a blue bird. So pleased he was with the blue bird, that he kept on until all different colors and sizes of birds appeared. But, he had one more thought as he looked at a rainbow in the sky and saw some red. 'Yes! Let's give the sky a jolt and yes, there appeared the knock-out red cardinal.'"

After relaying the story to Gap, "In my usual way, Gap, I got carried away with my words. I laughed when Monty started pulling on my arm. She said, 'Papa, when can I open my eyes?' She opened those beautiful eyes and laughed with joy. Monty was a good audience, she would have sat for hours with her eyes closed, with me going on and on."

Gap and Papa hugged. Gap as she reached for her hat, sighed, "Papa, there is always something new to learn when you talk. You take the wagon to pick up Plaid. Emilio decorated it and the horse with wildflowers. I am sure Plaid will delight when she sees it. I will ride the Appaloosa. Maybe I will share my horse on the way home. I doubt Plaid has ever been on a horse."

Gap turned back as she reached the screen door. Papa was slowly closing Monty's treasure box. Gap knew her father treated nothing as ordinary, always taking in as many of the senses as possible.

Father and daughter seemed calm on the way to meet the

Millhouses and Plaid. The pouring rain from last night had left muddy puddles all along the drive.

Chase and Talker as the third generation now pups were still called Chase and Talker. "We will always have a Chase and Talker," said Papa Lee. They were now smeared with red clay as the two ran ahead of the wagon. Usually, they wandered on some side adventure and would be waiting for Gap and Papa at the gate when they returned home. But the two new dogs seemed to sense, today is extra special, they decided to stick close by. And rode with the wagon.

CHAPTER 34

Plaid Goes Home to Georgia

June and Jazzy had discussed the best way to get Plaid to her family. All involved agreed, Plaid would be most comfortable traveling with the Millhouses, since June had scheduling conflicts with her job. Jazzy was grief-stricken over the loss of Monty. Also, Plaid had never met Jazzy. The Millhouses with concern for Plaid's welfare going into the unknown were more than happy to take the journey to Georgia with Plaid.

June met with Plaid and told her of the circumstances that would send her to her grandmother and great-grandfather in Georgia. June exclaimed, "Plaid, I knew your mother, at first I didn't understand her reasons for the unusual decision to abandon her child. But I grew to understand how much she had suffered with her acute mental illness. And the people she loved were so helpless to help her. Monty's imaginary world was a place no one else could enter to understand. The extreme stress upon her, we will never know."

"Please, June Bug. Tell me all you can about my mama."

"Plaid, she loved you so much. The pain of not telling you was almost unbearable, but it was really for the best."

June knew Plaid held no crossness. Her young age belied Plaid's knowing.

"I would love to have a picture of my mama, so I can carry it with me back to Georgia, I want to know every feature of her face."

June held out her arms to encircle Plaid, "I do, and I feel my life has been so enriched from knowing your mama and you. One more thing you should know, if you look into a mirror, you will see your mama's face. And from what Monty said, you both look like your grandmother."

June opened her purse and took out a picture of Monty that Jazzy had taken in Central Park. Monty was barefoot and intently painting away, looking beautiful. She opened Plaid's hand and laid the picture in it.

"Her family," Mrs. Millhouse mused to her husband. "All these years, then suddenly she has family? I know that there are extenuating circumstances, but it certainly seems peculiar."

Mr. Millhouse thoughtfully drew on his pipe. He knew from long years of experience the wisdom of silence. The Millhouses had, after long and careful consideration, decided to adopt Plaid. Mr. Millhouse had spent a great deal of time searching for the perfect art tutor for her and carefully checking references. They had considered her age and theirs and were about to approach June when she'd called them and told them that Plaid had a family who was eager to claim her.

Mr. Millhouse let his wife wind down, then said to her softly, "If it was meant to be, it would have been. I am sorry. I know how disappointed you are. I am too."

"Her place is with her family. Now we need to decide whether or not to invest our hearts in another foster child. Do we take the risk again?"

Plaid, on the other hand, was over the moon. Her heart hammered with the news that she could scarcely dare to believe. "Home! I have a home and I'm going there! I knew it! I just knew it! I have a family and my mama saw me, was proud of me, I look just like her." She held the picture out in front of her that June had given her of Monty.

The penciled drawings that Plaid had made during her stay with the Millhouses caught Plaid's eye. Mrs. Millhouse had taken down her daughter's fashion prints and replaced them with Plaid's sketches. Plaid stopped her frenzy of packing and carefully removed the drawings from the wall. She selected the ones that she thought the Millhouses would like to have. These drawings were put into two neat piles on the desk. Plaid took out her drawing pad and wrote a thank you letter to the Millhouses. She told them how much they meant to her.

Plaid knew that she would miss them. They had been kind to her, interested in her, loving and supportive. For the first time ever, she'd been given a bedroom of her own. The Millhouses had been wonderful, and she would always be grateful.

Plaid realized with a little jolt that she would be leaving New York, the only home that she had ever known. June, Hanna McCray, Central Park, all of it would be left behind — for what? Plaid had no idea, but she was wildly eager to find out. "I am going home! I am!"

The Millhouses accompanied Plaid to Central Park. Plaid wanted to tell Hanna how much Hanna's friendship had meant to her. But when they asked around, no one had seen Hanna for a few days. Plaid asked the Millhouses if she could go into the small church, just off Central Park. "The priest is a friend of Hanna's. Maybe he will know where she is. Mrs. Millhouse I really need to tell Hanna goodbye." Plaid had a pleading look in teary eyes.

But they received no satisfaction from the priest. "I am very sorry. I know how much Hanna treasures her friendship with you, Plaid. If you will leave a forwarding address, I do believe Hanna will show up. I will be happy to give her your address." Mrs. Millhouse wrote Plaid's future home address for the priest. He gave Plaid a hug, wished her well.

Plaid thanked the priest profusely for his kindness toward Hanna.

* * *

The Millhouses decided to take the train, Plaid was excited, and chattered her head bobbed fighting sleep. The train rolled into the town of

Darnell. The Millhouses had wary looks on their faces, being skeptical in the middle of the deep south. He hyped up his talk to get his wife's mind on the town, and a little off Plaid.

"Take notice of the architectural details on the charming railroad station. Each building seems to hold its own beguiling look. The stone sidewalk is unique. The sign at the start of the walk reads, 'Each stone was lovingly and carefully found and placed by the citizens of Darnell.'"

Plaid was the first to exit the train. Mr. Millhouse cautioned, "Wait right here. I understand your excitement in trying to take everything in—but for now, we are in strange surroundings. You remain close by."

Plaid said, "Cal's Hub looks like a busy place. There are horses, wagons, buggies, and even several trucks. And a large statue of a horse in front."

Mr. Millhouse softened his voice, "Yes, Plaid. I see. Are you hungry?"

"Maybe I could eat a nice, big piece of cake. I am so excited; my belly is moving around inside. I know you want me to eat more nutritiously, but this is a once-in-a-lifetime day. I am in a town that holds my name."

Mr. Millhouse smiled and thought, I am going to miss Plaid. "Plaid, how about we have a big piece of cake. Maybe they will have your favorite, coconut."

Cal's hub was now operated by Liza, Cal's only child. It would always be called Cal's Hub, in honor of Liza's mother. Cal was found dead, half-frozen in the creek that circled around the Hub and by her cabin. The talk was Cal lost her will to live after Mr. Ward died. She would close the Hub each night, sit by the fireplace, strumming on her guitar and drink until she was numb. Liza was old enough to go to the cabin, do her homework, and retire to bed. Cal's dogs were Liza's constant companions and would check out any noise that came remotely close to the cabin.

Liza awoke for school that painfully cold morning. The fire had gone out in the fireplace. No matter how much Cal drank, she never forgot to throw another stick of wood on the fire. Liza quickly dressed in the cold cabin; all the while she felt a sense of doom. She let the dogs out, and they quickly returned, barking with a disturbance. It was an unusually cold winter that year for Georgia. It was a grim scene Liza walked upon. Cal was surrounded by ice. She had apparently fallen, hit her head, and froze to death. All knew Cal was to have a graveside service and have her final resting place next to Mr. Lee Ward, and so it was.

Cal's spirit would forever be in Darnell. Generations had grown up in and around the Hub and most families experienced Cal's generosity in one way or another. Liza didn't look like her Mama, but she did get her fearless nature and was making her mark in the hearts of the citizens of Darnell. Nothing was moved or changed in Cal's cabin. Friends, such as old Sam, and people hired by Lee, were to keep the Hub operating while Liza went to school. She dropped out and continued to live in the cabin and run Cal's Hub. She wanted to live out her days where she was born and where her mother was laid to rest. Liza had dropped the E from her name.

Gap had informed Liza of Monty's child. And the date she was to arrive. Her foster parents will be on the train with her.

The small town was a buzz, as usual. Men in overalls with sun-worn faces looked mighty content seated on the Hub's porch playing chess. Colorful quilts hung on the rails of the Hub. The porch was a pleasure of crafts for the eye and some top-notch artwork lined the walls of the Hub. Mr. Millhouse commented to his wife, "This artwork could grace any gallery in New York City. And I know it would sell."

Two outsiders and one newcomer stepped onto the porch of Cal's Hub. The curiosity of the two chess players and a few people now milling around was intensifying.

Plaid had been taught chess by Hanna, and she was a very smart and savvy player. She started walking toward the men playing chess.

Mr. Millhouse said, "Plaid, I understand your great curiosity, but please, Dear, stay by our side until we know more."

"I understand," and she moved in close to the couple.

Mrs. Millhouse said to a gentleman standing close by, in her highly polished voice, "We are heading to Mr. Lee Darnell's place. This is his great-grandchild, Plaid Patience."

The man, having lived in Darnell for years, looked at the child. "Why, that child's the spitting image of Gap's kid, Monty. That girl just up and left. Sure looks just like her." The old man continued, "Keep walking toward the Hub sign and go in and ask for Liza. She's a good friend of them Darnell's. She will serve you up some great food. Bet you folks are hungry. Come all the way from New York, did ya? Those stock market people — crashing — all in a panic — sure glad we live on our little self-maintained farms."

The Millhouses listened and answered with politeness, Mr. Millhouse said to his wife, "I really can't argue his point." then turned their attention back to Plaid.

Mr. Millhouse and Plaid noticed the sculpture honoring Mr. Ward's circus and his performers that stood in the small park area of town.

"Oh my! How wonderful is that? It equals anything I have seen anywhere. We must take a closer look. I repeat my words, Darnell is an extremely interesting place," said Mrs. Millhouse.

Plaid was bounding up and down with excitement, "May I go and look at the circus sculpture?"

Mr. Millhouse answered Plaid, "Soon, Plaid. Let's first get a bit of food in us and a bathroom would be welcomed."

"Looks like my ancestor built a good town. Don't you think so, Mr. Millhouse?" Plaid reached for his hand. He felt deep emotion on the thought of not seeing Plaid grow up. His thought, I do pray this is the right thing for this exceptional child, leaving her in this small southern town.

"The town looks prosperous, farming in the rural areas is mostly self-sufficient. I like it." I don't believe any bank is going to be foreclosing here," said Mr. Millhouse with a gratifying smile.

Mr. Millhouse did not want Plaid to know that he was a little worried. This country life felt slightly strange. Mr. and Mrs. Millhouse nodded to each other. Seeing the joy on Plaid's face, both said, "We are happy for you, dear Plaid."

Liza walked out on the porch and one of the old men said, "These folks brought Lee Darnell's great-grandchild home all the way from New York."

Plaid walked between the Millhouses. She was on the adventure of her life. The train ride to Georgia was stimulating for Plaid. She asked the Millhouses questions about everything that came into her view. Before, she had wondered where people were going. Now, she was the one who was going somewhere.

Papa Lee and Gap craned their necks forward as the wagon and Gap on horseback entered town. They spotted the girl. Was this their granddaughter? Oh, yes. The young lady coming towards them was little Monty all over again. Gap jumped off her horse and threw her arms open and said, "Welcome home, Plaid Patience."

Plaid did not hesitate… she ran into those arms. All her years in New York conditioning her to be cautious of strangers flew out the window. Plaid, round-eyed, declared, "You look like me!" The Millhouses shook hands with Papa Lee and introduced themselves. Gap rocked her granddaughter back and forth, unable to speak.

When Gap finally let go and stepped back, Papa Lee stepped forward and said, "My turn." With one scoop of his arms, Papa picked up Plaid and sat her on his shoulders. "Plaid Patience, I'm Papa."

Plaid put her arm around his head in a fit of giggles. "I felt like I took off just like a bird, Papa. You smell good!" This was so… right. Plaid knew in her heart that she really had come home.

Gap steered the Millhouses away from the parking lot, "Are you folks hungry?"

"Yes, we were headed toward the Hub."

Gap answered, "Our dear friend will prepare a meal for us. Most likely she had it ready. I told her that you were from New York, and she said that she'd cook a southern feast. I can tell you, we're all in for a treat." Gap and the Millhouses walked to the Hub.

"Oh, how charming," Mrs. Millhouse said when she saw the log cabin building with the wrap-around, covered porch with honeysuckles climbing up the posts. Mr. Millhouse spoke, "My, what is that intoxicating sweet smell that's engulfing us?"

Plaid spoke, "I believe that's Georgia honeysuckles I read about."

Mr. Millhouse replied, "Well! I can understand, it sure sucks one in wonderfully."

Mrs. Millhouse reached and snapped off a few sweet blooms and turned and stuck them in her husband's lapel.

Liza, like her mama before her, was multi-tasking in high gear. She balanced three orders of coconut cake on her left hand and arm while her right hand gave a long-awaited letter to a farm couple from their son who had been drafted. From the tiny Post Office inside the Hub, Liza scanned the Hub for empty coffee mugs while tending to her Post Office customers. As they left, she delivered the cake, then refilled the basket lined with a yellow checked cloth on the buffet with golden, moist fried chicken. Not one to tarry, she removed lemon pie from the oven while thinking ahead, measuring her supply of clean crockery against the number of people that she'd already served.

Suddenly, Liza was aware that the Hub had fallen oddly silent. Carefully sliding the pie onto the cooling rack, she looked up and saw that all heads were turned to the entrance. Entering the Hub were Papa Lee, Gap, a tall, sophisticated-looking couple, and an enchanting little girl, the spitting image of Monty riding on Lee's shoulder. The Hub freeze-framed.

Liza walked toward the entrance, aware of dropped jaws all over the diner. She called out a rowdy welcome. "Hi, folks. Welcome to Darnell. I'm Liza." She stuck out her hand, first to the little girl, then to Mr. and Mrs. Millhouse. To Liza's surprise, the little girl gripped her hand in a firm handshake and looked her squarely in the eye. Sure enough, this is Lee's great-granddaughter, Liza thought. Gap had confided to Liza that she was expecting her granddaughter.

Plaid almost shouted to Liza, "I am Plaid Patience. My Mama was Monty, Gap is my grandmother, and Papa Lee is my great grandfather." Plaid was trembling she was so excited.

"Yes, Miss Plaid Patience, some quip you have there, good handshake. Did you folks have a good train ride?"

"We did. Plaid is very entertaining and doesn't miss much. Plaid pointed out all the passing landscape."

"How 'bout a bowl of chicken and dumplings and a big, fat piece of special coconut cake?" asked Liza in her husky voice. She eyed Plaid with merriment.

Plaid was still looking toward the Millhouses for direction.

Plaid was tugging at Mr. Millhouse's arm, "Mr. Millhouse, may I just have coconut cake and walk over to the circus statue?" He turned to see how far the statue was.

Liza spoke, "Oh, she will be fine. Plaid, the little boy statue on the strong man's shoulder is your great grandfather Lee. Come, let's get you folks seated and get Plaid her cake, then she can go explore."

Mrs. Millhouse took a letter out of her purse and handed it to Gap. "Our letter of introduction from a friend of Monty's. A gentleman named Jazzy. He was unable to make the trip and asked us to bring Plaid. We have been her foster parents for two years. She is a dear, super smart, enchanting, kind child and we will miss her dearly."

"She is now entering a fascinating life with the best of people," commented Liza.

Disturbed by the gaping stares throughout the room, Mr. Millhouse put a protective arm around Plaid's shoulder and pulled her close. Mr. Millhouse straightened into his full military bearing and countered the stares. It was a small town.

Liza smiled down at Plaid, fully aware of the intense scrutiny of their exchange. "How does it feel, Plaid Patience Darnell, coming home to a town that bears your own name?"

"It feels very heavenly, Miss Liza. I will do Darnell proud," replied Plaid.

'Good for you,' thought Liza. Well done. Glancing up at the Millhouses, Liza was not at all concerned for Plaid, but rather for the surprised citizenry seated all around her. She said under her breath, "Mama, you should be here to see this." Liza missed her mama Cal.

"Come on, folks. I'll set a southern table the likes of which you've never seen. We'll ruin you for that Yankee food."

Mrs. Millhouse was defensive in response to what she felt was unwarranted attention to Plaid. Most of the town seemed to be in this room. It was unthinkable to leave this child here; Plaid was not an oddity to be picked apart by a small town — a town where everyone seems to address each other by their first name. Can all this niceness be real? Liza showed everyone to their seats at the choice table in front of the big window. She offered Plaid the honored seat at the head of the table. Plaid looked at the Millhouses for approval. Mr. Millhouse said, "It's okay, Plaid. Your grandmother Gap and Papa Lee are your authority now. Let's all enjoy our last meal together."

Papa declared, "No, let's pray, Mr. Millhouse, you and Mrs. Millhouse will visit us in the years to come."

Plaid was still pleading with Mr. Millhouse to go and explore the circus statue.

Liza scurried to serve the tea. People were getting up to visit the buffet table as before. Liza hustled double-time to bring steaming bowls of the Hub's best fare to Papa Lee's table. If there was ever a VIP dinner at her establishment, this was it. She was determined to see her little Hub superior to any five-star restaurant that New York had to offer. She knew her mama Cal would be proud of her little Liza Jane. She smiled. Liza did not have the flair or sex appeal her mother Cal had. Liza was a big, muscular woman. As far as anyone knew, Liza had not had any affairs with the men of Darnell. Whispers were she had rather kick the man in the rear end than crawl into bed with any of them.

All the protective maneuvering on her behalf was not lost on Plaid. After everyone had taken their seats, Plaid stood, "I have something to say." She looked around the table, "I want to say thank you to all of you. Mr. and Mrs. Millhouse, thank you for giving me a home when I needed one, and for all your care. I'll never forget our conversations. You gave me a room of my own. I am grateful for having a say in decisions about my school. Thank you for letting me go to Central Park, and for meeting Hanna McCray to be sure that I was safe, and for a million little things that you didn't know I noticed. Living with you both is something that will stay with me forever. Please, pretty please, come back and spend some time in Georgia with my family." The Millhouses were deeply touched and made a promise to Plaid they would return for a visit.

Plaid turned to Gap and Papa Lee and continued with a catch in her voice. "You'll never know what it is to come home. Somehow, I always knew that I would."

Plaid now felt a little embarrassed. She sort of shrugged her shoulder and grinned as her gestures said, "Oh well. That's it."

Plaid turned to Liza, "Miss Liza, may I have my cake? Would you tell me about the statue, Papa Lee?"

"Sure, you take your cake. Then I'll meet you at the sculpture."

Plaid gave the Millhouses a hug, picked up her cake in her hand, and ran towards the statue.

The sculpture was of dimensional life-sized figures, all having to do with the circus. It was made of marble, wood, and cast metal. Mr. Ward completed it one month before he passed away.

Papa joined Plaid who was now seated on the horse, Princess, who had carried her great, great aunt Azzie. He briefly went through each character. "Plaid it will take time to tell you all the great stories of Mr. Ward and my days with the circus. The sculpture gives them honor. The handsome little boy on the strongman's shoulders is your Papa."

Plaid was talking nonstop, "Coconut is my favorite. But I never ate one this good. Maybe Liza will show me how to make a cake. I have never cooked anything."

"I am sure she will put that task on her list. I believe your friends are about ready and I know your excitement is jumping out of you."

Mr. and Mrs. Millhouse were finished with their food. Liza refused any money. All thanked her and said their goodbyes.

"Plaid, I'll be seeing you soon," said Liza.

"May I give you a big hug, Miss Liza. June Bug, my friend from New York, says I give the best, true hugs."

Plaid felt shivers at the gladness she felt. "I am finally home. The empty parts of my heart are starting to fill." As the Millhouses' waited for the train, Plaid continued, "Mr. and Mrs. Millhouse, I am grateful from the bottom of my heart. I will keep the time we spent together forever. Maybe someday I can repay you both for your teaching and your kindness to me."

Papa and Gap had stepped aside to give Plaid the private talk of saying goodbye to the Millhouses.

"Plaid, this is your home. We are delighted for you!"

Before the train arrived, Liza walked out to the train station with icy Nehi orange sodas and a bag full of food. "For the road. Been a pleasure. Safe travels." And she walked back towards the store, a proud standing woman as her mother Cal was.

Plaid was talking with no pauses. "Oh my! I am so grateful for this blessing on me. My belly is fluttering. I will be saving these feelings for later, to give proper attention to each one."

Plaid continued her parlay, "In my short eight years, my spirit has sat mostly without song. I want to be like the birds from this day forward. I will never, never let my soul live a day without music. Some may not be such a pretty tune, but like the birds, no matter the weather, they find it in them to sing a few notes."

The Millhouse's stood tall. Mr. Millhouse had his arm on his wife's shoulder. The two were listening to Plaid, who was so excited she was talking non-stop.

Mrs. Millhouse spoke, "My, my, Plaid. Such deep thoughts for one so young. But we understand so well. We have seen people, even under the most ugly and dire times, use song to lift their spirits out of a powerless life. Maybe that's why we still have faith. God gave us this amazing joy that we exude in dance, music, song, and love of family. We, too, have carried on, under all types of weather."

Mr. Millhouse spoke, "All the folks we met today made us feel welcome. I suppose we are a mysterious-looking threesome. You, Plaid, looking like cotton candy and Mrs. Millhouse and I with our darkness in hair, skin, and clothes. I realize this is the deep-seated south. But I seemed to have had a useless worry. My view of the southern states seems to be rooted by my not understanding who the southern people are." Mr. and Mrs. Millhouse were affecting. They had a great carriage. Handsome cut faces with ripe expressive mouths. The curious had a right good reason to look long and hard.

Plaid said with a tremble in her voice, "I will forever carry the lessons you both have given me; to know that being different is special. You both gave me a guidance to understand why my mother abandoned me. I will recall our adventure in life, when I am sitting on the riverbank and my horse is grazing close by. A well-dressed bumble bee will light on my arm and the two of you will be dancing in my memory."

Mr. Millhouse was always awed by the gift of talk Plaid possessed. "Plaid, I have no doubt you will be a great writer and artist. This I know. And if all goes well in our life—we will make sure we will be there to applaud you."

"Thank you for your belief in me."

Plaid liked Mr. Millhouse's voice each word, each given great importance. It soothed your ears like soft flute music she had stopped and listen to on a street in New York.

Plaid walked over to Gap and her Papa. She took Gap's hand and they walked over to the Millhouses. Plaid pulled on Gap's hand for her attention, "Grandmother, you are so very beautiful. Did my mother look like you?"

"Yes! And you are as beautiful as your mother?"

Papa and Gap thanked the couple profusely for their care, love, and the direction they had given Plaid. Papa kept hold of Mr. Millhouse's hand and said, "Please know these are not idle words I speak. You and Mrs. Millhouse and your family are forever welcome into our home. Maybe one day, you may decide to take a closer look at our southern life. It would be an honor to have you all visit us. Do think about it?"

Mr. Millhouse asked Papa Lee to excuse him a minute—while he talked to his wife. The two moved away from the others. He asked his wife—we have come this far—should we not see where Plaid is going to live her life. Mrs. Millhouse was delighted. "Oh yes—how wonderful—lets do take Papa and Gap upon their invite." The Millhouses walked back to Papa, Gap and Plaid—"We have decided to accept your invite, and spend the night maybe a few, we feel very welcome. All were jubilant.

"Mr. Darnell, there wasn't a moment since Plaid came to live with us that we were not encouraged to enlighten Plaid. She has an open mind and heart to know everything, and believe us, she is working on it. We now feel certain Plaid is in the best of hands."

The Millhouses said, "We have a bag or two. He walked inside the train station to get the bags."

All shook hands, the Millhouses somewhat reserved received several big hugs from Papa and Gap.

Papa said, "Come, Plaid, you may ride with us, or Papa had ridden his horse in, there was more enough room in the wagon for the Millhouse's. Your grandmother would love for you to share her horse for the rest of the way home. It's your choice."

Plaid took a look at the Millhouses'. Chase and Talker had hopped into the wagon for a lazy ride home. "I will ride with you and my friends Mr. and Mrs. Millhouse."

A recent rain shower had given a sparkle to the land. The sun's heat caused evaporation, giving the drive and ride to the property a magical look. Plaid was shaking she was so excited. Papa pulled her in close. She started to cry. Papa let her get it all out.

Mr. Millhouse put his hand on her head.

Plaid softly spoke, "May I take my shoes off and run? I want to feel the red dirt road, have the mud push between my toes. I have longed for this land, over and over. Please!"

"Okay, but not too far that we can't see you."

"You will be entering protected earth soon, then you may remove your shoes," said Papa.

Plaid had already removed her new boots the Millhouses had gifted her. As soon as the wagon turned into protected earth, Plaid jumped out of the wagon. She ran straight to a puddle and jumped in. The mud gushed between her toes. Plaid had joy coming out of her soul. A thought ran through her head, and she wondered if any mud people were here. She could almost hear Hanna say, "Of course, Plaid, of course."

She spread her arms, as if to take off any moment and fly above the pastures. She ran and ran—took in a few hurried breaths. Detectable odors filled her nose. Freshly plowed earth, foliage of sweet scrubs, honeysuckle, and cattle. Horses grazed on a hillside with their precious colts. Goats were gathered in a small valley.

If this wasn't enough for her, she looked out into the rolling hills. Boundless trees reached into the sky.

Plaid sat on a large rock to the side of a small spring that ran across the drive. She turned her face to the heavens, with her hand's prayer like, she said, "Can my heart take in more?"

The Millhouses asked Papa Lee question after question. They were completely spellbound by the building of the town, and Protected Earth. The day was a little wet, but perfect. Nothing could dim this day. Papa drove the buggy and Gap rode her horse. The sun's rays were beaming through the pine thicket, exposing bits of matter and small sediment of sparkling rock dust. All jiggling its way through the sun's ray.

Chase and Talker were nowhere to be seen. They were just as excited about the new person. The buggy splashed through the puddles.

Gap noticed the road had a few large gullies where it had washed away. The dogs came running back to meet them. Barking insistence that something was going on up ahead.

Plaid said to Papa, "My enthusiasm beats loud with each pulse of my heart. I want to hug each tree, lie down and roll in the fields, smell the wildflowers, and let the honeybee know I am home."

Mr. Millhouse responded, "Yes, Plaid, I agree with you—Mrs. Millhouse and I both feel like kids. The ride here in the open wagon was a delight for our spirits. Your Papa also had some blackberry wine. We feel excited for you and your family."

A small frog hopped out of a puddle and sat croaking at her. She picked it up. "Hello, my little friend. I am Plaid." She gently sat it down and watched it hop across the road.

The day was starting to brighten after the showers stopped. Gap had thrown some slickers into the wagon, just in case.

Papa said, "I always welcome a lovely, soft rain."

Gap and Papa Lee watched with great pride at the cotton-haired barefoot enchanter who stood in the middle of the road, now with mud splashed clothes, Chase and Talker beside her. Plaid Patience raised her head and looking into two faces she felt she already knew.

Plaid's backpack lay on the seat in the wagon. Papa picked it up and ran his fingers over the work worn plaid flannel, that had been sewed into the bag.

"Plaid, this shirt has a huge history. Your mama played in it, slept in it, wrapped it around hurt and abandoned squirrels, lizards, a baby fox, she nursed and loved them all back to good health. Monty would be beside herself with joy when the animals were well enough to run away."

"Yes! Yes! Papa—Mama wrapped me in it. So, I would be warm and protected. Papa can I have one of your flannel shirts. Maybe a blue one, the color of the sky."

"Of course, now let's get going so you can meet your new home and Mr. and Mrs. Millhouse can explore your new home. And all the remarkable people who live and take care of Protected Earth."

A soft drizzle had started, Plaid held her face up, closed her eyes and enjoyed the softness of the rain. "Grandmother Gap, your artwork on the porch was so nice. June bug said, 'My mama was a great artist. I am going to receive lots of her paintings.'"

"Plaid, your mama was a much better artist than me. I understand you're not so bad yourself." Gap had gotten off her horse, tied him to the back of the wagon and rode the rest of the way with her Papa, Plaid, and the Millhouses.

Papa put his arm around his overexcited great-granddaughter. "Plaid," he began, "you will soon enter Protected Earth. It is the place of Gap's birth, your Mama Monty's birth, and it contains the earthly remains of people we have loved. And the spirits of generations of people before us. You will get to know them through stories. Even though you will never hear their voices, they live in every part of Protected

Earth. But at this moment, we just want to feel joy in your presence here and all the discoveries that you will find each day. This place is in your blood, as it is in ours."

Plaid turned to her foster parents and said, "I am so happy you are seeing where I will be living—if I have never told you both I love you, I do. Thanks, from my heart for your care."

As they turned into the front yard, a handsome, dark skin, muscular young man came forward to take charge of the wagon. His cowboy hat was black, and his black hair hung to his shoulders. Papa introduced Emilio. Emilio welcomed Plaid with a strong handshake. Plaid thought he looked like he walked straight out of a cowboy movie. She waved goodbye as he walked the horses and wagon down the lane to the barn. Papa showed Plaid how to work the outside water pump so that they could wash their feet and boots before entering the house.

There was so much to take in. Plaid wanted to do everything at once, but even her seemingly inexhaustible energy was depleted. News of her family, goodbye to her New York friends, her foster parents the Millhouses, being on Protected Earth, and the long train ride had taken their toll. A thousand acres called to her to explore, but she could hardly hold her head up. Gap saw that her granddaughter needed rest but was fighting it.

Papa picked her up and carried her into the house and place her onto the settee. Papa and Gap looked at Plaid, Papa said, "Now that's a sight. How blessed are we?"

Gap nodded her heartfelt agreement. "She's only eight. What an astonishing few days this child has experienced. What strength that Darnell blood runs deep in her veins."

Papa said, "It's a clear night. Why don't we go out on the porch? Have a few drinks, get the Millhouses settled into the guest rooms, hopefully they will join us." He picked up Plaid and carried her out to the porch as Gap collected a quilt. On the porch, Gap sat on the swing first, reaching up to receive the sleeping child. Plaid slept on, oblivious, with her head on Gap's lap and her feet in Papa's lap. Gap covered her with a quilt and stroked her hair.

"Yes, indeed. We are graced." Chase and Talker, several generations from the original pair, were sprawled on the porch as the crickets and cicadas began their night song. Gap and Papa sat in companionable silence with their treasure stretched between them.

And waited for their two fabulous new friends and guest the Millhouses.

Friends were made, and all felt sure the Millhouses would return for visits.

Tears were not shed, the Millhouses felt assured Plaid was in a great home, and the radiant Plaid was enough to convince them.

CHAPTER 35

New Sounds

P laid was going to be settling into a whole new life. She had a broad range of experiences in getting accustomed to new surroundings.

The night sounds of rural Georgia coming through the window were totally foreign from the night sounds of New York City. Gone was the roar of the trains that had vibrated the entire Millhouse home and had caused tinkling, pleasing sounds from the crystal glassware in the china cabinet. The sounds of traffic never stopped in New York. Night and day, they were an integral part of the cityscape and totally natural to her, but this was different, she had her very own room and wanted to take in every detail of it. She removed her shoes so that she could feel the texture of the wide wood-planked floors. She closed her eyes while her feet and body took in the vibration from the floor. Then she ran her hand over each windowpane, feeling the burlap curtains dyed a soft, rosy pink. A tiny spider scurried into a corner. Kneeling at the window, she closed her eyes for a moment and let the cool, clean air blow over her face. The screen had a tear in it at the lower corner about the size of a dollar bill.

Carefully, Plaid wiggled her small hand through the tear in the screen and reached toward the large limb that crossed close to the window. Touching the leaves of the smaller branches with reverence. "My mother, Monty, must have crawled out this window, and sat on the large limb of this tree. Did she talk to you, Mr. Tree? Did Momma give you a name? The people that knew Mama said she heard voices from things, trees, flowers, tables, and animals. How brave she was!

"Please welcome me, giant oak, as you did my mother. I'm here. I am Plaid Patience Darnell. Did my mama fall asleep on your large sheltering limb? Tonight, when I talk to the almighty, I will ask him your name. I am sure the Almighty named all things He created."

The oak's branches spread from its trunk at a height almost level with the window. The branches made a cradle of sorts. Plaid couldn't reach the big branch without making the tear in the screen larger. The breeze coming through the window carried the night sounds from the insects, bobwhites, owls, and occasional coyotes. "I'm a little afraid, Mama, but I know I'll grow brave like you were. Soon, I'll call out to you, 'Look, Mama! I'm right here. You'll be pleased I am your daughter, Plaid Patience.'"

Plaid carefully pulled her hand back through the screen. She worked with the torn screen until it was almost back in place. She asked God to keep her mind from thinking about New York. As delighted as she was with her new home, she was overwhelmed with sadness to think that, because her Mama had died, she was brought to this perfect place.

Gap had said to leave the bedroom door open so that the two bluetick hounds could come and go. Chase and Talker would protect her with their lives. She believed that yes, they would, she could see it in their eyes. The dogs knew their job. The dogs finished whatever they had been doing, ambled into Plaid's room, and hopped up on her bed with tongues tolling. Plaid welcomed the dogs wholeheartedly as they made themselves at home. She giggled as she stroked them. Plaid talked to Chase and Talker who perked their ears at her and solemnly gazed at her with their liquid brown eyes. Talker periodically gave soft little yips and shuddered as he dreamed. She reached over and scratched behind their ears. The dogs sighed with pleasure and made themselves more comfortable on the bed. Plaid had to contort in order to accommodate both full-sized dogs and herself.

Still, she was glad to have their company. The sounds of their breathing and, soon after, their snoring, were comfort to her. The hooting owls and ear-splitting songs of the cicadas didn't make her afraid when the dogs were there on the bed with her. The cicadas were impossibly loud, considering that all the noise came from mere insects. She thought about what she had read. A wasp that lived just on the cicadas it caught. She said to Chase and Talker, "Maybe Papa can get some of those wasps and turn them loose here on Protected Earth. We can ask."

The cicadas answered each other. A cacophony of sounds rocked back and forth. Back and forth.

The very air was different here. Nice, just different, Plaid thought as she drew in a deep breath, adjusting to the new smells of home, her home. There were the clean, fresh smells of lined-dried bed linens, the sweet, heavenly scent of honeysuckle vines out in the yard, the earthly scent of the rich, overturned Georgia soil in Gap's gardens, and the smell of southern cooking that was continually wafting from the big country kitchen that lingered long after meals were eaten. Sparsity mostly always had something stirring in a pot. Yes, Plaid thought, I'll get used to this place pretty fast. Home! I'm home! The word was unbearably precious to her. Her dreams had come true, all at once. Maybe, someday, Gap or Papa can help me to understand why? My mama felt it was necessary for her to leave Protected Earth? "Oh mama," she said aloud. "I am not condemning you I just want to know—why you made the decisions that you did?

This was the life that she had visions of almost every day that she had spent in New York. Now that she was here, she hardly knew what to do with herself. Plaid felt she had somehow landed on another planet. How can I ever learn all there is to know and experience? I am sure going to give it my all.

She remembered a conversation that she'd once had with June Light. "Just take it one step at a time, Plaid. Just one step. Use that wonderful common sense that God gifted you with, and take one step—then another, and keep going. When there's a fork in the path, go where the peace is. You'll be fine. I believe that."

Plaid yawned, relaxed, and snuggled down into the covers. She wondered what adventures tomorrow would bring.

Plaid had asked Papa and Gap to please always awaken her early, "I don't want to miss a morning." Papa wanted to teach Plaid how to fire up the big wood cookstove for the morning breakfast.

"I want to learn everything, Papa. If I can split wood, I can cut up enough kindling for our stove. I love the smell of the wood. The good sound when you light a match to the pine kindling. Watching the yellow and gold flames jump up and send out the heat." Plaid stretched herself as tall as possible, put both hands on her hips, and took a deep breath.

This morning, Plaid wished to have Gap show her how to make coffee. As she stood by the warm stove she said, "Papa, doesn't a fire make you feel safe?"

Papa smiled, which he did a lot now that his beautiful unduly curious great-granddaughter was home.

Chase and Talker were close by, Plaid thought as she looked at the two dogs their look tells me they are happy I am here, and part of this great family.

"Gap, will you show me how to make coffee? I saw the coffee pot waiting on the stove and I set the wood in the stove, so it's all set up to be lit, but I didn't want to mess up. Where's Papa going?" Plaid would ask a question, not wait for an answer, and let her talk run into another subject.

"May I have a cup of coffee like Sparsity made for you last night, some of that luscious rich creme in it."

"Sure," said Gap, "But, let's start with half cream and half coffee. Also, add some vanilla, it's right there in the spice cabinet."

Plaid drank her special coffee, feeling very grown-up. She had tasted coffee once before. People look so content drinking coffee, but black coffee didn't taste so good.

Sparsity was busy moving around the kitchen. She moved so lightly, one could not tell where she would appear next.

Gap asked Plaid, "After we have enjoyed Sparsity's fine breakfast she has prepared for us, what would you love to do today?"

Gap's gentle voice put Plaid at ease. Plaid had become spellbinded watching Sparsity. She tried not to stare at Sparsity but she had never seen another person that looked anywhere near like Sparsity. Plaid imagined an angel must be comparable. All white, but maybe not have Sparsity's colorful clothes on.

At the large table was also a pile of papers and files. Gap saw that Plaid had noticed, Gap thought this kid sure is a Darnell, she doesn't miss a thing.

Sparsity understood the interest Plaid had in her appearance. Sparsity spoke, "Plaid, I made blueberry pancakes with a little lemon added, the way your mama liked them." Sparsity chatted lightly to Plaid.

"Thank you, Miss Sparsity. I look forward to them."

Sparsity was used to being stared at. Some folks used the word albino to describe her. White hair, skin, eyebrows, eyelashes, and eyes that looked to have a tinge of pink in them. But she liked the way she looked, and knew after a person was around her, they were under her spell. She was smart, read most every book she could get her hands on, and Doc Francis would say, Sparsity knows medicine and its healing power as well as me. Doc would loan her his med books on every kind of illness. She absorbed all she read and studied. Doc wanted her to go to school and felt she would make an outstanding doctor. She understood about natural healing and sent away for information on herbs.

Doc often called on Sparsity to help a patient that had an unusual rash, cough, or insect bite. Sparsity would know a poison spider bite from a harmless one, and what was needed to ward off an infection. A cough could be from something as simple as a certain weed that grew in their yard, or something eaten. She would work as a skilled detective to get to an answer, then a cure.

"Don't mind the mess. We're planning a party for Papa Lee and you. We're going to have a celebration and invite the whole town. Would you like to help?"

"Yes, ma'am," Plaid replied, careful to use her best manners.

Plaid wanted in. While Sparsity served the breakfast, she filled Plaid in on the party plans. Then, as Plaid polished off extra pancakes and vanilla coffee, once more she thanked the obliging Sparsity. "Miss Sparsity, thank you for that delicious breakfast. I understand why it was my Mama's favorite."

Gap told her about how Papa had come to meet Mr. Ward. "I want to know everything. I want to listen with my ears open so wide, all the history of this family will forever be in me. Then someday I will write it all in a story. I wish I had known all the wonderful good, fine interesting people in our family that have passed on. I miss them and yet I never knew them. When you can see a person physically and observe their face, color of eyes, skin, how they move their hands and mouth, when they talk, they leave a little more to how we remember them! Don't you think so?"

Gap smiled large, "Oh my dear Plaid, believe me, you are in a family of huge storytellers. You will know each one. The wonderful thing about memory—we can bring our loved ones back. We can go back in time to let them come into our life anew—through stories. I know you have so many questions it's hard to know where to start, but Papa and I will do our best."

Plaid helped clean up the kitchen and thanked Sparsity once more for the delicious food, then hand in hand, Gap and Plaid strolled around the house, barn, and gardens while Gap brought her up to the present and assured Plaid that in time her Papa would satisfy any of her wonderings.

As Gap and Plaid walked around, Gap introduced Plaid to their animals. Each one responded to its own name, even mischievous Push Me, the baby bull. Push Me gave Plaid a playful push as she went by. Plaid had great fun helping Gap feed the chickens, but felt a little uneasy thinking about if these would one day be fried chicken on a dinner platter. 'Now is not the time to ask Gap that question, I will save it,' she thought. Before they went back to the house, Plaid had dropped every shred of her reserve and was chattering away like a magpie.

"There's Papa waiting for us on the porch, may I run ahead."

"Sure, my dearest—your papa awaits."

Gap was as fascinated by her granddaughter as she had been by Monty. Plaid had a different personality than her mother or grandmother. There was no pain in Plaid's words. They rang out clear, only excitement and curiosity for each new day and the world around her. She didn't give one of her sense's priority over the others. All were in play.

Gap, lost in her thoughts, was jolted by Plaid's voice, "Gamma Gap, it sure would make this day even more lovely if we could spend some family time together. My questions just keep building up."

"Sure, dear."

Plaid's face pulled together with excitement. "Do you think Papa would have time to be with us? I don't know if I will ever catch up. There was Mr. Ward, Birchard, my mama, Great, Great Aunt Crow, her sisters, Dessie and Azzie and Cal. I am sure I am missing lots of people. I need to know who they were, what did they get excited about, on and on. Every beat of my heart says your and Papa's name."

Gap said, "Yes, what say I gather the dogs, cats, and wagon while you prepare our lunch. It's time you met Girlean. She is most anxious for the two of you to become friends. Want to pick her up? It's your choice. You are right, it's too sweet and handsome a day to pass it by."

Girlean was Leeward's child, one year older than Plaid. Plaid was beyond words, that with all of this wonderment, she would also be blessed with a best friend.

Plaid liked making decisions, but cooking! She had never even boiled water. But she loved the smells that surrounded food. Plaid hollered, "What should I prepare?" Plaid felt happy she was believed in, but still needed Gap's approval and direction.

"Use your fancy, you will make a good decision. Check around the kitchen, you will come up with a good lunch," Gap smiled and answered, her vibrant voice drifted through the screen door, hallway, and into the kitchen. Her granddaughter savored each word.

Plaid busied herself in the large sun-filled kitchen. Often becoming distracted from her chore, stopping to watch the tiny hummingbirds that were fighting over nectar from the purposely planted flower-filled window boxes.

Plaid knew she got easily distracted. She thought, 'So many things to see and do! How does anyone focus on one thing.'

She looked around the kitchen, picked up a large basket, filled it with crusty biscuits from a pan that was warm on the stove. Goat cheese, fig preserves. A quart mason jar of pickled peaches, and two jars of sweet tea. Knowing Gap liked iced tea, she picked up the ice pick, opened the box, and chipped away as she had watched Gap do. All secure in the basket, she turned to leave with basket in hand.

"Hi, Plaid." It was Girlean that had just walked into the kitchen.

"We were going to pick you up," Plaid said.

"I walked over. I should have taken my horse. Can I help?"

"Sure, take a couple of tablecloths from the linen shelf."

Plaid was staring at Girlean, "You are beautiful, and I hear fearless. I do want us to be best friends."

Girlean answered as she removed each tablecloth, gently admiring the embroidery that danced with herbs, wildflowers, birds, and angels. "I feel we have known each other for a long time."

Plaid walked over to her. She took corners of the tablecloth, Girlean the other end. It snapped open.

Girlean said, "Oh, my! It sure is pretty. Did Crow make them?"

"Yes! Don't you like the name Crow? My great-great-aunt; I feel her spirit throughout the house, watching over us. Papa talks of her and his other two sisters. He loved them so much. Oh, how I wish I could be surrounded by them."

"If we believe what Sparsity says about spirits, then you are," said Girlean.

"How did Crow die?" Girlean asked.

Papa said she was seated on the porch, after dinner, each had a few glasses of blackberry wine and just having a talk. Crow said she was sleepy, think I will turn in early. She kissed Papa and Gap goodnight. Didn't even take her nightly bath or change into a nightgown. She laid down on the bed, went to sleep, and never woke up. Pictures of her beloved sisters, Papa, and her mother, stood on her night table."

Girlean had tears rolling down her face, she wiped them away, with her shirttail. "Sounds like she made the choice," Girlean said.

The kitchen sat quiet, then Chase ran in and started pulling on Plaid's overalls. "Okay! Chase don't be so impatient." With a kiss on the head and a piece of biscuit, he was a delighted dog.

The two girls were immediate best friends.

Plaid walked onto the porch. She saw Papa behind the wheel of his Model T pickup truck, his full head of curly salt and pepper hair hanging long, blending into his full gray beard. The truck piled full with Gap, three cats, Talker, and Papa's rocker.

"Papa, wanted to take the truck instead of the wagon," said Gap.

Plaid could not wipe the happiness off her face. Girlean picked up the basket. Shaking her head with a large smile noticing how her new buddy could easily get sidetracked.

Papa was driving and all was secure in the truck, he spun the wheels and headed for the pond. Dogs and cats went flying to the other side of the truck bed.

Papa said, "Let's suck in this day."

Upon reaching the pond, Chase and Talker headed for the forest. The cats quickly checked out the edge of the pond for minnows, and sporadically gave a slap at their own reflection.

Gap laid out the pansy pattern quilt for relaxing and a nap. Girlean unfolded the tablecloths, admiring them once more as she laid them out.

Plaid positioned the lunch onto the cloths. Proud of her selection.

Gap commented, "A still life, a Chef d'oeuvre."

Plaid smiled and pulled out a word of French she had heard the Millhouses use, "Merci, my dear grandmother." They had a good laugh.

Gap was going to homeschool Plaid, and felt it was important for her to speak another language. Plaid said she liked French, "It is a romantic language. Maybe one day we will take a trip to France."

They were enjoying the lunch when Gap stopped eating. "What's the matter?" Plaid said, looking at the change in Gap's expression.

"Plaid, my beautiful child, it's time for better table manners. You are gulping that biscuit like it's your last meal. Slow down, child."

"Am I a letdown to you?" said Plaid.

"Never!" I only want you to stretch yourself in all areas of life's living. Then you will be able to dine with Kings and Queens or a lonely shepherd tending his sheep."

Plaid dabbed the side of her mouth with a napkin and said, "I will surely work on all my eating habits and anything else that needs improvement." All gave a smile and resumed their heart-to-heart talk.

Papa spoke from his rocker, "Plaid, we wish to know all about the life you lived in New York. When you are ready to tell us."

Gap commented, "Plaid, you have been blessed with your Papa's gift of story, you make us eager to hear more of your life." Third generation Chase and Talker sat curled at Plaid's feet. They too had become enthralled with the new gift to the family. All eyes were on Plaid.

Plaid would cuddle the two dogs and whisper in their ear, "Have you two been off disturbing spirits?" They turned their heads to the side, questioning.

The air was chilly, and fall leaves left a carpet of golds and reds on the ground. Soon all would disappear into a decomposing carpet of life-enriching mulch.

Gap called out to Plaid, "Plaid, take the hatchet and cut a small tree for poles to throw a blanket over for a lean to. We will have a nap later."

"Come, Plaid," said Girlean. "I saw the perfect little trees bunched up as we arrived. I will show you — they could be thinned out a little. To give them some breathing room."

Gap built a fire in the rock pit. The flames were now dancing about. Papa pulled his rocker in closer to the warmth, stretching his legs out to feel the heat on his bare feet. He sipped his whiskey out of a glass Mr. Ward had used every day. He let his thoughts drift away from the present and recalled his early years with Mr. Ward. Plaid disrupted his memories with a big long hug. She said, "I'll be right back, Papa. I will be just around the bend."

Papa smiled, but then he kept a smile on his face since his ever-delightful great-granddaughter had arrived. "Plaid, hurry back, I am hanging with anticipation to hear more of your adventures, and especially to hear more of Hanna's story."

"Sure, Papa. I love talking about Hanna—and I ask God to keep her safe and warm. I wrote her a letter, bringing her up to date with my life. June Bug will see that she gets it. June and Jazzy check on her. That makes me feel good. June Bug said Hanna was hesitant when they first contacted her. She always showed a cautious distrust of someone new.

Gap joined on, "We want to know everything and in turn, you ask us what you yearn to know. Now get those poles you two and let's get this lean to up."

The girls quickly delivered on their chore and then settled in.

Girlean had positioned herself between Papa and Gap, seated in a cross-legged position.

Plaid cuddled with the dogs and the cats. Plaid starkly repeating family names over and over, feeling a vibration in her body as their names entered her ears. When speaking to Papa or Gap, she said their name with deference, as if each letter was not to offend with importance to the next one.

"Papa - Do you think June Bug and Jazzy could visit."

"Of course, anyone that was kind to your mother or you is always welcome in our home."

"Gap...Papa! I don't regret my time in foster homes. The life I lived, I bring all that to my shining present and future. I welcome all those memories. Things have so much more coloring, because of New York. I never felt alone. Someone, now I know it was my Mama that also watched over me. I remember crawling along a cold, cold floor, seeing lots of feet, different colors of shoes, big feet, loud feet—then a man with a citrus odor lifted me high into the air, then I saw tops of heads, shapes of different color hair that was parted, on the side, in the middle, oily with comb marks, then he started swinging me around and around. I threw up all over the people. Throwing up got me out of that foster house early."

"In my next home, I remained cold, none of my clothes or covers made me warm. I cried and complained. I started talking early about being cold, they didn't want me. I wasn't very pleasant or happy, always curious about the feeling I had inside knowing somewhere I had a home and I would get there. No matter what anyone says, Hanna said, even small children have great awareness. So, off I go to another home. By now, it was horrifying to believe I would never be warm. I would start to tremble so hard, my lower jaw would knock against my upper jaw. One day, my social worker, June Light, came by to check on me. She was upset that I was in such a frightened condition."

"She shouted at the foster parent, 'Mr., give me a blanket for Plaid,' warming it first by a small stove. She then wrapped it around me. The warmth of the heat started to touch my skin. I was so happy, I started laughing—laughing hysterically. I think I was three. June kept me with her a few days. She broke the rules of her job for me. Strange my behavior, I would still crawl. I think because people acted like you didn't understand. You just heard more stuff crawling around on the floor. After a few days, I overheard June talking with someone at her door. I didn't want to leave. I really like living with June. June was saying, 'I can't keep her, I made a promise to someone. Besides, I have already grown attached, soon I will want her in my life forever. And, I know someday she will be leaving for her real home.'

"June found decent foster folks, the McMilly's, but they already had eight foster kids. Later, June said, 'Well, my! They sure were a disappointment. The McMilly's only wanted the money the state gave them. I am so sorry, Plaid, I let you down.' I did stay for almost two years with them, but I wasn't mad at June, she gave every effort for me, and Mr. McMilly did teach me to read.

"I was now five, and was reading far ahead of my years. He was proud of me, but gave himself credit for me being smart. In that house, nothing was a good idea, if you ate your bacon before your egg, Mrs. McMilly would say, 'Not such a good idea.' The children would ask maybe we could play in the park, go to the zoo, take in a movie... 'No! No! No! None of those trips are a good idea.' To ask why was futile. I would find a spot, which wasn't easy with so many people in the overcrowded apartment, then take out my very own two books June had given me, a Robert Lewis Stevenson Book of Poems and a book about birds and poets by John Burroughs. I had to keep them well hidden because most things in that house were destroyed. Nothing seemed to be treasured.

"One day, June was talking with ugly-tempered Mrs. McMilly, she said, 'Mrs. McMilly, I understand that Plaid has her own opinions about things, but she...' Mrs. McMilly would not let her finish her sentence. She was anxious to be rid of me. 'Sorry June, but Plaid does not comply with my house rules...' June laughed and said to me. 'Plaid, I think it's a very good idea to find a better suited home for you.' She got my hand and once more June Light came through for me. And we laughed about the good idea!"

Gap gathered Plaid in her arms and spoke into her face, "Tell us only what you feel comfortable with—any sorrow, adventurous times or happy. Don't ever, ever be afraid we will not love you. Slowly, you will also get to know your Mama through us recounting her life. We had the absolute joy of your Mama, starting with her birth in the pond, to the day she decided to leave."

Plaid watched Gap break down. Gap walked over to Papa, put her head in his lap, and cried. Plaid started to speak but Papa put his fingers to her lips—she knew then to keep quiet, which wasn't an easy thing for Plaid Patience to do.

Gap gave her Papa a hug and said, "Papa, I think I could use a shot of your sweet apple moonshine."

"Sounds good. Sometimes the heart needs a little help to calm the jitters of heartache. It's a good idea." With a big smile, Papa poured.

The two put two shots down, took some deep breaths.

Her grandfather spoke, "Plaid, there are many wondrous stories about your Mama. Through them may you grow to love her and treasure the wondrous person she was." Plaid shivered as Papa put a fringed shawl around her that had been Monty's.

Gap raised her head and said, "How about we jump in the pond and take a cold plunge. That always brings me back to life."

Papa said, "Not for me. I'll take a walk and round up Chase and Talker. You three enjoy. It will be Plaid's first cold swim; you all need the private time."

Girlean came up to join them. Plaid said, "We are going for a swim." First Gap shed her clothes. "It's okay, Plaid, if you feel shy. Swim in your underclothes"

"No, Gama Gap, I'm ready. Off came her clothes, and into the ice-cold pond she walked. Gap went under the dark water. Plaid and Girlean followed. Plaid felt Gap tickle her feet and thread her toes with reed. The water was warm at the bottom.

Girlean in her theatrical voice, bringing her head to the surface said, "My most blessed God of the Earth, I give thanks and gratitude for this moment with my protectors and newest buddy Plaid Patience."

Out they came with goosebumps and wrapped up in warm blankets that were warming by the fire that had magically appeared. They looked around for Papa, he came walking up with an armload of wood. Chase and Talker decided to take a turn in the pond. When Chase and Talker came out of the pond. Papa gave the doggies a rub with a blanket and they curled up by the fire.

Plaid said, "I will never be cold again!"

Gap asked, "Plaid, were you ever afraid or felt alone on the streets or in the park?"

"No! Well, maybe. Unsure in a few situations, but not afraid, not really. One thing that bothered me was telling an untruth to my nice foster parents, the Millhouses They gave me their trust."

"Well," Papa said, "l understand you not wanting to break trust, but sometimes we have to stretch ourselves beyond limits of the rules we have been taught, to experience the exhilaration of immediate life. We are allowed this to grow as a human."

Plaid drank her hot goat milk chocolate. After giving small sighs of pleasure, she once more started to talk, "My daydreams were about the forest — living in the woods, talking to the animals, having a tree-house high, high up, so I could see for miles to the end of the sky. One day in school, our teacher talked about Central Park, how a Mr. Olmstead, a remarkable landscape architect took a piece of land and built the extraordinary Central Park, tree by tree in the middle of New York City and it will be there forever. My constant botheration of my foster parents to take me to the Park came to no end. I was stirred to take action, so I did a bad thing and played hooky from school. I wrote my own excuse and signed my foster parent's name. The teacher had lent me her book on the making of the Park. I read every single word. Papa, can you believe Mr. Olmstead planted over 300,000 trees."

Papa smiled and said, 'Well, Mr. Flo beat me there."

"I thought about counting the trees but was overwhelmed by it. I stopped and sat on a big rock to enjoy my Zero candy bar. I was aware of a roar in the air. I looked around and watched people walking their dogs, a handsome man in fancy riding clothes on horseback. I thought the roar I heard must be the thousands of people talking away as they pounded the streets. I let the roar sink into my ears. I peeled away a little more of the silver and blue wrapper of my candy. My teeth bit into the caramel and nuts. Oh! Zeros are so good. I never want to be without one.

"An old woman with leftover beauty was pulling an old blue wagon piled high with stuff. Her clothes were wrinkled, her frizzy hair was in a braid, she approached me and said, 'Got another candy bar? I'm Hanna.' Her face was dropped. I gave her half of what I had not eaten. 'I'll save part for my late-night dessert. Thanks pretty one, you seem young to be in the park alone. I see you have books, why aren't you in school?' Hanna had such a clear voice. I trusted her right off. She didn't have an old gravel voice, it sounded spirited. English, I think."

I said, "I did a bad thing. And didn't go to school today. I cut through the Park because I wanted to see what Mr. Olmstead created after I read a book about him."

Hanna didn't judge me. She just asked, "Won't your parents be worried if they find you missing from school."

"You are so right, Miss Hanna."

"I will apologize profusely."

"Did you get to say goodbye to Hanna?" said Papa. "Maybe we can help her in some way or even bring Hanna to Protected Earth. We have empty cabins."

"Oh, I don't think Hanna would leave the Park. She has a secret little room hid behind the bushes and trees. A priest from a nearby cathedral keeps a watch on Hanna and when it becomes freezing weather, he brings Hanna in to sleep in the cathedral. I can write her a letter and June will find her and give it to her."

Papa said, "You must write Hanna tomorrow and bring her up to date on your life."

"I will, Papa."

"Good, now tell us more."

"After I met Hanna, I would finish my class studies early and hurry to the Park to see Hanna. I would save half my lunch for her and buy her a Zero bar from the newsstand, when I could get together enough money." Sometimes my foster parents would let me do small chores for a quarter. And even the newsstand man would treat me once in a while for credit on a Zero bar. It was extremely welcomed.

"Hanna told stories from her heart and acted out facially her feelings. God gave me the power of great visualizing, and Hanna's stories were entrancing.

"I got a great idea to spend the night in the Park with her. I left a detailed note for my foster parents, Mr. and Mrs. Millhouse, you saw how nice they were. I didn't want them to worry.

"I knew they would be upset, but sometimes in life, things are worth the punishment for the adventures. I didn't feel I was in danger.

"I put extra food in my backpack, two Zero candy bars, some tea bags. Hanna could make hot water for tea on a little camping stove the priest had given her."

Plaid paused, "Papa, are you tired of my constant talk? Should I stop? I have been talking nonstop."

"No! No! My Plaid. I can't afford to get tired. I want to take in every word about the moments you have lived, as I wish you to know our life."

"Papa, have you ever had a Zero candy bar? Maybe they could start selling them at the Hub. Maybe, maybe, maybe!"

"We can ask." said Papa. "Seems like I should try one. Go on, Plaid. We are all ears."

Just as Plaid was continuing, Gap said in a commanding voice, "Don't move anyone. Plaid, don't panic—a large water moc has crawled out of the pond onto the moss."

Plaid was frightened but sat still, she said to Gap, "Will it attack us? It sure is a sad unbecoming-looking serpent."

"No! If we don't move and it doesn't feel threatened, it will go on its way." Girlean chimed in, "I think the moc is about the ugliest thing I have ever seen."

Each one froze, the large smooth skin dark water moccasin showed no noticeable signs it even knew the group treaded upon its territory. It moved across the edge of the quilt and disappeared from view, into the reed bed.

"Gamma Gap, snakes sure get a person's respect. I often think that maybe animals, consider us strange creatures that are treading upon their land."

Papa chimed in, "As well they should, dear Plaid." The incident with the water moc did not deter Plaid.

Plaid went right back talking. Papa and Gap gave each other a knowing smile. Gap thought without a doubt, Plaid is a Darnell, give her a chance to be heard, and she was off and running.

"I took an extra sweater and a little threadbare baby blanket with birds, bees, and butterflies on it. June gave it to me when she took me from the hospital to my first foster home. I now know my Mama gave it to June. I treasured it, but I wanted Hanna to have it, don't you think a gift means more if you value it a lot and give it to another?"

"Yes, Plaid, and was that little blanket ever special. It was a gift to your mother from your great-great-aunt, Crow. She made that blanket for Monty," Papa and Gap answered together.

"Anyway, I put my broken binoculars, one of God's blessings someone had left on the train. Even though it only had one good side, Hanna and I would share them and look into the faces of birds, squirrels, chipmunks, hawks, and sometimes — people. But, Hanna said we shouldn't tread upon people's privacy, so we restricted our viewing. Much too soon, darkness came upon us. I had never spent overnight outside, my heart started to beat fast until I almost lost my breath. I was so excited to experience the night with Hanna in her secret hideaway nestled away in the thick bush."

Girlean had fallen asleep. Plaid didn't mind. She knew girl sometimes stayed awake all night worrying about all kinds of stuff.

"Girl, get our things together. Pack up the truck along with Papa's rocker, and Plaid dear, we will continue your story, you certainly aroused our curiosity."

Papa laughed, "Nice to have some strong arms to pick up my rocker." He sat his boots in the rocker and walked to the truck, pushing his bare feet into the earth with each step.

Gap continued, "I have an appointment with Emilo to fill a large goat cheese order for the Hub. Liza is now using goat cheese in most everything. It sure is good, people love it."

Chase, Talker, and the three cats came slowly out of the woods and took their places in Papa's truck.

Papa said, "Yes, we better get a move on, a lightning storm is approaching, nothing for one to scoff at. Plaid, you drive home. We can beat this storm." Papa had a big mischievous look on his face.

"But Papa, I don't know how."

Gap gave a laugh at Plaids surprised face, "It's okay, Papa will make sure we are safe."

Plaid slid behind the wheel, her heart pounding as it often did when she was overly excited.

After directions about the clutch, gas, and steering, she still didn't get it, and rabbit hopped the truck all along the drive. All were happy as Plaid worked to learn. Out of the blue Girlean said, "Plaid, you must feel sad if you don't know what has happened to Hanna. How lucky to have such an adventure in Central Park in the middle of the night. I am so excited to know what happened."

"Tell me, Plaid, what kept people away from Hanna's hut?"

"Girlean, let's let Plaid finish this story at home. Otherwise she will drive us into the woods," Papa said with a laugh.

"She scattered pine needles from balsam fir in and around it, rubbed the oil on our clothing. Hanna would say, 'It's those silly dogs always sniffing around. I tell you things not to put fear in you, Plaid, but you must stay alert and know good sounds from bad.' Hanna was very smart.

"Anyway, Hanna took me into her hideaway. She put a candle under her little warmer and heated a can of soup for us. After dinner, Hanna could sense my nervousness with all the strange sounds outside. She had a lovely voice, made a little weak by her pained life. With a concerned voice, Hanna said, 'Plaid Patience, there is nothing to fear, the mud people are all about, they will protect us. They stay hidden. Shy of most people. I felt Hanna told the truth, even if I couldn't see the mud people. I had never seen God either, but I know He exists by all the wonder around me. Hanna continued to explain the night. Listen closely to each sound, and once you know the night songs of the frogs, insects clicking love calls, owls sounding power over their territory, and many other forest creatures crying out for their voices to be heard, along with the voices of a few sad lonely people walking by, Hanna reassuring me, I was starting to feel safe by understanding."

"I took out a bologna sandwich and my last Zero candy bar. Hanna made the tea and we shared my dinner. Hanna told me to always speak softly, as the mud people had small ears and harsh loud voices made them vibrate. If they vibrate too violently, they could dissolve. 'You will love the mud people, you may have felt their presence and not even known it. That move in the space that we feel but do not see. They are experts at watching eye movements, and where humans focus. And are the quick shadows that swoosh past into the dark spots. They dance in the tops of trees or hide in the bubbles in mud puddles that grown-ups avoid, but children are drawn to, they tickle bare toes as children splash about in joy. Mud people are our friends, they connect only to open, loving spirits. We never have to be afraid, God gave them power to watch over us, as they sprinkle us with dew drops from trees and drop leaves and flowers on us as we walk by."

"Yes! Hanna convinced me there are mud people."

Papa spoke, "And you, dear Plaid, have convinced us. In fact, I heard a few swooshes as we sat by the pond today."

"Oh, Papa! That makes me so happy mud people are right here on Protected Earth."

"Hanna had leftovers in her face of being a great beauty, she showed me pictures of her when she performed on the stage. Now her skin hung on her long graceful fingers, veins showed through her thin skin as she moved her hand and arms in dancing rhythms, while rambling on, even if no one was listening. I would often walk upon her in this state, her hair sometimes stood out from her head, like she had been frightened by a monster, other times, it would be braided, neatly wrapped around her head, showing off earrings of green and blue stones that I had found on the train, and gifted them to her.

"Hanna would say, 'Plaid, I used to dazzle the people, seven curtain calls.' I really wanted to know why she got curtain called. But Hanna didn't like questions, they frightened her, and she would shake and say, 'Can't tell you! Don't ask! Don't ask Hanna questions. Hanna pains in her heart.'"

"It's hard to drive and talk, but I think I may have got it, Papa. What do you think, Papa?"

"Well, you certainly have the talking down. But the driving needs more focus. Let's finish your talk about Hanna. Girlean, honey, how about you spend the night. I'll send Emilo over to tell your family. It will be fine."

Thank you, Papa Darnell, I sure was disliking ending my day by going home," said Girlean.

After all settled in, dinner, baths, clean kitchen, then back onto the porch to sit and let Plaid continue her New York experiences.

Papa Lee sat in his rocker, pipe lit, shoes off, resting his bare feet on the side of Chaser.

Girlean spoke first, "Plaid, please continue your story of Hanna and your night in the Park."

Plaid jumped right in, "I left the Park at daybreak before Hanna awoke—kissed her on the head—surprised her hair smelled so clean, lavender I think. I left carrying with me all the night sounds of the Park, along with the spirit of Hanna and her soft breathing as she slept. With a new feeling of being protected at night by the tiny fearless mud people and memories, I now hold for a lifetime. They will live in my heart as I live out my life on Protected Earth."

Girlean sat spellbound, then she finally spoke, "Oh my heart, how I wish I could have shared Hanna's experience with you. Plaid, if only I could have been in that Park to meet Hanna McCray. What did your foster parents do when you came home? Bet they were upset and worried."

"My foster parents were extremely worried, but for some reason, they had not contacted the police. I did feel sorry, but I still would not take anything for my adventure."

All were ready for sleep after a long day. The storm had come and gone.

"My darlings. 1 am saying goodnight to each one. It's a full moon tonight, don't howl too loud. How about you and Girlean join me on an early morning ride?" The two girls looked at each other and knew they were blessed. In unison the two said, "We will have your coffee ready."

CHAPTER 36

Plaid Vignettes

Plaid and Girlean rode their horses along the pine thicket ridge. Papa couldn't make the ride, a problem came up and he was needed. Plaid was a natural on a horse. Girlean, who grew up riding, would say, "Even in this short time of training, Plaid out rides me. She is one with her horse."

The horses slowed and pulled back. Animals tend to become aware of danger quicker than humans. The girls stopped to check out what was making the horses feel uneasy from the woods. They could hear an animal cry. The sound was of an animal in pain. Dismounting, they tied up their horses. Girlean said, "Plaid, we need to check this out." Plaid stood and looked into the darkness of the woods, not sure if it was a place she wished to enter.

"Why don't we ride back and get Papa or Gamma? They will check out the cry." Plaid stood back, Girlean kept trying to remove Plaid's doubts and any fear she had.

"No, Plaid. Sounds are close and not deep into the woods. We need to do this." Plaid, trusting her brave friend, said, "Fine," and they walked toward the sound.

Plaid was not prepared for what they found—a baby coyote in a trap. On closer look, its leg was almost chewed down to the bone as it was trying to get its leg out.

Plaid said, "How did this happen? Papa has signs all over the place."

"Some people just do what they want without any guilt; they don't care about others," said Girlean to a distraught Plaid.

Girlean was calm and said to Plaid, "I will ride and find Emilio or

Gap to come and release the trap. Take off your sweater and wrap the pup up. We don't want the pup to go into shock. The S.O.B.'s. I hope Papa or Gap catch them and break their ankles, just like they did to the coyote pup. I'm sure its mama must be looking for her pup. Oh, I am so mad! I'm off. Just keep giving it soothing talk, but don't put your hand near its mouth. With it being scared, it could bite."

Plaid trusted Girlean and followed her directions.

Dusk was approaching. Girlean didn't like leaving Plaid alone but Plaid was learning the woods and the many dangers quickly. She will be fine. But then, Girlean thought, what if the trapper returns to pick up the furs? If there is one trap, you can bet there are plenty more. She thought about how upset Emilio was going to be that he didn't find the traps on his property checks. Girlean was already on her horse, Messalina, but hollered back at Plaid, "Plaid, if the trappers come, make sure you don't freeze. Tell them your Papa will be along with his shotgun."

"Okay, Girlean. Go, go, go! And get help!"

With that said, Girlean left in a full cantor. Plaid had been in the woods alone after dark before; she wasn't afraid. In fact, she now loved it when Gap would take her on night walks. Papa told her there were forest spirits that watched over Protected Earth. And in nature, what seems like a cruel happening might just be the spirits way of teaching humans' lessons they couldn't learn otherwise. Plaid kept talking to the little pup. She even took a chance and rubbed the top of its head. The pup seemed glad for the attention. Looking out into the forest, Plaid felt sure she saw a figure behind a tree but felt it must be the spirits and mud people that Hanna had told her about. The mud people were also very protective of someone doing good. Maybe they were coming closer to watch over her and the pup.

The fireflies were starting to do their sparkling. Still keeping her hand on the pup, Plaid talked and soothed the pup. She was talking as if the animal understood every word, "We will take care of you until you are well. Gap will clean your hurt paw and Papa and Sparsity will take care of you until you have mended. Then you can go back into the woods and I am sure your mama will find you all well." The fireflies came in very close and settled into the trees above her head. Plaid looked up into the trees, now sparkling with firefly lights. For a moment, she lost herself in the beauty of the fireflies.

Plaid heard her name being called. It was Papa's voice. Had she dozed off? He gently touched her shoulder. Her hand was still resting on the pup's head.

"I am proud of you and Girlean for taking control. Not only for yourself but for the pup's life. It's a wonder she isn't yelping in pain. You seem to have soothed her."

Plaid felt good inside when her Papa was pleased with her.

Girlean and Emilio rode up. Emilio quickly sprung the trap and the pup was free.

"Emilio, if you will put the pup in the carry cage, we will let her sleep in the barn tonight, and Sparsity can take over its care. If Sparsity feels she needs more help, we will go for the vet."

"But Papa," said Plaid in a worried voice, "won't she need someone to be with her? Girlean and I will stay in the barn with her until she is well. Not only is she hurt, she must miss her Mama."

"Okay, but only for tonight. I will have Emilio clean her up and bandage her paw. He can take her to Sparsity's in the morning. Maybe we can save the paw. Leeward is good with all the animals; he knows his stuff. Sparsity will confer with Leeward. Together, the two will work out a healing plan for the pup."

"Papa. It's incredible Leeward has such concern for animals because he doesn't seem to have it for his own family," said Plaid. All was silent except for some night sounds and a few drops of rain that started coming down. Papa figured Girlean must have confided in Plaid about Leeward's temper.

"I know, Plaid. There are a lot of human behaviors that can't be explained. It isn't that Leeward doesn't care for his family. He cares too much. You may not understand how destructive over-caring can be sometimes."

"Okay, Papa."

The injured pup was now resting and had fallen asleep in Girlean's arms. It was unbelievable that her little paw was not torn off, but now she was in caring hands.

"Gap will bring you girls some quilts and some food."

"Thanks, Papa, for letting us watch over the pup," said Plaid.

Papa walked toward the house, feeling confident that his caring, smart granddaughter would take care and the coyote pup was going to be fine and would live to run, play, and hunt another day.

Amazing the pup with all its hurts was sleeping well. Maybe it was the liquid Emilio gave them to pour down it. Sparsity had set up a healing cabinet in the barn for any sick or hurt animals.

Gap left food for the girls and a warm bottle to put with the pup.

"Goodnight, girls."

"Goodnight, Gamma Gap. Love you around the world." Plaid sang out. Best friends and injured pup slept through the night.

A Lazy Day

Papa felt proud as he rode silently behind Plaid and her pal, Girlean. Plaid's horsemanship had come a long way in such a short time; she was a natural. The three rode leisurely toward a most-liked spot by the creek. An old weeping willow spread its branches out far and low to shade part of the swim pond and let the sun have the other half.

Upon reaching the creek, all dismounted expertly. The horses were eager for a cool drink of water and a free run.

Papa gave directions to the girls, "Remove the saddles, then walk the horses to the small field. Just let them loose, harness and all. They love the feeling of being free. Don't worry," Papa said as he saw the girl's faces with lifted eyebrows, "they will stay close after a run of play."

Plaid felt a little reluctant to release Morgan. She thought maybe he would like freedom so much he will just keep running. But she trusted her Papa. The joy she felt at seeing them so happy and running was worth any doubt she may have had.

The girls watched the playful horses for a few minutes and then walked toward the pond.

The three were looking forward to a fine day of delicious fried bologna sandwiches and the girls' favorite: apple and red cabbage slaw, and fresh blackberries with some condensed milk poured over them. Heaven. Both girls were hopeful that today Papa would introduce them to his special perked coffee. Gap had asked Papa if he felt they were old enough. "Don't believe it's harmed Gap. She was finishing my cup at three."

Gap laughed and had said, "Yes, I do love my coffee."

Papa had spread Plaid's quilt upon the soft moss. "Go, girls. I will lay out our food and put the coffeepot on." Papa smiled to himself at the girl's excitement of feeling grown-up enough to now have a cup of coffee. He built a fire in the small rock pit that had been used so many times through three generations, now the fourth. He placed his well-used large cobalt blue swirl graniteware coffee pot on the hot coals. Then he decided to rest his bare feet in the cool, soft bottom of the pond. Sparsity often said, "The reason Papa has such beautiful feet, clear of any bad toes, is the walking in the bottom of the pond with all its good nutrients."

As the girls walked back from watching the horses, the wonderful aroma of Papa's coffee floated toward them. Plaid said, "Girlean, that coffee aroma sure welcomes some good talk as we partake of some of Papa's famous coffee today."

Papa was wading around in the pond, most likely massaging his toes in the marshy, healing bottoms.

"Hi girls. Are you ready for some good talk and a cup of coffee?"

"Yes, Papa. We were ready before we even left home," said Plaid.

Papa smiled, "Girl, why don't you do the honor s and pour me a half cup and fill two more cups half full. Then Plaid, open that can of sweetened condensed milk and pour a generous amount into our coffee cups."

Plaid thought, as she watched her beloved Papa, 'Papa is so free and easy with his movements. He enjoys everything. I want to grow up and be just like Papa.'

After giving the coffee a few stirs of the scrumptious milk, Plaid and Girlean drank sips from their coffee mugs, licking their lips.

Girlean gushed, as she once more lifted her coffee cup and made a toast, "To our many blessings for such great days."

Papa and Plaid agreed.

Papa said, "Before we start our food, let' s listen for a few minutes and eavesdrop into the sounds of nature." So, they did. Papa in a low voice, "Plaid, what do you hear?"

"The wind moving the willow branches as they do a slow, elegant dance. The crow flying noisily across the sky. Some other sounds floating out of the forest I am not sure of."

"And you, Girl?"

"Some frogs jumped into the pond. Cows mooing in a distant pasture. The horses gave a whinny."

"Keep your ears open," Papa said as he reached and pulled Plaid's ear.

The quilt that the food was spread on was a gift to Plaid from Girlean's mama. In the center was the Lord's prayer. Leaves of oak and maple and a variety of wildflowers exactly like the ones you found on Protected Earth were embroidered in a circle around the Lord's prayer. Plaid dearly loved the quilt and it had become her almost constant companion.

Papa told the girls how Monty loved walking the creek bed. "Laughing and sliding off that same mossy rock right over there into the pond. All the time begging me to come in 'Come on, Papa. Get all soaked like I am!' So, what do you think I did?"

"You jumped in and you both laughed and laughed until your sides hurt," said Plaid.

"That's right."

The three drank coffee, ate, and talked.

Girlean said, "I want to ask a question. My first question is for Plaid. Plaid Patience, tell us some things you see in nature as magical."

Plaid was feeling very grown-up, took a sip of her coffee, then said, "I knew it would not be a simple question."

"Why should it be? You are smart. You can handle it," Girlean said with a huge grin.

"My answer to that question could go on a long time, but I will try. Let's start with the honeybee. The bee transfers pollen from the wildflower and comes up with honey for our biscuit. The small quail protecting her nest in the field is fearless against my horse. Who gave her that? The cow makes milk from grass we sweetly drink with an oversized piece of cake. The rain runs off a leaf, the bird's feathers, and my face. Yes, I do think those things are magical. What do you think? Did I satisfy you with my answer? There is so much more." Plaid continued to talk, "Squirrels and all the animals that transfer seeds to help plant the forest. The cycle of life is endless. How could I not believe in magic? I am now convinced there is an almighty God conducting it all. God is the magician."

Plaid waited to see if Girlean would say something after what she felt was a very clever answer.

They looked, and Papa Lee had fallen asleep. Gap had said, "A Darnell will not pass up a good spot for a nap."

"Girlean, let's save our other questions for another day. Let's wade in the pond, then lay on the moss and drift off to sleep like Papa."

And so, they did. To dream of another day.

Plaid and Papa Day

On a cement-looking winter day, Papa and Plaid went searching the field and woods for some hanger on wildflowers to accompany them inside. Maybe the flowers will sit in a small vase on Plaid's nightstand or be pressed into the pages of one of her favorite books. There it will be a remembrance to last.

"Papa, if I press some flowers, I will be by the pond reading one day when I am old and I'll open the next page and there that lovely flower will be. I will close my eyes and remember every detail of our day."

Papa Lee reached out and pulled her long braid and said, "Let's get busy and find some beauties."

Plaid ran ahead, missing a tiny yellow flower. Papa Lee raising his voice to get Plaid's attention, "Behold! I found a beauty!"

She swirled around and ran to the tiny flower. Taking out of her leather pouch was a pocket magnifier Gap gave her to use for getting a little closer to her subject. Plaid held the magnifier close to the flower, taking in each little detail. After her observation, she tucked her magnifier away safely in her pocket. She looked at her Papa and said, "Papa, I feel a little sad depriving the field of its jewel."

Papa Lee reached down and snipped the flower. He placed it in some paper and stuck it into his bag. Continuing on the walk, Plaid said, "Save for a good memory."

"You bet," said Papa.

When the two finally reached a lovely shade tree standing alone in a field, underneath was Papa's rocker. A breeze was blowing the rocker. Papa teased Plaid, "Looks like someone is enjoying my rocker."

"Oh Papa, that's the sweet breeze doing that."

"Maybe," Papa replied.

Plaid was amazed how Papa acted like it was completely natural to find a beautiful, ornate rocker just waiting in the wilderness.

Plaid smiled, "Gamma Gap sure thinks of the nicest things to surprise us. Got an appetite, Papa? I sure have. Ready to unpack our lunch?"

"Sure," Papa replied as he removed his boots and stretched out his long legs as the rocker kept moving.

Plaid moved around with little wasted effort and soon had their lunch set out. She asked question after question. "Oh Papa! There is so much to learn, and I wish to know all about my ancestors and people in your past, like Mr. Ward. And many questions about life I don't understand."

"In time, dear one. In time."

"Papa, Girlean told me, her two brothers are being drafted into the armed forces. She cried when she talked about it. Girlean said when she asked her mother. Tess said, 'Her brothers can die if there is a World War II. Papa, will you have to go fight?' Papa said, 'I believe the president is working hard to keep America out of a World War II, but we can't let bad men take control.'"

"Papa, can I listen with you when the president talks. I may understand more why men have to go to war?" said Plaid.

After a good lunch of crust biscuits, goat cheese, crisp bacon, and sweet tea. Papa said, "Plaid, find your papa some small pebbles and twigs, pile them up at my feet. I need to exercise my feet—they seem to be getting a little tight."

She made a nice pile. Papa preceded in an acute way to pick up the items with his toes.

Plaid continued to talk non-stop. She looked into Papa's eyes and said, "Papa, your eyes are like a miniature globe, the bluest of skies, softest of white clouds, amber spots dotted like little bitty planets and on the move."

"My, how you flatter me."

"Papa, do you remember I told you about the cat that took up with Hanna at the park? She named it Spy. Spy could see an ant crawling way far, working its way across a path."

"Yes, I remember. You miss Hanna?"

"I think about her, but the mud people watch over her."

Plaid sat at her Papa's knee, removed her shoes, put her head on his knee and fell asleep.

They were awakened by Gap riding up with their horses behind her, attached to a lead rope.

"Thought you two might like a ride home."

"Does sound good, daughter." Papa put their lunch dishes into saddle bags and said, "The spirits may enjoy my rocker for a night."

"I'll pick it up tomorrow. Looks like a beautiful day was had."

"Oh yes, Gamma Gap. A satisfying day, indeed."

Plaid Patience and Girlean, Luster of Friendship

Plaid and Girlean's friendship was growing into, for certain, a long-standing one. Each day the two looked forward to new adventures.

Plaid said to Girlean, "Papa says each adventure should hold uncertainties, and bring into play all of our senses."

Girlean stood by her horse, listening to her pal Plaid giving multitudes of quotes from Papa.

Girl pressed her brown skin face against her horse, giving him some long rubs along his neck. "Plaid, your Papa is so wise, I do find it hard to take in so much information. His concise conversation does make me think about stuff."

Plaid answered, "What kind of stuff?"

Plaid led her horse Morgan over next to Girl, "Horses are the most phenomenal creatures, I love Morgan, and never do I tire of taking care of her or watching her run free in the pasture." declared Plaid as she gave Morgan a hug.

The horses the girl's rode were of the stallion Prince's bloodline. Prince was born of the incomparable mare Princess that Mr. Ward brought with him when he sold the circus. Princess had been Azzie's show horse. When Azzie left the circus. She took a larger horse, leaving Princess behind. Princess was never again willing to cooperate with another bareback performer; consequently, the new circus owner had been much relieved to sell her back to Mr. Ward.

Though Plaid was now an excellent rider, sitting strong in the saddle with her confidence growing each time she rode, she still found it hard to keep up with Girlean. Girlean had spent years of considerable time with Gap. Gap taught Girl the finer points of equestrian form. In turn, Plaid imitated everything that Girlean did on horseback.

Surrounded by nature, the two girls let their thoughts flow out through long, rambling conversations, little realizing that they were in turn building memories to endure.

Plaid felt secure and protected with her fearless friend. Girlean's common sense was backed up with her innate knowledge of nature. Because of Girlean's undesirable home life with Leeward, even from a young child she spent hours roaming the woods. She knew the land well. The girls' friendship was growing into, for certain, a long-standing one. Each day, new adventures were looked forward to. Lazy afternoons were blissfully spent in total harmony on long horseback rides. Girlean introducing Plaid to the many trails and open fields of wildflowers. Sometimes, the river ran rough and scary to Plaid; other times, though, it was gentle enough for the horses to cross. These were the times when the girls had the run of the full one thousand acres of Protected Earth.

Plaid felt at times Girlean put herself in dangerous situations.

Maybe Girl's years of beatings and constant belittlement from her father was behind it. How else could Girl feel?

Plaid thought as she looked at her beautiful friend, sitting like a young warrior on her horse, "No!" She said out loud, "I don't believe her mean father will ever kill the fire in Girl's eyes. Eyes that bear the truth of who she really is."

At the same time, Leeward took stabs to his heart when he looked into Girlean's eyes and that would never change. He would always see his wife's betrayal.

You could hear the river before you could see it. It sent its measure alright, it was up to the person if they took heed or read the river right and then made a decision. Gap sustained Plaid's word never to attempt to cross the river alone. "Even if it appears calm, it can deceive a person with a hidden undercurrent. The torrent had claimed numerous people, some never to be seen. It took my Starling," she had said with a trembling in her voice, brought about by the still strong emotion of her lost love. The father of my only child, and Plaid's other grandfather.

Plaid held a strong mind, but under these circumstances, she followed Girlean's lead.

"Let's stop here Plaid," Girlean said as she was already sliding off her horse. "I need to check Cloud's leg, his gait seems a bit off."

Plaid, eager to share memories in the making, held Clouds leg as Girl checked it. Sure enough, he had picked up a thorn which Girl easily removed. "Plaid, reach in my saddlebag and get that tin container holding Sparsity's special healing black salve. That stuff cures most anything it's put on."

After Cloud was taken care of, the two good buddies were quiet.

Plaid walked away from Girlean, took the ropes off their horses, proceeded to wrap, first around one tree then another, stopping to tie the ropes together, before closing off a marked place for their horses. She led the two horses in, gave their strong long shiny necks a few rubs, kissed them, and released the two into her makeshift corral.

Girlean stood with her mouth open, "What brought that about? You sure took control. You were great."

"I followed my feelings. Let's sit and talk." Plaid held a small metal container with a particularly noticeable red, gold, and blue emblem on it.

"That's interesting. What is it?" said Girlean as she sat on the ground.

Plaid unscrewed the top, handed it to Girl and said, "Taste it."

Girlean, trusting her pal, turned it up after admiring the flask, taking a big mouthful, then she slowly let it pass down her throat. A big smile came on her face, then she laughed, and what a glorious laugh Girlean had, it gave more life to the surrounding area.

Plaid said, "Girl, I can just see the birds, squirrels, and all the bees stop whatever they are doing, look at each other, asking, "What is that marvelous sound pulsating through the forest and over the fields? Girlean, with all the grief Leeward forces you to live with, God gave you that beautiful laugh. You are blessed and so is the rest of the world that will hear it. Gap says she gave you a guitar with twelve strings for your birthday. I haven't heard you sing, but if your singing voice is anything close to your laugh, watch out world. Here comes Girlean."

"The flask was given to me by Dame Hanna McCray, my friend from New York's central park. I admired it. Not knowing what it was," Hanna said, "The emblem represented her motherland. The drink is Crow's Muscadine wine. Papa Lee makes it in honor of my Great Great Aunt Crow. I asked Papa could we sample the wine. He said, 'Sure, but be slow with it.'" In the background you could hear the horses chomping away on the grass. Out of the blue, Cloud would run around the small area and kick up his hoofs in play. Morgan, Plaid's horse, was more serious.

"Plaid, tell me about the sound of the streets of New York. What was it like riding the subway. There must be a million stories to tell. Maybe one day we will go to New York together for a visit."

Eager to talk, Plaid spoke in meticulous form. She had been blessed with her family's gift of story and from living with her last foster parents, who spoke beautifully and corrected Plaid on her grammar.

"Most of my stories I made up, I was told by June not to get too friendly with strangers. But there existed a relaxed friendliness around me, which made it hard to be detached from people. Most people seemed in the middle of nowhere. But a lot were curious about me. My long cotton candy-looking braids, as one lady described my hair. After they talked with me, they would ask, "How did a little southern girl come to live in New York?""

Girlean popped a question, "How did they know you were from the south?"

"My southern accent. I have always had a southern accent. And I was born in New York City, I would tell the person. Hanna said a person's accent can be inborn. In my case, I believe she was right."

The two talked some more, then laid back on the grass. Keeping their eyes open, they stared into the blue sky. After their rest, Plaid turned to her best pal and said, "Let's visit Sparsity, I love the path to her stone cottage and the satisfaction I get just being around her. I must admit I was taken back when I first met Sparsity. But I think she looks like what an angel must look like."

Girlean started babbling, "Sparsity makes me question almost everything. One day she said to me, 'Girlean, you have to do more than just take up space.' Now I believe that's good advice for all. Plaid, I want to be a singer and musician. Gap thinks I have talent. The new guitar Gap gave me, I have been working very hard on. I keep it hidden because Leeward would destroy it and me. He tries emotionally and spiritually, but I will never ever let him. Plaid, I believe I will meet my blood father one day, I bet he was a musician."

"You will, I just know it. What say we saddle up and visit Sparsity?" Plaid spoke in a sweet voice with concern.

After they saddled Morgan and Cloud, Cloud being somewhat

reluctant to leave his new playground, did soon consent. Girlean and Plaid both smiled at the playful Cloud. They gave him loving rubs and kisses.

Plaid felt secure and protected with her fearless friend. Girlean's common sense was backed up by her innate knowledge of her surroundings.

Surrounded by nature, the two girls spent lazy afternoons in blissfully harmony on long horseback rides exploring the countless trails and open fields of wildflowers. Plaid was still afraid of crossing the river on horseback. Once in the beginning when she was just starting to ride, she followed Gap into the river, panicked, and fell off Morgan. Gap was watching her, ready to jump into the river if necessary. But Plaid swam to the riverbank where her grandmother waited for her.

"You were terrific, Plaid," yelled Gap.

"Yes! Well, I thought for a moment there you were going to leave me."

"Plaid, I will always be here with an outstretched hand for you to grab."

The horses were never that fired up about entering the river, but followed their rider's command. The horses would get that crazed look in their eyes, like the wooden horses on the merry-go-round.

Girlean's horse, Cloud, was stabled at Papa's. The stable was Girlean's haven, as she spent most of her time there to get away from her toxic home life. The arrival of Plaid to Protected Earth was a godsend for the beautiful, lonely girl.

Each time the two rode through the creek, Girlean would say, "Watch out for those water mocs. We'll ask Folly to make a snake stick for you, then you can fling those snakes right out of your way, onto the bank or further downstream. That old ugly snake will just go on about its business. Easy, when you know how to do it. I'll show you," explained Girlean.

Plaid said, "I think I can wait for that lesson on water mocs." Plaid made a little shiver just thinking about the whole thing. "Ain't nothing much uglier than a water moc."

Girlean and Cloud took the lead when they reached the river, they stepped into the fast-flowing water. Plaid called out her voice, sounding a bit nervous. "Girlean, this is the life I was meant to live. Hanna McCray read my leftover tea leaves; she was so right."

"You may be right, Plaid, but now let's cross this."

The river was high and running red from recent rains, the current was swift.

When Plaid's horse Morgan's hoofs left the bottom and were swimming free, Plaid leaned forward and whispered in Morgan's ear, "Boy, wish you had wings," when the two reached the middle, Morgan was swimming strong, but started to drift sideways in the current. Plaid let out a holler, she knew better, but it just came out, she couldn't breathe. Girlean was almost across, but twisted in her saddle to check on Plaid.

Girlean called out to her. "Stay with your horse. Let Morgan know you trust him. Come on, Plaid, you can do this!" Girlean saw Plaid's face turn from panic-stricken to confident and knew that all was well. With Plaid encouraging Morgan and praising him, the beautiful white horse brought her safely to the riverbank a bit downstream.

Both horses now on dry land, Girlean cheered Plaid for pulling through. "Plaid, you were great! Very brave. Never again will you not trust Morgan, or me either. Good job!"

Plaid was impressed with all of them. "I'm proud of you, too! Thanks for talking me through. These horses are the best! Even in the middle of it all, it was exciting."

They rode along the river then turned back across to reach Sparsity's. A person had to take it slow to appreciate all that had been planted or placed on the lane leading to Sparsity's. Rock formations, driftwood, fragrant, colorful wildflowers, blocks of salt for deer, and special berry bushes to attract birds, and all sorts of other treasured delights to spike the senses of Sparsity's visitors. The creatures of nature around her cottage knew they had no reason to fear people so they didn't run away, and a person could enjoy watching the variety, from little chipmunks to trained skunks.

The wooden bridge that arched over the marshy area caused Hanna and Morgan to tense up when it came into sight. The horses didn't care for either the sound their hooves made, or the way it felt.

All were relieved when they reached the other side.

Soon they rounded a curve and entered the grove of fruit trees that surrounded Sparsity's place. Her cottage was made of fieldstone collected from all over the property. A square piece of marble was built into the stonework just above the front door. Chiseled into the marble were these words.

Enter with an open heart
Linger and talk will start
Dine, laugh, and rest your head
Leave enriched, your soul well fed

A meandering herb garden outlined with rocks encircled her cottage. The open porch held a treasure table with articles collected over the many years. Sparsity would say, "Each one carries a memory of the day, sealed into my soul."

There were turtle shells, an assortment of bones, antlers, some broken Indian pottery, that the Indians living on and around Protected Earth, knew Sparsity had found. But the Indians wanted no part of anything the strange albino woman touched. They called her 'snow spirit', which was fine with Sparsity. She treasured the arrowheads, and even some jewelry. There was also glass colored from river sand, petrified wood, and fossils.

Girlean admitted that visiting Sparsity was exciting. Girl took most of life as that's the way it is. As a child, Girlean thought Sparsity was a creature from another planet that happened to land on the porch of a strange old woman and her twin sons. But now she related to Sparsity, and understood more that being different was not an easy life.

Sparsity didn't mind talking about her childhood with Granny Dalia and Granny's sons. They were good and kind to her. When she reached her teens, they sent her on her journey alone, because of their love for her, and she would say, "Look where I landed." She credited her survival to their care. Another Fortunate Abandonment.

The two girls dismounted and let the horses drink from the trough not far from the well. They giggled together as they unsaddled and walked the horses to cool them down, then released them into Sparsity's small paddock.

Walking toward the cottage, Plaid asked, "Do you think that Sparsity will invite us to eat lunch with her? She always prepares such interesting tasty things."

Girlean replied in a low voice, "Couldn't say. You never know what you may be eating." They stifled their giggles and rang the set of small bells that hung off the front porch.

Sparsity wore colorful layers of taffeta skirts that whispered in a ruffle whenever she moved. The girls thought that Sparsity's skirts made her even more mysterious. Plaid once remarked to Girlean that Sparsity's skirts were like looking at a merry-go-round. You felt happy. Girlean had never seen one, so Plaid had to describe merry-go-rounds in great detail.

Wide-eyed, Girlean had listened with rapt attention. About the merry-go-round in central park, Plaid described the wooden horses and the many wonderful colors on them. "What a thrill my first ride was, but I did get sick and threw up on everyone. Hanna said, 'Your belly can't take that around and around.'"

The girls dug in the pockets of their pants, which were still wet from crossing the river. They never came to Sparsity's empty-handed. Sometimes they brought a bouquet of wildflowers, or an unusual stone, or even some item that Chase and Talker had dug up in the forest.

Once, the dogs had uncovered a buried cache of broken pieces of sundry household items. Pretending that they were archeologists, the girls had dug around the area for days. Plaid declared that the site had been a campfire from a long-ago wagon train that had passed through. Plaid's imagination could come up with a story for anything. Working the site had rendered part of a delicate porcelain teacup with a yellow rose painted on it. The broken teacup had inspired a prolonged, intricate story from Plaid and later, it had ended up on Sparsity's treasure table.

Plaid brought out a thimble that she'd been carrying around, found at the cache site. Girlean produced a perfect staurolite stone that she had found near the river. Fairy stones, folks called them. Girlean thought that Sparsity was doing good to get this; she'd intended to keep it.

Sparsity came to the door in response to the sound of the bells. She greeted the girls. "Come. I have prepared our meal. We will eat outside."

"How did you know we would be here? We didn't even know," Plaid asked, puzzled.

Sparsity smiled and reached out to give the girls one of her special, life-assuring hugs. She winked at Girlean, who nodded, resigned to her belief that Sparsity knew everything, somehow. "Come," Sparsity said, shepherding the girls around the side of the cottage to her outdoor table. The table was already set, with small pottery vases of fresh flowers at each place. On each of the girl's plates was a little note card on which Sparsity had written their name and listed the menu. "Saves answering your questions," she laughed.

Plaid stood with her mouth agape at the sight. She repeated softly, "How did you know?"

Plaid made each hand into a fist and crossed them hand-over-hand. "Guess," she said Sparsity chose the right hand and found the thimble. Girlean was next, hiding the staurolite in her left hand. Again,

Sparsity guessed correctly. Plaid shook her head. "You never get it wrong. How come?"

Sparsity laughed in response. "I believe growing up in the wild with wild animals and people that raised me unrestricted, I do possess a sixth sense of things. Thank you for these lovely gifts. I will find a special place for them on the treasure table."

Girlean read their lunch menu aloud. "Mint tea, wild strawberry biscuits spread with goat cheese and lemon butter. Butterbean soup. Oh, wow, and fried green tomatoes with a fried egg on top."

Sparsity went inside. She returned moments later with a tray laden with their picnic feast.

The two girls ate with fervor. They all pitched in to clean up after their meal. Then Sparsity spread a thick quilt on the stone porch and produced fluffy pillows to rest upon. "Let's all sit. What shall be our talk today? Let's start with Plaid. Girlean, you ask our question of the day."

Plaid waited. Girlean closed her eyes and asked, "Why do you believe in God?"

Plaid launched into her answer with no hesitation. "I have thought about God a lot, even when I was wrapped in my Papa's Plaid shirt in Grand Central Station."

"Do you remember when you were born," said Girlean. "Wow!" She said excited, "How wonderful is that? Maybe someone just told you the story of your birth in such a special way."

Plaid continued without acknowledging Girlean's skepticism. "There was nothing to interest a human to pick me up, so I decided that I'd better make some noise. Now, who told me to do that? Not something that I evolved from, the vibrations from the heart and that kind woman connected to a helpless baby. Just think about the perfection of a sunrise, the rainbow, a single wildflower, the rock you hold in your hand, Chase and Talker finding stray spirits that you know are nearby, and you are not afraid."

While Plaid was talking, a swallowtail butterfly landed on the coneflower in front of the porch, mere inches from where they sat. Plaid pointed to it. "Right there, look at that. Perfect. Not to mention she is pollinating the flowers and food plants, earthworms turning over the earth so the rain can come in, the crows sounding their alarm, the birds and animals planting seeds along the fences to enhance the beauty of our planet. A cardinal making you stop in your tracks from their beauty that knocks you out, red against a blue sky. The squirrels planting acorns that will become the future mighty oaks, the wind carrying seeds miles and miles to spread their beauty, the beautiful writing spider catching a breeze to attach her web to a limb and building a web that can withstand a violent windstorm, the ants who attend all peoples' picnics across the world, the sun shining into the river. The wind and casting dancing diamonds so beautiful your eyes can't believe and can hold your attention for hours. Then casting dancing shadows from the trees on the waters. Is this all an act of science? No! No! I can never believe that. That's all I have to say on the subject for now." Plaid stopped to catch her breath. Sparsity and Girl sat silent. Plaid had taken their breath away.

Girlean finally spoke. "Next time, Plaid, my question will be, 'Did you sleep well? What did you dream last night? For a simple answer."

Sparsity said, "Girl, I have a feeling there is nothing simple about our Plaid."

The three laughed at the wonder of the mind and the luster of friendship.

Plaid Walks Alone

After Plaid ate breakfast, she received repeated words of encouragement for her first lone walk on Protected Earth. She had taken some short walks and listened with open ears to every word from Papa and Gap for guidance.

Gap continued, "I want you to let your surroundings saturate each one of your senses. Smell the flowers, break off a branch of evergreen, pick honeysuckle, taste it. Pick up a handful of dirt, feel the texture, smell it, observe the color. Look at the sky, take in the horizon, watch the breezes that make the tall grasses dance. But remember, the walk is strictly for your pleasure. Yes, you will always be learning. There will be times that you are scared. You can possibly become petrified. Try not to panic. Your good sense will tell you how to handle the situation at hand. If dangerous, bring Chase and Talker close, blow your whistle. Most likely they will sense any potential problems before you are aware of any, and be right beside you. You will rub their heads and know all is good."

Gap put her strong hands-on Plaid's shoulders and continued, "If your guts are telling you that you aren't ready for the walk. Don't!"

Plaid took one of Gap's hands, held it close to her cheek, lifted up her shoulder and pressed it into Gap's hands, and said, "I am ready."

Plaid's mind was always going. She asked herself, "Why am I now thinking of somewhere else? I am happy right here. Why question myself so strictly?"

Papa Lee was watching his child and great-grandchild with a wide smile on his face. Papa counseled, "All is okay, Plaid. My mind goes off all the time."

Plaid hugged her grandfather. "Plaid Patience, we will be waiting to hear even the smallest detail of your day. Know we are always with you. And to repeat, Chase and Talker will be close by, just call out their names or blow your whistle and they will be right by your side so fast you will believe you blinked them to you."

The day was anything but sunny. Clouds covered the sky. The morning dew was still heavy on most everything outside, even the windows in the kitchen were fogged. But Plaid was glad. Anyone can feel comfortable when the weather is perfect. Papa says, "Take weather as it is. It's beautiful, rain, shine, hot, cold — just live it."

She slipped her backpack on, with food and gear in tow, she turned once more to look at Papa and Gap. Chase and Talker were waiting, their tails beating out their impatience to get started. A little Quester ready for new exciting undertakings. Papa looked at Gap and said, "Like her mother and grandmother, she has all the qualities that delight the eye." Father and daughter sat in the old red swing and were silent as they watched their granddaughter walking away... and trying extremely hard to be brave.

Plaid walked and searched the rim of the woods with her eyes, her heartbeat a little faster. She stopped a few times, once to pick up a bluebird feather and a smooth black rock that looked at odds with its surroundings. Chase and Talker were nowhere in sight. She remembered what her Papa and Gamma Gap assured her with... "We are with you every step."

It wasn't fright she felt. It was the darkness of the unknown. But today was not the day of venturing into the deep woods. She was not sure she thought that day will ever come.

She was not ready to call out to Chase and Talker. They know I am here and under their protection. Plaid knew Papa and Gap would not let her take a long solo walk if she was unsure.

Plaid liked to think that nature waited for her, the robins trilled, bluebirds flew across her path, and someday may even light on her shoulder and sing a song. The low-hanging branches of the willows next to the river picked up a breeze and danced only for her.

A mallard paraded her babies up the river for Plaid's approval. Two bumblebee's played chase around her head.

The river was stirring. Plaid thought the river looked very much in control of its turf. She stayed a good distance back from the edge. A little shiver went over her as she remembered Gap had said the river had taken Starling and others that had never been found. Chase and Talker had joined her once more. She gave the two some hugs and kisses and thanked them for checking on her. Next, she wanted to walk the tall grass fields of oats and wheat. Soon the fields would be cut for harvest. She was almost hid from view. Her hands caressed the grasses, as the three continued across and up the hill to reach her ancestors burial ground. She surprised a small, frightened field mouse that was being chased by a red fox. The fox stopped, made eye contact with Plaid, Chase, and Talker, then hurried along in another direction. The dogs were trained to wait for an indication of hand movement before they would go after any animal. Plaid calmed the dogs.

"It's okay. The fox is only looking for lunch, which we robbed her of. Let's move along. We will have lunch soon." Chase and Talker were not composed, but they obeyed.

Plaid put her attention back on her walk and soon she would be alone with her thoughts and seated beside Monty's graveside. Also, she would say hello to her deceased great, great aunts, Azzie and Crow.

She was learning about each one from Papa Lee and Gap. She wondered if Papa would ever know what happened to his sister Dessie.

But it›s mainly my mother I have come to visit today.

She thought the ornate white wrought-iron fence looked quite grand, it wore a new coat of paint. The dogwoods that outline the fence were in full, glorious bloom, dropping their white blood stained blossoms. That's how Girlean described them. She said the red that dotted the blossoms were a symbol of Jesus' blood because the cross that he died on was made from a dogwood tree. Girlean sure can come up with some mighty heavy stuff. Whatever the truth, the graveyard was covered in a carpet of snow white dogwood petals.

Chase and Talker were clamoring to enter the meditation and prayer room. The dogs rushed in as Plaid opened the door. The two were waiting for her to unfold a quilt from a shelf and spread it on the floor for them. They curled up and gave a relaxed yawn and fell asleep. 'Not even waiting for their lunch,' Plaid thought. 'I suppose age may do that, preferring a nap over food.'

Plaid decided since a little mist of rain had started, and to take the chill off the room, she would build a fire in the small rock fireplace.

She took some starter kindling which she had helped Papa look for and they had placed it in neat, small bundles inside the room. The hearts of pine sure did smell nice and grabbed a flame fast. Soon, the fire's warmth filled the room. Next, she lit a few candles. First for her mother, then for her great aunts Azzie and Crow, then Mr. Ward, Cal, Birchard, and Mickey. Also, a corner of the graveyard had been set aside for all the departed generations of animals that had passed away.

She sat on a pillow close to the fire next to the dogs. Their soft breathing was a comfort. Closing her eyes, she moved into a meditative pose, as Gap had shown her, and welcomed each one of the spirits into the room. She said out loud, "Thou art with me, thou comfort me."

"Mama." Plaid felt such joy when she heard her own voice calling out to her mama.

"Mama, I want desperately to believe you hear me, that you reach out and catch each of my words and place them in your pocket. If you have a pocket, Gap says you always wanted a shirt or jacket with pockets, you would say 'How can I collect so many little treasures as I go through my day' if I don't have pockets. Papa tells me you are in every flower, blade of grass, even in the fragrances that float along with the breezes. Especially in the overly sweetness of the honeysuckles that the bees love so much. That was a favorite of yours. I believe that honeysuckles will be my favorite also."

Plaid shifted her attention to Talker. He started howling softly. "You feel Mama's Spirit don't you, Talker? She is here with us. Oh, Mama, I am so glad you saw me growing up. And knowing that everyone says I look like you. You can let your spirit rest. I was never really unhappy. I felt your love around me. I am sorry you suffered. I see your perfect face and carry the picture of you with the baby goat. Oh! How I love that picture. I want to crawl into it and live that moment with you. Papa and Gap say the most beautiful part of you was your kindness to all things. You are living with me through their gift of wonderful stories. I want to be as brave as you were. Mama, the dogs are hungry and I'm a little hungry also. We will talk more next visit. Bye, Mama."

Plaid spoke each person's name as she blew out the candles. Then she took out the food. She put another log on the fire. The three ate, feeling warm and safe. She curled up on the quilt after lunch with Chase and Talker and fell asleep.

The next thing Plaid knew, Emilio was calling her name and the light from his flashlight hurt her eyes. The hot coals glowed in the fireplace.

Papa and Gap had sent Emilio to ride the trails, check the graveyard, but they didn't wish for Plaid to know they were checking on her.

Emilio had smelled the smoke as he rode close and saw the glowing lights from the fire. "Miss Plaid, you are all right, are you not, Miss

Plaid?" Emilio did not want to frighten the child. Chase and Talker welcomed Emilio.

"Oh, hi, Emilio. We fell asleep by the warm fire. Sorry if we worried anyone. It sure was a good day. Did Papa send you to find me and bring me home?"

Emilio smiled, "To check on you. He felt it's your first walk out alone and staying all night would be a bit too much."

"Let's get rid of the fire. You can ride back with me. The dogs will follow. They know the way home."

Plaid fell asleep against Emilio's back. She had done a lot of walking. Emilio called out her name, "Wake up, Miss Plaid. It's a full moon. You should enjoy its beauty."

"Thanks, Emilio. Sorry I fell asleep." She looked at the full moon and wondered if Hannah was looking at it. Hannah loved a full moon. It lit up the darkness of Central Park.

"Emilio, were Papa and Gap worried about me?"

"They will always worry about you, Miss Plaid. You are such a dear treasure to them. Let's make Sadie here trot. I know two people who are eager to hear about your day."

Girlean's Chicken Reprieve

Leeward's imposing thumbprints covered Girlean's skinny arms. She was a wiry child of nine and carried a well-deserved fierce loathing for Leeward. Her lovely, shy mother and siblings had mostly given up on the handsome, hard-working, talented, noxious daddy, ever changing his ways. The family walked in fright.

Girlean collected these bruises because she dared to oppose him, knowing the consequence on herself was huge. She felt she was the main cause of Leeward's anger and jealous rages toward her mama. Her mama had no struggles left to defend herself and Girlean thought that faraway look on her mama's face was maybe for a lost love that most likely was Girlean's real father. She was right.

Tess would often touch Girlean's fierce but perfectly featured face, surrounded by a head of dark long ringlet hair and see the image of the kind, handsome gentleman that fathered Girlean.

Girlean was the lovechild of a short-lived, flawless, taboo love affair that was a lifetime lived in a few weeks between her mother and a man from up North, the son of an interracial couple. The people that knew Girlean's mother well felt she deserved a piece of happiness, even if it came about from a frowned-upon affair. When Leeward, the man that raised Girlean looked into the child's face, he only saw his wife's betrayal. Love can arrive at times and knock a person off their feet. Certainly, the love between Girlean's ravishing, timid mother and the exceedingly attractive stranger was a love that two people had no control over.

Leeward worked his hurt and anger out on Girlean.

An early Sunday supper is often served in the South. After church services of folks just sleeping late, resting a weary, hard-working body from a non-stop week, this meal was looked forward to.

On most Southern tables each Sunday, there is a tempting platter of fried chicken, each family frying up their own guarded secret recipe. Each golden piece was served on the prettiest platter, passed down from generation to generation. The most sought-after piece on the platter is the wishbone. Family members sit with anticipation that they will get the wishing part. After breaking the bone under the table with your sibling and to heighten the wish even more, you close your eyes, wrap your sticky hand around that bone and make a wish you have been holding for a long time. It's all yours; you never have to disclose it. Only you will know if it ever comes true.

But one child was filled with dread and trembling when she opened her eyes on Sunday mornings. Her head full of ringlets was laden with sweat, even before her feet touched the wood-planked floor. The foreboding situation that awaited her was harrowing.

Leeward, with his unhinged ways, decided the duty of catching the chicken that was to be killed for Sunday supper was now Girlean's. Leeward received evil gratification from subjecting Girlean to any chore that he knew petrified her. Girlean had become his target since her first day on Earth.

Each Sunday, his voice would ring out as he banged on the girl's door with a tin pan, which made the mingle noise and voice more freakish for Girlean. "Girlean," he hollered as he dragged out the 'lean' in her name. "Bang, bang," went the pan. "Girlean, the chickens are waiting. You don't want me to come into your room, do you?"

"No, no! Leeward, I'll do my job." Her voice working to sound strong.

"Get a move on, NOW! I'll watch you from the kitchen window. How many times must I say don't call me Leeward? Is it so hard to say Daddy?"

Girlean would sit like stone at the family's Sunday supper as her siblings chatted to each other, eating away at the fried chicken. When she was lucky enough to get the wishbone, her wish was always the same, and it wasn't a very nice wish. So what, she put no accountability to God. She had refused to be baptized as her siblings were. That is, all but Clancy and Girlean. Her oldest half-brother understood her. Before Girlean had the job of chopping the chicken's heads off, it was Clancy's job. Clancy had the softest heart, like his mother. One particular time when Clancy was stressed and only ten years old, he went into uncontrollable yelling at his daddy. Clancy missed the chicken and cut the tip of his finger off. He threw down the axe, swinging his arms, blood flying all around him. "Someday, Daddy Leeward, you will get your payback! I will not do this anymore. Beat me, even shoot me, but never again will I kill a chicken." He never did to anyone's knowledge. But this put Girlean in the position of taking over this disastrous duty. And Leeward grabbed the chance. Knowing she would be terrified to kill a chicken. It was a grisly act.

Today, Plaid was to experience firsthand her blood-bonded friends dread on Sunday mornings. Plaid was out for a ride on Morgan. She decided to ride by Girlean's. Girlean was the best companion for rides because there were places on Protected Earth that Plaid didn't yet feel comfortable riding alone.

It was a perfect day. The sky was luscious blue, and a soft, sweet breeze caressed one's face. As she rode up, she saw Girlean in the chicken yard. While trying to tie Morgan to the chicken fence post, Morgan started acting perturbed. His ears were pinched back, his eyes narrowed, switching his tail. He let out a high-pitched whinny. Plaid tried to calm her horse down. "Calm down, Morgan," she repeated as she rubbed his neck and tried to soothe him.

The chickens appeared terrified. They acted like a fox was in their yard. All Plaid saw besides the chickens was her best pal, Girlean. Plaid unlatched the gate and went into the chicken yard to join her friend. Plaid felt a little uneasy around chickens and somewhat sad for the creatures. They have wings but can't fly, only very short distances, and live in fear of being a Sunday supper.

"Hi, Girlean. Thought you may join me for a ride along the river. I feel sorta edgy down in that area alone." Plaid quickly sensed that something wasn't right. Girlean was crying. She didn't know Girlean ever cried or was afraid of anything; she seemed fearless. Sweat was beaded on her face.

"Believe me, Plaid, there isn't anything I would like better than riding along the river," her voice breaking as she spoke and all the while wiping her wet face with the tail of her shirt.

"So what's the matter? Why can't you go? I'll help you gather the eggs. Why are the chickens so crazy?"

"Plaid, I have to catch two of the handsome, sweet chickens for Mama to fry for Sunday supper," Girlean said in a voice that Plaid had never heard her use before. Plaid noticed the chickens huddled in the corner, restless, squawking, and walking in circles. It was the first time she had taken notice of what the chickens really looked like. They were covered in full, soft, speckled grey and white feathers that Plaid thought looked really pretty as they spread out over and around the chicken's feet. She had once seen a fancy lady on a New York train with a feather shawl wrapped around her shoulder. The feathers were not necessarily of the same size.

Girlean bent down, putting her head in her hands. "Oh, Plaid. They always know when death is near. When I walk in to gather eggs, or kiss the baby chicks, or feed them. The chickens are happy to see me, but on Sundays, they know. Will you help me? I can't do it anymore."

"Yes, I will. I have never seen anything killed before." But Plaid, wanting to assist her blood sister, walked toward a chicken — a big, fat, fluffy one. It took off running around the chicken yard, its eyes bulged, squawking, knowing the Grim Reaper was approaching.

Girlean rose as it ran past her into a corner. She caught it. The frightened chicken looked her straight in the face, begging for its life.

The two girls stepped outside the gate. Plaid put her hands on her stomach and threw up.

Girlean, still holding the chicken under one of her arms, walked over to Plaid, took the wet tail of her sweatshirt, and wiped her face. Then she sat the chicken down, but it just stood there, looking very confused.

Plaid started yelling, "Run! Run! Run for your life!" It took off and ran into the nearby cornfield. Plaid took the tail of her own shirt, wet it in the horses watering trough, and wiped her face.

Girlean put her arm around Plaid and said, "This means I get a beating for letting the chicken loose. But I don't care. Leeward can beat me until I die but I won't catch another chicken to be killed. Those chickens frightened faces haunt me in the middle of the night. He is probably watching us from the window."

Maybe to lessen the situation, they started to laugh, then took off running into the cornfield, running up, down, in and out of the corn rows, feeling free and happy like that fat, fluffy, beautiful chicken was now doing.

"I never knew a chicken could run so fast," said Plaid. Every once in a while, it would make an attempt to fly.

In the distance, in the direction of Girlean's house, they could hear Leeward hollering for Girlean.

Girlean told Plaid, "Go on home. I will see you tomorrow."

Plaid with tears now running down her face, "What can I do? Can I get Gap? Maybe she can do something."

"Yes! Go tell Gap and Papa Lee what happened here. Gap made me promise to tell her if Leeward ever tries to use his belt on me again. It's sure to happen."

Holding hands, the two girls walked toward the house. "Plaid, today, I am not running when Leeward calls my name." They saw Leeward standing in the driveway; the chickens were running every which way. The girls had left the chicken yard fence door open.

Plaid gave Girlean a hug, then got on Morgan and took off in a gallop to inform Gap and Papa Lee.

The pretty, speckled chickens ran into the cornfield, the little chicks alongside their mamas. Girlean smiled, her fear had oddly left her. What a gladness, to see all the chickens running free, up and in and out of the corn rows.

Bravely, Girlean held her head high with feelings inside of righteousness and walked right by Leeward into the house, as if he didn't exist.

Plaid gave Morgan a small push with her heel and he sped up. Thinking out loud, she spoke her inner mixed thoughts to God, "God, do I need to be forgiven for having eaten fried chicken, baked chicken, and chicken and dumplings? Why did I never think of how they died? I have never felt as sad as I do at this moment. Sad for my friend, Girlean, and sad for the terrified chickens. Come on, Morgan. My friend needs Papa's help."

Plaid was in a highly emotional state when she reached home. She had such fear as to what was going to happen to Girlean. She tied Morgan up and ran into the house, calling out to Papa Lee. "Papa, Papa! I need you!"

Lee was in his studio. He walked out covered in marble dust and had a concerned look at the sound of his great-granddaughter's terrified voice. "Slow down, Plaid. What's wrong?"

Plaid jumped into his arms, "Oh Papa, please help my friend Girlean. She may be in harm's way."

He took out his clean, white handkerchief and wiped away her tears. "Now, you are safe. Tell your Papa about Girlean."

"Leeward makes her kill chickens. Oh, Papa, it's awful, seeing those chickens so terror-struck, knowing Girlean is going to chop their heads off. She is so sad. Papa, maybe you could talk to Leeward. Why can't he do that job? Girlean says he is punishing her."

Plaid was a bit unnerved. Holding her head in her hands, putting her hands in a prayer position, she pleaded, "Please, Papa."

"You go make yourself a cup of sweet vanilla coffee. Then, go on the porch, curl up on the swing and wait for Gap. She will return shortly from her ride. Tell your grandmother what happened. I will take care of your friend and see that Leeward behaves himself from now on."

"But Papa, maybe I should be with you."

"No! You stay right here."

Lee reached for his shotgun standing in the corner.

Papa Lee swirled off the porch. Chase and Talker, sensing the excitement, were standing by Papa's truck. The hair on their backs was in a bristle position—ready to defend their loved one from danger. The truck spun out of the driveway, throwing Chase and Talker around.

When Papa reached Leeward's, he came out of the truck, shotgun in hand. All these years, he had kept Leeward somewhat contained and put up with behavior from a person that he didn't approve of but needed. And he had made a promise to his dear Birchard.

Leeward was Birchard's son, not that Leeward ever really accepted Birchard as his father, but he was always respectful towards him.

When Papa Lee walked into Leeward's house, Leeward was seated at the kitchen table. Papa Lee took hold of Leeward's collar and dragged him onto the porch, down the steps and into the truck. Papa pulled out of the yard, dirt and gravel flying. Leeward didn't try to talk or give Papa Lee resistance.

Girlean's family gathered on their porch, around their mother. "We will just wait. This has been in Papa Lee's belly for a long time. Now that Birchard has passed away, he no longer feels he is being disloyal to Birchard and Mickey," said Girlean's mother.

No one ever found out exactly what happened that Sunday afternoon. Leeward returned home walking, without his usual confident, arrogant manner. Whatever did happen on the ride with Papa Lee turned Leeward's hair completely white.

Leeward stood on his steps and said, "Girlean, saddle your horse. You will now live with the Darnell's." Girlean's mother sat silent as Leeward continued his speech. "It's for the best. Don't bother taking a thing and don't come around here. Gap will pick up your mother and she will visit you at Papa Lee's house."

Girlean rode away, her head up, back straight. She did not even bother to saddle her horse. She rode bareback as fast as she could to a safe place.

Gap and Plaid — A Surprise Nest

Mornings are a beginning. Venus, a morning star, could be seen in the eastern sky. Gap pulled the quilt in around Plaid; Plaid had gotten up early then fell asleep on the old red porch swing. The swing had seen lots of life, been repaired many times.

The early morning air held dampness, the grass and flowers were sucking up this nourishing dew.

Gap stood drinking her coffee and focused on the world around her. The ever-changing sky, a pile of stacked tree limbs with chipmunks playing chase in and out, a moth lit on the screen door, Chase and Talker peacefully sleeping close to the swing. Papa Lee's boots left at the front of his rocker. A lone empty mason jar still sat on the porch; holes punched in the top. It had been Monty's; she would catch lighting bugs and then release them before she went to bed.

Gap encouraged her granddaughter to talk about her years in New York and to ask any questions about her mother and ancestors she wanted to know. Plaid was not short of questions. What was lifelike when Mr. Ward purchased the thousand acres and started life on Protected Earth? Who were Cal and Birchard, Mickey, and all the others that were a part of Protected Earth?

Plaid wrote notes in a book she kept by her bed about her talks, and details of all that may enter her life each day. She soon realized there were no dull moments on Papa Lee's land.

Plaid had the same soft, clear voice that her mother, Monty, had possessed, and it was a voice that was determined to be heard. Gap unhurriedly listened. Gap smiled all the way through while listening to her granddaughter talk about New York or waiting for another question.

Plaid sat up, rubbing her eyes. "Morning, Gamma Gap. Sorry—I wanted to surprise you with coffee on the porch, but I fell asleep."

"You gave me a lovely surprise, to see you at such peace. Now have a small breakfast and off we go for a lovely walk." Gap reached and touched her head.

Today as they walked, looked, and listened, Gap came upon a spot where she had sat with Monty. She asked Plaid, "Would you like to build a nest like your mother did?"

Plaid stopped with great interest at the thought of people building a giant nest.

"How, Gamma Gap?"

"This is a great spot, we have all the makings to gather evergreen tree branches, pinecones, pine straw, leaves, mulch from the spring bottom and rocks."

Plaid, so excited she could barely contain herself, "Oh my, how wonderful. Where do I start?"

"Take the small foldup saw from your pack and start with the evergreens. Cut some small full branches. I will mark off our nest right here; looks like a good spot."

Gap outlined the nest with picked up pinecones. Plaid enjoyed the smell coming from the evergreens as she cut the small limbs. She piled them inside the outline of the nest.

"You continue, Plaid, then start placing them to make a nice cushion bottom for us." Gap cut some small trees and made poles about three feet long to hammer around the nest.

"When finished, we will intertwine some kudzu vines, then a few more evergreens."

Grandmother and granddaughter walked along the spring and pulled kudzu vines from the trees, cutting the vines in different lengths. At one point something started falling on Plaids head. It was muscadines. Plaid picked one up. "What is this, Gamma Gap?"

Gap reached down and popped two in her mouth. Plaid watched with great interest. "Go ahead and eat one, it's a muscadine. We will come back and pick enough for Papa to make us some delicious wine."

"Taste a little musky, but good." said Plaid.

Plaid was beyond excited. "Never, never did I think I would be helping my grandmother build a nest in the forest in Georgia and at the same time discover muscadines."

Now let's walk the spring and find a couple of stones that we can carry for our seats."

When completed, they stood back and admired their nest. "How 'bout we enjoy our ham and biscuits?" Gap removed a quilt from her pack and covered the evergreen.

The two were silent as they ate and let the beauty of their creation and the forest sink in.

Plaid spoke first, "Miss June, my social worker, kept trying to remove any doubts that I may have had that there was a special home and family waiting for me. My visions were of a place like Protected Earth."

"She is such a special person to have befriended Monty and kept her word on looking out for you. We may return sometime to our nest and find some animals have exercised dominion over it."

"Oh! I don't mind," declared Plaid, "it will give me great pleasure that we helped the animals out a little."

"You don't disappoint." Gap quipped with great pride. "Your mother would be so proud of you."

Grandmother and grandchild admired the nest, and their faces showed contentment.

"Gamma Gap, do you think a person remembers being inside their mother's womb?" Gap replied, "Maybe, if not inside my mama, very shortly after my birth. I remember the smell of strawberries. When I asked Papa about my birth, he pointed out Garrison had laid me in Sparsity's basket that she used to pick wild strawberries in."

Plaid was excited. "Oh my, what wonderful births we experienced. You had mama in the pond. My mama gave birth to me in Grand Central Station. Sparsity was left on an old cabin's porch with hound dogs. Papa was abandoned at Mr. Ward's circus door. Mr. Ward was left in a trunk on a ship. How special we are. I am so proud to be in this family with all this great history."

"Yes, Plaid we are Fortunate Abandonments," Gap said with contentment in her voice.

Gap disclosed, "Papa didn't know my mama was pregnant with me. Sparsity and Crow suspected Garrison was pregnant but felt it was Papa's business. She told Papa and asked to move in with Sparsity. Your great grandmother Garrison wrote in her note that I was to explore the world and had one request, that I be named after her. When it was time for me to be born, I was fast to enter the world. Sparsity and Aunt Crow cut the cord, cleaned mama and myself up. Crow stayed with mama and Sparsity went to fetch Doc Francis.

"Maybe the story has been repeated so many times, I just believe I remember."

Papa was overjoyed, "Now Crow, just look at the pretty gift Garrison left behind, how can we ever think ill of her." He repeated this statement often. While looking at Sparsity and Crow's faces of disdain that Garrison had left her child and maybe put herself in danger; after all, she had just had a baby. Papa disclosed my mama was beautiful, smart, a really good artist, and left great artwork behind, but she desired to be free. She wanted to travel. My mama would not hold me when Sparsity tried to place me in her arms."

"Why?" Plaid burst out.

Garrison had explained, "I don't want that remembrance in my life of her heart beating in rhythm next to mine."

Plaid hugged Gap, "Does it give you any pain, Gamma Gap?"

"No! Does it you, Plaid?"

"No! From the time I can remember, as I told you, I knew that someday I would go home. Then after my Mama Monty died and June Light told me her story—as much as she knew about my mama and my family in Georgia, and me—I understood my mama and why her actions were as they were. She was ill and June told me mama said, 'You and papa did all you could to help her.'"

"You are so young to be so smart," answered Gap.

The two rested in their new nest and fell asleep. Gap woke first, then gently touched Plaid's shoulder.

"We should head towards home."

"Thank you, Gamma Gap, for this experience. I will never, ever forget it."

They gathered their stuff and headed toward the main house.

CHAPTER 37

Plaid Talks Foster Homes

G ap looked at her granddaughter and thought, 'She is everything I like in a person, but so was my Monty.' Gap wanted Plaid's trust.

Gap spoke, "Plaid, Papa and I are eager to know each moment you experienced away from us. How painful to even think you were hurt or in trouble."

"Gamma Gap, I don't recall any pain, at least not physical. I would, at different times, have a huge tugging in my heart. As if a part was missing. I now believe it was my mama, trying to let me know how much she loved me."

"My first remembrance of foster parents is a family who had three children. My foster mother home-schooled her children. I don't know exactly how old I was, but I am grateful she taught me how to read at a young age. After learning to read, I lived through books. When I was lucky and got a book of my own, my book became a valuable jewel. I kept it with me or tried to find a hiding place for it. The household was clean and organized, but no real love did I feel. But not knowing how to love was supposed to be, I… have a great ability to adjust to what is."

None of the Darnell's cried easily. But, listening to their eight-year old granddaughter and her mature, sweet conversational prose, brought tears to their eyes, proud tears. Gap said, "Come here and give Papa and me the biggest hug you have in you." All were trying to put lost years behind.

Gap sensed Plaid was getting anxious, because Plaid was starting to twitch, a habit all the Darnell's seem to have.

Papa jumped in and said, "Gap, why don't you and Plaid pick some strawberries, I'll get the ice cream maker, the milk, etc. and let's make some good for the taste buds and the soul ice cream."

"Papa, can I finish this story?'

"Oh, sure darling, I felt you were ready to stop. We are interested in every word. I close my eyes and try to pull into close view the people and places you encountered. Proceed, dear."

"When my social worker, June Bug, told me the foster parents didn't want me anymore, June assured me their decision was nothing personal, the family was moving to another state. I wasn't hurt or broken hearted; I wasn't happy with them anyway."

Plaid said, "Papa, I feel as if any minute I will lift off the ground, miraculously my feet are still touching the porch… Oh Papa, you are so wise, could life be any better?"

Gap said, "I'll get the baskets, but Plaid, if you feel up to it, spill it all out about these foster parents, and then, your life will be ready to move on, but only if you agree."

"Yes, Gap. I do. I'm ready."

Gap and Plaid walked toward the strawberry fields and Papa readied the ice cream maker, mixed the ice cream, and waited for Gap and Plaid to return with the freshly picked strawberries.

After they had finished off the entire batch of strawberry ice cream, along with Chase, Talker and the cats, all laughed at their biggest joy and took naps of contentment.

Plaid was curled up on the floor with Chase, Talker and the cats. She had covered the dogs with a quilt; just their sweet speckled heads were sticking out.

Papa woke from his nap, called softly to Gap, "Feel like making your Papa a cup of coffee with hot milk and vanilla?"

"I was just gazing upon the two people I love so dearly, and that sunset." Gap went in to make coffee.

The animals became restless, wanting to go outside, pawing Plaid to wake up. Plaid woke up, "Okay! Okay! Hi, Papa, that was a lovely nap. I really like an afternoon nap; it makes a person feel they have seized just a little extra out of a day. How do you feel, Papa? I smelled a wonderful cup of coffee. Do I get one, Papa, with vanilla and hot milk?"

Lee smiled, "Let me start with the first question. I could not feel any better. I agree with your assessment of a nap in the afternoon, completely pleasurable, and I am sure Gap will see we all are taken care of. Here is our coffee. Now, are you ready to get back to your story?"

"Oh, yes! Thanks, Gamma Gap, the coffee smells like the first feeling of a good morning." Plaid lifted a cup off the tray, took a drink, closed her eyes, took a deep breath, and said, "Perfect."

The animals went outside and the three settled in, enjoying the coffee.

Once more, Plaid started to talk, "After the first foster family, June Bug placed me into a high society family on Park Avenue. I was mainly the companion to their special needs child. My dress was now fluffy clothes, but I did love that I was sent to school, and I got to ride the train. I had captive people for my stories, and I eavesdropped on many conversations. My little writing and drawing pad was kept busy. Papa and Gap, do you think that a person should be content for where God has placed us at any given moment? I know I am young, but something inside me just knew my life would not stay where I was, and here I am."

Gap said, "Yes, Plaid, I do think you are correct on that subject." Gap got up to let the animals back on the porch. "I didn't mind keeping the sad boy entertained, but what I disliked was him going through my backpack, which I know now, was made partly from your flannel shirt, Papa, that I was found in. I will treasure it forever."

Lee gave a large smile, stood up and stretched toward the ceiling, "Plaid Patience, you possess some of each one of the Darnell women's traits and my dear one, you can feel blessed for it."

"Papa, do I not have any of your traits?"

"One for sure, you are a good story-teller, and Gap feels you have lots of my traits."

"Oh, I am glad and I'm glad I have my Mama and Gamma Gap's looks."

Plaid became intrigued at the thought of being made up of all these different people.

"How, Papa? Please tell me how I am like them."

Your Great-Great Aunt Azzie was an individualist, with an extreme quest for adventure. Dessie I believe loved her life with gypsies. She never returned to us. Her music was dear to her heart and soul. She was a talent and Monterey, much later, was called Crow."

"Why Crow? I like it, I love my name also. Don't you, Papa?"

"Yes, it's a fact I love everything about you."

"Oh, Papa, how thrilling to look at it that way… Me a gypsy, and beautiful and exciting like my aunts. I will be a great artist, like my Mama and Gap. Maybe I will never help build a town, like you Papa, but there must be other brave goals I can achieve."

Papa looked at his great-granddaughter; she could barely contain the hunger in her to know who she is and where it will take her.

"To answer your question, Crow always wore black."

"Thanks, and Papa, could Aunt Dessie be alive?"

"Maybe, but I have never given up. Crow came home and our beautiful Azzie returned. When you visit the resting place on the hill, talk with their spirits, you will be welcomed by them."

"Not sure I believe in spirits, Papa. But when I was alone at the resting place, I talked to Mama and I did feel her spirit was close. Papa, you will tell me all about their extraordinary lives, and how your heart loved them so much. My mind finds it difficult to think of everyday chores and school when there is so much to fill my thoughts." Plaid took a deep breath.

Papa and Gap gave each other a look that said, "We have heard this before."

Papa stood, looked around and turned Plaids face towards him, with his hand, "Why don't we change this scene. Saddle our horses and check on our land, and all the wonderful creatures that inhibit it. It's a perfect time for viewing. If you like, Plaid, we can stop by Sparsity's; Girlean is staying with her a few days."

"No, Papa, I think some other time. I want to ride with you and Gap. I will see Girlean soon.

"Well, let's get our butts up and riding boots on and saddle up."

The three headed for the barn.

A Library Trip, "Beyond First Sight"

The town's library porch was a nice place to sit and relax in a rocker, the railroad station was in full view, as well as the small park, where the town's children played on the circus statue and fun games in the streets.

"Papa, my Papa Lee!" Plaid Patience sang her great grandfather's name again and again, as she danced around him. She hopped over his bare feet which protruded from his stretched-out form in the rocking chair. In all his years, Papa Lee had never seen such energy. Plaid was positively ablaze with it. When the sun was behind her cotton-top hair, he could swear that she radiated her own corona. The light surrounding her seemed to sparkle and flash in her exuberance. She was a rare, unexpected gift. The same as her grandmother Gap and her mother Monty were when they came into his life.

The giant oak beside the library's porch slowly showered its golden leaves over the cabin, some drifting on the breeze to fall upon Papa Lee's outstretched hand. Gently, Plaid reached and turned her Papas hand over and traced her fingers along the raised veins, pausing at his enlarged knuckles. Plaid asked in an almost whisper-soft voice, "Papa, I have my mama, and Gaps, and your blood running through my veins, Are we not a family chain?"

"Papa, does anyone know who my father was? Did you know him Papa?"

"Your grandmother will tell you all about your grandfather when she is ready. His name was Starling. But your father was not known to us, and Monty never revealed who he was."

"Yes, my Plaid. We are. Your voice is so much like your mama's. I feel your hand right here so like hers—and know that she is also here with us. We never really die. We move on into another matter."

Papa knew well that having Monty's child here in Georgia was a miracle. He stopped his mind from asking the question why Monty felt the necessity to leave Georgia and have her baby in New York. Monty wasn't coming back in the physical, and this dear, delightful, spirited child is here. He silently prayed for a lot more years to share. Papa wanted every moment that God would grant him to teach her...

so many things. Plaid needed to know to be aware of each moment, even the smallest things, and appreciate the miniscule as well as the vast, grand scheme. "Try not to miss any of it." Papa said. Plaid lifted inquisitive eyes to his. Monty's eyes—Gap's, and his own. "Plaid Patience," he continued, "look."

"Look at what, Papa?"

"Watch that batch of crows," Papa pointed to the sky.

Plaid was eager to listen, watch, and learn. She quickly located the congress of crows gathering in the oak tree.

Papa Lee let her observe silently, then he said, "Plaid, remember: no matter what moment you are in, never lose sight of the wonders happening around you. Feel the air moving across your face. Take in the smell of fall. Now, let's watch the crows and see what they do."

A group of small boys barreled down the street, immersed in a game of kick the can. Gleefully hollering, each competed to make the long shot. As the boys approached the library oak tree in happy bedlam, the crows squawked in ear splitting protest. The den of the spirited game and the outraged crows continued until the boys disappeared around the far corner of the mercantile down the street. The crows, thoroughly riled even after the disturbance was gone, disdainfully lifted into the air one by one. Their shiny black bodies highlighted as they flew into the crystal blue sky.

Papa, on occasion, would drift into a snooze. Now, in spite of the ruckus, he had managed to do just that. Plaid burst out into a panic, "Papa! Papa, are you in there? Don't leave me!"

Papa Lee came to with a start and a little snort. He continued as though uninterrupted, "Tell me—what do you see?"

Plaid looked toward the retreating crows winging their way to the river. "They seem to be annoyed as much with each other as with the boys. They sure did not like to be bothered with all that noise, did they? I think that they believe they own the place, and they just tolerate us—barely. They're both regal and ridiculous, and every bit as rumpus as the boys were." Plaid turned and looked at Papa, longing for his praise.

"Very good," Papa responded, proud of Plaid's quick mind. He continued, "You know what else I saw? I saw that they depend on each other, communicate freely, and stick together. Like a great, big family."

"We were lucky to see them," she continued. "There were crows in New York, but they're different, somehow. Maybe it's all the space. I think they adapt wherever they go. Sorta like I did, Papa, being in a big city." Plaid lifted her arms and twirled around to emphasize just how big this space was. She kept twirling, "I love to see your smile when you look at God's world. I love your long, white beard. And I looooooooooove crows!" Papa Lee watched her … thoroughly enchanted with his loving, intelligent, and interesting great granddaughter. He silently gave thanks for the hundredth time that day. Then he stood. Oak leaves fluttered to the ground. Plaid cried out in delight, "Papa! You're an oak tree!"

Questions came bumbling out, one after another. Papa Lee was hard pressed to keep up. "Papa, do you think my mama was proud of me?" "Papa, when mama gave birth to me in Grand Central Station and wrapped me in your flannel shirt, what were you and Gamma Gap doing at that particular moment?" "Papa, when did you find out about me? Were you glad?"

Plaid didn't wait for answers from her Papa, she moved on.

Plaid suddenly went still, "Papa, would you mind if I sketched you? That way, I can always keep this afternoon that I shared with you and learned a lot about crows. Maybe I will put a few crows perched on you. It's nice to be an artist. I can paint the world anyway I want it."Inordinately pleased, Papa positioned his rocker so that the sun would illuminate his face, then sat back down and said, "Sure, sketch away." He displayed his profile. Plaid collected her sketchpad and pencil from underneath the library books she had selected. She sat in silence as she dashed off her sketch.

"Done." She reviewed her work with satisfaction. "See?" She showed him her sketch pad. She had drawn a remarkable likeness of …. his bare feet. They laughed together. "Wait. I'm not finished." Plaid turned the page and began another sketch. This time, she produced a full-body sketch of Papa Lee in his rocker, authentic right down to the missing button on his shirt. She painted some crows sitting on his shoulder and even shaded in the raised veins in his hands and his enlarged knuckles. Oak leaves in such detail, they seemed to move on the paper. Her talent was undeniable. Papa Lee nearly burst with pride.

"Do you like it, Papa?" Plaid pressed her cheek on his shoulder.

"Yes, my dear one. Very soon, you will be as good as your Gamma Gap and your Mama. I am sure your mama is proud of you. She's watching you." At that moment, the wind picked up and produced a whirlwind of dancing oak leaves. Papa thought *I am not sure about heaven, but I sure do like the thought.*

Plaid excitedly hopped onto one of the rockers on Papa's chair and grabbed his arm. "Papa, do you think that was mamas' spirit? Was that her saying that she approves of me?"

Papa put his arm around Plaid's shoulders. "I'm sure that she does, honey. But you know, I do not believe that we are meant to know all the mysteries. A lovely part of life is to question. Let us head for home." Papa put on his boots. The two of them gathered up their things, which included several library books for each.

They reached the lot where their wagon was waiting. Papa had purchased one of the first new pickup trucks but preferred to use the wagon. Maude, their mule, wagged her long, silky ears at them. The big brown mule arched her neck down to Plaid, who scratched her behind the ears as Papa loaded their books and readied the wagon. Maude squeezed her eyes closed in contentment. A couple of men hailed Papa as they came toward the neighboring wagon. Papa proudly introduced them to his beautiful great-granddaughter. He helped Plaid up, then swung himself up on the wooden seat. As Maude headed out, Plaid turned to wave goodbye. When they were out of earshot, Plaid peppered Papa about questions.

"Where do they live? Do they have children? How old are they? What do they do for a living?" Papa patiently answered every question.

"Whoa, there, Maude. Whoa." Papa pulled the buckboard to a stop in front of the mercantile. Emilio had done the shopping for the farm and was waiting. Papa and Emilio loaded the wagon while Plaid scooted over to the driver's side.

"Papa, may I hold the reins on the way home?"

"Don't see a problem there," Papa responded. When his back was turned, Emilio and Plaid exchanged a look and a quick smile. Emilio had been coaching Plaid on the reins already. Also, he knew that Maude was reliable. Emilio swung up to the wagon in one fluid motion and climbed into the back.

The wagon was loaded and ready to go. "Looks like rain, don't it?" A disheveled man said as he shuffled up to Papa. Plaid looked at the man's face and saw the same look that the street people of New York had who slept in boxes on the sidewalks. A look she thought said, "Just put your hand on my shoulder, a touch." But it is much deeper than I understand.

"I'm Lee Darnell," Papa introduced himself to the man. "And this is Plaid Patience, my granddaughter, and Emilio."

The man responded, "I am Carl." A bit surprised, he looked down at Papa's outstretched hand, and then shook it. Carl seemed at a loss for words.

Papa said, "Carl, do you need a place to rest your head?"

Carl lifted his head and straightened his shoulders, "Yes, Mr. Darnell." Plaid noticed that his voice was clear and unbroken, and he had the kindest, bluest eyes she had ever seen.

Papa told Carl, "Behind the library, a cabin waits, it has a clean bed, a fireplace with logs laid out, and food in the cupboard. There's a well pump and a good pile of stove wood out back. You can heat your bath water on the stove. For today, Liza at the Hub will serve you a hot meal. Tomorrow, you can rake some leaves for the town. Or talk to Liza, she may have other chores you can take care of. That'll take care of any expenses for your food and sleeping quarters. Liza usually knows about anyone in the area who's looking for a worker. Tell her that Papa and Plaid sent you."

"Much obliged," Carl replied. Papa pointed out the way to the Hub. "Carl's shoulders were straighter," Plaid noted. Carl took a small, broken comb out of his pocket and combed his hair as he walked towards the Hub.

"Sometimes folks just need a hand," Papa told Plaid. Papa preferred to teach by example. "Plaid, you must look beyond your first sight in all you observe." Plaid was proud to be related to such a man as her Papa.

She lightly slapped the reigns. "Get up there, Maude. Papa, tell me more about what you mean."

Papa paid careful attention to Maude's responses to Plaid. Satisfied, he said, "It's like when you look into a pond—first you see your reflection. Move the water, and the reflection disappears as the water tries to right itself. Reach into the pond and let the water slip through your fingers. Take in the smell. Know how much its nourished you and all living things."

"I understand," Plaid responded. A moment later, she said, "Now, tell me about when you were a boy and got abandoned at Mr. Ward's circus. I want to know everything about you, don't leave anything out."

Papa chuckled, then complied with her insistent questions. He understood that she was filling in the gaps in the foundation of her identity. On the slow ride home, he regaled her with family stories. He told her about how her mama, when she was about the age of Plaid now, ran backwards and fell into the creek. Gap ran to the creek and jumped in with her. They splashed water on each other and laughed until they fell down together in the creek. It was wonderful to see such love and joy.

Plaid listened to every word. These stories were sinking into her soul. Maude, sensing Plaid's distraction, slowed almost to a stop. "Giddy up, Maude." Plaid came back to attention and Maude instantly responded to the light tap of the reins. "Papa, I've waited so long to say that, 'Giddy up'."

Papa Lee couldn't trust his voice for a while. When he could speak, he said, "I love you, Plaid Patience." Emilio, lulled to sleep by the gentle sway of the wagon, napped on sacks of feed as Maude took them home.

Night Walks

After the incident with Papa Lee having a major situation of disagreement with Leeward, Papa informed Leeward that Girlean would now be living on Protected Earth. Her mama and siblings were welcome in the main house, but he was no longer to set foot in the main house.

"Leeward, your father and mother were dear to my heart, and such a large part of building this land we live on. My promise to them, as did Mr. Ward when Mickey was giving birth to you and your brother, she asked us to take care of her boys. I have kept my commitment, and you have also been a great asset, having improved so many things that has made the farm run at a good profit and also improved the beauty of the land.

"Because of the anger you carry with you, there have been some problematic times. But as much as I value your work ethic, if you ever lay a belt or a hand on your wife or children again, you will be on a train to nowhere. Is that clear?"

Papa Lee, when provoked, was a force to deal with. "Your insulting and unjust language towards your family is offensive in every way. I do believe you love them, and in a very small way, I understand your feelings of rumination when you look at Girlean, but the child has a right to a sanctum. We will give her one."

Leeward was a talent. Capable of building anything and could repair most anything. He knew the land's use for wheats and oats and gardening, rock bridges, inventing supply water systems for crops, knew trees and how to maintain the beauty of the land, and was extremely handsome. An odd part to Leeward was his gentleness toward animals, insects, and flowers. He cared for all these things with care and precision.

But it seems his family is where all the pent up mental suffering was released. After Papa had talked over the rules with Leeward, Leeward looked at Papa and said, "I know I don't deserve all that I have. Inside me, there is something distorted and it eats at me each day. I understand your reasons for the restrictions."

Girlean flourished living on Protective Earth. Plaid and Girlean were inseparable. Plaid brought her New York experiences and Girlean knew the land and was fearless. Both girls were eager to share their knowledge.

Leeward, a healthy man, came down with a mysterious sickness that plagued him. He blamed Sparsity and her "witchy ways." His face broke out in big red boils, his ankles swelled so big, he could not get his boots on. He told anyone that would listen that Girlean had Sparsity put a curse on him.

Sparsity would have gladly, but she said, "Mr. Lee, I may have special powers, but my grandmother Dahlia told me never to use any of my powers for bad. Only for good."

On full moon nights, Gap would take Plaid and Girlean on walks and set up camp by the pond. This was a favorite time for the girls. Gap taught them about the beauty of night creatures, as her Papa had taught her. She felt the love from the girls, of reliving all the treasured times, of pleasant memories she had shared with her Papa and her beloved Monty.

On this particular walk, Gap took the girls to a special spot that she often had shared with Monty. The girls set up the tent while Gap built a fire in an overgrown fire pit. All three would rub their clothes with leaves and mulch from the marsh, so the animals couldn't smell them. Gap always took her gun along. It was only used to scare off a too close curious bobcat or coyote.

Plaid and Girlean would shiver with delight when a bobcat, raccoons, or maybe a wild fox would walk right by them, sniff the area, and then move on, leaving their hearts racing.

As they nestled in, the darkness surrounded the edge of the thick forest. The many night sounds were active and Plaid was proud that she was beginning to identify many of them. She often thought of her friend Hanna and said many blessings for God to keep watch over her. Gap would remind them to listen to any disruption or motion in the night. The animals stay alive by their keen ears and eyes. As you two must learn to do.

Plaid stood, reached into the wet mulch and marked her face on each cheek. "I feel so much a part of the animal world at this moment."

Gap felt all warm and glad at her granddaughter's observation. She said, "Use all your senses, girls. All things around us are in a total system of communication. The night is full of wonder, but panic and fear can get one hurt."

Gap always waited for the girls to respond, making sure the information soaked in. As the moon went behind the clouds, the fire lowered to embers. Each said 'good night', pulled their blankets up around their ears, and gave a small sigh of comfort.

Learn How to Make Soap

Today, Plaid and Girlean vowed they would visit Sparsity at her stone cottage. Every stone had been picked up from Protected Earth's land. The two girls were going to ask Sparsity to show and educate them on the different herbs in her garden. Not only the ones from the alphabetized garden but maybe she would take them on a wild herb gathering walk. Both girls were wanting to gain knowledge on herbs and their healing power. Plaid and Girlean had decided they wanted to be special doctors; not only like Dr. Francis, but combined with Sparsity's knowledge. Now that would be a good doctor, they felt, but a small hitch—Girlean was a really good singer. Plaid laughed and said, "A traveling, singing doctor. Why not?"

They wanted to check on the coyote pup that Sparsity was taking care of. They felt sure with Sparsity's healing powers the pup was now healed.

When Mr. Ward purchased the property, he posted signs throughout the 1,000 acres, that read:

No trapping of any kind. Hunting only with my okay.
This is private property,
But you may pick wild blackberries, blueberries, plums, or mulberries.
Eat some honey—if you dare.
Be warned: a knowledge of mushrooms is vital. Some can kill you.
Mr. Ward.

But some folks paid no attention. Then, animals die from the traps if not found in time.

Plaid and Girlean saw Sparsity working in her herb garden, the cute coyote pup was playing alongside her. Today the girls had hiked instead of taking their horses. They stood and watched Sparsity and the pup for a few minutes. Sparsity had a habit of rolling up her colorful skirt on the side with her hand, then unrolling it, over and over this could go on. When Plaid asked Papa and Gap about it, Papa said, "Oh, it's just nervousness. She isn't aware of it. Never mention it."

The path leading to the herb garden was blocked by a large writing spider. She had built her web completely across the path. Gap had taught them a lot about spiders and the vital job spiders had to controlling insects. The two went off the path to meet up with Sparsity and avoid damaging the hard work the colorful spider had put into its web.

Sparsity didn't look their way but said, "Hi, girls. Nice surprise visit. What's on your minds?"

Plaid spoke up, "We thought, that is, if you can take the time, we could help you gather some herbs."

"Well, it's a little late in the day and I see you girls are on foot. I know Gap and your Papa want you to be home before dark, unless he knows right where you are. Do they know?"

"No. We finished our chores and decided to come see you," said Girlean.

"Well, I was gathering herbs to mix some soap for Emilio to wash the different animals, to ward off fleas and ticks. Want to help for a short time?"

"Oh, yes! That would be wonderful, Sparsity," gushed Plaid.

The girls picked up an empty basket. Sparsity gave them a list of herbs to gather; easy to find with each herb planted in alphabetical order. A gift to them was a small pair of snipping scissors.

"Now, it's up to you to take care of them and don't lose them or I will be disappointed."

"We promise," the two spoke in unison.

"Are you going to keep that pup? He is growing big." Girlean smoothly spoke, as she rubbed the pup's head.

"I will let the pup make that decision. She will know what's right for her, she sure is smart and sweet, doesn't like to be outside at night and that may be a problem, but I do believe I caught a momentary view of her mama hanging nearby."

"Will you name her?" asked Plaid.

"No! Not yet. Let's wait, maybe her mama will still fetch her."

Sparsity was impressed with the great energy the girls put into each task. As the three worked in unison, the coyote pup seemed to be studying their movements. Plaid turned around to pick up the long-handled spoon used to stir the pot of herb soap being made. The pup was holding it in its mouth.

"Look, Sparsity! The pup is helping!"

"Yes, she is extremely smart, observes constantly. We may have a problem on sending her back into the wild." Sparsity fiddled with her bright orange skirt as she went about her work.

Plaid wondered how old Sparsity was, and had she ever been in love.

"Girlean, do you know how old Sparsity is?"

"No one knows her age, we are hoping she will live forever. She was about twelve when she came to live on Protective Earth, before Gap was born. She helped deliver Gap. I don't know about romance — Papa says love is what Sparsity is, and a highly intelligent woman."

Plaid thought of what Gap had exposed to her of Sparsity's life, Plaid said, "Let's ask her to tell her story — it is a fascinating one. Papa says stories are what we are made of, stories give us guidance, insights, hopefully teach us bravery, and a boldness to face life each day."

Plaid asked Sparsity, "Will you tell your story about growing up to Girlean and I someday? The sooner, the better. I am so anxious to know."

Sparsity kept working, pouring the newly made soap into pans to set and then to be cut into bars. She would make some additional bars for sale at Cal's Hub, pinks, yellows, blue, all with added herbs and goats' milk. The rest was made for the care of the animals that lived on Protected Earth.

Sparsity appreciated the girls help. But, with all of their questions, she just didn't feel like reliving her days with the twin boys and Granny."

"We are done. My thanks for your help, great workers, the two of you are going to be powerful women. Now go home, you have time before dark sets in. When the soap is ready for cut, I will gift some to you both."

"Our thanks!" said Girlean, "We had an informational day and fun."

"See ya!" yelled Plaid.

The two walked away feeling proud of a good day's work, and

looking forward to a nice, long bath in a few days with the soap they helped make.

The girls paused to inhale the wonderful scents that were filling the air around them.

CHAPTER 38

A Better Man

The day could not have been more perfect, an extraordinary blue sky, blended into the green long-haired pine trees that lined the ridge above where Sparsity stood. The fields were golden with oats that were ready for cutting.

Sparsity circled the tractor a few times. The tractor was moving like it had a pulse. She looked around, then climbed up and cut the engine. She had seen Plaid and Girlean in the meadow. The two girls might have seen the whole accident. Yes! It was an accident. Sparsity knew in her heart; she had often wished Leeward ill will.

Maybe he was still alive. She crawled under the tractor and checked

Leeward for a pulse. His bloody mangled throat showed no pulse. Still, she repeatedly checked.

Standing by the tractor, her hands red from Leeward's blood. She reached her arms toward the sky and said, "God of all, I lived a very good life on this land. I have seen lots of happiness and pain and part of that pain was inflicted by Leeward. Yes, he cared for the land and all the animals that inhabited it, but God, he continued each day to torment his sweet wife and Girlean. Did he not deserve punishment for that part of him? Maybe not death."

She thought, well he did get that one beating from Cal. The time he hit his wife on the Hub's front porch. But Cal didn't finish the job of giving Leeward his due.

And he was warned with a shotgun by Papa Lee to behave, that frightened him so much, his hair turned grey.

But, when I chased the tractor and tried to stop it, hollering out to Leeward, did I do enough? I may always ask myself.

Sparsity turned back toward the scene, a gas smell was strong. She moved closer in to make sure there was no danger of fire. Then she slipped out of her white petticoat and covered Leeward as best as she could.

She ranted, "Leeward, it never appeared you paid a price for being the cause of great suffering to your family. And showing shame that Folly was your brother and your beautiful soul, Father Birchard. Now tell your troubles to the devil, because I am sure that's where your soul is making its last journey."

Sparsity picked up the bottle of moonshine that Leeward had left by the huge rock. For some unknown reason, even to her, she turned that bottle up, and finished it. Then went on her knees looking up she asked, "I don't ask for forgiveness, for in my soul I feel this may have been a deed long overdue. Only you know why Leeward was allowed all these years to torment."

Earlier Sparsity felt the girls were watching and as she turned in the direction of the moving tall grass, Plaid and Girlean stood up.

Sparsity walked alone in the darkened area of the woods. Age may have slowed her down a bit, but she thought slow is a good thing. It now lets me take in every detail of what I walk through and the world around me. She watched the two young pals, Plaid and Girlean. They would ride for a short while, stop, get off their horses, give the horses a rub, then talk. Watching the best friends together, she felt a little tug in her heart. Even though she grew up with no playmates, she had the love of hunting dogs and the milk goats. Granny Dahlia and the twin brothers were much older and treated her more as an equal instead of a child. The brothers always made her feel protected. Sparsity's mind would jump back into her childhood, and sweetness and adventures. She had a good life since coming to Protected Earth. She often went back to the first time she met up with Birchard, and her life changed forever. She could remember every detail of that day as she sat in Birchard's wagon. Mr. Ward, Birchard, Mickey and Lee, and later Crow and Gap, accepted her as one of their family. Plaid and Girlean didn't know that Sparsity was anywhere close by, they were content in their newly bonded friendship. Both had plentiful stories to share.

Sparsity's aging eyesight was good some days and other days she saw two of everything. It didn't keep her from tending to her herb gardens. She still made her healing salves, aromatherapy, and soothing tonics for young and old, and had treated scores of ailments for the citizens of several generations, as well as their animals. She had worked alongside Doc Francis for years on the birth of many babies, earning her a well-deserved respect. After Mr. Ward died, she put her time into caring for the young Lee. Birchard and his twins also needed her after Mickey died. Her medicines were always handy, carried in a brown leather fringed backpack. Lee made it for her one Christmas.

When Cal was alive, she would say, "Wonder what's in that nasty smelling stuff Sparsity takes out of those vials. But I must say, at one time in each of our lives, we have depended on Sparsity's wisdom, to take care of some need. Maybe even saved a few lives."

Still observing the girls from a distance, and rolling in her own thoughts, Sparsity felt at peace.

Girlean loved telling stories about Cal, and there were many. Tales passed down. Girlean would say, "I keep my ears open for a good story. Most adults believe kids are not listening." Girlean started, "Once mama said, when Cal got drunk and fell into the creek, a big ol' snapping turtle bit her on the head, almost taking her ear off. Sparsity just showed up and found Cal almost dead on the creek bank. Cal's face was swollen three times its regular size, her tongue hung out the side of her mouth. Many things befell Cal after her great love, Mr. Ward died. Cal went sort of funny in the head. Mr. Ward was everything to Cal. Her sweetheart, sidekick, best friend. Gap says Ward and Cal's soul rhythms were the same, there was no barrier between the two. Cal said to people they both told each other all they knew and could dream. They had found the ideal love. Who wouldn't have lost it—when one person in a love like that dies. Sparsity told me Cal wished herself dead. But knowing she had Liza Jane to raise kept her going.

That day of the turtle bite, Cal told Sparsity, she had been calling her to come. All Sparsity said was, "Rest now I am here, I'll take care of you. But, you mean old gal, I should let you die after all the mean, ugly things you have said about me."

As much as Cal was hurting, she didn't lose her spunk. She ranted on and on. That Sparsity was the one that was mean, "You told Mr. Ward I slept with old Sam."

"Well didn't you?" asked Sparsity.

Sparsity says, "Cal and I were always bantering back and forth, all in fun."

Cal passed out. Sparsity got her into the wagon and took her back to her cottage and took care of her. Cal's daughter was being looked after by a neighbor. Liza Jane was growing up.

The underlying truth was Cal and Sparsity really loved each other; they were both such distinctive people. Sparsity says Cal would say, "What the hell has my past sex life got to do with my one and only true love Mr. Ward? And Sparsity if anything is wrong with my head now, or my strange behavior, it's those herbs that you gave me, not losing my love or that snapping turtle trying to take my head off."

Girlean continued, "Papa Lee says his father knew who Cal was, he loved her just that way, he had no desire to change her. She excited him. Plaid, do you think we will be exciting women?"

Plaid shook her head, "Girlean, we are unique, of course we will dazzle this world."

Girlean reached down and tied her cotton, rose printed dress up in two knots. Her long, skinny, brown, green bean legs, sticking out of her new boots Gap had gotten her.

"Come, Plaid, we will lead the horses through this wet area. They don't like it when the mud clumps up on their hoofs. And we have to watch for water mocs. If they see one, they will panic. Plaid was not thinking about anything but the ugly, deep scars covering Girlean's legs.

"Girlean, I am so sorry."

Girlean didn't respond to Plaid's comment. She said, "You can't be too careful when it comes to a water moc. When we cross that marsh area you have to look up as well as down, those water mocs have been known to drop off onto a person from those hanging kudzu vines. Just take your new snake stick and push it away. Far away as possible."

Plaid watched her best buddy, Girlean, not blink an eye as she crossed. The mud made a sucking sound each time the horses put their hoofs down. As much as Plaid's heart was in her throat, "Do you remember what I told you Hannah said about the mud people, I bet there are mud people in this place. Listen, there was a whoosh, another one, oh yea! They are here." A calm came over her. She stepped out onto the bank behind Girlean and shouted, "That was grand! Girlean, did you hear or see the mud people? They were there, protecting us. Hanna said they love the mushy mud."

"Yes, Plaid, I believe I did, and you were very brave. I do love the thought of tiny mud people. Are the mud people from the orient?" Plaid gave her luscious laugh, a laugh that Gap said had been passed down from four generations. It was a laugh that sent vibrations to the earth, it rolled over a person, making all ears that received it glad to be alive.

"Very intuitive, yes Hanna did say they were and also dressed in colorful tiny beads that covered their clothes. They do not get dirty, even though they live in mud."

The girls stood in the middle of a thousand acres, surrounded by fields of oats, cattle, pine thickets, white and pink clouds against the sky, could there be any place on Earth more perfect.

Girlean spoke reassuringly, "Plaid, when you get to know each part of this land, you will understand how it does communicate with us humans. We are blessed to have your Papa, Gap, and Sparsity. They understand the woods. Sparsity says the process of the life of the forests is death, and renewal, and we walk through the sky each day because the sky touches the earth. A person can smell, touch it, and embrace its spirit if you leave all your senses open."

"Oh! But I do know the meaning of it all. I felt this way in Central Park. The woods have called my name as long as I can remember."

"Come, Plaid, let's run towards the river, it's magical to pass through the wheat fields, we can find a spot, press it down, it makes me feel safe, nothing around you but the tall grasses and looking up into a beautiful blue sky. Let's go, I will tell you all my secrets." Off they ran.

Both horses had wandered toward the forest edge on the far side of the wheatfield. They heard the hum of Leeward's tractor in the background.

Girlean had taken a small quilt from her saddle bag. Plaid pressed some more wheat down, then laid the pretty quilt, adorned with birds and honeysuckle vine. Girlean reminded Plaid about her gift her mama was making for Plaid. "Mama's almost finished quilting your quilt, Plaid. It sure is going to be a pretty one."

Plaid jokingly shook Girlean by the shoulders saying, "Tell me! Tell me what it looks like!"

"No! Can't. Mama wants it to be a surprise for you."

"Let's eat." Plaid gushed, bringing attention back to her appetite. Plaid laid out two apples and goat cheese sandwiches, made with Gap's grain bread, a thermos of milk and coffee, and two moon pies.

Girl said, "Lunch fit for royalty."

"Girlean, I sure love this feeling of friendship, want to become blood buddies?"

"What's that?"

"First let me ask, have you never read Tom Sawyer and Huck Finn? We prick our fingers with a pocketknife and rub our blood together. That bonds us in a pact for life." Plaid reached in her pocket for her newly gifted, Swiss knife from Gap. Along with hands on instructions on how a person could survive with the knife, she handed it to Girl.

Girl didn't hesitate, she opened the knife and pricked her finger. Bright red blood rolled out.

Plaid stuck her thumb to Girlean's. Plaid's finger poured blood from such a small cut. Girlean removed her neck scarf, pressed it against Plaid's thumb. The bleeding slowed and the girls rubbed fingers.

No words were spoken during the ritual.

Plaid reached to close the knife. "No! No! Plaid," Girlean cried, "It's bad luck. It may only be a myth, but why take a chance. Whoever opens it, closes it. Keep that finger wrapped."

The two girls stood and pushed aside more tall wheat. They saw Sparsity walking down from the pine ridge toward the river. It wasn't unusual, Sparsity often scoured the land for herbs or just maybe to discover an undocumented herb or flower. This was a special dream for her, and the horticulture society would name it after her.

Sparsity was a sight as she walked the trails. Today she wore a purple skirt and a yellow blouse. She had always been very slim. She now wore braids wrapped around her head. Her hair had turned grey—which gave a halo effect on her head. Her eyes were clear, and a color that seemed to change. Sort of blue with specks of pink. She looked straight into your soul. Sparsity knew behavior in humans and animals.

Plaid and Girlean lay under a sky that sparkled.

Plaid said, "I love to watch Sparsity. When I see her coming toward me, my heart races for a moment and I always feel better about the world."

Girlean replied, "I feel exactly that way. A magical person lives among us. I think maybe she may live forever.

It was harvest time and the glorious tall wheat was being cut.

Plaid whispered to her pal, "Tell me, now that we are blood buddies, about Leeward, why on earth did he beat you with such an unpardonable vengeance?"

"I defied him, and he wanted complete power and influence over me, as he had with my mother and sisters and brother."

As the girls continued their depth talk, Sparsity had disappeared, and the tractor sounded like it was coming closer.

"It's obvious to everyone, Leeward isn't my Daddy. Look at my skin. He hates the sight of me. Mama never said who my daddy is or what happened when I was conceived. I have asked Gap, but she says she can't betray my Mama."

"Why don't you just ask your Mama?" Said Plaid, her face taking on a puzzled look.

"No! I can't. Plaid let's not talk about this subject now. Anyway, things are better now that I live with Gap and your Papa. Papa Lee has had it out with Leeward several times over the years. Papa Lee depends on Leeward's many skills, as Mr. Ward did with Leeward's daddy, Birchard. Even with Leeward's tormented, stinky ways, he is a smart, capable man. There is a tender part to his soul. He cares more for contented rides, sitting by the lily pond, watching the sun cast magic shadows, long walks, reading his favorite books and spending as much time as possible with my mother. Leeward loves working and living on Protected Earth."

Plaid was engrossed in what Girlean was sharing with her and wanted to know more, "But, does he still torment your mother?"

Plaid had completely forgotten where they were. But as Girlean continued to talk, Plaid thought, 'Sounds like some folks really feel the world would be a better place with Leeward out of the way.'

Girlean was rubbing her hands together faster. She said, "There was talk around the Hub, Liza Jane said, Papa Lee told some folks, 'Sorry for Girlean and Leeward's wife and the rest of those beautiful children. The thought slips into my mind, maybe I should have finished with Leeward. Given him money to get started some other place.'"

Girlean, still talking, "When Leeward would be in a drunken stumper, I knew he was going to come after me, I would squat into a ball and start screaming like a bobcat, sometimes it worked. He stumbled away, other times he continued to beat me, hollering out, 'Girlean! Why honey do you make me do this?' When I could get away, I would take off on my horse and head for the goat farm. It always makes me feel better, holding those sweet little baby goats. My mama is so broken in spirit, she can't help. She sends my brother to get Gap when she can't take care of something. Gap had enough and took me home with her. Daddy wouldn't dare put his foot in Gap's door. I am so shamefaced. But since I've been at Protected Earth, I laugh, eat, play games. I never want to leave here. I even sing and play my guitar."

"Maybe we should pack up and call it a day—you can't help the meanness of Leeward. You didn't ask to be born. Girlean, you are innocent, but I believe you were conceived out of love. I just know it."

The wind played with the long grain grass that circled the girls.

Plaid pointed, "Hey! There's Leeward, he is off the tractor. The motor is still humming away. Where do you think he is headed? We better stay put." Plaid poked her new blood buddy in the side.

"We will stay," gasped Girlean. "He keeps a supply of moonshine in an old beaver hole by the river, marsh area that isn't frequented by many. Leeward knows the land and understands, few people if any, are going to stick their hands into those dark snaky looking holes. Your Papa has never tolerated him drinking and operating the farm equipment. But I believe we all hide some secrets; even from the people we love."

Plaid whispered, "I am no longer hungry. How long should we stay here?"

They closed their eyes, packed up, but laid back and both felt exhausted. The two fell asleep surrounded by a golden sea of wheat.

Plaid awoke first, "Girl, wake up. I see Sparsity running alongside of Leeward's tractor. As Girl stood, she grabbed Plaid's hand. They watched as Sparsity was trying to stop the tractor that had started rolling. Sparsity was screaming, "Today I was led this way!" She made it to the side and tried to jump on. Hollering to Leeward, "Jump! Jump Leeward! Out of the way!"

The tractor had picked up speed and was headed straight for the spot where Leeward was slumped over on a stump. It was unusual for the moonshine to take over. Most times he could still take care of the cutting and drive the tractor with no problem. Little did Leeward know, today he would take his last breath, Leeward never looked up. For one thing, his distrust for Sparsity caused him not to give attention to her warning.

He was a man tormented with love for his beautiful, sad wife.

Being of an insanely jealous nature, even of her thoughts, his aspersions eventually became a reality.

Girlean wanted Plaid to understand, "After I was born, Leeward went nuts. Papa Lee had the sheriff lock Leeward up until he cooled down. Mama forgave him because she felt she was the worst sinner."

Girlean and Plaid were perplexed as to what was happening. They saw the tractor was headed for Leeward. Plaid started to warn him, Girlean put her hand over Plaid's mouth. Girlean was shaking. It was a gesture she would question often in her life. Plaid took her hand away, removed her sweater and wrapped it around Girlean. Plaid forgot the tractor for a moment — "Breath, take a big gob of air. Now blow it out, close your eyes and keep breathing." Girlean could feel her body calm down a bit. She tried to speak; nothing came out. Their brain said, 'Run, Get out of here.' Then they saw Sparsity at the riverbank — the front wheel of the tractor was over the bank and the tractor had dragged Leeward along with it. Sparsity was knelt down, trying to help Leeward.

Plaid and Girlean were perfectly still — the beats of their hearts were working overtime after what they had just witnessed.

Plaid pleaded, "Girlean, lets crawl until we reach our horses. I am sure Sparsity knows we saw her; she will be in a real bad situation." Slowly they made it out to where their horses grazed peacefully. The girls didn't realize the wheat moved about as they crawled. Sparsity knew they were there.

Fast and furious, they pushed the horses. Girlean stopped her horse and it reared up, Plaid thought just like in the movies. Plaid stopped and turned toward Girl. Girlean spoke, "Plaid I could have screamed, but my thoughts were of a new life, freedom to sing, to take care of Mama. I may even see her smile once more, Oh my! Plaid, I am so incredibly glad you came into our lives, and to think you were walking this earth and your Papa Lee and Gap didn't know you were alive. I love you, blood pal, and I will honor our friendship forever. May I ask forgiveness?"

Plaid urged, "Let's go find Gap and Papa. He might possibly still be alive."

Girlean was feeling anguished joy at seeing Leeward hurt. Did she wish him dead? She wasn't sure, just out of their lives. He had been the only daddy she knew, but it was mostly all bad. She could never bring herself to confront her beautiful, mistreated mama. "Now maybe she will tell me my story." She thought as she rode along, "Am I dreaming—will I really awake and be able to go back home. Wake up, and go down to breakfast, and Leeward won't be sitting there at the table. Mama will say, 'Isn't it a beautiful morning?' and her sweet voice will echo throughout the house. We won't be subjected to his ungodly temper, but maybe he is alive and will be paralyzed. Mama will be in a worse position. Oh, dear God, I should have hollered out, gave a warning, what have I done?"

As the two arrived at the barn, Gap was pitchforking hay into the stalls. The two girls were down off their horses, and both started talking at the same time.

"Sparsity's in trouble down at the river trail, she needs you real bad. Leeward has had an accident."

"Give me your horse, Plaid. Where exactly is Sparsity and Leeward?" Plaid answered as to where Sparsity was.

"You girls go to the house. Tell Papa Leeward has had an accident and to get Doc Francis. I will pick up Emilio on the way."

"Okay," said Plaid and took off running to inform Papa.

Girlean was shaking, "Miss Gap, I am going to be with Mama, she will need me if the news is bad."

"Go, Go."

Sparsity felt she didn't need to understand her behavior, sometimes in life there isn't a comprehension of a person's conduct. She sat and waited, knowing the girls would ride to get Gap. Gap always knows what to do.

"I tried to save Leeward, but something would not let me move fast enough," she said to no one. Her mind went back in memory. I have gladly helped generations of families with my power to heal. Sparsity thought of Cal, I do miss that crazy, wonderful woman. Cal left us her precious daughter, Liza, who is filling her Mama's shoes quite well.

Gap rode out to the pine thicket trail where she knew Emilio was checking and tagging the pines for beetles. He needed to be informed of Leeward's accident. Even as Gap rode carrying such disagreeable news, she still noticed the beauty of the pine tree trail.

The sun was sending its precise rays through the trees, a light breeze created a delightful sight of sparkling decomposed matter in the air. Monty had called the pine trail the fairy dust trail. Gap thought about how when she rode the trail with her daughter, she would turn back to catch Monty's face that was filled with wonderment. She came to a clearing, Emilo's horse was grazing, she gave a whistle, and soon Emilo walked out of the woods. Emilo would take over Leeward's duties and was quite competent to run the farm in all areas needed. Gap felt secure he could take care of things. Emilo was a striking man, long hair to his shoulders, shiny black with grey intermingled. His face was kind, tan and a strong, square jaw. His muscular body used quick and direct movements. He rode like a dream, a sight for the eyes when one sees him coming across the field on his horse.

Emilo approached, "You look terrible, Miss Gap."

"I believe Leeward might possibly be dead. The girls said they watched as the tractor hit him. Sparsity is with him."

"Not typical for Leeward, no matter how much he drank. I never saw him lose control of any equipment. He shows a great respect for his tools. Where did it happen? Most everyone knew he had troubles. Sorry! Does his family know? What can I do?"

"Girlean has gone to tell her Mama. You can accompany me to

check on the set of circumstances." Emilo's actions showed he was ready to handle any situation. He swung onto his horse without putting a foot in the stirrup. The two headed toward the river trail.

In the meantime, Girlean met her older brother in the field cutting wheat. She gave him the news. For some reason he said, "Girl, you go back to Gaps, I'll take care of Mama."

Papa Lee had been asleep on the porch. Plaid was calling his name, "Papa. Papa."

Hearing the distress in Plaids voice, he woke up promptly. He soothed his great granddaughter. Plaid told all that she and Girlean had witnessed. "Papa, all I just told you transpired right before our eyes."

Papa hugged Plaid close and said, "I am sorry you had to see a man maybe die."

"I am okay, Papa—but I think maybe I should be feeling some sadness for Leeward. Did he have some niceness about him? I want to understand."

"There will be a lot in life you may not understand, child."

Papa, holding Plaid close, asked, "Has Gap gone to the scene?"

"Yes, Papa!" Plaid answered with a shaky voice.

Papa felt Plaid deserved a better exclamation. He knew Gap would handle whatever had happened. "My dear, dear Plaid, sometimes in life a person makes a promise. I made one to Birchard and Mickey, that I would see that their boys were taken care of. I couldn't go back on that obligation. Birchard was Mr. Ward's partner and loyal friend. Besides, Birchard helped build a major part of this land. As Leeward grew into a man, he took over a major running of Protected Earth, which freed me to be concerned with my own needs and wishes.

"Your Papa has always been under the spell of nature. The change of seasons brings the animals out to view and sketch. Yes, I have worked hard, but when I hear the song of a bluebird, or the barking of a fox, I want to put all chores aside, and be in the midst of the wild creatures.

Knowing Leeward could take care of the land and animals, he freed me up to enjoy the birds, and not worry about all the responsibilities that needed attention each day. Sorry my sweet, but I want you to understand why a person will allow such behavior to exist, and not protest, just enough. It was not a noble position I put myself in. Leeward never forgave Birchard and Mickey, his parents, for being Little People."

Plaid asked, "Papa, will I ever understand all there is to know about why people do what they do?"

He pulled her in close, "Probably not. No one has. If you figure it out, you will be hailed a genius."

"Now go put your horse away."

"Gap rode my horse to check Leeward."

"Plaid! You asked a question, maybe I didn't answer in the best way—yes, Leeward did have some good qualities. He showed great care for animals, our farm animals and wild ones. He loved the earth and treated it with great respect. Sorry to say this didn't carry over always into the people he loved. I guess that would be it."

Girlean rode up and joined Papa and Plaid. "Brother is with mother."

Papa told the girls to sit, he would make some coffee. He said, "We will wait for Gap to bring us news."

The two friends sat, talked, and moved the swing with a nervous motion. Girlean whispered to Plaid, "Sparsity can't be held answerable for this act. Ever since she was bitten by an old ugly cottonmouth."

Plaid gave a shiver for a moment, forgetting she may have just witnessed another human die. "Papa, Sparsity ran after the tractor, even climbed on it, and gave a holler to Leeward, a warning."

Plaid now had the copperhead on her mind. "Tell me how it happened, Girlean? Where and how was Sparsity bitten by a copperhead."

"She was on a herb search in the forest. This particular herb she was seeking likes to hide itself along, old rotten logs and such. When Sparsity reached down to cut the herbs…" Girlean reached out her arm, demonstrating how Sparsity had done, then continued. "That copperhead sank its fangs into her wrist, bit her several times. Gives me the willies even to think about it now. She never was the same in the head after that happened."

All of a sudden, the sky turned dark, and lighting danced over the top of the trees. It hit the road, cutting a long deep slash that ran into the woods, cracking a pine that burst into hundreds of pieces, flinging chips everywhere. Plaid and Girlean pulled the quilt over their heads. Papa knew Gap could take care of any situation. His concern was for the young girls. Papa returned with hot coffee, laced with hot milk and brown sugar. "The good man is telling us something." Night was moving in momentarily.

Out of the unexpected, Plaid said, "I am afraid of the shadowiness edge of things, such as the pond corners, hallways, the back of barn stalls, and most of all the woods deep. Mysteries dwell there and tiny beginnings of all kinds of life that I can't see. Papa, you told me Gap was also scared of the same thing when she was a child. But each day you would let her venture a little bit further into the woods alone. I am sure going to work on my fears."

Papa understood why the girls were talking at random, aimed at no particular purpose.

"Oh Plaid, the woods are enchanted with all kinds of wonders, most likely the safest place on earth. We will go in together." Papa moved his rocker in closer to Plaid and Girlean. Papa wanted to keep the subject off Leeward.

"Chase and Talker know all the spirits that walk among us in the forest. The wilderness has a voice, we just have to learn how to listen."

"Girlean, I think Papa and I had better ride with you. Your mama will be needing comfort." Girlean's horse was waiting close by, nibbling at some loose hay that had dropped from a wagon. "Plaid, get your Papa's boots." The sky had quieted.

Girlean added, "I will saddle Papa's horse."

Papa was a little hesitant to leave, but Gap would have sent Emilo for the Doc, and would know where to find them. The three of them headed toward Leeward's house, with Chase and Talker running behind. Since Girlean's brother had already told their mother of Leeward's accident and almost certain death, all thought she seemed surprisingly calm.

Plaid and Papa gave their greetings, Papa said, "Gap and Emilo will be along shortly with the complete story as to what happened to Leeward."

Papa noticed a table set up under a large oak in the yard, one of Girlean's mothers beautiful quilts was spread on it, with a bountiful vase of wildflowers on it. It was rather an odd setting considering the present situation, but people do react differently when under extreme stress.

Girl's mother had a lovely, soft pink fringed shawl around her shoulders. She softly asked, "Would you like to join us in some iced tea, or lemonade, Papa Lee?"

"No! Our thanks, as long as you and the children are fine, we will be heading back. I will have to meet with the sheriff. He will be wanting to know about Leeward. If you need anything, just send Girlean or one of the boys for us.

"My thanks, Mr. Darnell. You are always so kind. I will call on you shortly to ask where we stand as a family, after we hear how this turns out."

"My dear, nothing will change, you and your children have a home for life. Mr. Ward gave his promise to Birchard that his children and grandchildren would always have a home. Leeward is a complex man, most talented people are. He has worked hard. No one can deny him that and he has given lots of good years to Protected Earth."

Girlean stood at the table drinking lemonade, deep in thought. Tonight's the night. I want my mama to tell me about my real father. Mama is feeling loss, but I have endured as much misery, almost to my doom, from Leeward. She owes me that much. Maybe I could have saved Leeward, but I will live with that.

Papa and Plaid got back on their horse, Plaid patted her heart, a gesture toward her blood pal, Girlean, and they rode away. Girlean upon entering the house realized how different she felt. That constant pain in her belly and the knot in her chest had left. She felt light, as if her feet were going to leave the floor. Her mama and siblings were now seated at the dinner table. The family would always wait for Leeward before they would have dinner. A soft knock came at the door. It was Gap. She glanced at all seated at the table. She walked close to Tess. "I am sorry! Doc and Sparsity did all they could. Doc felt Leeward died instantly and felt no pain. Would you like for me to stay?" Girlean felt as if her soul left her body upon hearing that Leeward was dead. She felt ill, she walked to the back yard and threw up. She had the cold sweats. How could this be that Leeward is dead. She had to get herself together for her dear mother, who seemed very much in a calm state.

Tess stood and gave Gap a hug, "Our thanks, Gap, but we will deal with all of these mixed emotions." Gap observed no tears from any of Leeward's family. Odd that Girlean seemed more distraught than anyone.

"Do you wish me to make the arrangements for Leeward?" Gap asked. "Leeward wanted to be cremated, is that right?"

Tess answered in short, "Yes."

Gap left and on the ride back thought about Leeward's beautiful family. She would check on the arrangements and then inform Tess when all was taken care of. Leeward had informed Papa of his wants, be cremated, his ashes spread throughout Protected Earth—and a small marker anywhere on Protected Earth.

Leeward had remarked numerous times, "I was born here and wish to die here." Papa had asked Leeward, "and what would you like written on your head stone."

I was a flawed person,
but I gave my all to
Protected Earth.

Tess's oldest boy, Clancy, spoke, "Mama, you go rest. We'll clean the kitchen and close the barn and house up for the night."

Girlean started to say, "Should we put a plate for Leeward in the oven…", but it hit her that part of her life is over.

Girlean couldn't help but notice her mama kept the pink lace shawl around her shoulders. Leeward despised the color, pink. Oddly Leeward and Folly were both wrapped in pink blankets when they were born, and it was Mickey's favorite color.

When all were in bed, Girlean knocked on her mama's bedroom door. "Come in, dear." Her mama's lyrical voice had magically returned.

"Come, it's time you knew your story." Tess went straight into who Girlean's father was. "What I did wasn't right, and I believe Leeward with all his meanness, never cheated on me. With that said, your daddy's name was Ajay. His mother was from India and an English father. Do you understand how unique you are? I can't undo the pain I brought onto Leeward or you, you must know you were conceived out of love. Before your father, the depth of my sorrow was deep. At times I didn't wish to live. I have your father's story written down for you—Gap holds it."

Girlean was crying and hugging her mama. "I am so happy you loved my daddy, and I am glad I am me. Adults and kids whisper behind my back—but it's okay. I would not change who I am."

"Yes, you are beautiful and so was your daddy." Her mama wiped her own tears, then her daughters.

"Do you wish to read his story, or do you wish to wait until you are older, and maybe will understand more?"

Girlean sat silent for a few minutes, then expressed how she felt. "Mama, I want to know now. But, for whatever reason, I think I should wait until after Leeward's funeral. I just feel that would be the right thing to do. I now understand why Leeward carried his anger toward me. You loved someone else."

It was time mother and daughter released all the hidden secrets. Girlean was young but had a maturity beyond her years. She took her mother's hand and asked if she could share with Plaid. "We are now blood sisters."

Tess agreed it was right to wait, Leeward was the father of four of her children. He was very different then, "Little Folly." But he protected him, but did not treat him as a brother.

"I love you, Mama, it's good to be home."

Girlean walked to the room she shared with her sisters and slept without nightmares. The next morning, she asked her Mama about Folly. "Does he know about Leeward's death?'

"Papa Lee will see to Folly, dear, now go have a peaceful day. Your brother could use some help, so check with Clancy."

Tess had spent her night wide awake as her children slept peacefully. She knelt by an open window, a full moon shone brightly, a shooting star showed itself. Her words to God were private.

Going over in her thoughts were all the details on Leeward's accident. Gap reassured Tess all arrangements for Leeward would be taken care of. Sparsity had secluded herself in her cottage, dealing with her feelings… that maybe she could have done more to save Leeward.

Doc Francis says he died instantly, and believed somehow, Leeward set up his own death. Leeward was too systematic in thought and behavior to be careless.

"Girlean," her mother lovingly spoke, "it's important you know that Leeward took me out of servitude. I was no more than a slave. I wasn't in love with Leeward, but very grateful. He gave me a home and respect. Along with all the people on Protected Earth. His fear of my initiative to sell my quilts and lace work were frightening for him. Knowing I would be exposed to meeting people and feeling less dependent on him. In all truth, he was right. As much as I loved your father, and it was a once in a lifetime love. I could never have left my children and Leeward. I was indebted to him. And I believe he wanted you to love him as your father, but you were your father's child. And born out of my love, but Leeward saw it as I sinned against God and him."

"Mama, I understand all of this now, and feel no hate toward Leeward. I will make you proud of me."

Leeward's service was held outside at the wildflower pond and cabin. Liza and the neighbors furnished tables of food and drinks.

To all's amazement, the town turned out for Leeward's funeral. The testimonies of the people of Darnell that Leeward had extended himself to over the years went on and on, Mr. Smith's fields were plowed and planted when he fell sick. The Jones's barn was rebuilt from a fire, sick animals cared for, unbeknownst to most all who lived and worked on Protected Earth and for sure his family. His good deeds seemed endless.

Doc Francis told how Leeward would stop by his office and ask for news of anyone who needed help. Liza at the Hub, said the same thing, Leeward had asked her to keep him posted of any citizen in need. How did Leeward keep this side of him so well hidden? Most every person who Leeward had given help to said Leeward asked them not to say anything, and they didn't. Girlean was open mouthed and wide eyed upon hearing how the people of Darnell loved Leeward and called upon him so often when a problem arose.

Plaid whispered to Girlean as the girls stood holding hands, "I feel so much better about Leeward after hearing all the good deeds he did."

Gap had put her arm around Tess's shoulder and marveled, "We never knew, and Leeward never uttered one word, that he often extended himself to neighbors. How sad! Maybe doing the good deeds gave his anguished soul relief."

Papa Lee, Gap, and family walked away with a different feeling in their heart. Wildflowers were in bloom, Gap gathered a cup of Leeward's ashes to be scattered, Leeward had planted so much that grew on Protected Earth.

Gap started to scatter the ashes into the wildflowers, she offered words, "Rest in peace, Leeward, I am sure you would stand tall and smile seeing all the people that were beholden to you for being such a good neighbor. How sad none of us knew. "

As the people left the field, gladness was in each heart, that Leeward was a better man than all knew.

Papa Lee praised the dedications and said he would ride out early morning and scatter the rest of Leeward's ashes. He had a few private words to say to Leeward. Sparsity did not attend the funeral for the better man.

Neither did Folly. Folly stayed with Sparsity for an extended time.

He felt the loss of his brother for reasons only Folly knew. But his emotions were high, and he felt much confusion.

Sparsity let him talk, if he wished, but mostly he was withdrawn and slept. When he felt better, she told him about the nice things Leeward had done.

"But Miss Sparsity, Leeward didn't like me because I am a little person."

Folly did crave a small cross, with flowers on it. And asked Gap to write, "May God know his good deeds. This was done and the cross was placed next to his marker."

CHAPTER 39

Goat Kidding

Today Gap asked Plaid and Girlean to help with the goat kidding, not only did they love the baby goats, but it would give her an opportune time to talk with the girls about Leeward's accident that resulted in his death. They had been witnesses to it and were trying to figure it all out.

Girlean's loss was of a man who desired for her to call him Daddy, like his other four children, but she never could bring herself to oblige. It was always Leeward.

There were grounds to loathe him because of his mean treatment toward her. But, since his funeral, where he was praised by so many of Darnell's citizens, she felt better about him.

Girlean asked Gap, "How can this be the same person? Are all persons made up of such good, but capable of such bad behavior?"

"It's very hard for anyone to understand, Girlean, but humans can be complex, and often we may never know why a person acts a certain way. I do believe Leeward loved you, but he was so torn with his love for your mother and you being the image of her betrayal it ate away at his heart and reason."

Girlean felt tears starting to flow, "Gap, maybe if I had called Leeward daddy like he asked, do you think he would have treated me different?"

Gap took the end of the white apron she wore and wiped Girl's tears. "I don't know, but I do hope you feel better toward him, now that you see all of his kindness."

Girl reassured Gap, "I am so glad I can remove any hate from my heart." Plaid was feeling a little uncomfortable with the talk and she said, "Excuse me, I am going to release our horses into the field, be right back." She felt it was a private talk between the two.

The goats were in an affectionate way, right before kidding. Sparsity had walked in with her special mixture of molasses and raspberry leaves with water. This was a procedure to be given to the mother goat, believed to assist in delivery.

"Hurry back, Plaid," shouted Gap. "We have lots of work to complete. We will be here all day."

"I will," and she was. The girls walked around giving hugs to the mother goats that were ready for delivery after five months.

Gap wanted to change the mood and suggested, "Let's sit and have a cup of tea." Plaid took the thermos and all sat on the milking stools. The goats on Protected Earth were the Alpine and LaMancha dairy goats.

"Gap, when can I start helping with the cheese making. I treasure the goats and love caring for them and I sure do love goat cheese," gushed Plaid.

"I understand, but remember our shepherd Folly, he's watching over the goats. He takes his position very seriously. Our Folly has fooled all the doctors and outlived his predicted longevity. He loves people and his life. His carved pieces reflect his joys and Liza sells them faster than Folly can carve them. The money he receives he buys cupcakes and cookies for the children and old people that visit the circus statue. He loves to hear the sounds of joy.

"Very soon. You have to become more enmeshed in your studies. I understand how easily it is to be distracted. We live on a magical place. Your education comes first, the hands-on learning will be in your daily life. One day, you, Plaid Patience, will be in charge of Protected Earth."

Gap gave Plaid a huge hug and wiped away some tears. Plaid was so much like Monty.

Girlean spoke, "Miss Gap, why are you sad today?"

"The tears are happy ones. I was born on the sunny side of the hedge. I have this unimaginable life. I lost Monty but gained Plaid."

"Now you both have had extraordinary lives for your young years. The life-promoting experiences and the hurtful ones are making you both people to be reckoned with. Sometimes in life we come upon things that are best left in that dark little secret place of our mind because to expose it could cause harm to others. So, we must try really hard to make the correct decision."

Plaid and Girlean hung onto Gap's wise words. "Now, let's turn all of our attention to the birthing goats."

Ryan McKlveen

CHAPTER 40

Tess Tells Girlean

Tess had not been on a horse in years, even though she loved riding and sat beautiful in the saddle. She held Girlean's face in her hands, "We are going for a long ride in the morning and a picnic. You are going to hear more of my story with your father."

Girlean could not sleep, she was so excited, never had she had a real conversation with her mother. Both were up early. Clancy got the kids ready for school and Tess and Girlean saddled up. And off they rode, Girlean knew all the trails on Protected Earth, but she had never experienced the 1,000 acres with her mother.

Girlean knew exactly where she would guide her mother… to the pond. Once they arrived at the pond, Girlean took care of the horses, gave them a pat on the head, and released them into the field. Tess had put a quilt on the heavy moss.

"Mama lets go for a swim," squeaked Girlean. Tess's blue eyes opened wide. "We do not have a swimsuit." Her mouth standing agape, eyes almost full of terror.

"Mama, we don't need one. We are exposing our hearts; this will be a good way to not hide anything." Girlean was starting to take off her clothes.

Tess was in a shiver. Girl waded into the cool pond and floated to the other side. "Come on, Mama, this is the right time to let everything go. We are going to wash away any hurt or guilt."

Slowly Tess disrobed and waded in. She stood with arms crossed over her breasts. Then she went forward into the pond and floated on her stomach, she then went under and swam over to Girlean.

Tess shouted, "What a great feeling, the mud between my toes, the cool water washing and cooling my body."

"Come, Girlean, we have more to talk about. I will start from the beginning so you will never wonder any more where you came from."

Girlean jumped in and swam to the other side. The two dried off, dressed, and spread their lunch out. Tess began…

"Leeward kept me in an overly protective household. I took care of the children and Leeward liked it that way. He came home to a beautiful, depressed, mostly emotionally shut off wife. I didn't speak about our differences. I was raised in different homes, as a servant cleaning, cooking, and caring for babies. That had been my life, and Leeward came along and removed me from that misery. He was more of a father figure and a rescuer, but Leeward didn't see our marriage that way. I was very young and was grateful for the rescue. Liza and Gap gave me material to make stunning quilts and I made tablecloths, bedspreads of embroidered fabric, quilts that told a story. After Papa Lee had a long talk with Leeward about his anger, I was able to express all those hidden emotions on to my fabrics. Gap sent some of my quilts to New York along with some of her own paintings. All were sold. I was discovering I had a talent. But along with this new freedom came problems.

"Liza let me spend one day on the Hub's porch with my quilts to sell. Leeward would time me in and out of Darnell. And he often rode into Darnell to check on me. But I could live with that. It was nice just being where I could talk with people and see their joy when they purchased one of my quilts.

"But one fateful day, love showed itself in a handsome man called Ajay. As I told you earlier, your father was part Indian. His mother was from India and his father was English. For an unknown reason, he was on an adventure and got off the train in Darnell.

"I was delighted when Papa Lee had some huge projects that were keeping Leeward occupied and he had very little free time. Clancy showed me how to harness the horse for the smaller wagon, which happened to be painted a bright yellow. When I got behind those reins, it was a joy I didn't know existed. I was beyond myself. On my free day, Sparsity would come and watch your brother and sisters.

"Leeward didn't approve, but would not come around when Sparsity was nearby.

Sparsity would shine the house, take the children for long hikes, the children were happy, and I was given some breathing time. Sparsity was not affected by him, she just shut him off.

"On my ride into Darnell, I would guide the horse and wagon in a leisurely manner, to stretch out my day. There is a pull-off by the Creek. I would tie up the horse and walk the pathway to the spot by the Creek. I would break off a piece of greenery from a Cedar, take whiffs, splash handfuls of cool water on my face, then walk back to the wagon and continue my drive."

Girlean asked, "Is this painful for you, Mama, to remember?"

"No! I want you to have the story, then we can move on."

The two finished their lunch, laid back on the quilt, closed their eyes, and rested from the strong talk.

Tess softly woke Girlean who had drifted off to sleep. "Wake, dear, and let's finish your father's story, today.

"I was seated on The Hub's porch and Liza brought me out a nice big piece of coconut cake and iced tea. Little did I know she had spiked my tea with some white lightning. Never ever having whiskey, I must say it did relax me and loosen me up.

"The interesting looking dark-skinned man kept looking at me. Finally, he walked over and said, 'You are the loveliest woman I have ever seen. I am Ajay.'

"Taken aback, but the white lightning gave me some courage to accept such a compliment. I merely said thank you.

"He asked if he could join me, I nodded yes. I said my name."

"Oh Mama, you are beautiful, and Gap says you have the power to captivate anyone, please go on."

"Did Liza try to talk you out of an affair with my father."

"She was worried. Liza knew how hot tempered and crazy jealous Leeward was. She felt the situation may get someone killed. Most of the citizens of Darnell were tolerant of different races. But Liza was afraid someone would tell Leeward. And they would not approve of a known and respected person like Leeward and the town knowing his wife was having an affair.

"But dear, dear Girlean, it was too late, we were deeply in love, and nothing could have stopped us getting together. Not even the terrible thought of Leeward killing us."

Ajay

"When Ajay's father died, he sold the business and had wanted to travel and explore the USA. He had been raised well in London; he headed out for the unknown.

"His train was now in the Deep South. He was excited by all he observed, the red clay covered banks, pine thickets, cotton fields that seem to go on forever, vines called kudzu that covered trees and even some houses. The vines often made large, strange animal shapes in the trees. Trees with hanging moss; a majestic blooming vine, with outstanding purple flowers, he learned was called wisteria. He said he questioned why he was particularly drawn to this land.

"When the conductor called out, 'Coming up to the charming town of Darnell,' he felt strongly this is where I get off. The train pulled into a well-designed station, an architect design he had seen back in London. The town looked as charming as anything he had left behind.

"The station was busy with people picking up all kinds of goods from the train, some waiting to load cattle. He observed no plantation homes. Wagons lined up at the station, pulled by healthy looking mules and horses, resting under shaded trees. After retrieving his carpet bag and unloading his motorized bike with a sidecar, which had gathered a small bunch of onlookers. And along his journey he had also collected a stray dog. He had named the spotted dog Buddy. The dog was smart and quickly endeared himself to Ajay. Ajay abhorred violence of any nature. That's not to say he couldn't protect himself if an incident arose. He was a crack shot with a pistol and skilled in the art of boxing. After asking the men gathered around his motorbike, which Buddy was guarding but had already made friends with the locals, if there was a hotel or rooming inn in town. A man replied, "Best start out at the Hub Cafe. Ask Liza, she will best guide you."

"Ok if I leave my bike, bags, and my dog right here."

"No problem we will get Buddy some water and a few vittles."

"Thank you, kind sirs," and Ajay walked toward the Hub, little did he know he was headed toward an event that would change a number of lives forever.

"Ajay had somewhat of an animal walk, as if he was stalking a prey. Dark hair, dark eyes, stony jaw, brown skin, Ajay was not raised as a

Buddhist, but he had studied both Buddhism and Christianity. He did often wear a simple sandal that seemed odd to the men in Darnell.

"Women stared and blushed when he walked close to them. And men stepped to the side for him. He carried a strong aura. He tipped his hat to women and men. Liza set the handsome stranger up in the library cabin. Her instructions to him were, 'Ajay, just sit on the porch for a few days, with a book or drink in hand, and, by the way, do you play chess or checkers?'

"'Sure do. And love a good talk.' He smiled, showing white teeth.

"'You will meet up with most of Darnell's citizens. We are a curious bunch, but a lot of nice, sweet folks. Your bike will be fine on the porch if you wish to take it out of the weather. Looking forward to a ride in that sidecar,' Liza joked.

"Ajay asked if it was okay if Buddy came inside.

"Liza replied, 'Yes, of course.'

"She walked back towards the Hub, thinking Ajay will get more company than he most likely will want.

"Ajay was a doer, and never shied away from testing his abilities. He immediately observed some repairs that were needed to the cabin. After a few games and drinks on the porch, the men were more than happy to supply him with all the tools he needed. In return he would repay them with building a porch, adding a room, plowing, and cutting fields of hay. He gained respect from Darnell's citizens quickly. Yes! They asked about his roots. Who were his parents and on and on. He felt 'I am a stranger in their land, why shouldn't the citizens be curious?' His dog buddy became known in the town.

"His father had left him well off, but he desired to live a simple life. Simple food, no meats, nuts, grain bread, lovely rich preserves made from fresh berries and peaches. He did grow to indulge in southern pecan pie. Mostly at this time of his life, he wished to live one day at a time. He enjoyed hard work, most any kind of activity that took physical labor. His father had taught him good lessons, he repeated his father's words, 'Son, don't talk without action and have kindness for all creatures.' Ajay was ready for new adventure, and from what he could observe, Darnell was going to give him a new start.

"On several occasions, he watched me as I brought out my quilts as I seated myself on the porch at the Hub. He approached, but still kept a distance. He talked to the customers, but always was glancing my way.

"Ajay was kept busy doing all kinds of repairs. Liza had started a vegetable and herb garden. He had great ideas and she put him in charge of the garden. Liza had asked Ajay to extend the porch of the Hub all the way around, and to add a separate room.

"It was officially the new post office. She even hired a local to be the postmaster a few hours. Ajay kept asking Liza about me.

"When we finally spoke to each other, there was no turning back, it was as if we were thrown off the earth, there was no one else.

"Liza was worried I had upped my days to a few days a week and would come in to see Ajay. Lee and Gap found him to be a gentleman. Lee picked up on Ajay's attraction for me and I for him.

"Papa Lee told Liza to keep a close eye on the situation.

"Leeward had already come in to check as to why I was spending more time at the Hub, but for some reason didn't seem that upset.

"One early morning when I arrived at the Hub, not really knowing why, I hid the wagon and horses behind the Hub. Ajay's motorbike was parked in sight, I displayed my quilts as usual.

"What would I say and do if Leeward showed up? And yet inside a part of me was fearless. I was taking some happiness and excitement for myself. Wrong yes, but it was too late. Ajay showed up and I got on his bike, and we took to the back roads, I even took the pins out of my hair, and let it hang long, blowing. No two people had ever been more attracted to each other.

"In spite of all the dangers, we somehow managed to sneak in some time. We were able to have an affair for about two months. Liza knew it had to stop - today! Liza said, 'You and Ajay must end this now.' Liza begged us. Our hearts torn, he begged me to go away with him. 'How can I have a life without you, Tess?'

"With my heart breaking, I tried to explain, 'I just don't know, Ajay. I don't know how, Ajay, but there isn't a choice, I will live with this ache in my heart for the rest of my days. I can never leave my children, and Leeward will hunt us down and surely kill us both.' I took his chiseled handsome face in my hands, 'How can I describe my heart; you will forever live with me.' I didn't mention I was carrying his child. That baby was you, Dear, Dear Girlean. I did confide in Liza who decided to keep my secret, knowing when my baby was born only God will have the answer as to what my life will be like.

"Once more Ajay pleaded, 'Is there anything I can do, you are the only woman I know I will ever love, this time together carries a lifetime with it.'

"When the lovers arrived back at the Hub. Liza had loaded Tess's quilts onto the brightly painted yellow wagon; it was now painted with sunflowers. Leeward hated it saying, 'That wagon does not belong on this farm.' With a broken heart, I headed the wagon towards Protected Earth. Liza took charge and saw that Ajay was on the noon day train out of Darnell forever. 'You must never return,' she told him. A few miles out of Darnell, I slowed my horse down and pulled off the main road into a secluded, shaded spot close to the rolling creek. After I tied the horse up, I walked down the green moss-covered damp path to the creek. Leaving my shoes on the path, I cupped my hands full of the sweet water, splashed my face several times, removed my clothes, slid off the large rock where I was seated, and lowered my body into the cool water. Closing my eyes, I must have fallen asleep. I was awakened by a pinching on my toes from little crawfish. The sun was going down. I kept up a chatter with myself, 'It will be close to dark before I reach home, most likely Leeward has been into town searching for me. I can envision the rage on his face, it would be a combination of jealousy and concern.'

"I thought I will give him no explanation of my actions. I am resigned to remain mute, no matter what happens. Nothing will ever move me to tell him the truth. My child will be born, from my intimate encounters with Ajay. This baby will show Ajay's genes. But Leeward's mother was dark, so the appearance of his child could be explained from his or her lineage. But all of this doesn't matter, this child will be mine, and the citizens may continue with their quiet gossip and whispers. I have no thoughts how Leeward will react when the baby is born.

"I knew I would never be free of Leeward. Leeward was a hard-working, driven man and of great value to Papa Lee and Protected Earth. Papa Lee knew that Leeward loved the land and the animals, and Leeward cared for both with great attention. But that inner core of anger could give way at any time. Yes, my dear Girlean, I was afraid, but I knew I would protect my baby with my life, if necessary.

"I pulled myself out of the water, dressed, and curled into a fetal position. I let go into a dark, safe, and peaceful place. I smelled the musty water, and the life of the trees around me. A granddaddy spider crawled across my leg, stopped, then went on its way. With darkness almost on me, I started up the embankment toward the main road. I halted after hearing a hard gallop of a horse on the road. I knew it was Leeward headed for town. After being sure he had passed, I quickly untied the horse and wagon and headed for home, knowing I would have to face whatever the consequences of my affair would bring.

"Liza later told me Leeward rode into town carrying a fury inside, not knowing where I was. He burst into the Hub with a wild look. Liza was aware of Leeward's jealousy and temper. He shouted, 'Liza, have you seen Tess today? She left at daybreak to get supplies and show her quilts. Enough is enough. I have been a patient man, but she will not be coming into town alone anymore.'

"Liza told him, 'I left some goods, picked up her money from the sale of her quilts, I gave her a take home lunch. Most likely she stopped at a spot by the creek, had lunch, and maybe fell asleep. I bet she is home.'

"'What goods did she leave?' asked Leeward.

"'Why? Go home Leeward.' Liza saw his anguish and laid her hand on his shoulder. 'Go Leeward, I am sure she is fine.'

"'Thanks.' He leaped on his horse and took off.

"Liza said, 'She put me in her prayers, and Ajay as well. Liza knew that Ajay would be a dead man if Leeward caught him with his wife.

"I had my baby girl. It was obvious to all that you were not fathered by Leeward.

"Leeward knew and showed his disdain by his actions toward you. I am so sorry, Girlean, please forgive me for the hell you lived with. Now you can know my story and yours. May this ease your heart, and know you were conceived in love."

Girlean hugged her Mama and said, "I love you dearly."

CHAPTER 41

Spring Comes to Tess

Girlean was satisfied with Tess's story. Tess had made known all she knew of Ajay, Girlean's father. The family was still adjusting to their daily life without Leeward, as well as the Darnell family and all that had depended on Leeward's expertise on nearly all things that concerned life on Protected Earth.

Tess wanted a life that had rightness to it. She now had conversations with her children, her oldest Clancy wanted to remain on the land and to continue his education of farming and care of the land. But plans changed for Clancy—he had been drafted to fight in the second world war. His family prayed each night the war would end soon, and he would return home. The little ones were too young to set goals at this time.

Girlean was flying six feet off the ground. She had shared all her mother told her about her father Ajay with her best friend Plaid Patience. She had won a talent contest that her mother had taken her to enter in Atlanta. All felt she had the talent, beauty, and style to become a famous singer. Girlean certainly maintained her own look. Nothing about her said "Fashion of the week." She wanted to go for it. She would stay in school. Darnell's public school now had a music department. Not a huge one, but it had a teacher who showed great interest in her students. Gap had met with the teacher to discuss setting up a small theater for live shows and maybe a jamboree once a month. Any talent could perform, and the citizens could dance on an outside floor. The building was under construction, and all were excited.

Liza had a suggestion box on the Hub's porch to name the new theater. The Ward Theater was the most suggested name — and so it was. Tess offered to make any costumes that were needed.

Tess told her children, after the house was scrubbed inside, and painted inside and out. "We are not in any way celebrating your father's passing. Of course, we wish God to be merciful, but that is between Leeward and God. As we heard the testimonials from the citizens, now we know your father was a good man in lots of ways. Each one of you can be proud and hold your head high. When older, you may understand the pain Leeward lived with."

Tess was emerging a new person. Papa Lee asked Sparsity to stay with the children while Tess went to New York to meet with some of her quilt clients. A northern paper gave a write up with a lovely photo of Tess. Liza had posted it at the Hub when Tess returned, Papa Lee, Gap, Plaid, Sparsity, and the children were all waiting with flowers, and some citizens also welcomed their new celebrity.

Tess had not lost all her shyness, a bit overwhelmed, she thanked the people and got into the wagon with her children. After Girlean was excited to get home, she came bouncing in and couldn't believe her mother had moved a newly acquired desk in front of the sunny window in the kitchen. She hollered with exhilaration, "Mama, Mama, you look so pretty, who are you writing to?"

"Writing the proprietress in New York thanking her for all her purchases, and for her kindness while I was there." Girlean gave her mother a hug, "I love you so much and so proud I am your daughter. Oh! And by the way, Plaid wants to write a play about you and your quilts."

"We will see," Tess said.

Each morning as Tess struck a match to the pine hearth kindling, pushed the iron cook stoves eye to the side, it made noise. The old sinking feeling came over her, am I going to wake Leeward? She stood, waiting to hear that nasty voice from down the hallway to the kitchen but there was silence. She sat at the table waiting. Nothing. No stomping footsteps. Nothing but the percolator starting its dance with morning coffee. She thought, this is the way mornings are supposed to be. The sun was breaking through the heavens. Grass damp and lush, birds scooping a drink from dewdrops. Oh, how I look forward to mornings and what's around the corner.

Soon Tess would know what true joy was, Ajay was to return to Darnell.

Years had passed since Ajay's affair with the lovely Tess. He knew in his heart there would never be another love. Moving to a large city like New York kept him extremely busy.

He often strolled the streets of New York, especially Madison Ave, checking out the many interesting shops. An extraordinary display quickly caught his eye. In the middle of the display was a frame article about the woman that made them. His heart pounded. Yes, it was Tess, every part of her lovely face was etched in his memory.

He walked into the shop. The proprietor approached him. "Hi, you look a bit shaken, sir, are you ok?"

"May I possibly sit for a moment?"

"Of course, would you like a glass of water. Better still, I was just making a cup of tea, may I prepare one for you?"

She put her hand on his shoulder. Ajay answered, "Yes, thank you, that would be nice."

The store owner walked to the back of her store leaving Ajay alone in the shop with his thoughts. He touched a quilt nearby draped over a chair, "My Tess did this," he said to no one. Never did I let myself dream I would be given the opportunity to see or hear from Tess, dare I hope."

The store owner placed the tea, on a small table, beside Ajay and said, "I took the liberty of pouring you a brandy. Please relax, finish your tea and brandy."

He thanked the woman for her kindness and said, "I knew Tess the maker of these beautiful quilts. She is the only woman I have ever loved, circumstances separated us, years back."

"Are you married, Ajay?"

"Oh, no."

"Do you feel like talking about your captivating story?" She handed Ajay the article about Tess then walked to her shop door and turned the store sign to closed.

"She is now a widow; her husband was killed in a tractor accident."

Pulling a chair up beside Ajay. She said, "I am all ears."

Ajay spoke of his love for Tess, and how the love affair happened.

Wiping tears from her eyes she said, "You must go to her, no notice just catch the next train to Georgia."

"Once more my many thanks for your kindness, rest assured I will be on the first available train to Georgia."

And so, he was.

CHAPTER 42

Protected Earth Lives On

After Leeward's death, Papa Lee once more picked up the reins. Gap took care of all finances and managed the cheese makings. The different delectable cheeses were most sought after, not only by the locals but Atlanta restaurants, and throughout Georgia.

Liza had built onto the Hub and opened a specialty shop for meats from the locals, canned goods, such as peaches, all kinds of jellies and preserves, French bread and rolls, her famous coconut cake, and Protected Earth cheeses and milk. In season vegetables were made available from the local farmers. Tess's quilts and Sparsity's herb salves for all kinds of ailments, not only for humans but animals' ailments.

Darnell was becoming a very desirable place to live and visit, for hiking and river canoeing. Doc Francis still held his practice but, his capable assistant, and a new young doctor, had taken over lots of the care of patients. Doc was ready to fully enjoy retirement.

Clancy had been wounded but was now home and was becoming efficient, along with Emilio and all the personnel who had stepped up and met every challenge.

Plaid pleaded with Gap and Papa to let her take more responsibilities, "I know my schooling is important." Tears running down her face, she was desperate to do her part. Gap reassured her how important she was to Protected Earth. Plaid, like her mother and grandmother, felt they were needed each day for chores, and school was conflicting. Gap had many talks with Plaid explaining she was limited to the time she would be home to school her.

Once more she approached her grandmother on the subject. "No, Plaid, you must be understanding," Gap explained. To Gap and Papa Lee's surprise, Plaid became very interested in writing plays. She remembered Mr. Millhouse, her New York foster parent, had told her, "One day, Plaid, you will be famous, either for your writings or your paintings, maybe both."

The small, new playhouse was completed and local talent performed on Saturdays. It was a happy and enjoyable time for all again. Girlean had become a standout with her singing, and Plaid had written most of her songs. The new art teacher found Plaid's writing of great interest, and had accepted one of her plays to be performed in the new Playhouse. Tess had volunteered to make the costumes and some local carpenters were available to build anything that was needed for the stage. Gap had written to June Light, Jazzy, and the Millhouses about Plaid's play that would be the first play to open Darnell's new playhouse. If at all possible, we would love for you all to be our guest. We have more than enough room to accommodate, with private rooms. How lovely it would be, and such a glorious surprise for Plaid! You are welcome to visit and as long as you desire.

Liza had taken in a partner, the Hub's business had increased, and it was of necessity. After all the years, she decided one day to pry up the board in the cabin and take out her father's journal about his life.

To her surprise, there was a picture of him stuck in between. Why she waited so long was a mystery. Within the pages was an old post that he had written if Cal ever wished to reach him. This was something Liza felt she would have to think long and hard about.

Today while sorting the mail, Liza kept staring at the letter, postmarked all the way from Switzerland, addressed to Papa Lee. The handwriting looked very familiar. Liza had seen Gaps handwriting over the years and her heart beat a little faster, could it really be from Gaps mother. She had seen Emilio earlier at the supply station and knew he would be stopping by with a cheese supply. She could barely wait to send the letter to Papa Lee. When Emilio handed the post to Papa, he purposely had put the Switzerland letter on top.

Gap had gone for a ride, but Papa, containing his curiosity, felt he should wait for Gap's return so they could read the letter together. As soon as Gap stepped onto the screened porch, Papa Lee said, "Daughter, mix two blackberry shine's and come sit. A letter has arrived from your mother." Gap was surprised she felt a quickening from her heart to her jaw.

She said, "Papa you open the letter."

They both took a few large gulps and some deep breaths. "Papa, what do you suppose she has written and it is amazing my handwriting is similar in every detail."

Papa Lee opened the letter and started to read, it wasn't a long letter, it was to the point.

Lee Darnell and Gap,

I write Gap because I am sure you kept your word, Lee, and named our daughter Gap at my request.

When I left Protected Earth, you gave me an open invitation to return at any time. Understanding it has been some years, I am sure Gap has be-

come quite a woman, having both of our genes. Curious if I am a grandmother, even looking at the word grandmother seems out of sorts.

Lee, I do not need money. My paintings have sold throughout, even during my most debilitating times. I feel strongly my winter days are close, and I have a strong pull to spend time with you and Gap, and also, is Sparsity still alive? I am in a keenly expectant state of mind that you will say yes. I will wait for a letter from Protected Earth,

Garrison Anne Polly, the woman with the three first names.

Gap was shaken, and not many things shook Gap. "Papa, I would like to answer Garrison's letter." Papa looked at his daughter.

"I leave it up to you, I feel it should be your decision."

"I wish for her to come and live out her days with us. Do you agree?"

"Yes! I am not sure what we will face, but as always, nothing has beaten us so far."

Gap answered with a direct letter.

Mother,

I write mother with deep excitement. Papa Lee, your great granddaughter, Plaid, and I will greet you at the Darnell Train Station with open hearts. Yes, Sparsity, is very much alive and sends well wishes. She offers you her cottage. And looking forward to you chopping some firewood if you are up to the task.

We have great hope Sparsity will live forever. You had a granddaughter named Monty. To our broken hearts she passed away. She left us an outstanding grandchild. All will be talked about upon your visit. Or if you decide, Mother, our hope is you will live out your life on Protected Earth.

PS. With some celebratory blackberry shine.

Your daughter Gap
with three first names